Copyright ©2023 by S.A. Heiden

All rights reserved.

No portion of this book may be reproduced in any form without written permission from the publisher or author, except in the case of brief quotations used in critical articles or reviews.

This book is a work of fiction. The story, all names, characters, and incidents portrayed in this production are fictitious. Any resemblance to actual persons, living or dead, events or locales is entirely coincidental.

1st edition 2023

For more information contact: http://www.saheiden.com/

Book Cover by Etheric Designs

ISBN: 979-8-9882709-3-5

THE ARCHER'S ALCHEMY

THE LUMEN LEGACY
BOOK TWO

S.A. HEIDEN

For my Dad —
The strongest man I've ever known.

CONTENTS

CHAPTER
ONE

LUCY

Ash and debris covered Lucy from head to toe. From her long, dark curly hair, across her light, freckled skin, and over her torn tunic—everything was smudged in a deep gray ash. Everything except for the arrow she clutched tight in her hand.

Her fingernails dug into the palm of her hand, but she refused to ease her grip. That bloodied arrow was the only thing grounding her. It stood as proof that she wasn't a feeble Fae female, but rather someone who could not be tamed. It was the only thing that reminded her that what she experienced was real.

As she made her way up the path to the Baum Estate, uneven breaths of panic pushed her further and further away from the calm and composed exterior she knew she would need for entering the halls.

The salvaged branches from The Elderwood were wrapped in canvas and held tightly in her other hand. Getting the bag into her bedchambers and out of sight would be difficult, but she nearly died trying to retrieve them.

The dark night covered her on her journey, and the rose bushes that lined the path back to her home rustled gently in the breeze. On any other night, she'd appreciate their delicate scent, but not tonight. Nothing could soothe her—not with death and flame so heavy on her mind.

A hurried footstep shuffled from the nearby garden archway as Lucy entered the courtyard on the east wing of the estate. The sudden realization that other Fae were near caused an uneasy sensation to bloom in her stomach.

What if they see me looking so disheveled? Did they realize I was gone?

Too tired to think clearly, all Lucy could focus on was that she needed to quickly get back into her room. First, she needed the privacy to look at the strange mark The Elderwood placed on her. More than that, she needed to prepare for the inevitable discussion with her father that could change her life forever.

The loud snap of a tree branch came from off the path. Lucy stopped and turned toward the sound, a rush of adrenaline surging through her body. An odd magic began to flow through her veins, slithering through her, preparing to strike. Her Fae hearing picked up on a slight jangle of gold chains and relief filled her; though it was soon replaced by repulsion.

Jasper.

"I know you're there," she announced to the Fae male hidden in the shadows. The overwhelming feeling of her strange magic receded as she spoke. "You can tell my father I've returned."

She turned her head and continued inside, not needing to confirm that the lurking male had heard her. Lucy knew her father's second-in-command would make it to Corvus to inform him of her presence before she even stepped foot into her bedchambers.

"I'm done running," she said in a mumble, and though Jasper was sure to hear it with his Fae senses, she wondered if she said it aloud for his benefit or for hers?

Lucy may have been done running, but her plan was far from over. She needed to convince her father that the marriage he arranged for her must be called off immediately. If she could not do that, then her real battle would soon begin.

Lucy stared at the space she had called home for over one hundred twenty years. Her bedroom was exactly how she had left it, everything in its respective place.

Her ornate gowns were hung in her wardrobe hiding the pants and leggings she vastly preferred, the window overlooking Denora lay open with the soft breeze wafting through, and the wedding announcements that made her stomach churn were still in a pile on her bed. She sat on her bed, pushing the announcements to the side, looking at the space that seemed frozen in time. No matter how hard she tried, she couldn't comprehend how so much within her had changed.

Time moves differently throughout the realms, so her

absence from her home in Denora allowed her nearly a week in the mortal realm of Joterra. Two days ago she was begging her father to allow her to take on the roles of the family business. When he said no, and instead discussed an arranged marriage, she ran away from home to try to prove herself. Now, she had returned as someone internally changed. Someone who had taken on the burden of saving her entire family's legacy and came out stronger in the end.

The breeze carried through her room to where she sat on her bed. Upon her return, she had hastily placed the branches from The Elderwood under her bed and out of sight, then freshened up for her meeting with her father. His second-in-command, Jasper DeValey, had already delivered the news of her arrival, which, knowing her father, would surely prompt an urgent gathering. Restlessly, she began pacing her room, waiting for her father's summons ever since, panic growing with every step.

Crossing the room to her window, Lucy leaned against the brick wall looking out to her family's courtyard and the landscape beyond. The Baum Estate was in the Central Territory, near the outskirts of the city. From her bedroom window, the expanse of the Nilban Woods unfolded in the distance, reminding her of her journey that felt like a lifetime ago.

In those woods, she had her first experience with death as she fought for her life against a small pack of wolven. Her eyes darted to the wardrobe that concealed the bloodied arrow she hid, nervously ensuring it remained out of sight.

She could never have predicted that she'd encounter so much death and violence in such a short span of time. Lucy mindlessly rubbed the palm of her right hand as it throbbed—the feeling of The Elderwood's unparalleled magic writhing inside of her.

Why did you do this to me? she asked the strange magic, still so lost as to how this immense power lived within her. Her heart raced as each memory sliced into her like a knife, tumbling through her at a speed she could no longer control.

Her perfectly poised exterior threatened to crumble at the thought of everything she was trying to hold together.

Lucy smoothed the skirt to her red gown, took a deep breath, and turned away from the open window in an attempt to calm her nerves. A glance in the mirror was all it took for her memories to play in her mind on a loop.

Red.

The blood of the wolven she slaughtered on her way to Joterra.

The bandana Micah wrapped so delicately around her eyes as they played seek-and-find.

The wine they shared in the privacy of the study.

The flames of the fire as it overtook Abe's house.

The bloodied and burned mortal she struck down.

The brand that burned into her palm as she made a vow to The Elderwood.

Her lungs seized and she couldn't breathe.

She walked away from the mirror, trying to shake the memory, bracing the wall, begging for breath.

Her fists balled tightly as she forced her mind to

refocus on the upcoming meeting with her father. She needed a clear mind if she were to sway him into understanding what she did. So much was riding on him finally accepting her for who she was. However, many things had happened in such a short period of time, and someone would have to be held responsible for the damages to the forest—and for the loss of life.

I am the one who saved the entire Elderwood, but I'm sure my father won't see it that way. Instead, I will be the one at fault for it all.

Lucy uncurled her fist to inspect the magicked scar from The Elderwood tree. It was either a curse or a gift, but she was unable to tell which. The deep red lines that formed the Baum Bowyer sigil filled the palm of her hand—though she still didn't understand why or how it happened.

With a feather-light touch, she brushed over the marking with her left hand, willing a concealment charm to keep it hidden.

Pacing the room, her body renewed its panic. With each passing thought, her heart pounded harder. *What will happen in these next days? Micah is so far... The only way back to him is to convince my father to just hear me. Really hear me.*

She stopped and sighed as she listened to the wind. The soft breeze on her face reminded her of working in the shade of The Elderwood trees. Closing her eyes, she took a deep breath in, and with it, the scent of Micah seemed to float to her on the wind—the warm earthy smell of the man she yearned for.

Lucy followed the aroma, her head tilted up, toes

gently guiding her, but when she opened her eyes, she stood alone in her room, seeing nothing but the sprawling vista of northern Denora through the window.

Her eyes caught the glinting snow in the mountain scape far beyond the city in the Northern Territory. There, protected within the Leithe Mountains, was where Lord Laurent Sloan resided with his military forces. Lucy grimaced at the thought of him—the Fae to whom she was promised.

It was difficult enough that Lucy did not approve of the arrangement to Lord Sloan, but when the betrothal was made public, the servants of the Baum Estate had no qualms with whispering their gossip in the halls.

"Did you hear what Lord 'Slain' did this week?"

"Another attack on his own people."

"When will the King step in and do something?"

No one knew for sure if the rumors were true or not, but it was worth keeping in mind. On the other hand, these were the same Fae who gladly spread erroneous gossip that Lucy was overjoyed at the love-match. *Don't believe everything you hear,* she reminded herself.

A knock on her door drew Lucy back into reality. She took a step closer and nervously tugged at her gown. "You may come in."

Her brother, Wes, entered the room and she exhaled a soft sigh of relief.

"Lucella," he said in greeting, but the formality of her full name made Lucy's heart fall just a little.

He's upset with me.

He stood within the doorway, clad head to toe in his customary professional attire—long dark slacks and a crisp white tunic underneath a silver suit jacket with greenery embroidered on it. Always the perfect Baum son.

"Wesley," she replied in mock sincerity. She crossed her arms to conceal her hand and leaned against her bureau, waiting for her brother to give the scolding she was sure he had planned in his head hours ago.

Wes was the only brother in her family who had ever bothered to spend time with Lucy. Until her father recently put an end to it, Wes had allowed Lucy to accompany him on his trips to Joterra when she became restless at home and was avoiding her studies. It was during those travels that Lucy reunited with her friend, Abe, and felt as though she had found her calling within the Baum Bowyer family business. Now that she was older, Wes often needed reminding that she was no longer the little girl who needed an attendant.

Wes sighed and looked at Lucy with an irritable scowl. "How could you have been so careless?"

Lucy knew there would be repercussions for her taking the amulet to travel alone to the mortal realm, but she wasn't expecting Wes to be the one who would dole out the first chastising. It went without saying that her acquisition of the family heirloom would be a source of contention once others found out. Though in reality, if she had to do it again? She would. Burning a mortal to death, on the other hand? She wasn't so sure. The memory of his gruesome death made her squirm with unease. Lucy pushed the thought aside, not ready for others to know about it just yet.

"Yes, yes, I know. Get on with it." Lucy fanned her

hands at Wes as she sat down at the edge of her bed, stilling herself. "Proceed. I'm comfortable and ready for the lecture."

"This is not a joke, Lucella," he said to her sharply, walking toward her. "You could have gotten killed out there! Then what would Mother have done? And with the amulet, no less! Father would have been beside himself!" His anger was palpable, but Lucy refused to hear it.

"Father would have cared about the missing amulet and the broken business deal. Nothing more," Lucy said dismissively as she turned away from him. Her fingernails bit into the skin of her flesh as she looked out the window on the other side of the room.

The words sounded cruel and vindictive, but she thought them true nonetheless, and the pain of that stung. Truthfully, everything inside of Lucy hurt, and her spiraling thoughts came crashing from her mouth.

"They care for nothing except the business. They don't care that there is a new guardian there, as long as one exists, correct? They do not care that Abe is gone. That he's- he's... dead." She gasped for breath, the hard truth of those words making her ill.

"He's dead?" Wes asked in a faintly He looked up and ran a hand through his dark brown hair. Slowly, he walked over to her and knelt on the wooden floor in front of her.

"Lucella."

She refused to look at him.

"Lucy," he said, his voice a whisper.

At that, she finally turned to him, traitorous tears in her eyes.

Don't cry, she told herself.

"I'm sorry about Abe," he said to her, solemnly. "I know he was your friend. I'm sorry we weren't made aware in order to support you through this." Wes gently took her hand in his and her heart threatened to crack right in half.

Lucy inhaled sharply, choking on the tears she held back with all of her might. She blinked furiously, her heart sinking with each passing second.

"But you have to know that our parents do care; deeply. Our parents loved Abe. And they love you, Lucy. We all love you."

Unable to hold it back any longer, tears poured from her eyes, each drop a memory of her dearest friend, Abe. With everything that had happened, she barely had any time dedicated to grieving her most treasured friend in all the realms. And beyond that, her thoughts of Micah left her strained. It had only been a few hours, but she already missed him more than words could describe.

"Everything has gone so wrong," she whispered, taking deep breaths to calm the tears. He raised his hand and a small burst of silvery light swirled out from his fingers. A delicate gust of air dried her tears, carrying them away on the shimmering wind until it dissipated.

"Then let us meet Father so you can tell him every-thing," he said. He stood up and carefully straightened out his clothes. "He is ready for us in his study." Wes's attentiveness toward her faded with each word.

Lucy looked up at him in question, apprehension

clear upon her face. Wes, however, called on his rehearsed stoic expression, preparing for the audience with their father. Lucy recognized the facade he donned, knowing it was her turn to do the same. Her father did not appreciate overtly emotional displays from his adult children, and ensuring that she was up to his standard would allow the meeting to progress without additional complications.

Wes extended his hand and Lucy wrapped her fingers around his arm as he escorted her to the study where Lucy's actions would be judged.

Please, let him listen. She wasn't sure what she would do if her father didn't understand the risks she took and why. There was no other plan for her to attempt.

Please. She squeezed her fist tightly, begging for strength.

"Father, you don't understand," Lucy tried to explain for the third time. "I had no other choice!" Her patient exterior crumbled with each passing second.

"You talk of choices as if your future is not yet defined," Corvus Baum scoffed at his daughter. "You took a prized artifact that does not belong to you, traveled without an escort, and masqueraded as a true representative of the Baum Bowyer industry. Each step of the way you deliberately defied Denoran tradition. And your poor mother! She was worried sick!"

"I was gone for less than two days, Father," Lucy replied in frustration. "Surely *worried sick* is an exaggeration. By the time either of you realized I had gone, I was already back by nightfall."

Lucy paced around her father's study, trying to find the words to make him understand. She did everything she could to hold her tongue, but her father's Denoran views of females made each and every word from his mouth harder and harder to take.

If one of her brothers had made this choice, Corvus would have forgiven them immediately. However, because Lucy was a female, his expectations for her were skewed.

Lucy took a deep breath in, centering herself with the smell of bow varnish bottled on the shelves. She was astounded that they weren't listening to the crucial findings from her journey: Abe was gone, The Elderwood was unguarded and at risk, and there was now a new guardian who desperately needed support. She didn't dare mention that in her attempt to save The Elderwood, she had slain a mortal. It would have to come out eventually, but she wasn't ready for the emotional onslaught.

The meeting felt never-ending with the conversation going around in circles, Corvus never truly listening to what had happened while she was gone. He could not understand that her six days in Joterra had been filled with more than just her mistakes.

She sagged into the worn leather chair across from her father's enormous wooden desk as Jasper DeValey and Wes sat off to the side. Jasper's usual oily sneer was slick on his face as Lucy received her scolding, but she contently ignored him as she was apt to do.

Instead, she looked to Wes, desperate hope buzzing

through her. His face hardened and he looked away, siding with their father. Lucy pursed her lips and forced her eyes straight ahead, realizing that, as usual, she was alone. *Here I am again, back at square one, trying to prove myself to every male in my life.*

Corvus sat at his desk—the same desk that Lucy had meddled in without his permission a few days prior. His colossal frame filled the space as true power exuded from his stature—it was one of the reasons the family business remained successful. Not only did the Baum Bowyers have exclusive access to The Elderwood, but Corvus Baum was a powerful Fae, and there were few who would dare to cross him.

"Please," she begged, "please, listen. I just borrowed the amulet. Then when I got there, The Elderwood was at risk, I—"

"The Elderwood is none of your concern," her father boomed, his fist pounding the desk. "If you had not gone to the mortal realm, we would not be in this dire situation."

"If I had not gone, the realm would have been destroyed," she challenged, her voice rising to meet his, a flare of fire thrumming in her veins that she did not expect. With shaking hands, Lucy stood as she held her ground, refusing to back down to her father. "Abe was not there to defend the property and if I wasn't there, all would have been lost!"

Corvus looked at her with wide eyes. Lucy had never known for someone to raise their voice to him before, and it was clear that he did not approve. His eyes narrowed and he quieted as she continued her tirade, her face flushed with anger.

"You should be *thanking* me, not punishing me, for doing my duty to protect our family's legacy." She stood stock-still, keeping the raging emotions at bay, unsure of the tingling sensation now writhing under her skin.

"This is *my* legacy, Lucella," her father replied with bone chilling calm. He gripped the edge of his desk and stood, a deep purple aura of magic radiating from his large stature, threatening to explode. "Your place is with your soon-to-be husband," he said as he stooped his tall frame to make himself eye level to Lucy. "It is not traipsing through the realms pretending to be something you're not."

Lucy took the reprimand like a slap to her face, physically taking a step back from him and his hurtful words. "And what is it you believe me to be, Father?" she asked, poison lacing her tone. Her blood simmered just below the surface. She pushed the rage back down, her fingernails digging into the palm of her hand as she desperately tried to regain her composure.

"Not a bowyer as you so often pretend," he said with a sneer. "The marriage to Lord Sloan will continue and you will not be leaving the grounds anytime soon," he declared. He sat and went back to the paperwork on his desk, the magic receding back into his body like smoke being filtered through a summoning charm. "You are not to return to Joterra, you will not travel with your brother, and all pretense of what you think your life should be ends now. Have I made myself clear?"

"You cannot mean that," Lucy said, breathless in her

response. Her father had never spoken to her this way before. He had never made her feel as worthless as he did just then. "I have to go back! Please, Father."

Corvus did not look up to face her and Lucy's shoulders sagged beneath the realization of the truth in his words. His dismissal of her was absolute.

"Jasper," he commanded, still focused on the paperwork at his desk, oversized quill in hand. Wes and Jasper immediately stood at attention. "You and Wes are to go to Joterra to gain control of the situation. Inform the new guardian of his role and restore the power between realms. Prepare a formulated spell to repair the home. Report back as soon as you've returned."

Jasper nodded and looked at Lucy with a derisive grin. "Of course. I'd hate to see any more mistakes being made on behalf of the business. You should be ashamed to call yourself a Baum."

The lights flickered and the room darkened as Corvus slowly stood up, his shadow growing tenfold on the wall. His eyes narrowed as darkness seeped from the far corners, like spilled ink—Corvus's trademarked move. A promise of violence loomed in the air in dim candlelight.

Only the strongest Fae of Denora had an additional power or skill set. Corvus owned the ability to manipulate the shadows with his purple aura to make his presence seem more menacing.

And it worked.

"What did you just say to my daughter?" he asked Jasper with a deadly expression.

Jasper gulped down his next words, his eyes looking

wildly around the room, nervously turning the gaudy rings on his fingers. "I just meant—"

Corvus's hand flew up in front of him as his gaze narrowed at Jasper. Ever so slowly, he pulled his fingers into a fist, squeezing so tightly they turned red.

A strangled cry left Jasper until he was wordlessly moving his lips. The ascot Jasper wore every day clamped around his neck, pulling tighter and tighter, making Jasper's already bulging eyes widen more.

"You will never speak to my daughter that way, ever again," Corvus said, emphasizing each word slowly. "She is a Baum and she is my blood. You will never disrespect a single person in this manor again. Is that understood?"

Jasper gasped for breath, pulling at the scarf around his neck, straining for air in a chaotic frenzy.

"Is that understood?" Corvus repeated, squeezing his fist tighter, his magic closing off Jasper's breathing completely.

Jasper nodded his head frantically as he turned purple beneath the pressure.

Corvus released him and placed his hand on the table. The shadows scurried off as the brightness returned to the room.

Lucy stood rooted in place, eyes wide and unblinking, taking in what had just happened with quiet, hyperventilating breaths.

He stood up for me.

Her shock must have been apparent, but she wasn't sure how to grasp what she had just seen. She had never seen her father display that sort of violence before, though she had heard the stories and knew he was capable.

Jasper quickly left the room, coughing and gasping for air. Wes looked between his sister and father with trepidation.

Corvus gave Wes a nod. "You're all dismissed."

Wes bowed and quickly followed Jasper out into the hall.

"Wait!" Lucy rushed after them, abandoning the idea of trying to convince her father. "Please Wes, please listen to me!"

Jasper rubbed his neck resentfully. A taunting curl of his lip made its presence known as he watched their interaction.

Wes faced Jasper, aware of his prying eyes. "I will meet you at the front gate when I have packed and changed for the journey."

"Don't be late," Jasper said hoarsely, rearranging the ornate golden necklace around his reddened throat. "We have a mess to clean up and I'd like to get it over with as quickly as possible."

Wes turned his back on him in dismissal, a rude gesture no matter what realm you were from. Lucy looked at Wes, hopelessness filling her heart. She needed her brother to be on her side. Without him, there would be no one else who could help her.

Wes hasted across the estate, not speaking a word to Lucy. She followed after him, afraid to break the silence.

He strode into Lucy's chambers, and as Lucy closed the door, he pulled her into the center of the room with urgency. He lifted his hands in the air and spoke the

Denoran words to materialize a privacy charm, his hands swooping into a large half circle enclosing the entire room. A shimmering sheen filled the space around them, proving the charm to be in effect.

"Thank you, Wes," Lucy said, relief filling her voice. "I just need to get back and there is just so much to—"

"Lucy," he interrupted. "I have a feeling you are withholding important information and I am very curious to hear what it is you so conveniently forgot to tell Father." His serious expression bore into her soul, his knowing eyes alight with purpose. This was one argument she was sure to lose. "Why are you so desperate to return?"

Lucy looked up to the ceiling of the room, gave a heavy sigh and turned back to her brother, nervous to admit that he was right. Her thoughts were in turmoil, wary of what she was willing to tell him.

"Well," she began, hesitantly. "The new guardian is named Micah. He helped me to protect the property, and we..." Lucy paused, unsure of how to describe the enormity of what happened between them. "We, connected?"

Wes took a quick step closer to Lucy, looking at her in disbelief. "Surely, you did not do what I think it is you are about to admit." He paced the room, running his hands through his straight brown hair that always fell so perfectly it made even Lucy jealous. "In fact, maybe you shouldn't share with me."

This is so typical. If she were one of her brothers, the males would be sharing in cheers for the power of her magic and the bonds she had tied with Micah. However, since she was a female, they would hear nothing of it. She preferred not to dig herself into her own grave, so she went about this withheld knowledge from a different angle.

"He is my friend, Wes," she said gently as she placed a hand on his arm. In her mind, she was Wes's equal, and the constant belittling was pushing her closer to her breaking point.

"Friend," he said flatly.

"He is mortal and barely aware of any of the knowledge he is supposed to have of the realms and of magic. He needs assistance to learn what he is meant to do there."

Wes stared at her blankly, clearly unimpressed with her response.

Lucy withheld a frustrated groan and instead huffed out a sigh.

"I will talk to this new guardian for you," Wes said hesitantly.

Eyes bright, Lucy looked at Wes with the faint hope that she finally had someone on her side.

"I will tell him the basics of what he needs and set up a way of communication in case of emergencies. Is this acceptable?"

It was not a perfect plan, but it was something. The weight of the realms left Lucy's shoulders, and she pulled him into her arms for a hug. It was not an ordinary act to show this kind of familial affection, but Lucy was tired of doing things the Denoran way.

Wes's body first stiffened at the gesture, but after his initial surprise, he wrapped his arms around his sister, returning the hug. They held onto one another for just a moment, and Lucy reveled in the feeling of being just a little less alone.

"Thank you," Lucy whispered, tears threatening to pierce through the barrier she was tired of holding.

"I'm glad you're okay," Wes responded in a murmur. With one last gentle squeeze, Wes turned and walked from the room, dismantling the privacy ward as he left, and a flood of tears crashed down Lucy's cheeks.

TWO

MICAH

Nearly three days had passed since Lucy left. Micah spent his time cleaning up the charred debris of what remained of Grandad's home during the day and he slept in the crowded confines of his car at night.

The trunk of his car was filled with his grandad's belongings Micah had sorted through before Lucy had come into his life—but that felt like a lifetime ago already. He was glad he was able to save the important documents for the lawyers, but signatures and legal jargon didn't seem to matter in the grand scheme of things.

Of everything he was able to save, it was the picture of his mom and grandad that he was grateful for. Micah had propped it up on the dash so that it watched over him as he slept each night, reminding him that he was on the right path.

He just had to be patient.

The vow he had made to protect The Elderwood meant he couldn't leave the property for long periods of time, and since someone had just come and torched half of the land, he was hesitant to leave it unoccupied for more than an hour or two. He took a few quick trips into town to get basic supplies, figuring it was safe enough, but he really didn't know. There wasn't much of a plan in place. All he knew was he was stuck here. Alone.

Under the heat of the sun, he sat in the yard near the fire pit, looking out into the ancient trees that got him into this situation to begin with. Most of the grove had evidence of char, and many trees were destroyed from the devastating fire from the arsonists. Only one patch of land was salvaged, and the green leaves of those magical trees swayed gently in the breeze.

The tree that held the portal was safe, and Micah would remain here to ensure it stayed that way. He just wished that Lucy would hurry up and come back to him, because he didn't know what to do next.

He took his time sorting and piling the destroyed wood, preparing it for the fire pit. He reached down and grabbed another branch and a strong zap coursed through his arm.

"Ouch!" He dropped it and shook his hand. *What the hell was that?*

The piece was a lighter color than the other branches.

He looked around at the trees nearby, all of them a deep brown. This small branch was pale; almost gray compared to the dirt it laid upon. He searched the littered ground around him. There were a few more pieces in a small stack off to the side, as if they were thrown there in a hurry.

It was then that he realized where it was from.

Lucy and Micah had traveled to The Elderwood to gather wood for Lucy to bring back to Denora. During the fight to save The Elderwood, some branches broke. Lucy took the pieces that were big enough to use, and the rest were left here in this pile. He stepped closer and pushed the stray branch back into the heap with his leather boot, careful not to touch it again with his skin.

He sighed in dismay as he looked at the broken branches. Lucy told him this wood was unique, with special, magical properties.

This is all I've got left of her, huh?

He assumed throwing it into the burn pile was probably in poor taste, so he left it to the side of the tree line, deciding to deal with it later.

He was exhausted and his body was sore from sleeping in his car, so he abandoned his task and sat by the fire pit. *I can't keep this up.* He put his elbows on his knees and ran his fingers through his hair, drowning at the thought of what to do next.

"Hello there," a voice said. Micah jumped to his feet, startled to see two men standing in front of him. He hadn't even heard them walk up. How could he have missed them?

The first one who spoke was tall and lean, with long brown hair. His light-gray eyes complimented his pale skin, and his dark blue uniform was emblazoned with silver and gold leaves. He stood with an air of confidence so different from what he had ever seen before that Micah considered he may not be mortal.

The older of the two looked closer to his father's age.

His dingy long blond hair was swept into a low tie. He wore a white, high-collared shirt framed with tacky gold chains.

"Who are you?" Micah watched the strangers cautiously. "Where did you come from?"

"My name is Wesley Baum," the younger man responded. He spoke in a cadence that reminded him of Lucy. *Were they from Denora?* "I believe you've met my sister Lucella?"

"Lucy is your sister?" Micah asked in disbelief. He wasn't sure if he was relieved or worried. "How is she? Is she okay?" He took a quick step toward Wesley as he asked. He tried to keep the desperation out of his voice, but failed miserably.

"My name is Jasper DeValey," the other man interrupted before Wesley could respond. "Seems to me we have some business to attend to now that you are the new guardian of the portal." Jasper took an assessing scan of Micah and the land around—distaste evident upon his face.

The only proof a house ever stood on the property were the large beams of wood, charred and destroyed. Jasper eyed the tree to The Elderwood, an emotion flashing over him that Micah couldn't identify, but it was gone as quickly as it came.

"I'm not sure how we are supposed to work in these conditions," he said with disgust.

Micah looked at the older Fae, wondering if he ever made a pleasant expression.

"Then let's get on with it," Wesley said with no intention of friendliness. He nodded toward the ruins, then glanced at Micah. "Please stay out of the way."

Micah took one step back and then another as the two Fae moved to stand ten paces apart, facing the wreckage that was once Micah's safe-haven. The duo lifted their hands high into the air and tilted their heads toward the sky, taking deep and steady breaths.

It started with a calm, velvety breeze racing through the trees, brushing against Micah's bare arms and sending a chill down his spine. Looking to the sky, he watched as the clouds slowly moved to block the sun. The two Fae were frozen in their peculiar stance, making the hair on the back of Micah's neck tingle.

Suddenly, the wind picked up around them, sending leaves and debris flying through the air. As the Fae men dropped their gaze to the ashes and destruction that was once Abe's house, they whispered in another language. Swirling light came from their hands and soared toward the empty space in front of them. The shimmering light twisted and turned around the broken remains of the cabin, covering each piece in a radiant luster.

The wind around Micah grew to a brutal current, crashing into the surrounding trees and making them bend and sway violently. He crouched down low, trying to avoid the magic bolting around him. The forest shook in the squall, the chaos threatening to uproot the trees.

What the fuck is happening? He watched in a panic as the shimmering magic picked up charred pieces of the old front door. They floated midair for a moment and then, caught in the gust of wind, zoomed past him again and again as the torrent circled around them. The Fae men remained with their hands outstretched, having to shout the spell over the sheer volume of the wind.

Micah froze as the Fae men pushed more light from their hands, the radiance building with each erratic beat of his racing heart. He put a hand in front of his eyes to block the blinding light and swirling ashes, nearly falling to his knees from the powerful magic on display before him.

As if the wind ceased completely, the ashes and debris calmly came to a halt and floated in the empty land before them. The wind raged on around him, while he stood in the quiet eye of the storm, as though an invisible sphere protected them from the chaotic whirlwind just beyond.

This is unbelievable.

The ash and remains bathed in the magical light, bending to the will of Jasper and Wesley as they twisted their hands ever so slowly. As they pushed their magic into the space before them, the rubble and debris formed spiraling shapes that spun in the air above them, whirling around faster with each rotation.

"Close your eyes," Wesley ordered Micah loudly, keeping his attention focused on the house.

Micah wasn't sure why he needed to close his eyes—he had seen Lucy control magic before. Nevertheless, he obeyed, and did so just in the nick of time. A bright light abruptly flashed before him, making him cover his already closed eyes with his hands. Complete silence followed the radiant blast.

No more wind, no rustling leaves, not a sound to be heard.

Micah carefully opened his eyes and was astonished by what he saw. In front of him, where his grandad's house once stood, was a large wooden cabin, modernized and breath-taking. It fit in the outdoor space as if it had always been there.

"Now that's done, let's go inside to sit and go over the paperwork, shall we?" Wesley asked, dusting his hands with a clap as if the power he had displayed was a normal run-of-the-mill thing.

Jasper was a bit breathless as he followed Wesley into the house, ignoring Micah completely. He patted his sweaty forehead with a handkerchief as he walked.

"Uh, yeah," Micah replied, dumbfounded. *What the hell was that?*

Jasper and Wesley made their way into the newly built house as Micah trailed behind them, completely baffled by what had just happened. This was nowhere near the kind of magic Lucy had displayed in her time with him. Was that normal for Fae?

If Micah was speechless as they built the cabin, he was even more so now that he walked through the fully furnished house. The living room had a small wooden table, two brown leather chairs, and a couch. Across from the hall, where the dining room used to be, was an office. Micah's heart ached with the gentle reminder of Abe's old study. Empty bookshelves lined the walls, and the desk seemed to be stocked with parchment and quills—Micah didn't see a pen or pencil.

Peeking up the stairs, he noticed a hallway with additional bedrooms. He couldn't see inside of them, but he was sure they were likely supplied with the same modern furniture as the main level.

Walking to the back of the house into the kitchen he noticed the biggest changes. The old cabinets were replaced with walls of windows and the appliances were updated with the most modern technologies. A large, white marble island sat in the middle of the kitchen and a wooden table with chairs were off to the side along a wall that held an oversized window which looked out into the wooded grove that surrounded the property.

Micah ambled around the house with his mouth hanging open. It was so different, yet the wide windows that brought more of the forest into the cabin just seemed to fit.

You would have loved this, Grandad. His heart ached.

"Sit," Jasper commanded as he sat at the wooden table in the kitchen. With a flourish of his hand, he tried to push a chair from the table back a few inches, but all it seemed to do was wiggle a bit. On Jasper's third attempt, it was clear that he was directing Micah to sit, and Wesley used his own magic to pull the chair back with a roll of his eye. Jasper huffed in annoyance while Wesley maintained a smirk.

"H-how? How were you able to do all of this?" Micah sputtered, looking around in amazement.

"Magic," Wesley said with an air of impatience. His arrogance was hard to read. He didn't seem as mean as the older guy, but there was something about him, like there was something he was hiding.

Does he know something about me and Lucy? Does he know about the man Lucy killed?

"Yes, obviously," Micah snapped back. "But Lucy's magic looked different from that. It wasn't so…" he tried to find the word.

"Amazing?" Jasper supplied smugly.

"Extravagant," Micah replied, wiping the smile from Jasper's face.

"Lucella should not have used her magic here with you," Wesley said before Jasper could speak. "As for the magic you saw just now, it is predetermined magic. Prewritten, if you will. Lucella told us about the destruction of your home. We came prepared with the things you would need here in the mortal realm. A wooden home. Bedrooms, living areas, a kitchen with the common technologies." He waved his hand in the air. "The rest you can buy as needed." Wesley walked away from the table, inspecting his work with a self-satisfied grin.

"Like a pen?" Micah joked.

"A what?" Wesley replied, bewildered.

"Never mind," Micah muttered.

Jasper cleared his throat dramatically, shifting himself in the kitchen chair. "Now, as I was saying." He looked at Micah and pointed to the chair across from him with a jabbing finger. Micah sat slowly, still keeping his eyes on the two strangers. He didn't know them, and even though they said they knew Lucy, how could he trust them? He promised Lucy he wouldn't work with anyone but her.

Wesley was the brother Lucy spoke of regularly, but why did he keep calling her Lucella like she was a child being scolded?

This Jasper guy though... Micah couldn't put a finger on it, but there was something off about Jasper, something that made him stay on alert. Maybe it was the way his eyes bulged when offended; he looked like an insect being squished.

Normally, Micah had a good sense for reading people. Call it a trick of the trade or just practice being around people as a detective, but he could usually sense when people meant him harm and when they were not a threat; it was how he knew to trust Lucy, even when he first fought against that instinct.

Keep your cool, he reminded himself. *You don't know anything about these two or what they want from you.* He contemplated another moment longer. *Or what you want from them.*

"Abe held this position for many years before his passing. Our condolences," Jasper added in a flat tone. "I'm not sure why you are unaware of the transference process for the guardians at the gate, so I will try to be as succinct as possible."

Jasper spoke quickly and without remorse for Abe. Micah tried to listen as intently as he could, not wanting to miss any important information.

"You are not to leave the premises for more than a few hours at a time. You are compensated by the Baum family and we will send all funds to the same financial institution Abe used—your name is already on the account. I suggest the next time you go into your town, you stop in to provide any other contact information needed." He paused as he sniffed the air with disgust.

"Ensure you stop by a merchant to buy some soap," he added, then abruptly stood in dismissal.

"That's it?" Micah looked at him, eyebrows raised. "I know nothing about this job and nothing about your realm. What is it that I'm supposed to be doing?"

"You have nothing to do except stay here and wait for someone to call on you." Jasper walked over to the living room, preparing to leave. "Other than that, follow the few simple rules left to you. We have nothing else we need of you."

"I won't work for anyone else but Lucy," Micah said stubbornly.

Jasper paused and turned, his eyes glinted with violence. "Miss Baum will not be here to help you. You will figure it out without her, as is ordered by her father."

"You want to talk about ordering someone around?" Micah asked angrily, standing from his chair and striding up to Jasper. When face to face with him, Micah stood nearly a head taller than the greasy, arrogant Fae. "I refuse to do shit for you, and you can tell that to your boss as well. If you expect me to work with you or your business, *Miss Baum* better be part of the equation."

Jasper's sneer grew with each word until his teeth were bared at Micah. He rubbed at the rings on his hands angrily.

Micah was happy to face down this snobby old Fae who clearly didn't realize what Micah went through that week. In the past seven days, his entire world was turned upside down thanks to these Fae and their bullshit rules. He wasn't about to let them control his life any longer.

"If you need any help, we will assist you," Wesley

spoke for the pair. He looked between Jasper and Micah as they continued their stare down. Micah didn't move from his spot.

"Help? What kind of help do you need?" Jasper scoffed. "You are a mortal hired to oversee a *tree*. I think you'll be fine." He turned away from Micah and walked to the door once more.

"Lucy helped me. Her magic was more powerful than even yours," he told them. Wesley looked at Micah with interest, but Jasper had a completely different reaction.

"What did you say?" Jasper asked in a hiss, facing Micah once more. "Do you dare insult me?" Jasper met Micah's stare with his eyes bulging. "Are you insinuating that my magic is—"

"Lucy's magic is incredible," Micah interrupted. "When those thugs came and threatened The Elderwood, she was the only thing to stop them. Without her, the entire forest would have been in a blaze of fire," Micah said to them, proud of Lucy's determination.

"Pfft," Jasper scoffed. "Lucella Baum is nothing more than a disobedient child."

"Do not call her that." Micah squared off with Jasper again, his broad shoulders rippling under his thin cotton shirt. He refused to stand back as someone insulted Lucy. Not after everything she had risked, not after everything they went through together.

A vein popped out of Jasper's neck, his face ruddy and distorted with fury. Just as he opened his mouth to speak, Wesley stepped between the two and put his back to Jasper, looking directly at Micah.

"Agreed. She is not a child—far from it. However, she

has made many mistakes we are here to correct," Wesley said to him evenly. He pivoted his body to Jasper, speaking to him sternly. "Remember your warning. Go outside and ensure the premises is secure while I go over the last few items with the guardian here."

Jasper gaped at them both, his mouth opening and closing like a suffocating fish, his hands stroking the scarf around his neck. Clearly, he had more to say, but decided to keep it to himself.

This Jasper guy is unbelievable. Micah kept his guard up, clenching his fists, prepared to take him on to defend Lucy's name.

Wesley, however, waited patiently as Jasper stormed out of the house. Once he was gone, Wesley turned back to Micah with a hint of a smile in his eyes.

"Jasper regularly forgets that he works for my father, and therefore works for me. Not the other way around."

He led Micah into the living room and stood before an undecorated wall. "I appreciate you standing up for Lucy like that," Wesley said—it was the first time he called her that in front of Micah, and it didn't go unnoticed.

"Of course," Micah said. "If she were here, she would have done it for herself."

"Would she, now?" Wesley tilted his head to eye Micah with curiosity.

"She's a spitfire, that one," Micah said with a grin, remembering her fierce temperament toward him in the woods. "Lucy doesn't deserve the hand she is being dealt. She's an amazing woman. She just wants to be heard."

"That she does," Wesley replied with a crooked smile. "She took care to ensure you would have what you needed here. She wanted to say goodbye in person, but it is not something that can be done."

"Goodbye?" Micah asked in alarm, his heart racing as dozens of questions flowed through his mind. "Why goodbye?"

"My father will not allow it," he said simply.

Micah's heart fell.

"In the face of an emergency, this mirror will allow you to contact one of us for support." Wesley ignored Micah's obvious disappointment and continued the conversation as if he didn't just turn Micah's world upside down once again. "This will help in times of need."

Wesley faced the empty wall, stretched out his right arm, and spun it in a circle three times. On the third rotation, an ornate mirror appeared on the wall.

Micah took a step back, but said nothing. Each new expression of magic put a bit more fear in him, but he knew better than to ask how the mirror came into existence. Instead, he asked a question that would hopefully help him. "How does it work?"

"You look into the mirror and say the name of the person you are looking for while sprinkling this powder in front of you," Wesley said as he handed Micah a small drawstring bag filled with a pale powder, almost like sand. "If there is an emergency, call out that The Elderwood is in distress and someone will come to your aid." With finality, Wesley turned on his heel and strode to the front door.

"So that's it, then?" Micah asked in disbelief. He shook his head and again was forced to follow Lucy's brother out the door.

Wes paused to face the house with admiration. "This is probably the best and most intricate spell I've ever written," he said, ignoring Micah's question.

Micah saw Jasper walking around the grove of trees that held the portal to The Elderwood, looking between them intently. He bent down and touched something, but Micah couldn't make out what it was.

"The property is protected from any unwanted visitors," Jasper shared as he approached Micah and Wesley. "The house has also been charmed to withstand the years, just as the previous dwelling was. Keep the fires to a minimum," Jasper said, as his lips curved up into an unbalanced smile. "A female with a bow and arrow can't keep all unwanted people away, but now that we are here with real magic, far more sophisticated deterrents were put in place to keep mortals like the J. Pearson Land Developers at bay."

He turned and walked into the forest with Wesley, the words leaving Micah feeling uncomfortable. *What does he know about that day?*

Wesley looked back with a stalwart smile and nod to Micah, as Jasper turned to look at the portal with a leering grin. Micah watched as they left down the same path Lucy took back to Denora.

Micah retreated into the cabin, marveling at the brand new home he was given. Sitting back on the new leather couch, he tilted his head to look up toward the ceiling. *Magic did all of this,* he thought to himself and chuckled with disbelief. *Magic.*

He bolted upright.

Magic.

He ran to his car.

In the front seat, under the other papers, hidden away from view, lay the great, leather-bound book, filled with the knowledge from his ancestors.

Alderic Lumen created the book and it was passed down for generations from guardian to guardian, sharing the secrets of the portal to The Elderwood and the magic that surrounded it. There had to be answers in there somewhere. Answers to help him understand his place in the world now; to give him purpose.

He walked back toward the house, tucking the book under his arm and holding it close. The trees that started all of this seemed to dance in the wind, taunting him as he passed.

Those trees hid the woman who pushed him to face the hard truths about his life. The one who called him out on all of his shit and opened his eyes to a completely new world. Those trees were the basis of his relationship with his Grandad, and his mom, growing up in their shade, the shadow of their power bearing down on his family. Yet, here those trees were, still thriving, thanks to Lucy's powerful magic that had pushed the fire away from them in order to spare the portal.

From the corner of Micah's eye, he saw the light change, almost like a shadow. He jerked his gaze toward the lurking darkness to investigate, but when he looked, there was nothing. Just trees.

He shook his head, swearing to get a better night's sleep in an actual bed, and headed back into the house with the book in hand. There, he pored over every word he could understand, desperately searching for more answers that could lead him back to Lucy.

THREE

LUCY

The morning was not going as planned and Lucy was in her room alone, yet again. She never realized how much she hated being alone until now.

After meeting Micah, she craved that closeness that she had felt in his presence. She lay back in her bed, closing her eyes and thinking of the mortal who held such a large piece of her heart. *How do I get back to you?* She pictured his broad smile beneath those deep brown eyes.

Lucy had so many things on her mind and wasn't sure which answer to search for first. She was desperate to know why The Elderwood seared her family sigil into her palm. It was nearly all she thought about since her return—that and Micah.

Even with the concealment charm, Lucy could feel the raised lines of her scar. From a quick glance, you couldn't see that anything was different, but Lucy knew what lay hidden.

She released the charm and stared at the lines glistening in the daylight. Her finger lightly traced the arrow circling the tree with a bow for its roots; the Baum Bowyer family crest, now feeling like a lie.

Surely, there must be a reason for this... gift.

However, for all her contemplation, she couldn't fathom an answer. All she knew was that on her return home, when she came close to the portal, the lines on her hand glowed a bright green. Was it to remind her of her promise to watch over Micah? Was The Elderwood angry at her for channeling its magic during the battle?

The magic slithered through Lucy's body, reminding her it was still there. It was a quiet, silken graze beneath her skin, though every once in a while it felt more active, dancing wildly.

She wasn't sure what it all meant, but she found comfort in the power coursing through her—reminding her of her strength in Joterra and how she faced any threat to The Elderwood head-on, no matter how dire the outcome.

The memory brought a jolt of anger. She remembered the men trying to destroy the portal and hurt Micah. Visions of the fire flashed in her memory, heating her blood. Her newfound magic churned within her in response and rose to the surface like a wave crashing through her and exiting her palms; a slow jade mist danced around her scar.

Lucy gasped—it had never done this before.

She watched curiously as the green swirling haze glided over her hand and up her arm, twirling around her playfully. It moved from one arm to the other, caressing Lucy in a feather soft embrace. A giggle sprung from her lips in fascination.

"Why are you still with me?" she wondered aloud.

It slowly drifted back toward her right palm and dissolved into her skin, becoming a part of her once more.

Lucy waited with bated breath, wondering if the spirited magic would return, but nothing happened. Her hand displayed its round scar, and the magic resumed purring under her skin.

A knock on her door startled her back into reality, and she quickly returned the concealment charm.

Madame Baum entered with a polite smile of contentment on her face, but Lucy knew better than to believe that. Her mother had been upset with her from the moment she was made aware of Lucy's disappearance. However, following proper Denoran etiquette, Lucy's mother would never admit her grievances. She would move about her day as though she was not bothered, silently withholding any negative feelings.

"Hello, Mother," Lucy offered kindly, sitting up on her bed to greet her.

"Good morning, Lucella," she replied tactfully. Her mother pulled out the small stool in front of the vanity with her beautiful gold swirling magic. "Come. Sit."

Her mother's usual light and cheerful smile seemed pasted on, her brightness dimmed somehow.

Lucy nodded in reverent compliance and sat before the vanity, allowing her mother to dote on her. Lucy felt the distance growing between her and her mother, and wanted to mend it if she could. Despite knowing her actions would hurt her family, Lucy had hoped they would understand upon her return.

"You must look your absolute best today, Lucella," her mother told her as she fussed at Lucy's lavender gown, flattening imaginary creases and wrinkles. Picking up a brush, she arranged Lucy's hair.

Lucy held back a groan as she straightened her shoulders, preparing for the day's events. The arrival of her magic distracted her from her impending meeting with Lord Sloan.

"Remind me again why you believe I must marry this male?" Lucy asked.

Anita stopped mid brush stroke for just a quick second, but it was enough for Lucy to notice. Her hands shook as she continued.

"This marriage will be a beautiful way to bring Denora together once again, Lucella, you know this," she explained. "You will be the Lady of the Northern Territory and have a prosperous marriage to Lord Sloan."

Lucy looked at her mother in the mirror's reflection —it was only at times like this that Lucy felt like she could truly look at her. Her face was tight with her lips pursed, trying to withhold something.

Does she really believe the words she says, Lucy asked herself. *Or is she trying to convince herself, too?*

"Mother." Lucy turned to face her, holding her mother's hands in her own. "This isn't what I want," Lucy spoke plainly, hopeful that her mother would listen this time.

There was no time to speak in riddles, no reading between the lines—at least one of her parents had to understand that she did not want to get married. In fact, it was the last thing she wanted. She had spent so many hours dropping hints at the fact with no success.

Lucy never wanted to come across as disrespectful to her family, but at some point she had hoped that someone would really know Lucy for who she was and see that this was not the future she wanted. Unfortunately, no one noticed, and since no one else was speaking up for her, she had to do it herself.

Anita's face was painted in confusion. "What do you mean, dear? This will be a wonderful opportunity for you."

"No, Mother, it won't," Lucy said sternly, standing up now to speak to her. "I want to be a bowyer. I want to be part of the family business." She walked across the room to the window, looking out to the Nilban Woods. "I want to create and explore—I want to find my own path." She turned to her mother. "Why is that so wrong?"

"Lucella, you understand Denoran tradition more than you pretend to," she began harshly. She used her magic to float the hairbrush back to the dresser and quickly returned the chair to the vanity. "Enough with the foolishness."

"Because I enjoy crafting bows, I am foolish?" Lucy challenged.

"Yes, Lucy," her mother said sharply. "You are foolish for the ridiculous choices you've made. I will *never* understand why you felt as though leaving to another realm on your own was a wise choice. It is completely outlandish behavior."

The words knocked the breath from Lucy, the pang of betrayal more than she was prepared for.

The pained look on Lucy's face was enough for her mother to turn to leave. "I'm sorry you're so lost right now," she said over the shoulder of her gray gown, then she left the room.

Lucy took a deep breath, her blood rushing through her ears, unable to even hear as her mother closed the door.

How could she?

She tried to reason with herself as she looked in the mirror—trying to shake the feeling of devastation that swirled in her heart.

Why is there no one who will support me? Why is a business deal more important than my life?

Her long lavender gown was adorned with silver filigree along the bodice, with sheer, flowing sleeves reaching just past her elbows. It felt absolutely beautiful, and nothing like herself. She thought back to the woods on Abe's property... with Micah. When she could wear clothes that felt much more comfortable. Clothes that allowed her to run around in the forests and chop wood to create her elegant bows. She'd never be able to run in a gown like this.

And that's all she wanted to do—run away.

"It's time," Jasper's muffled voice came through Lucy's closed door. "Make haste."

"One more moment, please," she called, staring out

her bedroom window, trying to find the courage to withstand the next few hours. Her stomach roiled with unease and every breath she took felt more and more shallow.

You can do this, she reminded herself. *Have the semblance of strength in front of Father and get through the day to make a plan back to Micah.*

She took a deep breath.

"You may enter," she called.

Jasper entered with an impatient huff, his permanent sneer on his face drilling holes through Lucy. "Why are you taking so long?" He asked icily.

"My apologies. Of course," Lucy replied with mock sincerity. "It would be so unfortunate for Lord Sloan to have to wait on a female. Goodness, we can't have that happening."

Her scathing reply left Jasper's eyes bulging, and Lucy kept her smile hidden. He spent so much of his time making Lucy feel like a worthless Fae, she thoroughly enjoyed pressing every one of his buttons.

"Your father and I have already cemented this union that will spread the Baum Bowyers throughout all of Denora. You should thank me for my business prowess, yet you are ungrateful."

Lucy eyed him suspiciously. It was rare for him to make more than a few commanding remarks to Lucy. She was thankful that he was usually not much of a conversationalist.

"What if I don't want to thank you? The business was fine without the Northern Territory—my future did not need to become a bargaining chip." There was fire in her response and in her soul.

"Your future means nothing to me," he replied as he waved her off impatiently. "The Baum Bowyers will take over the whole of Denora and beyond with this union. You'll see. Your father will see it, too." His arrogant grimace made Lucy uneasy.

What part did Jasper play in this betrothal? Why is he so concerned?

As usual, Jasper kept two steps ahead of Lucy on the walk through the estate to meet her parents and Lord Sloan's entourage. As they crossed the foyer, she released a sigh of relief. There were no carriages, no soldiers, and no hustle and bustle of the staff.

He isn't here yet.

Lucy considered the royals in Denora as nothing more than over-served, demanding Fae who held the citizens of the realm to an unrealistic standard. Being that Laurent Sloan was the Lord of the entire Northern Territory, she was sure he was just as bad at the rest.

His reputation for being a malevolent leader echoed through the homes of the Kingdom, but the Dukes, and the King himself, were all too afraid to do anything about it. Whispered voices talked of Lord *Slain*, and his wrath among his people.

The citizens of the other territories were thankful that he kept his people in the North, rarely needing to come into the Capital for any business. Although, that was to change with the marriage agreement.

Some of the fire in her dimmed with a sigh. Lucy

couldn't understand why everyone thought her life was theirs to negotiate.

Her reality felt so small now that she had encountered so much beyond her realm. Here in Denora, she knew the expectations of a female Fae—and they were less than inspiring. She was to be a silent, beautiful figure who nodded subserviently to each request. Her mother, Anita, played the role wonderfully. Lucy preferred to live a life beyond service to her potential husband.

But in Joterra?

Her heart fluttered at the possibilities of a life in Joterra with Micah. In the mortal realm she could be exactly who she wanted to be, with no one there to try to change her. There she could shoot her bow and use her hands to create the most beautiful weapons for future archers. Dresses would be for special occasions only and she would never be looked down upon for wearing pants. Lucy could be exactly who she wanted to be without a Fae male, or anyone else for that matter, telling her she could not.

Jasper swung the doors to the garden open and stepped aside for Lucy to enter before him. His bow to her was negligible.

"There's my little flower," Corvus exclaimed as Lucy entered the room. She did her best not to blanch at the childish affection, curious of his change of tone from earlier that day.

The room was bright, with long oversized windows that stretched from the vaulted ceiling to the tiled floor. It was her mother's favorite room to host guests because of the beautiful view of the garden terrace, which was always expertly tended.

The sun refreshed Lucy, bringing her a sense of calm that she craved so very much. Her life had been turned upside down from the moment she left home, and she still had questions about this new magic that flowed within her. Her fingers dug into her palm as she remembered the soft green mist that made its swift, but short, appearance.

Lucy scanned the room, trying to prepare for the uncomfortable afternoon that was to unfold before her. Her father was seated comfortably before the fire, though the weather outside did not call for the additional warmth. Corvus liked to show off his power and influence by flaunting his wealth and his extravagant home. In his mind, a fifteen foot fireplace was a show of power, especially when he used a unique spell and a flourish of his hand to start the fire with golden sparks that crashed like thunder.

Jasper took a position behind her father and her mother stood near the plush armchairs and settees, awaiting her arrival.

One male stood at the far wall, but Lucy had never seen this Fae soldier before.

"Come, Lucella," Corvus called out to her. With a wave of his hand, a gray chair floated from one side of the room to the other, inviting her to sit. Lucy walked gracefully to the chair in her ornate gown with no hint of the clumsiness that she was so used to in the previous week due to the uncomfortable boots she wore in Joterra. She stood quietly and kept her lips pressed in a thin line, determined not to speak unless absolutely necessary.

Corvus, smiling like a pig in shit, turned to a man sitting across from him in a high-backed chair. She didn't even notice this stranger who sat with her father, still as a statue.

"This is my daughter, Lucella," Corvus proclaimed proudly.

The stranger stood to greet her with a sly grin and a boyish charm at odds with his regal stature. "Hello, Miss Lucella, it is a pleasure to formally meet you."

He was a handsome male, with long blond hair, nearly white as snow, and a straight, long nose over a thin mouth. He stood tall and elegant—beautiful in a way that Lucy had never seen in Denora; poised and quiet. Everything about him reminded her of the cold; even his posture was stiff. His commanding ice-blue eyes and the silver clothing hugging his muscular frame only added to the starkness of his pale skin.

Lucy wasn't entirely sure who this male was, so she curtsied obediently and sat, keeping a facade of pleasantry about her in order to appease her mother. She looked around the room distractedly and wondered when Lord Laurent Sloan would arrive with his entourage of soldiers and servants at his every beck and call.

"Lucy," Corvus began again. "This is Lord Sloan."

Her eyes swung toward her father at his declaration. Surprise painted across her face as she carefully observed the stranger across from her.

How is this man in front of me the terror known as Lord Slain?

Corvus smiled proudly as he turned to his daughter. "I thought it would be best for you two to get to know one another before we send the announcements out next week."

Her heart stopped, and she fixed her eyes upon her father.

Next week?

Lucy looked to her mother who was picturesque, propped on the plush settee, smiling placidly as the males spoke.

She knew... She knew, and she didn't even tell me.

As if reading her thoughts, Corvus continued. "We have moved up the wedding. We will hold it in four months."

"Why are you moving it up?" Lucy blurted, still staring at her father, the first words out of her mouth in front of Lord Sloan.

No, this can't be happening, she thought to herself, bile rising in her throat.

"Lord Sloan accepted my suggestion to have the wedding before the snow falls, as the long winter is on its way. We wouldn't want to delay such an extraordinary event in Denora, now would we?" His cautionary gaze was fixed on Lucy, demanding her words to be picked carefully in the presence of the Lord of the North.

"I see." She bowed her head and kept it down, refusing to look up at the males responsible for ruining her life, doing her best to compose herself.

"I look forward to courting you this month, Miss Baum," Lord Sloan said softly, the kindness in his tone clashing with what she knew of his reputation.

"Thank you, Lord Sloan," she replied sweetly. If there was anything Lucy knew, it was how to play the part when the time called.

Her father was sure to be shocked by her play of obedience, but she was no fool. Corvus got all of Lucy's harsh words and acts of protest, because she believed that deep down he once loved her with all of his being. Though it seemed a lifetime ago, she knew the feelings were still in there. Somewhere.

Lucy dared to look at Lord Sloan, trying to identify why this male sitting in front of her was one that others dreaded beyond all measure. He was tranquil and polite. Though, even with his soft white hair and gentle way of speaking, his features painted a picture of a predator to be feared. His long, thin nose and pointed chin gave him sharp features reminiscent of a bird hunting their prey.

Regardless, she would never give away her true thoughts of contempt to a stranger, let alone one she was set to marry. No, instead she would focus her efforts on trying to learn more about Lord Sloan. If there was any small detail she could collect in order to help her rid herself of him forever, she would find it. Then she would free herself from the manacles that Denora kept firmly shackled to every Fae female.

She was not the weak Fae her father once knew her to be, and she never would be again. She rubbed the palm of her hand in remembrance.

"This evening I would like to take you to dinner at

the Capital," Lord Sloan said with a voice of velvet, his eyes sparkling. "I have some business to attend to in the city, and Tralont has extended his welcome to me."

Lord Sloan's familiarity with King Tralont surprised Lucy; she had never heard of anyone speaking so casually about a royal. Even the dukes spoke of the King with great reverence and respect.

"I will be busy and cannot return in time to escort you myself. My guard, Roger, will be there to greet you if I am delayed." He turned to speak to her father. "Corvus, will you handle the travel arrangements?"

"Of course, Lord Sloan." Corvus's smile faltered momentarily, not used to being told what to do. "Jasper," he snapped, directing him to begin the arrangements.

Jasper's face pulled into a grimace behind Corvus, but he quickly replaced it with a vacant look, prepared to serve.

Lucy eyed the silent guard, still standing at attention nearby. He wore Fae armor and the emblem of the North. *How did I miss that?*

"Wonderful," Lord Sloan replied with a curt nod. "I am also interested in protecting those *assets* we were discussing, so I will be arranging that today as well."

He stood and all the others in the room stood along with him, including Lucy. His height towered over everyone except Corvus. The ladies gave a small curtsey, Corvus and Jasper gave a deep bow, and Lord Laurent Sloan left with his guard in tow.

The door closed with a click, and Lucy whipped her head toward her father. "How could you do this to me?" Lucy's lips curled in anger.

"Lucella Baum, I will not hear another word from you," Corvus said, exasperated. "You are lucky Lord Sloan is willing to marry you and that the rumor of your escapades have not been dragged around the realm!"

"I have no other choice in the matter, do I? My life means so little to you." Lucy's eyes welled with tears as her anger filled her entirely. Once again, the tingling sensation of magic rippled through her, begging to be released.

To Lucy's astonishment, Anita stepped in before Corvus spoke again. "Your life means everything to us, Lucy."

Corvus stood, face flushed with frustration, preparing to lecture Lucy on her behavior once more. However, once he turned and looked at his wife, his anger faded from his features.

Anita stood tall, her hands folded tightly in front of her, with silent tears falling down her face. Her sad eyes fixed upon Lucy.

"This marriage does not mean we do not love you. Your father has only your best interests in mind, and we want nothing more than for you to be well taken care of. No female in Denora lives a happy and full life all alone."

"We will not continue to speak of this, and you will not bring it up again and upset your mother," Corvus demanded. "You will go to the Capital today to dine with Lord Sloan and you will be on your absolute best behavior."

Lucy looked at her mother with unbearable hurt.

How could she sit by and allow this to happen? The look

Lucy gave her father was enough to kill, and the vibrating aura of her magic tempted to follow suit.

She swiftly turned on her feet to get as far from her parents as possible before her magic acted of its own accord once again. Though this time, she was both fearful and exalted by the new power seated deep within her, knowing the possibilities of this new magic were yet to be discovered.

She would never use the magic to hurt those she loved—but she didn't love Laurent Sloan.

CHAPTER

FOUR

LUCY

S torming back into her bedchambers, Lucy slammed the door shut, rattling the metal rails on her bed frame. Then she did something that she had not done in nearly 75 years. She spread her arms wide, lifted both hands into the air until they touched, and brought a powerful privacy charm over her room, strengthened by her otherworldly magic. Once she saw the pearlescent barrier in place, she let out a heart wrenching scream.

In agony, she released every painful moment she was ever ignored and demanded her voice to be uncaged. She screamed for the unfair wedding arrangement that she refused to accept. She screamed for the loss of her best friend, and the fact that no one understood her grief. And she sobbed, as she thought of the only person who understood her, and how he was so, so far away.

Lucy crumbled to the ground, exhausted by the burden of loneliness she carried with her.

I can't keep doing this. I need Micah.

Her hands braced the cold floor as she remained on all fours, trying to find her breath. Tears streaked down the tip of her nose and dripped ever so gently to the floor. She watched with ragged breaths as her teardrops puddled onto the wood beneath her.

Her ornate lavender gown was sure to tear with her huddled on the ground, but she could not find it in her to care.

What does it matter? she thought to herself despondently. *Nothing will change my fate. A torn gown will not change the mind of stubborn male Fae who care for nothing beyond themselves.*

She turned, sitting with her back against the wall, feeling the cold brick. Her racing heart hammered in her chest and she didn't know how to stop the raging despair inside of her.

That's when she felt it again: magic bubbling from deep within, starting in her broken heart and pouring through her like a wave. Her chest heaved as she felt the strange magic surge through her center like a blast of lightning until an emerald mist burst from her palms.

With her arms outstretched, a small sphere of green pooled in her hands. She stretched her fingers wide, numbly watching, curious to see if it would stay in her palm without her cupped hand there to contain it. Tipping her hand, she expected to see the mist pour over, but instead of falling, it floated. It changed form from a mist to a more solidified shape as it rose higher into the air.

No longer a sphere, the hazy magic turned into

several small orbs, spreading through the room, circling Lucy as she watched in awe at the magic which seemed to have a mind of its own. Each orb began to stretch and divide, but right before it split entirely, the two rounded edges formed wings. The shapes then flapped in a graceful dance around Lucy's bedroom.

Butterflies.

Her eyes welled with tears again, as the beautiful, luminescent butterflies fluttered around her, bringing back a memory long forgotten.

Lucy and Abe, in the depths of the forest, adventuring while their fathers discussed business. They came upon a field of wildflowers during butterfly migration season. Running into the field, they startled the beautiful winged creatures, creating a whirlwind of magnificence around the friends as the butterflies soared through the air. Abe grabbed her hand and pulled her onto the grass. There, lying on their backs, they looked up to the sky and watched the butterflies as they flew high into the clouds.

"I wish I were a butterfly," a young Lucy told Abe, wistfully.

"I don't want to be a bug," Abe laughed at her.

"I don't want to be a bug either," she laughed, then sighed. "I just want to be free."

Lucy's sobs filled the room again as her magic kept her company, gliding through the air, allowing her to feel just a little less alone.

~

By the time Lucy calmed herself, she was still without an appetite. In just a few hours, Lord Laurent Sloan would expect her at the finest restaurant in Denora and the very thought made her ill.

She paced back and forth in her lonely bedroom that had become a prison to her. The ornate furniture and soft comforts of her bed were a dazzling facade to the fact that Lucy was stuck in this cell of a room, not allowed to leave the estate.

She stopped at her open window, the breeze and fresh air clearing her mind for just a moment. A beautiful black raven perched on her windowsill. Lucy almost didn't notice it for how perfectly still it was.

"Hello, little one," she cooed to the bird. She slowly stretched out her hand, seeing if the bird would startle and fly away. Instead, it took a tiny hop forward.

Lucy pulled her hand back in surprise. Tilting her head, she analyzed the bird closer. It seemed to be watching her.

That's preposterous. Birds don't watch people.

Then the raven took another small hop toward Lucy. She smiled and reached out, carefully petting the bird with two gentle fingers. It was soft as silk, with the most lustrous black feathers.

"Thank you for visiting me," she whispered. "I wish I had some crumbs to offer you, but you don't want to be in this prison cell. Fly. Be free." Lucy bit the inside of her cheek; feeling so isolated was getting to her, but she wouldn't fall apart again. She turned from the window, a new determination filling her.

Her body buzzing, she pulled out the thin branches of

wood she had hidden under her bed. Lucy touched the beautiful pale branch sadly. Her father would never accept this wood for the creation of a new bow while he was so upset with Lucy. He'd just as soon throw it in his fireplace out of spite.

His anger was unmistakable, and she knew he wouldn't approve any request from Lucy to construct a bow from the wood she collected from her journey. She'd rather ask for forgiveness later than for permission now.

Her hands skimmed the branches from The Elderwood with longing, and she felt the whisper of a shiver through her heart and down her arms. Her magic rose to the surface, as the bouncing green light slid from her palm, danced around her body and retreated into her skin once more.

Her eyebrows shot up in surprise, wondering why the wood triggered such a reaction.

You feel me, too... Don't you?

Unsure of what it all meant, she took the time to examine each branch as she took them out of their hiding place. She went through the steps slowly, analyzing each piece and determining which would be the best pieces to use for a bow.

It was the first time she was able to be herself without having to pretend that she was fine.

She was not fine.

Thinking about Micah filled most of her night; every inch of her hurt with longing. She needed to find a way back to him. As soon as she saw him, she would jump in his arms just to feel his strong embrace. However, the most frustrating part was that she had no idea when that could be. Her life was, yet again, under control of her father.

Control. That simple word put a fire in the pit of her stomach. *I won't let them control me again.*

The small strap of her tool bag poked out from under her bed. She took it by the handle and dragged the bag out. It had been so long since she had used these tools. Her father hadn't let her create any bows in nearly a year, and most of her focus had been on getting him to listen to her. The last bow she made with her father had been sold to one of the dukes for their son's 150th birthday. It felt like a lifetime ago.

Picking up her tools, one by one, she noted the familiarity of their heavy weight in her hands. These were sturdy and reliable instruments, and they had assisted Lucy in making more than one hundred bows.

What harm could there be in one more? she wondered mischievously.

Selecting the longest, sturdiest branch from The Elderwood, she sent a silent apology to Duke Renfro for taking the material meant for his sons, and decided she would have better skill with this bow than any of the Renfros anyway.

Then, she went to work.

For more than an hour, she shaped and shaved the wood, sanding it down to the perfect form. Lucy balanced it in her hands, watching it as it rocked back and forth, perfectly weighted. It was a lethal weapon of beauty and grace.

She picked up the engraver and paused, unsure what design to choose. Usually she engraved her family's sigil along with leaves, but something about that felt off. Her hand tingled in response.

Yes, I know you're still there. I don't think I need another reminder.

She held the bow in her hands and closed her eyes, thinking of how she had changed so much. She was no longer interested in flowers and leaves—that was behind her now.

In her mind, Lucy replayed her moments with Micah, the heat that rose between them, the flames dancing in the window. She thought of the fire she controlled to save The Elderwood.

That's it. Lucy took her time carving tiny flames up and down the limbs of the bow, connecting them with vines.

When she finished, she looked at the masterpiece that reflected who she was now. Lucy was not a timid leaf blowing in the wind. She was fire—ready to burn down anything in her path.

A smile played on her lips as she held the bow in her hands. She would play her role at dinner that evening, but she would not be the demure, silent female that a Denoran male expects. No. She would prove to Laurent Sloan how absolutely wrong she was for him. Then, she would find her way to Micah.

Her parents could try to carve her path for her future, but it was up to Lucy which direction she took. Would she follow the perfectly placed stepping stones to a future in the mountains as Lady Lucella Sloan? Or would she trample through the Denoran wilderness to get to the handsome mortal man in Joterra?

There was really only one option, and he had the most perfect dark brown eyes that she had ever gazed upon.

And he was waiting for her.

JUST LIKE BEFORE, Lucy refused to sit around and wait for someone else to save her. She would be happy to forge her own path and upset anyone who got in her way—no one else minded they were upsetting *her*, did they?

I may be on my own, but that doesn't mean I'm weak.

Closing her eyes, she focused all of her thoughts on the emerald energy that buzzed within her, asking it to assist her. The magic hummed with excitement as it answered her summons, pouring out of her palms in a rush. Lucy watched as the green mist swirled around her arms, waiting for her command. Lucy whispered the Denoran privacy charm, ensuring her footsteps would be silent as she traversed the estate, getting the things she needed for her trip.

Hmm, this feels familiar, she thought sarcastically.

She crept down the staircase that led to the kitchens, knowing if she were going to leave, she needed food to take with her. Last time she made the trip, she was less prepared than she would have liked. Lucy had already missed both breakfast and lunch and any risk of weakness would endanger her plan.

Once in the kitchen, she stalled, listening in wait to make sure she was alone. Unfortunately, she heard the voice of someone she definitely did not want to run into. Her mother.

"Bethilda, please prepare the fish for my husband's lunch, his meeting should be over shortly."

"Yes, Madame Baum," the kitchen master replied.

"And, has..." her voice trailed off. "Has Lucella eaten?"

"Not that I am aware of, Madame. She did not come down for breakfast and ignored the summons for lunch."

Lucy bit her tongue at the remark. *I didn't ignore the summons; I ignored Jasper. There's a difference.*

"Well, I would like you to prepare a meal for her. Some of her favorites, perhaps? I know she prefers the cheese and meat rolls from Durrant. Maybe some vegetable soup with warm bread and butter?"

"Yes, Madame. Right away."

"When it is ready, please find me. I would like to eat with her." A softness filled her voice that Lucy did not recognize.

Why does she wish to eat with me?

Lucy listened as her mother's footsteps walked away, then she waited rather impatiently as Bethilda prepared her father's lunch. Once the kitchen master left, Lucy had to act quickly.

Darting into the pantry, she gathered a large loaf of bread, dried berries and nuts that she often took with her into the woods, and a jug filled with water. It wasn't likely to be a long journey, but history proved again and again that her plans never quite worked the way she anticipated.

With her bag packed full of the food for her journey, a

determined smile made its way upon her face. There was no doubt about it; Lucy was going to Joterra to be with Micah. Only one question remained—when would a window of opportunity present itself?

LUCY WOULD BE LYING if she said she was excited to eat with her mother, but if she was going to be leaving soon, it had to be done.

"Would you like some sugar for your tea?" Anita offered.

"No, thank you," Lucy replied.

The air was stifling, with an awkward silence hanging between them. What was left to be said? Lucy shared her issues and her mother dutifully ignored them —there was nothing else.

"I was just down by the Reiniers' last evening. Did you know Shoshana will marry Duke Renfro's eldest son?"

"Oh?" Lucy asked politely, though in reality, she did not care in the slightest. Shoshana was lovely, but Lucy hadn't spoken to her since she was quite young and was still required to take classes with the seamstresses.

"Yes, Maryanne is quite pleased. You know the Reiniers were very hopeful to marry to a strong bloodline."

Bloodlines.

An idea rose in Lucy's mind.

"How many weak bloodlines are there in Denora?" Lucy asked.

Her mother was smarter than she let on to the rest of the realm, but Lucy knew her mother was very knowledgeable regarding history and the families of Denora.

Perhaps she knows more about Alderic Lumen.

"Truthfully, more than is known. Most families of weaker magic do their best to compensate in other ways so that others don't see their true shortcomings."

"What do you mean?" This surprised Lucy. She was only aware of a few families who had weak magical capabilities due to their bloodlines.

"Most families who have... more *fragile* magic are well-known in the realm and they attempt to make allies in other ways. The Reiniers produce some of the most beautiful females in Southern Denora. Duke Renfro has an incredibly strong family line—he does not have to worry about the bloodline weakening with the Reinier line. Ethan Renfro can marry Shoshana and together they will bear beautifully strong Fae."

Of course. An arranged marriage for the sole purpose of strengthening Denoran tradition. The thought made her nauseous.

"However, there are also families who are weak who have nothing to offer. They do their best to hide it—they find other ways to be purposeful to the realm." Anita's voice dropped to a whisper as she leaned in close to Lucy. "Take the DeValeys for example."

The bulge of Lucy's eyes could rival Jasper's at the mention of his family line.

"*Jasper* DeValey?" Lucy asked in astonishment.

"Yes, dear. Are there any others?"

"I had no idea he was a weak Fae. How is that even possible? He has been working with Father for decades."

"Exactly," Anita said with a wry smile. "He is known for being in league with your father's business, so of course he must be a strong Fae." Anita winked.

"He isn't?"

"Absolutely not," Anita laughed as she shook her head.

Lucy stared wide eyed at her mother. How had she missed that?

"Think, darling. When was the last time you've seen Jasper use any magic?"

Her eyes blinked rapidly as she tried to recall a time. "Wait, what about Micah? Didn't Jasper and Wes have to travel to repair the house?"

Anita took a sip of her tea, a note of discomfort across her face at the mention of her mortal friend in Joterra. "Prewritten magic, yes. It's the only way Jasper has any success—that and Wes carried the majority of that spell."

"How can that be so different?"

Anita placed her teacup down and took a moment to choose her words carefully. "Do you know how prewritten magic works?"

Lucy squinted. "I probably should know this answer, but I am going to assume my tutors explained it during one of the lessons that I missed."

Her mother's pursed lips were light with the hint of a smile. "I see. Well, in short, prewritten magic is created by the caster. Wes created the spell for Abe's cabin to be restored, so his magic supported it," she said, pausing momentarily. "I am so sorry for your loss, Lucella."

A wave of silence overtook the room. Lucy wasn't ready to talk about Abe just yet. The hurt Lucy harbored over her mother's view of marriage was still fresh, and it was hard enough to speak cordially as it was.

Lucy cleared her throat and redirected the subject. "How many strong bloodlines are there in Denora?"

"Too many to count," Anita replied, taking another sip of tea. "Why do you ask?" Her perfectly shaded eyebrows furrowed in question.

Lucy just shrugged her shoulders. "Which are the stronger bloodlines in Denora? Any families we know?"

"I suppose it changes over time," Anita replied, setting down her teacup gently. "Bloodlines can weaken when mixed with others who are less powerful—that's exactly what happened to the Reiniers."

"Any others?" Whenever Lucy was upset with her mother, she always felt it was easier to ask questions than try to carry on a genuine conversation. It allowed her to seem polite without having to share her feelings on any given subject. However, in the past, her fury was juvenile. Today, her anger threatened to spill over— though she did her best to keep it contained.

"Hmm... The Brightons, Nostellas, Cridettes. Many of the families we celebrate with at the Winter Solstice."

"Which families would you suppose were the strongest?" Lucy wasn't sure how else to ask, hoping that her mother would give the Lumen name on her own without bringing any suspicion to Lucy.

"Well, ours, for one."

"Ours?" Lucy was completely caught off guard.

"Yes, dear," her mother replied with a soft smile on her lips.

"Just Father's side? Or yours as well?"

"Darling, do you think I am nothing but a pretty face for your father?" Anita asked in false distress.

"No, of course not," Lucy said quickly. However, the more she thought about it... *When was the last time I've seen Mother use her magic?*

"It is wise for females to use their magic strategically in Denora, Lucy," her mother told her seriously. Her voice dropped as she continued, as if worried about being overheard. "I know you think less of me because of my public subservience to your father, but not everything is what it seems behind closed doors."

Puzzled, Lucy looked at her mother at this strange admission. "What do you mean?" Lucy asked in an equally low voice.

Anita put her finger up to her lips to request quiet, and Lucy carefully nodded. With that, Anita stood up and walked a few paces away from the bed and stopped at the window. Her smile was wide and bright—something almost foreign to Lucy.

For so long, her mother had played the role of a silent figurehead for the family, never giving her opinion over important matters. She her practiced smile for the male Fae who came to do business with Corvus and the fancy estate dinners. She always smiled as she doted upon her husband.

But this. This smile was magnificent. It reached from one rosy, high cheekbone to the next.

It was real.

Lucy couldn't help but smile along with her as she watched, bewildered by the behavior.

What is she up to?

Anita turned to the window and took a deep breath in and out. She brought her hand up to her mouth and kissed her fingers, ever so softly, then blew over the top of her hand as though she was blowing someone a kiss. Her golden, shimmering magic drifted out the window to something down below.

Lucy stood and rushed over to the window as quickly and quietly as she could. Anita's eyes were bright and full of life as she put her hands on Lucy's shoulders and brought her closer to the window. From over her shoulder, Anita pointed at a rosebush in the distance, then whispered in her ear. "Watch closely."

The warm skin of her mother's arms pressed tenderly against her as she picked up on the scent of her delicate perfume. Being so close to her mother was a comfort she had not experienced since she was a very small child.

With a content sigh, Lucy bent further, trying to see what her mother wanted to show her in the plant. Suddenly, the entire bush grew dozens of bright red rose blossoms.

"Oh!" Lucy gasped as she clutched the window ledge, watching the green bush drown in large, red petals. She looked at her mother with wide eyes, as if seeing her for the first time. "How?"

This made little sense to Lucy. Her mother was known for using her magic for superficial beautification —pinning hair, smoothing make up, placing small details on gowns. But this? This was something she had never seen another Denoran female ever accomplish.

She has magic that works with nature?

"I've always been able to do these things, darling," her mother said, staring lovingly into her daughter's eyes.

"But you—" Lucy didn't know how to continue. She had never seen her mother do this kind of magic. Why did she hide such a beautiful gift?

"I know," Anita said with a sad smile. "I keep my magic private, because there is no room for a female who is stronger than her husband." She winked at Lucy, but the playful act took on a somber tone.

"Mother, I can't believe you have such wondrous magic! Female Fae shouldn't have to hide their magic when it is something to be proud of! And just because you are—" she stopped. "Wait."

Anita huffed out a small laugh as she saw her daughter register the last comment she made.

"You're stronger than Father? You can't be."

"I am."

"This is amazing!" Lucy trilled with delight. "Who cares what Father says? You should utilize your magic whenever and however you want!"

"I do, Lucy. Keeping my magic to myself is my choice. If your father had his way, I'd be flaunting my power all over Denora," she laughed.

"He is in support of your magic?" Lucy asked. Each time her mother spoke she learned something brand new.

How have I missed so much of this? How did I not know?

"He is. Why do you think he was so happy to show you the artistry of being a bowyer? Your blood runs thick with some of the most powerful magic in all of Denora," Anita said as she hugged her daughter. "What we do for you is out of love and respect for you and your magic. A strong pairing with another strong Fae is important—it allows for you to find equal footing within the marriage." Her voice trailed off at the change of topic.

Lucy stiffened under her mother's embrace, pulling back slowly.

"You deserve someone who will understand your strength and your need to always challenge yourself," her mother continued. "Lord Sloan is an exceptional Fae with powerful magic... Within a marriage, concessions are made."

"I will not be a concession," Lucy's tone fell. "I will not be with someone who gives me *permission* to be who I am," Lucy said with disgust.

"That isn't what I meant," Anita shook her head quickly, reaching out to Lucy as she spun away from her. "Lucy, all I mean is that there is more to marriage than Denoran tradition."

"Then let me find it on my own!" Lucy nearly shouted.

The room fell still again. Lucy was breathing heavily as she turned to look at her mother. Anita's chest flushed pink, and the life that had once danced in her eyes was replaced with sadness.

"Mother, I realize you think you know what is best for me, but I am not you. And Lord Sloan is not Father." Her words that started out slow came quicker and quicker. "I am not promised a perfect love match and no matter how much I beg for you to let me make my own path in life, you silence me. Why? Why must I be silent?"

Her mother opened her mouth to speak, but then closed it again. They both knew there was no answer that could ever suffice. Instead, they remained face to face in a standoff. Two female Fae with unprecedented power: one willing to bend to the whims of Denoran tradition and one prepared the burn the entire institution to the ground.

"I will not divulge your secret, Mother," she said in hushed tones, forcing herself to breathe. "You are entitled to be as silent as you wish. I, however, refuse. I will not bend. I will not become something I am not simply because society deems it to be so." She took a step back and smoothed her gown, forcing herself to appear as calm as the magic writhed within her, mirroring her rage. "I will play Father's game, and I will smile serenely —but know behind each and every fake smile plastered to my face is a fire that is burning, ready to bring down anything that gets in my way."

Anita's footsteps fumbled. "Lucy, you misunderstand." She tried to find the words, but Lucy refused to hear anything more.

"Thank you for lunch," Lucy said with calm repose, devastated tears welling in her eyes. She stood next to her door, dismissing Anita from her room. "I will finish preparing for my evening alone now."

Her mother tipped her head down in defeat and took a deep breath, smoothing her skirts. Lifting her gaze, she walked to the door to leave. She paused only to wipe the tear falling from Lucy's eye with the back of her finger, staring at her daughter with sorrow.

Lucy held her pose, looking straight ahead, begging the tears to stop flowing, as she watched her mother walk through the door and down the hall.

FIVE

MICAH

There and back, he kept telling himself. *Lunch with Dad, turn in my badge, pack up the apartment and back.*

He paced the newly renovated living room of the cabin in the woods, knowing that this trip could be risky, but also knowing he had no other choice. Taking these next steps toward his new role as guardian was important to him, and hopefully the closer he was to that, the closer he'd get to Lucy. Maybe with her, things would make more sense.

It's just me here in this middle-of-nowhere-house trying to figure out how to guard a magic portal with no magic. Got it. Easy.

Micah clearly had no idea what he was doing.

Leaving the property meant leaving The Elderwood unprotected, but since Wes and Jasper had visited a few days ago, nothing had happened. In fact, the house was so unbearably quiet he felt like he was going insane.

He glanced around at the unfamiliar space, not

seeing any trace of who he was or where he came from. No mom. No Grandad. Everything was different now.

Micah wanted his own things to help him feel more like himself. His record player. His workout clothes. Hell, his own pajamas. He had never expected to stay at the house for more than a few days, and now it had turned into his entire future.

This is my life now and the least I can do it make it feel more like home. The thought hung heavy in his mind.

Home.

My life.

Neither of those things felt real anymore. Micah's life, and everything in it, had been turned upside down. He squeezed his eyes shut as he pushed the thoughts away. There wasn't time to deal with it yet.

He grabbed the paper shopping bag perched on the arm of the couch and walked outside. Earlier in the day, he ran to the local hardware store to grab some equipment that would hopefully put him at ease as he left the premises. He didn't want to be gone for too long for a multitude of reasons—most obviously, he couldn't leave the portal unguarded. However, the bigger reason was the hope that Lucy would come back. It didn't matter to him how ridiculous it was—there was no one else he dreamed of late at night. No one else he craved the way he yearned for her. He could figure out the rest, as long as he had her.

All of this was unusual for Micah. Pining for a girl was something he had left behind so long ago, he didn't even think he had it in him anymore. He had worked hard building a life with no attachments. His carefully constructed boundaries kept him always an arms-length away from everyone. He built his system so rigorously to keep himself from ever getting hurt again.

Much good that did, he thought as he prepared to visit his old life and say goodbye.

The paper bag contained a set of wireless cameras he purchased to place around the cabin. He didn't expect to be gone long, but with the J. Pearson cronies starting the fire, he wasn't sure what lengths they would go to get the property. He needed to keep an eye on things until he understood more of how to legitimately protect the land.

He placed a camera by the front door, one to spotlight the back door, and another on The Elderwood portal itself. He connected the cameras to his phone and once he was sure it was working correctly, he got in his car to leave for his weekend journey to the city.

Something tugged at his heart as he drove away from the cabin.

Is this the right move?

The question hung heavily on his mind… but he wasn't sure what else there was for him. His life at the police department was important to him, and leaving felt like giving up on everything he worked hard for… But something deep inside of him warmed at the thought of his family and having the chance to walk in their footsteps. This was the task given to him by his grandad and mom. By choosing this life, he accepted the reality of magic and other realms… Hopefully Lucy saw that and accepted it for what it was: Micah choosing her, too.

There was no other choice for Micah to make. There was only this.

Glancing back in the rearview mirror, he could have sworn he saw a shadow hovering near the base of the trees, but when he looked again, it was gone.

"YOU'RE SURE ABOUT THIS, SON?" Micah's father, Richard, asked him for the third time.

Seeing his dad was important to Micah. He shared the same last name as his mom, but when he looked in the mirror, all he saw was his dad; his bronzed skin, dark brown eyes, broad shoulders.

Looking at his dad now showed more changes between the two than Micah had ever hoped to admit. His father's once dark hair was now peppered with silver, and the fine lines around his eyes were proof of time passing. Micah's heart hurt as he looked at the man that meant so much to him. When would he see his father next? Months? Years?

For the majority of his life, it had been just the two of them together. Once his mom got sick, he stayed with his dad most of the time. Richard always helped Micah forge his path in the world, never playing the overbearing parent role.

When his mom died, Micah was lost. He didn't speak up in class, he stopped going to sports, and didn't make time for his friends. All the kids from his baseball team called each other by their last names, and he couldn't hear "Lumen" without thinking of his mom. He loved the connection he had to her, by having her last name, but the reality of the situation was bigger than his young heart could handle.

It was only his dad and his new wife, Lori, who were able to coax him out of his shell and bring him back into the world. They tried doing some things Micah's mom, Vanessa, loved to do.

They started with volunteering at local homeless shelters and soup kitchens, just to help Micah feel like he was doing something good in his life. Lori made it a habit to bring him to the library weekly so he could pick out books to read, just like his mom used to do with him. They upheld Thursday family nights with movies and microwave popcorn. These small steps led Micah back to life again, and now it felt like a lie to have to leave that life behind after working so hard to get it back.

"I know it sounds crazy, Dad," Micah tried to explain as he took another bite of his lunch. "Mom left me some things at Grandad's that I didn't know about. Being there really helps me feel connected to them again."

"Things like what?" his father asked, hoping to get more out of his reserved son. Micah had always been closed off and private, but these were things he really couldn't imagine telling his dad.

Yeah, Dad, I've got magical blood and have to stand guard over a portal in a tree. That wouldn't go over well.

"You seem so different talking about them now." Richard shook his head in contemplation, a smile playing at his mouth. "I don't think I've ever heard you talk about your mom so much in one sitting since before she passed away…"

It was true. Speaking about his mom caused him

heartache he refused to acknowledge. Somehow, forcing this path had made it easier for him to think about her without falling apart.

Maybe more good will come out of this than I realize.

The pair sat and finished their sandwiches on the outdoor patio of a local cafe, enjoying the sun. Micah looked around at the people bustling on the streets of the busy city, hurriedly going from one place to the next. This was sure to be the last big group of people he would be surrounded by for a long time.

He took a deep breath and took it all in. Soon, he would be alone again. The thought made his head hurt.

"I know. I feel different," Micah agreed with a quiet nod. "Grandad was smart with the property and did a lot of investing. His acreage is worth a small fortune, and he's set up an agreement with some farmers to use his land. I can live there and earn passive income while I get the land in good shape. I can really make it my own, you know?" Convincing his dad of this plan was important to Micah. He had to have his dad on his side.

"That house is so outdated. Does it even have internet access? If you are just looking to take a break, Lori and I wouldn't mind you coming to stay with us for a while."

"I've decided to take the money that Grandad left and make some major renovations," Micah lied. The property already changed, and it definitely wasn't done the way his dad would have guessed. "When it's all done and I'm settled, I'll have you and Lori come up."

Richard had spent the better part of their lunch hour trying to convince him to stay at his apartment and not to leave the police force, but Micah stayed calm and focused as he told his dad that this was really what he wanted in his life.

He was getting better and better at lying, and he hated every ounce of it. Hadn't he just told Lucy never to lie about who she was? And here he was doing the same.

He didn't want to lose his job at the department, and he didn't want to end his lease in the city—but what other choice did he have? The landscape to his future was clear; being the guardian of the gate was his life now. There was so much to say goodbye to, but there was also a bright new horizon for him. In time, he would get it all figured out. He and Lucy would figure it out together. Hope blossomed in his chest at the thought of a life with her.

Micah looked at his dad and took in the deep set lines across his forehead, the creases around his eyes every time he smiled. His father was aging with grace, and he was so happy that he had found love again after his mother. Lori was a nice woman, and she made Richard happy, too.

It made him think of Lucy. Her bright hazel eyes. Her soft smile that he had to earn. Her beautiful freckles that covered her nose and cheeks. The ache at the memory of her face spread from his heart to the rest of his body. He only hoped he could have the same kind of happiness with her one day.

"I'll keep in touch," Micah reassured his father, and he took in the moment, unsure of when he'd be able to leave his house to see his dad again. "Just a phone call away."

They both stood, embraced one another in a deep farewell, and went their separate ways.

Micah took the short walk back to his car, preparing to complete the last leg of his trip. He spent time with his dad, and now all he had left to do was resign from the police department and finish packing. His head was pounding—the stress of the last few days was really taking a toll on him.

Maybe a good night's sleep will make this headache go away, he hoped.

A SHARP PAIN knit in Micah's side as he gripped the steering wheel of his car so tight his knuckles turned white.

Almost there, I'm almost there, he coached himself, driving as quickly as he could back to the Lumen property.

Boxing up his life and moving it in one day proved to be harder than he initially imagined. His headache started at the lunch with his dad two days ago, and each hour it got worse. Speaking to the chief at the department was difficult, but he chalked up the nausea and dry mouth to nervousness, no illness.

Going through an entire upheaval of his life, he assumed the aches and pains were from the intense emotions running through him, but when he woke up in his empty apartment the next day, they didn't get any better. In fact, with each passing minute, things got progressively worse. He almost didn't finish packing—

the headaches turned vicious, making him dizzy and unable to stand.

When he finally decided enough was enough, he left with pains lancing through his body, feeling as if his whole nervous system was hit with a bolt of lightning.

His only focus on his long drive back was to return to the cabin and pray whatever made him so sick would pass quickly. The lines on the road doubled before him, causing his car to swerve, narrowly missing the ditch to his right.

When he saw his cabin, he could have cried with relief, but instead he cried out in pain—his headache was so intense that bright flashes of light were clouding his vision. This migraine was worse than any he had ever experienced before.

Micah threw the car into park and lumbered toward the house, praying for the moment he could finally lie down and rest. His head pounded and his eyesight was hazy as he squinted through the bright sunshine, making his way from the car.

From the corner of his eye, he saw a large shape barrel out from somewhere behind the trees. He couldn't see clearly and didn't understand what was happening.

He whipped around, ready to take on an attacker, like the day of the arson, but nothing was there. Blinking, he tried to clear the spots forming in his vision. Everything felt like it was spinning. He turned again, frantically waiting for the onslaught, when the world seemed to tip on its axis. He took a step toward his cabin... then everything went black.

THE SOFT PADDING of footsteps across the floor was the first sound to register to Micah, but his eyes were closed and his head was still pounding.

Where am I?

There were soft cushions beneath him, and a savory smell of something buttery cooking in the air.

Maybe I'm at the apartment? Did I end up going to Dad's? No. I've got to get back to the cabin.

The memories of his last few hours were a blur, but then he remembered his drive. He remembered getting close to the house, but did he make it inside?

Another clink of glass brought him to reality. There was someone with him.

He opened his eyes and sat up quickly, the side of his head pounding, sending a surge of nausea down to his stomach. Groaning, Micah lifted his fingers to his temple and a burst of pain followed.

Squinting through the pain, he realized he was home, sitting on the couch in his living room. But he certainly didn't remember making it back to his cabin.

The noise in the kitchen stopped.

Lucy?

The forbidden hope of her coming to his aid made his heart practically leap from his chest.

Micah stood and tried to walk toward the kitchen, but his body felt weak and lightheaded. Stopping to refocus, he looked down at the beautiful hardwood flooring. Trying to center himself before he lost his balance, he leaned into the wall for support.

"Easy there, buddy," an unfamiliar female voice came from a few feet in front of him.

Micah's eyes trailed from the wooden floor to the woman's feet; bronzed skin with strappy sandals made of leather were wrapped up strong, muscular legs. She wore a fitted pair of shorts and a tank top, all in brown, making it look like a second layer of skin upon her athletic build, secured with leather straps. His eyes continued their trek up as he spotted her straight, short, black hair, chopped right above her shoulder which gave her sharp jaw line an even more aggressive look. Her full lips and high cheekbones made her breathtaking. With deep brown eyes, shaded with thick black makeup on the edges, her gaze seemed to pierce through Micah's soul.

"Who are you?" Micah asked her, trying to stand up straight, but the pounding in his head made every moment torture. His eyes strained as he fought to keep them open without wincing.

"Sit," she ordered, her voice smokey, with the hint of an accent he couldn't place. She pulled out a kitchen chair for him so he didn't have to walk much further.

"No," Micah refused, but he took a step closer and held the back of the chair for support anyway. "Who are you? Why are you in my house?" He tried to add strength to his voice, but each breath was a chore.

"You can call me Brax," she said with a roll of her eye and a sway of her hips as she walked away from him. She looked like a soldier wrapped in seduction.

I must have hit my head really hard, he told himself as he momentarily closed his eyes to try to figure out what the hell was going on.

"Okay, *Brax*, why are you in my house?" Micah asked again, looking around to see if there were other surprises waiting for him, but all he saw was his perfectly furnished and updated home Jasper and Wes left him.

Is Brax one of them?

"I was sent here by my employer," she stated. She walked up to the stove and stirred something in the pan, an aroma of rosemary and butter filling the air and making his stomach growl. "You should sit so I can look at that wound on your head," she said. "That must hurt." She gave him a pointed look somewhere between sympathy and disgust.

"Did you do this to me?" Micah said, taking a cautionary step back from her.

She turned the stove off and walked over to him, a mixture of arrogance and danger in her gaze. "No, I'm the one who found you on the ground and dragged you into the house and onto the couch. I'm the one who made you dinner. And I'm the one who's going to make your headaches go away."

Brax then took Micah by his shoulders and, with unexpected strength, she shoved him down into the seat and stepped in front of him. His legs were spread and she stepped suggestively between them, pressing her thighs against his. He looked up at her, ready to push her away when she put her hands on his head and whispered a language Micah had never heard. He knew it wasn't anything from Joterra, but he also wasn't sure if it was Denoran; it seemed different than when Lucy spoke in her Fae language.

Suddenly, his skin heated slightly, gave a burst of

cold, and his pain disappeared. Micah groaned in appreciation and slunk his head back as he closed his eyes. It had been days with ongoing headaches, and being without it felt like the sweetest relief. "Thank you," he said sincerely, looking up at her.

Brax was still very close to him, and Micah looked around awkwardly. If he looked in front of him, he was face-to-face with her breasts, tightly wrapped a skin-tight cotton tank and leather straps and buckles. He tried looking around instead, and her smile grew.

"Am I making you uncomfortable, Lumen?" she asked as she cocked her head with a tease.

"How do you know who I am?" Micah asked, looking her in the eye. His stomach flipped and he became more uneasy as the interaction continued. "Who did you say your employer was?"

"I work for Lord Laurent Sloan," she said with fire in her voice, and Micah stilled. "He sent me here to help you protect his assets." She took a long step back, away from him, and turned toward the kitchen. "Seems you have had some issues with the portal, and I'm here until you figure out what you're doing." She winked at him over her shoulder. Her cropped hair swung with the action.

Micah couldn't breathe—Laurent Sloan was the man Lucy was expected to marry. Did that still stand?

Did she find a way to stop it?

"You're from Denora?" He tried to sound calm, but his emotions were at war. There was nothing in the entire world that would prepare him to hear that Lucy had to still marry that prick. If Brax were to say it now, he knew he wouldn't be able to keep his composure. Taking a deep breath in, he shoved those thoughts away. There wasn't time for them now.

"Look at you, a little mortal knowing about Denora," she said with a laugh. "No, I'm not from Denora, but I did take a quick stop there on the way to you. Interesting place." She stirred the food in the pan and served it onto two plates, licking her finger when a bit of the sauce spilled over. "Some of the most gorgeous males I've ever seen, though you aren't too bad to look at either." She gave him a long, seductive stare, biting her bottom lip, and Micah looked away.

It wasn't that he didn't appreciate her looks. She was alluring in ways he hadn't seen in a woman, but he had Lucy, and they had a connection that couldn't compare. He wouldn't consider risking that for all the ass in Denora.

There was only one woman for him.

"I could never live there, though," Brax continued as she brought the two plates of food to the table. "The males treat females like they are pieces of art. Statues formed out of the most beautiful marble. Breathtaking to look at, but they are expected to be nothing more than what the males carve them out to be." Her smiling facade was gone now, just simmering anger underneath her eyes so dark they looked black.

"When Lucy mentioned—," he stopped himself short. Was it smart of him to mention his tie to her employer's future wife?

Brax's eyes brightened in interest. "Lucella Baum? Oh, please continue," she purred. There was something unnerving about Brax. She was beautiful, but spoke as though she hid a deadly secret. She moved like a snake, ready to strike.

What is she supposed to do here? How does Laurent Sloan expect to use her?

He cleared his throat. "Yes, Lucy mentioned your employer, Sloan?"

"*Lord* Sloan," she corrected with a glint of violence in her eyes.

"Right," Micah said as he shifted in his chair uncomfortably. "Why did he send you here, exactly?"

"I told you already, I'm here to ease your headaches. I'm here to guard The Elderwood."

Micah didn't doubt it this time—there was danger in the air, and it all pointed to Brax.

SIX

MICAH

The wafting scent of bacon infiltrated Micah's room the next morning, waking him up. Micah's stomach growled in response—he was starving.

His new bedroom was all gray with dark green and white accents. It reminded him so much of the forest, which was beautiful, but he wasn't sure if his space reflected who *he* was just yet. The greens and grays were comfortable, but he had always been more drawn to the sky, with its bright reds at sunset and deep blacks at night. However, he was in no position to complain. Just a little over a week ago, he was homeless.

He had an awful time sleeping knowing that a stranger was in his house with him, but at some point in the night, he realized that if she wanted him dead, he would be by now. He still couldn't understand why Sloan sent her, but he also realized how powerless he was in changing anything about his current circumstances. No one seemed to care what a mortal man had to say in a group of powerful Fae.

Striding down the steps in his socks and sweat-pants, he heard Brax singing a song in another language. Her voice carried through the main level, deep and sensual, the rawness in her voice exuding emotion. The words tugged at his heart, yet he had no idea what they meant.

"What are you singing?" Micah asked kindly as he walked into the room.

Brax turned with a smile, wearing black leggings and a cropped black tank top. Her feet were bare and her face had no makeup. Without the black shadows around her eyes, she looked younger and less abrasive. Her hair was in two messy buns on either side of her head, giving her an even more amiable appearance.

"It's a song my sisters and I love from back home." Her eyes were bright as she spoke of her family. She turned to the pans on the stove. "The song's title translates to *Warrior Beauty,* and it talks about this amazing warrior's sex-ploits and her independence."

"Sex-ploits?" Micah laughed as he walked to the coffee maker to brew a pot for the pair. He had to look around the cabinets a bit to figure out where the coffee was stored—it was all still so new to him.

"Yeah, you know, the sexual exploits people partake in? Don't tell me you're a prude," she pointed the spatula at him with a mock serious expression.

He put his hands up in fake surrender, appreciating the banter after so many days all alone. With his head feeling better, he was in a much better mood, though his thoughts on Brax's arrival still made him apprehensive. "Nope, took care of that during senior prom," he laughed as he dropped his hands and continued to make the coffee.

"I'm not sure what the hell *senior prom* is, but I'm glad you took care of that. Vytyrians are very sexual Fae and we have no shame on the subject." She grabbed two plates and piled a hefty serving of eggs, bacon, and toast on each.

"Are you going to cook like this every day?" Micah said as he looked at the mouthwatering plate of food. "Because I really don't mind if you do." He placed a mug of coffee down on the table for each of them and dug into his breakfast.

"I like to be useful," Brax said, as she bit a piece of crispy bacon. "This place is incredibly boring."

Micah snorted into his coffee.

"I'm serious. I was sent here to protect The Elderwood, but it's just an old gnarled tree that doesn't even *do* anything. And they told me to keep an eye on you." She looked him up and down. "No offense, you aren't much of a threat."

"I have no idea how to respond to any of that," Micah said honestly. He also had no idea why she was there or what protecting The Elderwood even entailed. He just knew he had to stay on the property. He needed more time to read about his duties in the book his grandad left him. And him not being much of a threat?

I'm a cop, damnit. I should be at least a little intimidating, right?

"I really don't mean offense," she repeated with a mouthful of eggs. "The Vytyr are trained warriors—I could take any human down in like, six seconds flat." She snapped her fingers, then waved her hand as she held her mug of coffee, taking a deep drink.

The way she spoke with such candor caused Micah to think she probably told the truth, so he made a mental note not to piss her off too badly.

Her presence still did not add up to Micah. If he was there guarding The Elderwood, what made Brax have to be there as well? Why did Micah have to be watched to do a job that was passed down through his family? And what was Sloan's stake in the matter? Wasn't it Baum property?

"Trained warriors? Like a soldier?"

"Don't insult me, Lumen." She pointed her fork at him, then speared another bite of food. "No. *Warrior*."

"Throw me a bone here. This is all new to me. A few weeks ago, I was a cop in a city and now I'm the guardian of a tree and magic is real. I'm not really sure what I'm supposed to be doing here."

Brax looked at him curiously, putting an arm over the back of her chair, letting her guard down. She wasn't nearly as scary as she had seemed, but he realized there was just a lot about her and the rest of the Fae that he knew nothing about.

"I believe you," Brax said quietly, taking a sip of coffee, continuing to stare at him. "Alright," she announced louder, bringing her arms in front of her on the table. "I'll teach you while I'm here. It'll give me something to do." Her abruptness was a bit of a shock to Micah.

"Really?" he asked, relieved by the opportunity to finally learn more about his place among the Fae. He hoped he could get some real answers about what he and Lucy were up against. Words couldn't describe how badly he missed her. He had no idea what the hell he was supposed to do and feeling uncertain made him feel useless and weak.

"Why not?" Brax said, a bored look on her full lips. "There aren't any other humans nor Fae around, and the tree is out there, *being a tree*... there's no threat to hinder us."

"Thank you."

"Lesson one."

Micah choked on a bite of toast. He definitely didn't expect her to start helping immediately.

"Warrior is more than a soldier. A soldier works for a realm, like the kingdom of Denora. They are tied to that realm and must obey the command of the officers above them. Warriors, on the other hand, are bred for combat. The Vytyr are instilled with *lyfar*—combat magic. We are the only Fae who hold such a powerful force of battle magic, but we do not hold the same Fae skill as others. I cannot say a spell and create practical magic like Denorans. However, we hold an advantage, because no mere mortal or Fae can ever take down a Vytyr. We are trained from a very young age. I learned to throw a spear before I knew how to write my name."

"If you don't work for the realm and are not a soldier, then who signs your checks?" Micah asked, confused.

"We decide who we support, and we get paid well for our services," she said plainly.

The way she described her position reminded Micah of a bounty hunter or mercenary. However, the memory of the things Lucy had told him about Denora kept nagging at his mind. Did they allow this in Fae realms? Was Brax being entirely truthful with him?

"Women are allowed to work where you're from?"

"Females, like anyone else, can do whatever they desire. No one is in charge of them but themselves— something Denora has not honored."

Micah's thoughts hung in his mind, remembering the pressures Lucy faced. She took major risks just to make her own choices in her life, and here was Brax, able to do anything she wanted.

Why was Denora so different?

"So, it was your choice to work for Lord Sloan?" He chose his words carefully, not wanting to provoke Brax.

"Absolutely. He is a kind and fair lord. The best among all Denorans. Any would be privileged to live in his territory or work alongside him."

She spoke with such veneration for the man who stood in the way of his and Lucy's happiness. It left a bitter taste in his mouth, but he would never admit this to Brax; not when her allegiance to Sloan was so apparent.

"Let me get this straight... You are Fae with magic that makes you a good warrior. And other Fae have magic that is used with spells?"

Brax nodded.

"And, where you're from—Vytyr? They appreciate women and Denora is a bunch of crusty old men making decisions?"

Brax's laughter filled the room, bringing a smile to Micah. "Yes. I like that description."

"Do the Fae realms of Denora and Vytyr have anything else in common? It seemed like you were speaking a different language than Denoran?"

"I'm surprised you caught on to that, Lumen. You're smarter than you look."

"I don't think that was a compliment," he said with a smirk.

"No, we speak different languages. However, the warriors in Vytyr are trained in many languages, ensuring that wherever we contract our work, we can speak with our employers, or taunt whomever we're fighting." She gave a roguish wink.

"Not everyone in Vytyr is a warrior?" Micah asked, perplexed.

"No, you loaf of bread. Have you not been listening? Vytyr allows people to make their own decisions. My mother was a warrior, and my sisters and I have followed in her footsteps. That is, everyone except for my youngest sister." Her eyes came alight with warmth again, as they always did when she spoke of her family. "Noelia is the budding artist among us."

"My mom liked art, too," he shared.

"Maybe you've got some redeeming qualities in there, Lumen," she said with a tease. Then she abruptly stood and grabbed her sandals. She put them on, lacing the leather up her muscular calves. "I am going to walk the property and secure the safety of the border. Do not go anywhere."

She walked to the door and opened it, leaving Micah and the dirty dishes at the table. Brax looked over her shoulder mischievously. "By the way, I don't clean." Then she left.

Micah let out a deep sigh, relaxing his muscles and rolling his shoulders.

What the hell have I gotten myself into? He looked up, thinking of his family. *I hope one of y'all up there is keeping an eye on me, because I'm lost.*

He got up and began cleaning the dishes from breakfast and the previous night. The new kitchen set-up was much more practical for daily life. The room was brighter now, with windows on three of the four walls—the last wall backing up to the living area and holding the stove and counter space. Over the kitchen sink was a window facing out to the west side of the property. On the opposite wall, where the kitchen table and chairs sat, were two large windows next to one another, offering natural light into the updated kitchen. The third wall held the door to the backyard and the fire pit where he and Lucy spent so many nights. As he scrubbed the dishes, he looked out the window to see Brax in the distance, walking the perimeter.

He turned back toward the table and saw a dark shadow in the windows beyond. It was only there for a moment and then disappeared from view. From his position in the kitchen, he could almost make out the tree to The Elderwood on the east side of the house.

What was that? he asked himself. *It can't be Brax; she must be on the complete other side of the property by now.* His heartbeat quickened. *What if the arsonists came back?*

He looked around the room for a weapon, but kitchen utensils wouldn't likely help him in this situation.

He grabbed his phone to bring out the camera app he had installed before his trip. Micah pulled up the last five minutes of video from the recording directed at the tree, trying to see where the shadow came from, but nothing was there. The camera didn't pick up a single figure.

A loud cracking noise from outside made Micah's head jerk back toward the window. He waited silently, watching the woods, but nothing happened.

He sighed and shook his head.

It's just the forest.

He felt so on edge he wasn't sure what was an actual threat anymore.

Micah returned the phone to his pocket and finished cleaning the kitchen. When he went back to wipe the table, he saw the dark shadows again. He ran to the window to get a better look, and there, just beyond The Elderwood tree, stood a tremendous black creature with a feline body.

It had to be nearly four feet tall when on all fours, and its massive stature made it impossible to believe it was as quiet as it was. It slunk behind the tree that held The Elderwood portal and then disappeared.

Micah's heart was a jackhammer in his chest. He brought the camera footage up again to get a closer look. However, just like last time, nothing appeared on the video.

Am I losing my fucking mind? I swear, something was there.

Micah rubbed his hands over his eyes, trying to clear the confusion building within him. He grunted in frustration, pushing his hands through his hair and onto his neck, letting them hang there for a moment as he thought of his next steps.

Outside, he decided. *I'll just go look around the tree and see what I can find.*

The surrounding forest was quiet. The wind was soft. The birds were silent. Not a footstep could be heard. Part of that calmed Micah, knowing that nothing lurked in the distance. However, another part unnerved him even more, wondering where all the animals went.

He took a straight path to the tree that held the portal and kept aware of his surroundings. Whatever was prowling around earlier was massive—he didn't need that sneaking up on him when he was alone.

As he stepped up to The Elderwood tree, what he saw stunned him. He didn't know what to make of it. The sigil engraved high on the tree trunk had changed. It wasn't just a basic carving. Now it had black, ashy smudges spread all around it—like it was burning from the inside.

This can't be good.

SEVEN

LUCY

The Baum carriage was the epitome of extravagance. Crushed red velvet covered the seats and draped the windows, keeping the interior dark to the world outside.

Lucy pulled the curtains open to allow the light to enter the cabin. She watched as the children ran alongside the carriage, offering toothless smiles behind dirt smudged cheeks. She smiled and gave them a small wave. Lucy had not been to this area before. Usually when she had traveled to the Capital, they took a much longer, roundabout trip in order to visit extended relatives along the way.

"There is nothing to see out there except for penniless beggars and their run-down shacks," Jasper spat, snapping the curtains shut. He spent the majority of the ride fidgeting with his rings, clearly on edge. His temperament was worse than usual. She sighed and sat back; it wasn't worth the fight.

This dinner has to be worth it, she thought. *I need to*

focus on learning whatever I can about Sloan so I can use it to remove myself from this mess. Maybe leave Denora completely.

The thought of leaving played in her mind more and more since her return, and her current companion did little to change her views. Jasper had come to hand deliver her to Lord Sloan. Corvus no longer trusted Lucy off the estate, so he put his most faithful employee to the task.

The Capital was busier than Lucy remembered. She hadn't visited in quite some time, and the residents were in a flurry with the arrival of Lord Sloan. It seemed as though the dukes were desperate to strengthen Sloan's connections to the Kingdom as it was his first visit outside of the Northern Territory in over 85 years. Lord Sloan preferred for most of his business to be done within his region.

Corvus visited the Lord of the Northern Territories nearly a year prior and convinced him to try a few of his custom bows in exchange for ore from the mountains to create sturdier arrow tips for the legion. Lord Sloan was very hesitant at first, but seemed to warm up after talk of alliances. Lucy never did figure out whose idea it was to arrange the marriage; however, given that everyone besides her agreed to the proposal, it would not change her thoughts on the matter. Regardless of who had organized it, she had no plans on following through.

The restaurant where Lucy was to meet Lord Sloan was the most lavish building she had ever seen. The outer wall was made of pure white stone, not a smudge of dirt anywhere in sight. Fae magic illuminated ornate sconces, sending a soft glowing light out to those walking nearby. Elite Fae in breathtaking gowns and tunics crowded the entrance.

Lucy was never one to care about those things, but then again, she had never had the pleasure of being around so many beautiful Fae before while wearing such a luxurious gown herself. Most of her life consisted of tagging along with her brothers and father—or ducking out of her etiquette lessons without her mother knowing.

But this? This was a completely new world to Lucy, more different than even Joterra or The Elderwood. This was the world of upper class Fae: royalty and wealth.

Standing under the dazzling lights, Lucy pulled at her lavender gown, checking to make sure the silver filigree was still in place and shining.

It was customary to dress with grandeur when dining with Fae of high status. However, she made it a point not to change her gown from her earlier meeting with Lord Sloan. She knew he, like most males, would take it as a slight that she did not modify her wardrobe for him.

Let him, she thought as she again fussed with the fine fabric.

It was unusual for her to feel insecure, but with so many females gliding across the floor in precious gems and metals, she worried she would stick out like a sore thumb.

Maybe that's all the better, she considered. *Let me stand out as someone who doesn't belong in this crowd, and Sloan will see that he's made the wrong choice.*

Jasper escorted Lucy through enormous metal doors, adorned in bright red tapestries; fine silver thread adding beautiful embellishments along the corners. Lucy placed her hand lightly on top of Jasper's arm as he walked through the crowd, clearly knowing his way.

Normally Lucy would not have been appreciative of Jasper, seeing as he was largely overbearing and full of rude opinions that made her eye twitch. Yet, here in this bustling crowd, she found herself thankful she didn't have to navigate it on her own.

Tucked away in the corner of the restaurant was a large table, fit for ten, but with place settings prepared for only two.

Extravagance. This must be the place, she thought sarcastically.

Lucy forced a smile instead of an eye roll and did her best to play the part her father forced upon her. She would have this dinner if it meant finding a way back to Micah.

Micah.

It had only been a few days for her, but it was much longer for him. She longed for the man who captured her heart and opened her eyes to real partnership. When would she see those deep brown eyes again?

Jasper guided her to her seat, and she immediately felt out of place at such a large table. To make matters worse, the empty place setting for Lord Sloan sat on the complete opposite end of the table.

I guess that means he didn't have much interest in hearing me speak. All the better, she thought as she unfolded her napkin dramatically.

I'll stuff myself and leave lethargic and full, and I'll sleep on my return trip home so I can avoid interactions with Jasper.

Her repulsive chaperone stood at her side, waiting with the air of utmost respect and chivalry—though Lucy knew better than to believe that farce.

As minutes passed, Lucy tried to avoid the eyes from the crowded room and began to fidget, pulling at her dress and touching her hair. She anxiously sipped from the oversized wine glass placed at the table. They wouldn't bring the food until the guest of honor arrived.

Clearly, that was not her.

It was almost as if a wave swept through the restaurant and hushed each patron, for all at once, the room quieted. Lucy looked up from her reverie to search for the cause—surely something must have happened for all of these very important Fae to stop their chatter and focus on something other than themselves.

Through a gap in the crowd, she saw him enter. Long, flowing white hair, flawless pale skin, and iridescent blue eyes meeting hers as he descended upon her, giving only her his full attention.

"Miss Lucella, it delights me to see you here tonight. Thank you for accepting my invitation." He bowed, took her hand in his, and kissed it ever so gently with warm lips. For some reason, she had expected them to be cold; as cold as the rumors. But here he was, flesh and bone, warm and apparently delighted to see her.

"Thank you for the invitation," she replied compliantly. "It has been quite some time since I've seen the castle and the Capital. I appreciate the opportunity to visit and see them once again."

Lord Sloan went to pull out a chair next to her until he saw his place setting across the long table. A server pulled out the chair on the other end and offered it to him, but he gave a curt shake of his head to decline it. "I will take my dinner here, from this seat next to Miss Lucella." Everyone within earshot took a collective breath in, attempting not to gasp at the shock.

"Yes, sir. I can switch your place with Miss Baum right away."

Lucy stood to change seats to allow Lord Sloan to be at the head of the table.

"No, no need," he reassured the wait staff. "Here is fine. Miss Lucella may keep her seat. She was already quite comfortable in it before I came. There's no reason to change."

"But, sir," Jasper interjected. "Surely you'll want the head of the table. Lucella would be more than happy to give that to you, wouldn't you?" He gave Lucy a stern look, expressing his disapproval.

"Absolutely," Lucy began again. She gave a tight smile as she gathered her skirt in her hands and attempted to stand and switch seats.

"Enough of this," Lord Sloan said loudly. Lucy froze. "It is perfectly acceptable for a female to sit at any seat she wants. In fact, I would prefer for her to sit there. She is my guest tonight, and I am honored to have her. Now, there will be no more talk of seating changes." He sat in the chair next to Lucy and, with a dazzling smile, asked the server to bring the food. "I am sure Miss Lucella is quite hungry after waiting for me."

A blush of embarrassment covered her cheeks as she returned to her seat. Every Fae in the vicinity eyed her curiously, wondering why the notorious Lord of the Northern Territory was so generous to this unimportant Fae.

"I am terribly sorry for being late, Miss Lucella," he leaned over and murmured to Lucy. His ice-blue eyes held Lucy's with sincerity.

"No apology needed. I understand you are a very busy Fae. And please, Lucy is fine."

"As you wish, Miss Lucy," he conceded.

"Just Lucy," she repeated with an easy smile. If she was going to have to spend the entirety of her evening with him, she couldn't keep being addressed in such a formal manner—it only added to her anxiety.

Lord Sloan smiled at her and then gave a nod to the servers as they brought out their food: a delicious-looking feast of soups, platters of meats and steamed vegetables, and a large basket of assorted breads.

Heaving a great sigh, Lord Sloan stood, straightened the hem of his jacket, and looked out to the crowd around them. Every Fae there was pretending not to be eavesdropping, but only a fool would dismiss Fae hearing for being anything other than a perfect tactic for acquiring new gossip. The icy Lord from the North peered into the bustling crowd and with a click of his tongue and a soft shake of his head, he lifted his hands in the air.

Lucy wasn't sure what she was seeing at first, until

the crowd abandoned any pretense of disinterest to watch with wide eyes.

Lord Sloan's hands were above his head, and he murmured words Lucy could hardly make out. His hands spread apart, creating a half circle, and suddenly there was quiet; all that remained was a shimmering barrier like a bubble around the corner of the restaurant where they sat. The onlookers groaned with disappointment and turned back to their own sources of merriment.

"What magic is this?" Lucy asked, still staring at the shimmering sheen he had created.

Lord Sloan looked to Jasper and excused him from their presence with a wave of his hand. Jasper looked as though he might argue, but came to his senses and walked out into the foyer with a sharp look over his shoulder.

I'm sure that was for me.

Jasper wanted nothing to go wrong when he was ordered to escort her. Though what could go wrong in a room full of Fae? Besides, Lord Sloan's personal guard stood nearby at the ready.

"That, Miss Lucy," Lord Sloan began as he sat, "is a special privacy barrier."

The shimmering bubble reminded Lucy of the privacy ward Wes had placed on her room when they had spoken before he went to visit Micah. But this seemed different. For one, it was much darker than any other privacy charm she had ever seen before. Another thing, most privacy spells did not stop noise from both sides. In her room with Wes, she could still hear the birds outside clear as day. But this? She was in a room full of people, but the noise was much softer, as though a thick wall separated them.

"I don't enjoy an entire room of Fae listening in on my conversations and staring at me as though I am an animal in a cage on display. This ward is specialized so that we can see out, but they cannot see in. It will also stop prying ears from listening, so gossip should hopefully be minimized. I was never impressed with the Capital's obsession with gossip."

Placing her napkin in her lap, Lucy then took another sip of the fruity wine, eyeing her company for the evening.

This is... unexpected.

She was relieved to be rid of Jasper, but thankful at least one of Sloan's guards remained; for propriety's sake.

The pair helped themselves to the delectable food placed in front of them, and Lucy audibly moaned as she bit into a slice of warm bread with butter and jam.

"Are you enjoying the food?" Lord Sloan teased as he ripped a piece of bread and popped it unceremoniously into his mouth. Lucy laughed at his candor and wiped her mouth clean with her napkin.

"I don't think I've ever had more delicious bread," she said as she smiled. "I'm sorry for the theatrics, I'll be sure to keep it down." She laughed as she prepared another piece.

"It's refreshing," he said as he stared into her hazel eyes. He watched her with such interest and regard, it was hard to peg him as the same man that others called *Lord Slain*.

"What is refreshing? Oh, the wine! Yes, it's quite flavorful." She took another sip as he continued to stare at her.

"The wine?" He laughed, his ice-blue eyes twinkled with delight. "Yes, the wine is wonderful. But you…" His boyish smile returned as he spoke. "*You* are what is so refreshing. You're a wonder to behold."

At that, Lucy rolled her eyes. It was an involuntary reaction, and she internally cringed as she waited for the repercussions of such attitude in the presence of a great Lord of Denora.

Instead, he laughed! A big, hearty, full laugh that warmed Lucy down to her bones.

"You don't believe me, do you?" he asked her with a smile so wide, it made it hard for Lucy not to smile herself.

He scooted his chair closer to hers and leaned into her personal space to speak more intimately. "Look at the company we have." He directed his eyes to the rest of the patrons of the restaurant. "Each Fae here is a glutton for the delicacies this amazing chef has to offer. They indulge on the savory meats, exquisite wines, and mouth-watering desserts."

His voice was a low rumble, reverberating through Lucy. The warmth of his presence crept over her skin, her body reacting to their closeness.

"They take a bite and know it is delicious simply because this is the most prestigious restaurant in the realm. But that isn't what they are thinking about, now is it?"

Lord Sloan wrapped an arm around the back of

Lucy's chair to share in her space. The deep tenor of his voice made her skin tingle.

"They don't care about the food at all. That female?" he continued as he nodded toward a beautiful Fae in a pale pink gown adorned with opalescent stones. "She keeps checking her jewels among her neck and ears. As she does so, she compares them to the rest of the females present, ensuring hers look the most elegant."

Lucy watched the female as she laughed and subtly placed her hand on her throat, brushing her necklace discreetly. The Fae covered her mouth in a fake laugh, and her hand next went to her earrings, dangling from her ears.

Lucy's eyes opened wide with astonishment. Lord Sloan was completely correct. The female continued to scan the crowd, eyeing others' jewels draped carefully across unblemished skin.

"How did you know that?" Lucy twisted and asked him with a smile. She forgot how close he was, and when she turned, their noses nearly touched. She quickly looked back toward the crowd, giving herself a bit more space, her heart racing at the proximity.

"Look at that older gentleFae in the corner," he whispered, inching closer to her, his thigh touching hers.

Lucy didn't know what to make of it. Surely this closeness was not appropriate for any Fae, let alone the Lord of the North and his betrothed wife? Despite that, Lucy looked in the direction he suggested, shifting her body away from him slightly.

"He is here with his wife, and has absolutely no

interest in her, nor his meal. Look at the way he shovels the food into his mouth, just to get the dinner over with."

Lucy saw the aged male Fae hastily swallowing the food, checking his watch between each bite. In the time they watched the couple, the female didn't stop talking for more than a few seconds in between eating and the male never made eye contact with her at all.

A laugh escaped Lucy as the male outright rolled his eyes at his wife and called for the check, even as she still had a full plate of food. Lord Sloan shifted back toward his part of the table and Lucy inhaled deeply, calming herself with slow, deep breaths.

"See, Miss Lucy? These people are here as a show of wealth and what they deem as *importance*. They don't bother with the taste of the food or any appreciation for the work that goes into a meal such as this. I enjoy that you find that appreciation in such a simple function as eating dinner. It is refreshing because I do not see it often enough in the rare occasion that I visit."

Lucy looked at Lord Laurent Sloan as if seeing him in a new light.

Is he what others say he is?

He seemed so different from any other Fae male she had met in Denora, especially those with a high status such as his.

"You are not what I expected, Lord Sloan," she said before she realized the words left her tongue.

"I will take that as a compliment," he said with a wink. "I aim to be different than my male counterparts."

"In what ways?"

"Well, to begin with, this meal?" He gestured to the

food before them. "What a complete waste of resources. I hope you don't take offense, but you will not be taking the remaining food home once they box it up."

This caught Lucy off guard, unsure of his frank tone. "Of course not, Lord Sloan. I am here as your guest, it is yours."

"No, no, you misunderstand," he said as he leaned closer to her, reaching out for her hand. The tenderness of the action shocked her, making her heart leap. He held her left hand gently. "I also do not need this food. You and I, and everyone in this building, quite honestly, do not need food to this excess. However, on the trip here, I passed dozens of hungry families who could use this to feed their children."

Her mouth popped open in realization. She thought back to her ride to the Capital—the barefoot children, playing in the streets. "You're going to give it to them?"

"Yes, I was hoping we both could." His lips turned up into a smile. "Unless you would find that uncomfortable, then I understand completely."

"No, I would love to," Lucy said hurriedly, squeezing his hand in return. The warmth of his hands spread into hers, causing her core to flutter with excitement. "Honestly, I would find it more uncomfortable to ignore them as others do. They are worthy of our attention."

"Yes, they are, and I am so glad to hear you say that." Laurent's smile doubled, his white teeth gleaming from ear to ear. "I have always had many... issues, with the way that male Denorans conduct themselves. I find myself at odds with those around me."

"What do you mean?" Lucy asked, curiosity getting the best of her.

Every single thing out of his mouth from the moment she had met him had been the complete opposite of what she had been told to expect.

He was not the cold, heartless monster that others believed him to be. So far, he was the only male in all of Denora who thought of something other than status.

"We do things differently where I'm from," he said slowly, brushing her hand with his thumb, trying to find the words. "I take care of all the citizens of the North, no matter their station in life."

Lucy knew she was staring at Laurent with disbelief and that her unblinking gaze could easily appear as rude, but she just could not get her mind around what he was saying.

How could he be what I was fearing all this time? This must be too good to be true.

"I enjoy your fresh outlook, Lord Sloan. It's a pleasure to hear that someone is thinking of all of the citizens of their region, not just the ones who could fill their coffers."

"Thank you, Miss Lucy," Lord Sloan said with a smile and a nod as he released her hand. He took another sip of his wine and looked down at his empty dinner plate. "I apologize, but there is some small business I must attend to while we are here. Do you mind giving me a moment?"

"Absolutely," Lucy replied with a smile. "I under-stand." And she did. She didn't feel as though he was neglecting her, and she didn't feel that he would leave her unless he absolutely must.

Laurent stood and straightened his suit jacket. "I will have them send over dessert—you can start without me. Though," his voice trailed off as he leaned closer to Lucy, finishing his thought in a near whisper. "I would love to watch you enjoying the delectable sweets, so save a bite or two."

Lucy's heart leapt to her throat, a small gasp leaving her. Her cheeks flushed as she looked at Laurent, whose amusement lingered in the glint of his brilliant blue eyes. She watched as he left the domed privacy charm, walked into the main vestibule of the restaurant, and went out of view.

Lucy slumped back in her seat, reeling with the impossibility of how her night was unfolding. Laurent Sloan was nothing she imagined; in fact, he proved time and time again what a good and noble Fae he was.

How could the disparaging rumors be so mistaken?

A sharp sting in her palm caught Lucy by surprise. She dropped her hand into her lap, trying her best to be inconspicuous, even though no one could see her through the privacy charm. The imprint on her hand turned red, showing again through her concealment spell. She pushed more magic into the scar, watching it disappear from view, unsure why it decided to bother her.

The wine she drank coursed right through her, and she thought it was a perfect time to use the restroom. Unfortunately, with her elaborate gown, it could take a while. She asked Laurent's guard to show her the way through the unfamiliar restaurant.

"Of course, Miss Baum. And please, call me Roger," the guard said kindly.

She took his offered arm and he led her toward the foyer. More and more people were arriving—whispers and gossip met her ears every turn she made.

"Lord Sloan is here with a female Fae."

"No, she isn't royalty at all!"

"Haven't you heard? She's that Baum female!"

"What does he even see in her? There are so many others who are much more beautiful."

"She's so lucky."

The chatter amused Lucy. Earlier in the week, before Lord Sloan arrived, all the rumors were about his dark side and how vicious he was. Since he arrived, each Fae whispering to their neighbor wanted to gain the favor of the handsome Lord Sloan.

Funny how people's malicious words could change with the snap of a finger. I wonder what they will say about me next?

Their prattling about her didn't bother Lucy. She was not the most beautiful nor the most wealthy and she knew others would see her betrothal as a step down for Lord Sloan, but that didn't matter to her. Besides, Lucy wasn't planning on going forward with the marriage, anyway. There was still time to figure her way out of the entire arrangement.

Once Roger brought her to the middle of the foyer, he pointed toward the back where the restrooms were located.

Off to the right was a distinguished bar, stocked with the finest spirits available. The mirror behind the bar reflected dozens of fine cut crystal drink-ware in varying shapes and sizes. Some of the spirits were so rare, one tiny glass would cost a small fortune.

A flash of bright white hair caught her attention.

There, off to the side of the bar, was Lord Sloan, talking animatedly to another male Fae. She could only see the back of Laurent, his posture rigid with frustration. His shoulders leaned down, bringing his enormous height closer to the shorter Fae male in front of him. Lucy felt awkward watching the interaction. Realizing it was not for her eyes, she continued toward the bathroom taking one more glance at the pair.

She stopped dead in her tracks when she recognized the male. He looked right at her with rage in his bulging eyes.

Jasper.

Why is Laurent Sloan, Lord of Northern Territories, wasting his time with Jasper?

THE CARRIAGE ROCKED BACK and forth as the horses continued their return to the Baum Estate. Lord Sloan and his small entourage were en route ahead. The clip-clopping of the horses echoed down the narrow lanes in the Capital.

The ride home led through the outer cities, which were overcrowded and unsupported. With the summer months still underway, the sun was only beginning to fall, leaving enough light for the townspeople to roam about without difficulty. Lucy peered around the curtains, ignoring Jasper's scoffing, and took in every-thing she saw on the outskirts of a town she thought she knew well.

What she saw surprised her. The homes were stacked upon one another, leaving no space for children to play or for families to retain any semblance of privacy. The cobblestone streets were cracked, with weeds growing between the damaged rocks. Each street looked identical to the next: thin wooden houses with damaged windows, either broken and exposed to the elements or boarded up with warping wood, and doors that backed up to long, narrow alleyways that overflowed with rubbish and waste.

People sat outside of their homes, toiling over their work; whether it was scouring pots and pans, repairing old shoes, or washing clothes. One elderly female plucked the feathers from a dead bird laid flat in her lap.

Children in worn clothing were chasing the carriage in the streets; most had no shoes. They smiled, excited to see anyone of importance come through their small corner of town.

The distinct contrast between where Lucy sat and where the children ran outside made her heart sink. Lucy was clad in a beautiful, expensive gown with ornate jewelry, traveling in a velvet-lined carriage. The dress she wore was probably worth more than one of the homes on this street, and why? If she sold it, it would feed a family for a month.

Why does the King allow this? She shifted uncomfortably in her seat at the thought.

The carriage continued its trek away from the Capital, leaving the children and their weathered homes behind them. It hurt her to think about the poor children who were forgotten by the Kingdom. A nauseating sense of guilt grew within her chest.

How is this something we have allowed to happen?

It was just another nail in the coffin, finding Denora guilty of further injustices.

"Close the window. You're letting the stink in," Jasper barked, snapping the curtains shut, a look of disdain dripping down his face.

Lucy looked back to him with equal parts annoyance and curiosity. So many things about Jasper had never made sense to her.

Jasper's relationship with her father, Corvus, seemed most difficult for her to grasp. He had been riding her father's coattails for as long as Corvus had been in the bowyer industry. Even when they were young Fae, Jasper followed after him, always hoping to claim a position as his right hand.

It had worked, too. Jasper was so ingrained in the finances of the Baum Bowyers that, while many did not know his name, they at least knew his face, because he accompanied Corvus all throughout the realm.

Looking at him from across the carriage, Lucy recalled the day Duke Renfro came to the estate to arrange a business deal with her father. Normally, Corvus would travel to the dukes for their work, but on this occasion, since it was personal and not related to the Kingdom, Duke Renfro insisted on coming to him instead.

Lucy was speaking with her father, making yet

another bid for her place with the bowyers, when Duke Renfro walked in with Jasper at his side.

Jasper led him to a chair and Renfro nearly shoo-ed him away with a look of annoyance, dismissing him. When Jasper cleared his throat to speak, the duke interrupted him.

"Stop blathering on. I won't be needing a beverage, this is a short visit. You are excused."

The look on Jasper's face was enough to curdle milk. His eyes flared with rage before they glossed over and he introduced himself to the duke.

"I am Jasper DeValey. I manage the finances for the Baum Bowyer industry and will be assisting Master Baum."

Lucy remembered him saying it with such greasy affect, wondering how hard it must have been for him to have swallowed so much anger. When she glanced at her father, she realized he hadn't even noticed. He was busy gathering the materials he needed for the duke's visit and didn't think twice about the conversation Jasper and the duke were having.

That day Jasper flashed her a look of pure loathing, forcing her to leave the study in a hurry, not wanting to be anywhere near those toxic males.

That bulging glare was seared into her memory, and she often wondered when the rest of the realm would see the real Jasper. Lucy knew he was hiding under a threadbare exterior, ready to erupt at any moment, and since her mother explained his lack of magic, it started to make more sense.

The carriage bumped over the cobblestones and came to an abrupt halt.

Jasper's eyes danced with fury reminiscent of Lucy's memory. His revulsion of the outer city pressed on Lucy's nerves.

His obsession with wealth and status is sickening.

The last thing Lucy wanted was to be stuck in a stopped carriage with Jasper, yet here they were.

"What is happening? Why have we stopped?!" he shouted to the driver.

Lucy peered out to see Laurent Sloan walking in muddied puddles, with boxes of food in his arms. His guard, Roger, came to the window to speak to Lucy.

"Sir, what are you doing out there?"

"Greetings, Miss Baum. Lord Sloan ordered additional meals to be passed out on our return to the estate."

"Meals?"

"Yes, Miss. Lord Sloan hoped that you could join him?"

Lucy's heart leapt from her chest. He was serious about giving the food to the families... "Yes, I would love to." She gathered her skirts and reached for the carriage door when Jasper held the door shut, stopping her.

"Absolutely not," he spat with disgust. "It is not safe for you in the dark of the streets, Lucella. Your father would never allow such a thing."

"She is entirely safe with us, sir."

"There will be no more talk of Lucella exiting the carriage. We are leaving."

Lucy could only glare at Jasper with frustration.

"Yes, sir," Roger said to Jasper. He turned to look at Lucy once more. "Have a safe trip home." Roger offered an apologetic smile and caught up with Lord Sloan.

He's hand delivering food to the families in need, and actually invited me to join him. Lucy looked on in shock.

Only a moment passed as the rest of the carriages continued on their way, leaving Laurent Sloan and his barrage of guards behind as they dirtied their uniforms, taking time out of their night to support the neediest families in Denora.

EIGHT

MICAH

Micah looked at the sigil on the tree; the black, charred edges remained. The last time the sigil changed, Micah was in The Elderwood with Lucy and he saw the symbol glow a bright red when his grandad's property was under attack and set on fire. This, however, was different. It didn't glow or surge; the carving in the tree did nothing at all. It almost looked dead—disconnected to The Elderwood completely.

That couldn't happen, Micah tried to convince himself.

He was thankful that Brax went on another one of her endless patrols. He appreciated having someone around so that he didn't have to talk to himself. However, she was a stranger, and he was still figuring out this new life that got dumped in his lap.

From his place near the trees, he saw in the distance something that made him pause, but this time, not with fear. A soft smile made an appearance on his usually stoic face as he walked to the old tree house that was left abandoned in the woods.

When the fire occurred, the tree house was far enough away that it didn't get destroyed—though time and weathering seemed to have dismantled it over the years.

Micah jogged over and slid his hand over the ridged wood of the gnarled tree, seeing the small fort he and his grandad used to escape to.

"What I wouldn't give for a good escape now," he said to the trees.

Being in the forest on his grandad's property had been a challenge all on its own, even before Lucy's magic. Each day he came outside, he saw flashes of memories; both good and bad.

More often than not, he chose to ignore the flashbacks. Pushing them away from his mind, focusing instead on what he needed to do right at that moment. Evading those hard memories was something he was an expert at, especially when he spent his life avoiding anything that could ever force him to remember. However, being here in the midst of everything, his mind couldn't escape them anymore, and each memory was slowly breaking him down.

He sat down at the base of the gnarled tree, not trusting the rickety ladder to enter the worn structure. He propped his arms on his knees and closed his eyes, heaving a sigh and feeling a sense of hopelessness that sank down to his very core.

He was alone again.

He had tried so hard, for so long, to not get back to this place, both figuratively and literally. He avoided Abe's property because he was just so damn mad at him for so long. He avoided the feelings, because he didn't know what to do with them—he never did.

Before his grandad died, Micah was willing to die with the anger he harbored toward Abe. He never planned on forgiving him or giving him a second thought. In his mind, it was a sealed fate.

But when Lucy came... Lucy changed everything.

God, I miss her. I'd do anything to have her with me now, he mused. But then again, maybe that was him trying to find other ways to escape.

He opened his eyes to the forest around him. His forest. This was all his now, whether he liked it or not. And really? He hadn't decided how he felt about it at all. It was easier to push it away and just deal with it a moment at a time than to think too much about it. He was here, this was his job, and he would do it.

Since Brax had arrived, he threw himself into figuring out his new role. Micah looked through the book his grandad left him and searched for answers, but ended up with more questions than when he started. He kept an eye open for the weird things that kept happening at the property and for talk of shadows or changes in the portal symbol. Unfortunately, he couldn't decipher the language, so he got nothing out of it.

Every bit of this new life reminded him of Lucy, and he missed his girl more than he thought possible.

He shook his head again, refusing to think too much about her. Micah couldn't fall apart when things were still fine between them.

Time moved differently there, and who knew what

happened since she returned. Did her dad finally hear her out and let her join the family business? Was that why she was so busy? Or maybe she was in trouble? Maybe they found out about the man who died when she was defending The Elderwood? Was she okay?

The thoughts swarmed his mind, making his blood rage within him, thinking she could be facing something without any support. She was so far away and there was nothing he could do for her.

He couldn't help her.

He couldn't protect her.

Releasing a grunt of anger, he got up from the ground and began pacing.

Dwelling over this does nothing, he told himself again, reinforcing the concept of pushing away yet another issue from his mind.

With a final pat of the tree trunk, Micah turned back toward the house. He was thankful this new cabin looked so different from Abe's old one... He had a hard enough time keeping the memories at bay among a bunch of trees. Those rooms where he grew up would have been too much. It would have been too hard.

He sighed in relief, knowing he was going to walk into a kitchen where his grandad never sat, and sit in a living room where his mother never rested. But it was also a house where he never loved Lucy, and that part didn't necessarily feel fair.

He trudged past the small cluster of trees that surrounded the portal to The Elderwood. Looking at the carving, he expected it to look as it had for the past few days: charred with black. But this time, dark smoke slowly seeped from tiny cracks within the symbol.

He froze.

What the fuck is happening?

Shadows began to creep out of the engraved bark in bursts and puffs like it was being pushed through by an unknown force on the other side. Deep orange sparks jumped out as the smokey aura grew.

Micah's breath hitched. He took one step back, and then another as the ground trembled. Stumbling over the leaves and debris in the yard, he watched wide-eyed as a shroud of darkness encompassed the tree. Red sparks shot viciously in every direction.

"Brax!" he yelled. "BRAX!"

His head swiveled around, looking for a plan. Should he run? Defend himself? Wait for Brax?

Suddenly, the sigil on the tree began to glow an ominous blood red. The birds, who were once so quiet in the forest, began to caw and screech like mad, flying away as quickly as possible. Micah's eyes darted to the canopy of the tree above him, watching them flee.

A slow chittering began, and Micah whipped his head left and right, panicking as he tried to find the source of the sound. It wasn't coming from the air, and all around him was still.

Then a pulse rocked the ground beneath his feet. Micah bent his knees and spread his arms, trying to steady himself. *Boom.* Another pulse.

Boom. Another.

Boom. Boom. Boom boom boom. It turned into a rumble

so violent his feet felt as though they were vibrating. He stepped backward, moving away from the trees, fearing that they would topple over and crush him.

Then, a resounding *crack* echoed through the air; the sound so loud he dropped to the ground on his knees and covered his ears. With his eyes shut tight, came silence.

The chittering had stopped. The rumbling ceased. He opened his eyes and squinted through the haze. The shadows began to recede. The sparks disappeared, and the tree was back to normal.

Except for one thing.

At the base of the tree, around the roots, the ground had split open leaving a puddle of smoke and ash swirling within it like lava deep underground.

Micah was entranced, staring at the dark, misty abyss before him. He took a step closer to get a better look. The shadows from the forest made it hard to see, and the depth of the split was too far away. Micah stood only another step away when another rumble came from below him. This time, more violent than before.

He could have sworn the earth growled at him; the sound splitting his resolve. The trees were shaking and swaying with the thunderous bellow.

A deafening *snap* and a tree branch came crashing down behind him. He jumped to get away from it.

The ground roared in response, sending a more powerful shudder coursing through the earth.

Micah looked up with wide eyes, his body trembling, realizing he was in prime position to be pummeled by fallen tree branches. Just like the previous branch, more were sure to follow if the rumbling continued. He spotted another limb cracking from the vigorous swaying of the tree above. Taking a step back to get out of the way, he tripped over the oversized limb that had already fallen.

From his position on his back, he looked straight up and saw the swaying bough crack once more. It was falling from the tree and headed directly for him.

He scrambled, trying to get himself back up, but couldn't seem to get his footing. The branch was only feet away, and Micah was paralyzed with fear.

Screaming, he threw his hands out in front of him. He closed his eyes and prepared for the monstrous bough to crush him.

But nothing happened.

He slowly opened his tightly shut eyes, knowing that any second the enormous piece of tree would come tumbling down on top of him, but when he saw what really happened, he couldn't breathe.

The 12 foot tree branch hovered in the air before him, wrapped in a red swirling mist. It was less than four feet away from crushing him, just floating in the air like it weighed nothing. Micah tried to figure out where the red magic came from. Was it Brax? Did someone know there was something wrong with The Elderwood and had come to help him?

No. There was no one else there.

His eyes widened, following the magic from the tree to where it originated.

The red swirling magic danced around Micah's

splayed fingers. With each slight movement of his hands, the branch moved with him.

Gasping, he quickly shoved his hands to the side, throwing the limb away from him. The red magic let go of the branch and disappeared from Micah's hands.

He lurched to his feet, turned on his heel, and sprinted back into the house.

Once inside, he held the window frame with two hands. He leaned against the pane and scanned the trees for a threat. There was no evidence of any kind of disturbance. The forest was quiet and calm.

I'm going fucking crazy, aren't I? Should I call someone? He glanced at the mirror.

"Okay," he said out loud, talking only to himself. "Let's look at this logically. The Elderwood tree was smoking and sparking. The birds freaked out and left. A weird noise came from the ground, it rumbled like crazy and now there's a crack. And magic," his voice cracked on the last word. "I used fucking magic."

Micah released the window frame and paced back and forth. When he got to the end of the room, he looked out the window to The Elderwood and turned on his heel and walked back to the other wall. He continued this pattern of talking and walking until he calmed himself.

With each circuit, he peered out the window, though nothing seemed out of place. The tree still stood, the smoke was out of sight. His hands were magic free.

Did I imagine that?

"An earthquake," he said as he stopped mid-stride. "That's what this was. An earthquake. And there's some weird smokey shit because there's magic in the tree and the birds were afraid of the earthquake. And something must have hit my head."

He slumped down on the couch and closed his eyes.

Flowing brown hair, hazel eyes, and freckles invaded his mind. Lucy.

I need Lucy.

CHAPTER

NINE

LUCY

I need Micah.

It was the only thing on Lucy's mind as she trundled through the fallen leaves crunching beneath her feet in the Nilban Woods.

It felt as though she was walking in a dream—the last time she was here, she had battled and defeated one of the largest wolven she had ever come across. Back then, she traveled with nervous steps; but today, no fear ran through her veins. Instead, pure power pulsed in her magic, and she was ready to wield it.

Learning about this magic was vitally important and that realization danced heavily in her mind. There were so many possibilities with this new magic she had yet to master, and with a the risky plans she had in mind, she could use all the help she could get.

The dinner with Laurent the previous night was more confusing than helpful. She had anticipated an evening with Lord Sloan would have provided her with ample information to guide her away from him. Instead, she had found hope in the most unexpected of places.

It was all too much to manage and now what she needed most, more than anything else in all the realms, was to be in the arms of the man who understood her most.

Luckily for her, Lucy's plan thus far was working flawlessly. She woke early, bathed, and finished packing her bag. She attended breakfast so her parents wouldn't even bother to look for her until at least lunch, and even then, Lucy would not truly be missed until her absence from dinner was noticed. Either way, it would all work out, as she expected to be home before nightfall.

She pulled her bag a little higher on her shoulder and continued her trek through the changing forest. Denora had not seen a winter in decades, and now that it was on the horizon, the hint of autumn made its appearance in little ways throughout the realm.

It seemed to happen so suddenly; almost overnight. One moment the apple trees in the orchard were blossoming as they always did, and the next, the leaves were as vibrantly red as the apples that had fallen.

She gripped her bow tightly in her left hand, keeping a keen ear available to hear any prowling animals. Her magic seemed to dance under her skin, getting more excitable with each passing moment. Lucy wasn't certain how she would enter the portal without the amulet, but she had a theory she expected would work, and each time she considered it, her magic responded with a gentle flutter from somewhere deep within.

When she last returned home from Joterra, the

symbol that The Elderwood tree marked on her hand lit up with a green glowing light. It was the same symbol as the amulet and the tree carvings that activated the portals. If she guessed correctly, it would be enough to allow her to enter.

Lucy glanced down at the markings with a desperate plea for success. If this plan of hers didn't work, she would have to return home and plot out an entirely new strategy. And who knew how much time she had before she was sent off to see Lord Sloan again?

No. I will get to Micah.

There was no other option. There was no one else in all existence who could understand her the way he could, and she would do whatever it took to get back to him, if only for one moment wrapped in his warm embrace.

Beads of sweat peppered her brow as her anxiety grew.

This has to work.

Ahead on the path, she heard a scuttling of animals. She paused and focused her Fae hearing in the distance beyond. Gentle flapping wings. Small pattering feet. Then, a hushed caw.

Birds?

Lucy continued down the path cautiously, her bow in hand. She reached above her head and behind her to her quiver to count the arrows available to her.

Four.

She needed more branches from The Elderwood to create more, but four would have to do. Her heart beat erratically in her chest.

As she crested the small slope, she saw what caused the noise. A scant flock of birds hovered around the carcass of an animal. Ravens and vultures took turns pecking at the rotting meat, fighting over who got the biggest piece.

Lucy stayed off to one side, keeping out of the way of the birds and their meal. As she passed, she realized the carcass was the wolven she had struck down on her initial journey just a few days ago.

That means I must be close.

Her eyes darted down to her right hand; her palm was shining a bright green. Her heart jolted as she searched the trees for the same symbol glowing somewhere nearby. Looking left and right, she feverishly dashed around the woods, knowing the portal was just steps away from her

She stilled as the sight of the portal came into view.

A beautiful, large tree, leaves still green from the magic imbued within it, stood tall in front of her. Its brown bark displayed the glowing green sigil, signaling to Lucy like a lighthouse leading her in from the storm.

Her heart raced in anticipation; the only thing separating her from Micah was this.

Please, bring me to Micah.

Holding her breath, Lucy closed her eyes as she placed her right hand on the tree. The bark under her hand felt firm, and her heart sunk.

Please. Please, bring me to Micah.

Suddenly, the bark seemed to warm at her touch. She opened her eyes and was astonished to see the tree bark rippling under her fingers. Releasing her breath, she stepped through with complete confidence.

As she passed through from one realm to another, she was met again with the feeling of absence, unlike her previous trips to Joterra. No light, no color, no sound—everything was placid and empty. Except that tiny, familiar sound she had heard once before. Was it a voice?

Before she could analyze it any further, she stepped through the other end of the portal onto the lush grass of Joterra. Only, she wasn't where she had expected.

How did this happen?

As she exited the portal, she realized she was not on the outskirts of Micah's property, stepping out of the portal to Joterra, but was standing in the shadow of The Elderwood tree itself.

Lucy was directly in front of Micah's new cabin.

"How did I get here?" She asked herself quietly.

"That is a wonderful question," a female's voice spoke from behind her.

Lucy spun to see a tall, tan female, wrapped in tight leather as rich as her skin. Her short, chopped hair made her sharp features look threatening, and the kohl make up that lined her eyes helped to add to that image. She could tell that something fierce lay just beyond this stranger's sultry appearance, but Lucy was not going anywhere.

"Who are you?" Lucy demanded, pulling her bow and aiming it at the beguiling stranger.

Is this another attack on The Elderwood? Is Micah here? Is he okay?

Too many thoughts filled her mind, but she forced

them away as she took stock of the enemy before her. She was clearly Fae, and definitely not from Denora. Whoever she was, Micah did not invite her here, which made her an intruder; and intruders were not welcome.

The fire in her veins ignited at the threat, and Lucy felt the magic of The Elderwood slithering through her body, preparing to attack.

Lucy brought her bow up closer to her line of sight, and the enemy gave a feral smile as she bent into a crouch, ready to charge.

"Brax?" Micah called from just out of view. The Fae barely flinched. "Brax? Is that you back there? Be careful with the portal, something is going on. It's not acting right."

Lucy's eyes darted over to where she heard his voice and then back to the female in front of her.

Brax? Micah knows her?

"Stay back, Lumen," the female Fae called. "There's a trespasser that needs dealing with."

"I'm not trespassing," Lucy spat in reply. "You are."

Brax's eyes lit up with ferocity as though she enjoyed the possibility of a fight.

"Lu?" Micah asked incredulously. Lucy could hear his footsteps as he ran toward the trees, finally coming into sight. "Lu!"

She was hesitant to take her eyes off of this strange Fae standing in between her and Micah, but Lucy couldn't help herself. She looked at Micah and her heart leapt with joy. He stepped directly between the females to greet Lucy and a smile broke over her face.

Lucy kept her bow in one hand and an arrow in the

other as she flung herself into Micah's welcoming arms. His broad shoulders squeezed her tightly as Lucy clung to him. She could smell the familiar scent of him that lingered in the back of her brain since she had left him.

She pulled his face into her hands and she studied him. Micah seemed so different from when she saw him last. His hair had grown out and his five o'clock shadow was more of a short, scruffy beard, hiding the scar she had memorized. Her eyes landed on his full lips, then his chocolate brown eyes.

Those eyes. They pulled her in and kept her there, threatening to captivate her for all of time.

"I've missed you," she whispered, her eyes bright with adoration.

"Baby, words can't begin to describe how much I've missed you."

He grabbed her by her neck and pulled her into a deep kiss, making Lucy's heart explode. She couldn't get past the taste of him, the smell of him, the feel of him on her skin once more, but the sentiment was quickly doused as she heard someone clearing their throat.

Micah pulled back with a laugh and tucked his arm around Lucy's shoulders, facing the Fae.

"Lu, this is Brax," he said with a smile.

"What is she doing here?" Brax asked, stone faced.

"Who are you? What are *you* doing here?" Lucy retorted, taking a step toward Brax.

Brax ignored Lucy and looked at Micah instead. "If you were planning on having a female caller, all you had to do was tell me. You know I won't judge." She looked

Lucy up and down. "Though I am surprised she's Fae. Who is she?"

"*She* is standing right in front of you," Lucy seethed.

"That is not her reason for being here," Micah replied, trying to ease the tension in the air.

"Why do you care who he's with?" Lucy said again, her magic bubbling up inside of her, ready to unleash on this horrid Fae.

"I don't," Brax replied, arching her eyebrow with distaste. "But I have a job to do while I am here, and taking out the trash comes with the territory."

Lucy's magic jumped from her hands and crashed into Brax, throwing her to the ground in surprise. Brax looked up at Lucy and saw her standing with two orbs of green light rotating in her hands.

"What the fuck is that?" Brax asked, staring at Lucy's magic and then to Micah, looking for an answer.

"It's me taking out the trash," Lucy said with fake kindness. Lucy pulled her arms back, prepared to unleash another blast upon the Fae, when Micah darted in front of her with his hands outstretched.

"Whoa, whoa, hey," he said, trying to calm her. "This is one big misunderstanding. Brax was sent here by Lord Sloan to help me with The Elderwood. That's all."

"Why are you telling her about The Elderwood, you kumquat?" Brax scolded.

"Because it's hers as much as it's mine." Micah reached a hand out to bring Brax back to her feet and then stood between the two beautiful, yet volatile, female Fae. "Brax, this is Lucy Baum."

TEN

MICAH

"Baum? As in Lucella Baum?" Brax asked with amused curiosity.

"You work for Laurent?" Lucy asked her, eyeing her apprehensively. The swirling green mist whirled in her hands in a threat as she kept her body firmly in front of The Elderwood, blocking it from Brax.

Micah's head jerked back at the casual way she used Sloan's first name.

"Yes, I do," Brax said, smiling now. She cast a look at Micah in a taunt.

Does she know something I don't?

"I don't understand why you need to be here," Lucy continued. "The Elderwood is fine and Micah is completely capable."

"Sure he is," Brax laughed.

The forest floor crunched under Lucy's feet as she took another step toward Brax. Her magic flared in her hands as a hint of green light shimmered in her eyes.

Grabbing Lucy's arm, Micah gently tugged her closer to him. "Lu?"

When she turned to him, he saw the green more clearly, dancing in her irises as though the color was alive within her. Lucy blinked, and it was gone.

"I think I'll leave you two alone as I continue my rounds." Brax turned to Micah and pointed her finger at him in earnest. "I expect an explanation of whatever the fuck that was."

Micah nodded, his furrowed brow watching as Brax made her way across the trees and into the thicket of woods beyond them.

He slid his hand down Lucy's arm and stopped right before he got to her hands, then he cleared his throat.

"Oh," Lucy said sheepishly as she doused the orbs of green.

He grabbed her hand and led her to the cabin. He had no idea why she was here or what that standoff was about, but maybe putting some distance between her and the portal would help her clear her head... both mentally and physically.

Clasping their hands together, Micah felt a wave of contentment.

I can't believe she's actually here.

Brushing his thumb over the back of her left hand, he soaked in the feeling. When he last saw her, she tied him up and dashed through the portal without so much as a goodbye. He wouldn't let her go so easily this time.

As they entered the house, he watched as Lucy's eyes took in the new interior her brother and that older creep had designed. With each passing day, it had felt more and more like home, and now that Lucy was here, it was as though everything was complete.

However, at the thought, his heart tightened; he knew she wouldn't stay.

Unless...

"What are you doing here, Lu?" His voice was soft, not because he was trying to be quiet, but because he couldn't let the shakiness of his words be heard. He guided her to the couch and sat next to her, still holding her hand tenderly.

"I needed you." She said it so matter-of-factly, just as she did everything.

He smiled broadly at the response. "My warrior." He pulled her in for a kiss, their mouths meeting in a heated moment of desire. Lucy's body melted into his, her lips growing more needy with each passing second.

With his powerful arms, he moved her from the couch into his lap to better hold her. Her body felt strong yet soft in just the right places, while his body felt starved without her affection. But in the moment, it was almost as though no time had passed between them.

Lucy raked her fingers through his hair and a growl of appreciation came from his throat, making Lucy huff a laugh between kisses.

"I think you liked that," Lucy whispered in a tease.

"I like everything about you." Micah pulled her closer, reclaiming her lips with his.

"If I didn't know any better, I'd think you've missed me," she said, pulling back to look at him.

Staring into her hazel eyes, his heart pounded in his chest.

She's perfect.

From the freckles on her nose to the curve of her lip, there was not one part of her that he didn't worship. She could command him to do just about anything and he would obey, just to see her smile. She was everything.

"Words can't sum up what I feel," he whispered, changing the teasing tone to something more serious. His eyes bored deeply into hers as her playful smile faded to an understanding lilt of her lips.

She nodded, reading his heart. "I know."

Micah stilled, unsure of what to say next. Should he lay it all on the line? Confess his never-ending love to her? Should he wait for her to share why she came back? To see if she was going to stay this time?

The seconds felt like hours, but Lucy didn't give any hint as to why she was there. He sighed and pulled her closer. She wrapped her arms around him, hugging him tightly, and nestled her head in the crook of his neck.

Micah held her as close to him as he possibly could. Rubbing his hands up her thighs, on her back, through her hair; it would never be enough.

"Why are you really here?" Micah continued to stroke her hair, losing himself to her scent... *roses and honey.*

She sat up, keeping her arms around him; her fingertips teased the hair at the base of his neck. Then she sat down on the couch next to him.

"Things aren't going as smoothly as I would have liked, and I just... missed you. I wanted to be with the one who knows my heart."

She shied away as she spoke, but Micah didn't mind. The soft smile on his face grew, and he dropped his hands to hers and squeezed. "I'm here. What's going on? How can I help?"

"I'm not sure you can," she admitted.

It hurt that she didn't think he could help. It's what he did—he helped people. Didn't she trust him? He turned to her to ask, but stopped. He wasn't sure he was prepared to hear the answer.

She turned away from him to the vast windows, looking out into the woods. "It's so beautiful here."

Micah agreed, but that wasn't what he wanted to talk about. He wanted to know what happened with her father. He wanted to ask what she was doing there, and if this time she would stay... Not to mention the portal, Brax, and the swirling red magic. Damn, there were so many problems.

"It is, but there have been some weird things going on that we should probably talk about. It's The Elderwood..."

"What happened to it? Was it that Fae female? Did she do something?" Lucy stood in a hurry, ready to defend land that wasn't being threatened.

"No, not that," Micah said. "The portal. There's something wrong with it."

"Wrong? What do you mean?"

"The sigil on the tree. It's changed. It has a dark, ashy smoke that seems to seep out of it." He rubbed at his chin, trying to find the right words. "It looks almost as if something inside of it exploded. And there's a crack in the ground. I don't know if it was an earthquake or what, but something is happening."

"Exploded? Fire?" Lucy's lips popped open in shock. Her fingers twitched at her sides.

"No, it's different. I don't know how to explain it. All I know is that it isn't a good sign. Something's gone haywire with it."

Lucy took a step toward the door, clearly prepared to go see for herself.

"That's not all," he murmured. The hairs on the back of his neck stood rigid as he remembered the creature in the shadows. A shiver shot down his spine. "There is something lurking around the tree, and I can't seem to get a read on it. It looks like an enormous cat, and every time I try to get close enough to see it, it's gone. I can't catch it on camera. I can't figure out where it's coming from."

"A feline? Is it small?" Lucy asked, focused on their conversation. She took a careful step closer to Micah.

"No. It's massive. It looks like a giant black panther, but its coat is so dark, like it's made of shadows. "

"A shadow beast?" She gasped in surprise. "But those are unheard of in Joterra..." Lucy went to the window, looking out into the forest. "In fact, they haven't been in Denora for thousands of years from what I've read."

"I haven't been able to find much about it in the book yet, but I figure Brax will help me find more answers."

She spun to look at Micah with a glare. "You're going to let that stranger look in your ancestral book?"

"I mean, I guess it depends, doesn't it? Are you going to stick around and help me or will you be leaving again?" His words had a sharper edge than he meant, but he couldn't stop them as they came out. The harshness lacing them hid the heartbreak. He was tired of people leaving him.

Lucy didn't respond. Instead, she stared at Micah, causing his thoughts to spin wildly.

I'm pushing her away. She never wanted to stay, did she...

"You know there was nothing I could have done about that," Lucy finally said. The hurt in her tone was quiet, but the defiance in her voice was strong.

Micah was already putting a wall between them before they even gave the relationship a chance.

"I know. I'm sorry." He shook his head, trying to relieve himself from the headache that kept growing.

Reaching out, he extended his hand to her, hoping she would take it.

If she takes it, there's still a chance... Take my hand baby, he silently pleaded.

She took his hand, and he pulled her back to sit on the couch next to him, her thigh grazing his.

A relieved sigh left him, but he wasn't out of the woods yet. There were too many obstacles between them. He had to figure out a way to make the two of them work—he wouldn't give up when they had barely had the chance to begin.

Lucy looked down, refusing to make eye contact. He saw her putting up mental walls, too.

"Do you remember the night in the study?" Micah whispered.

Lucy's eyes met his. She nodded almost imperceptibly, and a stray curl fell from behind her ear.

Micah's heart ached as he recalled the night. He

needed to offer this piece of himself to her. He needed her to remember as much as he did.

"The flame from the candle lit up the wall in little shapes. We had red wine and cheese and you wore those soft, little leggings." He grazed a finger on the edge of her knee, not wanting to overstep, but wanting to touch her more than anything in the world. "You told me you wanted love—real love. You wanted someone who saw you and decided that they couldn't live without you."

Lucy's breath hitched as she lifted her head to Micah. They faced one another, their breathing erratic and shallow.

"That's me, Lu. I can't live without you." Micah's shaky words came out in a breathless tumble. "And it scares the fuck out of me."

Lucy's lips crashed into Micah's, swallowing his words whole. Her hands gripped his shoulders and she pulled him on top of her as they laid on the couch.

All at once, the pressure and stress that Micah had been carrying around in his tainted heart disappeared. Relief and love overwhelmed him, body, mind, and soul. The only thing he needed in this lifetime and the next was Lucy, there in his arms, as he made her happy every day for the rest of their lives.

The rest of mine, he realized.

Lucy was Fae and would outlive him.

He propped himself up on his arms, needing to look at Lucy. Her cheeks were flushed and her eyes were bright. There was no hesitation from her, so why did Micah feel so uneasy? He couldn't stand the thought of her running from him again. What if she left and found herself in the arms of Sloan instead?

She combed her fingers through his shaggy hair and looked at him curiously. "What's wrong?"

"I don't want you to close yourself off to me when things get hard," he whispered. "Don't run from me, baby."

Lucy's eyes welled with tears as she nodded. Then she pulled him in close and kissed him ever so gently, her hands exploring his body.

Micah tangled his fingers into her curly brown hair and kissed down the length of her neck, teasing with nips of his teeth and soothing strokes of his tongue. Lucy moaned as she encouraged him to continue, pulling off his shirt as he reached to pull down her leggings.

Micah needed more of her; he needed all of her. She was the sun lighting up his day and the moon and stars guiding him at night. She was the beauty of the wild-flowers in the grove and the foundation of the ground that nourishes his soul. Lucy was the answer to every-thing, and he made a silent promise to the stars at that moment that he would do everything within his power to always make her feel loved and seen.

Love.

The thought was nearly a shock to Micah.

This is love.

And for the first time in his life, he didn't run. Instead, he worshiped Lucy right there on the couch until the sun made its way down and all that was left were the shadows cast from the light in the hall.

~

"I'm sorry it took me so long to return to you," Lucy said in between soft kisses as they lay on the living room floor in a tangle of naked limbs.

"It's fine. Your brother, Wes, and some old dude named Jasper came and helped me take care of things here." He looked around at the new cabin they created for him. "Wes seems like he could maybe be nice if he wanted to be."

"If he wanted to be?" Lucy let out a reluctant huff of laughter. "Actually, that's a pretty accurate description of Wes." She sat up and began dressing, picking between the scattered clothes among them.

"Suffice to say, I don't think he likes me much. Did you tell him about us?"

Lucy paled. "No, of course not. I could never."

Micah's head jerked back in surprise at the admission. "*Never*? Why *never*? Am I not allowed to be something to you?" His voice was uncertain, with a pang of frustration that he tried to hide. He grabbed his jeans and began to clothe himself.

Lucy shook her head and offered a sad smile, scooting closer to him again. "No. It's not that. It's just… complicated right now. There's so much going on that I barely understand. I am doing my best to figure it out, but I haven't had many opportunities. I'm trying to find out more about your Lumen ancestry, but Jasper keeps following me around like a shadow—he won't leave me alone. Everywhere I go, there he is."

"Yeah, something about him rubs me the wrong

way." Micah's face softened, happy with the change of topic. "When he came here, I'm pretty sure he just said things to intentionally piss me off. It surprised me you told them about the land developers." He stood as he grabbed his shirt and pulled it over his head.

"Pardon?" Lucy looked at him curiously, straightening her clothes.

"No. Pearson," he replied, helping her up. "J. Pearson? Jasper knew all about it and was talking to me like I was crazy when I said that I was worried they would come back."

"Micah—I didn't tell them who the land developers were." Her eyebrows furrowed. "I didn't even use that term because I assumed they wouldn't know what I was talking about."

"Then how did he know?"

"I have no idea, but maybe we're missing something. Once I return, I will see what Jasper is up to. I've never trusted him, and maybe my gut is telling me something more."

His stomach dropped.

"Once you return? You're leaving me again?" The sting of that reality was almost too much for Micah to bear. Didn't he just profess his love to her? Did she not feel the same?

"Micah, I have to. No one knows I'm here and I need to be back before the sun rises in Joterra." She glanced out the window to measure her time. "Besides, we need to figure out this Jasper issue. It is too odd for it to be coincidence."

We. It was the only thing Micah could hold on to.

He'd never force Lucy into a decision she didn't want to make, and as long as she was still including him in her plans, that had to be enough.

"There have been some weird things going on here, too," Micah said to her as he dragged a hand down the front of his face. He took a deep breath, preparing to tell her about the red magic that saved his life.

"In Denora, as well," Lucy interrupted him. "My father is beyond angry with me, and he wouldn't let me come to say goodbye. I'm so sorry I couldn't come and see you sooner."

"Goodbye? What do you mean goodbye?" His response was faint, worry and confusion causing his voice to crack.

"Micah... I am doing everything to try to dissuade Lord Sloan from wanting to move forward with the arrangement, but my parents seem glued to the idea."

Micah's lips parted with disbelief, then quickly snapped shut. "Wait. Did you say you were trying to dissuade your parents, or Lord Sloan?"

"Lord Sloan," she whispered. "He arrived the day after I returned."

ELEVEN

"I don't understand. What are you doing with him? Why so soon?"

"My father moved things up—the wedding is arranged for the Spring... Just a few more months away. He set up a dinner in the Capital so Laurent and I could get to know each other."

Lucy did her best to keep her tone neutral, to list the facts without any emotion behind them, because that's all that it was: facts.

Right?

"*Dinner,* Lucy? You're telling me you're going on dates?"

"Dates? What are you talking about?"

"You're spending time with him alone? Getting to know one another?" The anger had bubbled over in Micah once again, a line of frustration wrinkling in his forehead.

"It's not my choice, Micah!" Lucy retorted in frustration. "I am obligated to accept his invitations. It's what's expected of me! If I am to solve any of this, then I need to play my part."

"And what part is that exactly, Lucy?" Micah jumped from his seat on the couch and stalked across the room away from her. "Are you Lucy Baum, badass extraordinaire, who doesn't take no for an answer? Are you Lady Lucella, ready to take on a suitor?" He spun around to look at her, pain in his eyes. "Or are you my Lu? My warrior goddess, who I would move the stars for? Who are you today?" His voice rose and fell with an onslaught of emotion.

"What is that supposed to mean?" Lucy countered angrily.

Who does he think he is?

She stood up and walked to the windows, putting space between them. "What do you expect me to do, Micah? I already attempted one brash decision and it landed me stranded in another realm with a stranger and caused half of the star-damned woods to burn to the ground," she said in exasperation, shoving her hands at the window and the forest beyond.

"A stranger." His nostrils flared as he tried to get a deep breath of air. "A *stranger*, Lucy? That's what I am to you now?"

"No, that's not what I meant." Lucy shook her head and huffed an air of annoyance.

Why won't he listen to me?

The magical power in her veins thrummed with hostility. She had to tamper it down before it acted on its own accord once again. "Please. Let's talk this out."

Micah looked away indignantly, refusing any eye contact.

"Micah, I am here for you. I've traveled across the star-damned realms for you. Doesn't that mean anything?" She took a careful step toward him.

"I guess that depends on what it is you want from me." His voice was withdrawn and quiet. He took a few steps toward her, meeting her in front of the couch once again.

Lucy's heart fell at the comment.

"What I want from you? You are not a commodity I wish to use for my benefit... Micah, you're my friend. I just needed my friend. Is that too much to ask of you?"

Is friend the right word?

It felt like a lie, but she wasn't prepared to consider the other option. Not now.

Micah sighed. "No, of course it isn't. I'm sorry." He rubbed his eyes and groaned with his face in his hands, falling back onto the couch with a thud. "I'm so sick of these damn headaches."

"Headaches?" Her annoyance with Micah ceased immediately at the thought of him hurt. "When did they start?"

"I went home to turn in my badge and see my dad, and I don't know Lucy... something happened. I got so sick." He dropped his hands and laced them behind his neck, reminding her of the many times he did that in the forest with her. Especially when she was driving him crazy. The memory tore at her heart. She grabbed his hand and laced her fingers through his, sitting with him on the couch.

Just like the other times, her heart sang with their connection. Something about his touch just felt right, like there was nothing else that could complete her.

"My head was throbbing and before I got back on to the property, I thought I was going to lose it. I stepped out of the car and immediately passed out from the pain. I was lucky Brax was here to cure me—I thought I was going to have to go to the hospital. I didn't even know if that would be allowed?" Micah ran his hands through his hair, looking at Lucy with worry-filled eyes. "What happens if I get sick here and have to leave?"

"I- I don't know," she stammered out at last. Fae didn't have the same health problems mortals faced.

"Lumen, why didn't you tell me this?" Brax chimed in, leaning in the hall entryway that separated the kitchen and living area.

"What the fuck? Where did you come from? Have you been there listening this whole time?" Micah asked in surprise.

"Of course I was here. Now answer the question. Why didn't you tell me?"

Lucy glared at the strange female, ready to tear her limb from limb. How dare she be lurking in the back listening to their private conversation?

Was she there while they were naked and—oh my stars.

"What are you talking about? You knew. You were here," Micah said as he turned to talk to Brax.

Walking into the room slowly, Brax stopped in front of them and crossed her arms; her eyebrows furrowed above menacing eyes.

Feeling her magic pushing at the surface, Lucy took a

deep breath, keeping it tampered down. She wouldn't have Micah injured in the crossfire if her magic went wild.

"You said it yourself—you were here to cure my headaches?" Micah finished tying his boots and stood, looking between Lucy and Brax with apprehension.

Yeah, you should be cautious. I'm going to maim this female, Lucy thought bitterly.

"I meant when you hit your head off the ground, Lumen. You bashed your head open and I had to heal you —but that's all I healed. Your body was perfectly fine before that."

"What?" Micah fully faced her now. "No, I passed out from the pain. I was definitely not *perfectly fine.*"

"My lyfar magic can sense sickness. We use it on the battlefield to find infection in wounds. But you? You were healthy beyond a head wound." Brax eyed him skeptically, her dark lined eyes narrowing in annoyance.

"That doesn't make any sense," Micah said as he took a step back. "I was dizzy, nauseous, and my head was splitting before you came around. Maybe your magic just didn't pick it up because I'm not Fae?"

"That's nonsense," Brax scoffed. "My magic does not discriminate like most Fae do. I am telling you, Lumen. There was nothing wrong with you."

"That doesn't make sense," Micah repeated louder.

"No, it does not," she agreed, turning to look at Lucy.

Lucy remained on the couch, watching the interaction and doing her best to keep control of her immense power. At the very sight of Brax, all Lucy wanted to do was blast magic into her chest and shove her out of the room.

"Maybe we can find some answers in my book?" Micah suggested, oblivious to the silent war being raged in Lucy and Brax's glares.

"What book would have answers for this, Lumen?" Brax asked him doubtfully, looking away from Lucy in boredom.

He walked over and uncovered the leather-bound book from behind the couch. "This book."

Lucy fumed. "I can't believe you told her."

"Who else is going to help me, Lucy? Do you think I look like a guy who can speak and read ancient Fae? Spoiler alert: I'm not. And you aren't always here, so someone is going to have to help me."

Lucy seethed with anger, but Micah wasn't wrong. She hated to admit it, but there was really no other choice in this situation, was there?

She had to continue to get close to Laurent to prove to him that there was a better fit for marriage than her. Micah had to stay at The Elderwood and figure out what was happening to the portal. They were both destined to carry out their tasks, far from one another, unsure of where the future may lead.

The reality of Lucy having to leave him hit her like a ton of stones. How could she leave the man who held her heart in the safety of his? How would she survive the night when she longed for his lips upon hers? How could she leave when she was finally exploring the possibility of real... love?

Her magic flickered in and out, anger fading with every thought.

Brax took the book in her hands and looked at it with great reverence.

"I will prepare this book in the study. You need to say goodbye to your visitor. I'm sure her daddy is wondering where she is," Brax said condescendingly.

Lucy took a step toward Brax, ready to unleash fury on her when she made a sharp turn around the corner and disappeared from Lucy's view. Instead, in front of her was Micah, with his hands up, ready to detain her from following Brax.

"So, you pick her to share all of your secrets with?"

Micah sighed, "I am just trying to do what I am supposed to: protect the portal. Sloan sent her to help me, so how awful can it be? I'm surprised you didn't know, with all of your time spent with him." His face was drawn, clearly unhappy with the turn of events in their discussion.

"Let me get this straight. You are judging me for being forced to spend time with Laurent and you are here cavorting with another female?"

"*Laurent*—first name basis now, huh?" He bit his bottom lip in anger, trying to withhold words.

Lucy stared at him as he did it—feeling furious yet also wishing she were that lip.

No, she told herself. *No. He is being ridiculous.*

"I'm going to pretend that you didn't make that last comment and instead leave you with this: I'm glad you're alright, and I am happy that there is someone here who can help you while I'm gone." The words pained her to say. "I can't necessarily say that I like her, but I don't want you to feel alone."

She looked out the window in a panic. The sun was rising, and if she wanted to get home without being caught, she needed to leave. Now.

"Work out what is going on with The Elderwood, and I will find a way out of all of this... Don't give up on me yet. Okay?"

Her eyes were fierce as she said it, but her shaky words betrayed her. Inside, she was falling apart, but she couldn't let Micah know. Not yet.

Micah's eyes remained fixed on hers as he nodded, his severe expression never leaving his face. Lucy couldn't be sure that he believed her, but there was nothing left to say.

She stood on the tips of her toes to reach up and kiss him softly; his lips didn't move. Her heart sank as he didn't respond, and as she turned away, he grabbed onto her waist and pulled her back to him.

His returning kiss was forceful and heartbreaking and she couldn't decide if it was a kiss that said "I'll miss you", or a kiss that said "goodbye".

Either way, she couldn't stay to find out, for as soon as her Fae speed could allow it, she reached The Elderwood portal and was through the gateway without even pausing to see it.

What mattered most was that Micah did not get to see the tears streaming down her face—and that was all she could focus on.

TWELVE

MICAH

Micah's balled fists pounded into the wall next to the door frame. "Lucy!" he yelled again, trying to will her back to the cabin. There was no point—she was gone, and he couldn't force her to come back.

"Let her go, Lumen," Brax said from her place in the study. "We have work to do."

Micah turned reluctantly, glancing back once more, hoping that Lucy would appear.

What the hell just happened?

He squeezed his eyes tight as he dragged his hand down his face.

"What have you been doing this entire time? Where have you been?" Micah asked her.

Brax opened the leather-bound book at the desk, analyzing each page closely. "Around."

Her flippant tone made Micah's eye twitch. He wouldn't be getting any more answers from her; she was more stubborn than Lucy, and that was saying something.

As Brax turned the pages, her eyes grew wider with each inscription. She mumbled to herself as she read through them, quickly flipping through, searching for information.

Micah propped himself on the desk next to her, resigning himself to the fact that he had no real way to help. He had to rely on Brax, and he still wasn't sure where he stood with her. "We need to find out about that shadow cat, too."

"Nonsense," Brax replied. "There is no such thing as a shadow cat."

"Yes, there is. Lucy said they used to be in Denora."

"Miss Baum said that once upon a time there was, but we don't live in a fairy tale, Lumen. What she spoke of has not existed in a very long time." She continued to page through the book, scanning through the inscriptions. "Beyond that, they don't live here in Joterra. It would be preposterous of them to come to a mortal land. Their food source comes from the souls of the ancient Fae—not from mortals." She raked her eyes up and down his body. "They would starve."

Micah paled. "They feed on souls?" His eyebrows shot up. "What does that even mean?"

Brax turned on him with a look, leaning in with a wicked whisper. "I'm not going to spell it out for you, Lumen. Use your imagination."

Micah gulped and Brax smiled at his discomfort.

She turned back to the book. "Now, like I said. There's no reason to fear the creatures you think you saw. I am sure you mistook it for a forest cat. But there must be some more information on why you felt so ill and why my lyfar didn't pick up on it."

"How long were you standing there listening to our... conversation?"

Brax shooed the question away with her hand.

He sighed. "What about the crack in the ground?"

"I'll look into it. It is likely nothing."

"So black smoke, sparks and a fucking *earthquake* is nothing? Why didn't you hear it, by the way?"

Micah's frustration poured out of him with every word, but he knew there was no point. Each and every part of this had become more complicated than the next, and he wasn't sure what he was supposed to do.

"I heard you, and I came," she said matter-of-factly.

Micah looked at her in disbelief. Though, the more he thought about it, maybe he was overreacting. It probably felt like hours for him, but really, the rumbling was a matter of minutes. Not much time had passed by the time he got inside and Lucy came. At the thought of her, his insides twisted yet again.

He wasn't even sure if being mad was fair. Micah had spent so many years of his life being upset with people who didn't deserve it—the least he could do was try to rein it in as he lived on his grandad's property. Micah would never be able to apologize to his grandad for refusing his calls and avoiding all contact. He'd never be able to make things right... Being here on his land had to mean something more than just following in his footsteps. Micah knew deep down in his heart, things had to change. He had to try to honor his grandad in some way.

Micah slunk into the cushioned chair across from the desk and groaned. "This is a fucking disaster."

Brax took a quick look at Micah as he sat with his hands over his face, at a loss for his next steps. "What is going on with you and the Baum female?"

"What do you mean?" He mumbled.

"Well, you've just had a lovers' quarrel, and while it was extremely entertaining, I don't quite understand it. She is betrothed to Lord Sloan—is she not?"

He dropped his hands to look at her, but she focused on the book. Micah was at war with himself—he wanted to tell Brax everything. He wanted to finally talk to someone about everything that was going on without having to hold back any details.

Who better to talk to about Fae magic and forbidden love than someone who understood the bogus Denoran politics? But Micah wasn't sure how much he could trust Brax. More than that, he couldn't risk Brax going back to her employer, telling him everything that had happened between the pair.

Or maybe he did?

Maybe if Sloan knew Lucy was previously involved with another man, he'd back off. Maybe he'd see that she isn't into him and would let her go.

"It's complicated," was all he ended up sharing.

"It's less complicated than a mortal man having a Fae book. Indulge me."

Micah heaved another sigh and tried to figure his way through the story. "Well, when I first saw her, we didn't want anything to do with one another. I wanted to sell my grandad's old place, and she wanted me to keep it. God, she was such a nag about it all," he laughed. "She was so fierce. So beautiful... She's unlike anyone I've ever met."

His voice trailed off as he got lost in thought, sighing deeply.

"We went through a lot to get to where we are now," he told Brax seriously. "Hell, without her, I'd be a cop in the city, miserably unaware that life was passing me by."

"What do you mean by that? Miserably unaware? If you are unaware of what you are missing, how can that be miserable?"

"Because if I'm being honest, I was miserable anyway." As soon as he said it, he knew it was true. "I didn't realize it until now. Until Lucy."

Brax stopped what she was doing and looked over at Micah, enthralled by his words.

"Your life was miserable? What made it so bad?" she asked, truly curious.

"I was just kind of living life on auto-pilot." Micah shrugged, not wanting to get too deep.

She gave him a quizzical look and he assumed it was the lingo.

"I was just doing the same routine every day? I did my job, worked out, came home and took care of my apartment, and repeated the same things every single day of my life. I didn't have many friends, so there wasn't much I did with anyone outside of work."

"What about lovers?" Brax asked as she pushed the book aside, leaning her elbows on the desk, cradling her head in one of her hands.

Being the center of Brax's attention made him squirm.

"I didn't have too many of those either." He shifted in his seat. "I had a girl for a while, but things didn't work out. I wasn't willing to change. I don't think I was a great listener."

Ugh. I'm seeing a fucking pattern here.

"So, what is this situation with you and Miss Baum? There is romance there?"

Micah wasn't sure he wanted to answer, but the look in Brax's eyes wasn't judgmental. There was a tender curiosity peeking from behind her tough exterior.

"Yeah," he said solemnly. "There is."

Brax nodded her head in understanding.

Micah had always been a good judge of character—it was one of the things that made him a good detective. He could read the intentions of a person by the inflection of their voice, the tilt of their head... He could always determine when someone was lying to him. He always knew who to trust; and he wanted to trust Brax.

The only person to ever make him question that was his grandad. He was the one person who didn't live up to who Micah thought he was... Though now, as he looked back, he realized he was able to count on Abe. That never faltered. Life just wasn't as it seemed, and Micah was too proud to just talk to him.

He shrugged off the thought, real emotion threatening to be acknowledged. "How about you? Got a guy? Or a girl?" Changing the topic was his best defense and he shoved the emotion away, refusing to bring it to light.

"Not at the moment. I have had many lovers who I've

taken to bed, but none who have had the courage to stick around. It is a difficult thing to be paired with a Vytyrian." Brax straightened her shoulders and brushed imaginary lint off of her shirt.

"Why is that?" he asked, leaning back and turning toward her.

"Warriors move around a lot; we go from contract to contract and find work. I have gone to bed with Denorans from every territory, Vytyrians, the Karroz — the list goes on."

"Karroz?" It seemed like every time he thought he was getting the hang of things, new foreign words kept popping up.

How am I going to figure all of this stuff out?

"Yes, another realm. You'd probably find it fun, Lumen," Brax said with a sly smile.

"And why is that?"

She leaned forward and looked at Micah with devious eyes. "Dragons."

"Dragons?" Micah choked. "They're real?"

"Of course, Lumen." She rolled her eyes and turned her body back to the book. "By the stars, you're like a giant, hairy baby. There are so many things you need to learn."

"Tell me about it," Micah said with a huff.

It was just a customary Joterran phrase, but Brax took it literally.

"We will begin here," she pointed at a page near the middle of the book. "What do you know of this book and Denora?"

"Well," Micah began, taken aback by her abruptness

once again. "I know there are Fae who live in Denora. They have magic. There is a Kingdom. And somehow I'm related to a distant Fae relative who decided to come here to live and then never left." He shook his head, listening to the words that came out of his mouth.

Magic. Fae. I'm not sure I'll ever get used to this.

Brax's eyes seemed to shimmer with mischief. "Alderic Lumen! I should have known you were related to him. He was a *beast* in the bedchambers." She leaned back with a smile on her face.

"What? How the hell would you know?"

"I'm older than I look. I've been around for thousands of years. Why do you think I am both so beautiful and knowledgeable?" She winked at him. "Only one who has seen the years that I have could be both."

Micah's eyes nearly bulged out of their sockets. "Thousands? More than one? "

"Yes. Four and a half, but the math changes with each realm you visit."

"You're four thousand years old?!"

"Yes." She rolled her eyes at his display of surprise. "Pay attention, you wet noodle. We have things to do."

She handed the book back over to him and he took it in his arms. Still dazed by their conversation, Micah remained silent.

"I will do another scan of the property to see what explains this crack you spoke of. You look through this book to figure out why your head ails you." Swinging the door open, she turned to speak to him. "Think about when it began, when you noticed it, and exactly how it felt. Then scan through the pages that you can understand. Look at the pictures, too. Maybe something will click."

"You can't go back out there. What about that shadow creature?" Micah was terrified of something happening to Brax and him being left all alone on the property. He didn't have anyone to rely on.

"Enough of that." She waved an annoyed hand in the air. "I will have my walk and be back soon. I'll put a call into my employer if it makes you feel better."

A look of hesitation crossed Micah's face before Brax spoke once more. "Don't worry, Lumen. I won't mention your fun with Miss Baum."

Then she left Micah alone in the house. He tried to look out the window to follow her, but her purposeful strides brought her to the trees quickly, and in moments she was far enough into the thicket that Micah couldn't see her.

What is she always doing back there? Am I right to trust her?

He squinted his eyes to see farther, but it was no use.

He lugged the book over to the kitchen table and plopped it down as he turned to grab a glass of water.

This is all so ridiculous. I can't believe that Lucy and I fought like that.

Closing his eyes, he tried to remember her beautiful face before it had turned to anger. Before he hurt her with his words. He had every right to be upset with her, didn't he?

Maybe this is why I was supposed to end up alone.

He shook his head again as he sat down at the kitchen table with the book, alone in the house that contained only wisps of memories, the dishwasher whirring the background.

For over an hour, he flipped through page by page, hoping something familiar would pop up. Carefully, he searched for anything that had the potential to answer his questions about his headaches or the mysterious creature prowling in the woods; something about the enormous crack in the ground. Better yet, he needed an explanation of what that red mist was—how magic came out of nowhere and saved his life.

Micah knew he wasn't making it up. It was there, plain as day. He didn't tell Lucy or Brax about the magic just yet, though. How would they believe that magic came to help him? That creature, though...

Why doesn't anyone believe me? If that shadow beast really exists, how did it get here from Denora?

More pages went by, and it was easier and easier for Micah to flip through. The majority of the entries were written in another language, and Micah had no idea how to read them. The pictures weren't very helpful. Every now and then there would be an image of a plant or herb, maybe some weapons? There were numerous entries with flasks and glass vials filled with liquids or powders. But for the most part, just ornate scrawl filled the pages, all written in dark ink on beige paper.

After what felt like an eternity, Micah flipped to a page and stopped. There in front of him was unmistakably familiar handwriting.

Grandad.

He brushed his fingertips over the words. When he read the inscription, Micah stilled.

The Curse of the Guardian

I am unsure who will see this after me, but I want it to go into record to ensure that no one makes the same mistake I did.

My wife is very ill, and I needed to leave with her in order to get her medical care. While I was away from home, I took a turn for the worse. It was a pain unlike anything I have ever experienced before. My head throbbed like it was in a vise; it felt like I was walking through a fog. I am mortal and have spent years experiencing many illnesses—but nothing like this. Once we got back to the property, all of my pain disappeared. It was as though I had imagined it all, which didn't make any sense.

A few weeks later, I had to bring my wife to visit family. The same sensations occurred. We had to shorten our trip due to my sudden symptoms, and again, as soon as I crossed over the property line to the house, all of my ailments vanished.

I spent time testing my theory, and discovered that extended time away from our home induces an enormous list of illnesses that I experienced, which were all relieved with my proximity to the grounds—though some took longer than others.

I was always told to stay to guard The Elderwood, and I was always encouraged not to leave, but I didn't realize there would be such a physical reaction. I never realized that is why my father, and his before him, never left the property. I didn't realize the ramifications of the curse placed upon us if we were to abandon our post—nor was I ever told.

So, to all future guardians—stay. The longer you are away, the more severe the symptoms become. I fear death would come to those who do not return to The Elderwood when beckoned.

ABE LUMEN

MICAH STARED AT THE PAGE, disbelief shaking him to his core.

Why would the Fae put a curse on someone just to guard a damn tree? An actual fucking curse?

He strode across the room with the book, dropping it on the small table in the living room. Heated anger rose to the surface. He balled his fists tightly and lifted them to his temples, his teeth clenching together in frustration.

I need to get out of here. If I don't get out of this fucking place, I'm gonna lose it.

Grabbing his running shoes and his phone, he stuck his earbuds in and ran out the front door, letting it swing shut behind him. He didn't care that he wasn't in his workout clothes.

He didn't think about the giant crack from the tree, the scarlet ropes of mist that sprang from his hands, nor the actual curse that threatened to hurt him if he left. Instead, he focused on the steady pound of his shoes on the earth. Each foot propelling him further away from that book, filled with a reality he refused to accept.

He ran from a cabin with no family, Brax and the Fae dipshit Sloan, Jasper, J. Pearson, everything. Even Lucy. He needed his mind empty of all the things crashing down around him.

Eventually, the music in his ears calmed him, and the quiet of the forest felt less foreboding.

His path around the property ended back at the cabin, and he walked in breathless. By busying his body, it quieted his mind. He was thirsty and sweaty, but clear-headed for the first time in days.

"Lumen."

Brax's voice startled him. She sat so quietly with the leather book in her lap. He didn't even see her there, sitting on the floor in front of the couch. Usually she was filled with movement, never still. But this… this was new. Her eyes held worry and sorrow.

The book laid in her lap, open to the page where he left off.

"I know," he replied, wiping the sweat from his brow. "The curse. That's why I was sick."

"No, that's not it," Brax replied seriously.

"Yes, I know I can die if I leave. I get it," Micah replied flatly, trying to forget.

"Listen to me, you overgrown turnip," Brax snapped at him. "The other side of this page is in Denoran and I assume you haven't miraculously acquired a lesson in Fae languages while I was in the forest, have you?" Her eyes were full of fire and impatience, hinting what truly lay beneath Brax's feminine exterior.

"Sorry," Micah replied with a defeated sigh. With a

raised eyebrow he added, "do I want to know what it said in Denoran?"

"It says if there is no guardian to watch over the portal, it is open for all the dark and evil things to travel through."

"What does that mean?"

"It means the shadow beast is the least of our worries."

THIRTEEN

LUCY

"Throw it higher," Lucy called to Wes. She held her new bow high and aimed her arrow at the clay plate. Upon her release, the arrow whistled through the sky, striking her target dead center, shattering the clay into pieces.

Since her return, her head filled with a never ending whirlwind of uncertainty. Her secret trip to Joterra lasted only half of one Denoran day. She sulked in her room for the remainder of her night which made for unrestful sleep and a dreadful attitude.

Thankfully, her brother Tristan sought her out and invited her to an early morning archery practice. It was precisely the thing she needed to get her mind off of her troubles, if only for a little while. With each arrow, her mind calmed.

"This is always how high I send them for you," Wes said with an edge of annoyance. "How often have you been practicing?"

"Not often," Lucy said irritably. "Now send it."

Archery never failed to put Lucy's mind at ease. The predictable and repetitive movements slowed her body down and allowed her to breathe freely without the pressure of her reality weighing on her mind.

Lucy dropped her bow and looked at her brothers across the grassy field. Wes stood next to a tower of clay plates they used during target practice, preparing to throw another.

Tristan lazily sent magic toward the broken shards across the field, bringing them back into a pile to be recreated into a target once more. She chuckled at his less-than-enthusiastic position, lying back in the grass, his arm over his eyes to block the sun, one leg crossed over the other.

"Yes, Lucy, how often?" Tristan called. "You're pulverizing these plates and making the clean up harder than usual." He flicked his hand in the air as more pieces joined the pile. "I'm going to have to call Henry and Simon out here to take over. You're making me actually work."

"Not that often?" Lucy replied, wondering how much she had actually improved. "How much higher can you project them?" She asked with a hint of mischief.

"What are you thinking?" Wes replied, sensing Lucy's devious intent.

A flicker of mischief lit Lucy's eyes. "For each plate I hit, throw the next ten feet further. We shall continue until I miss."

"What happens if you miss?"

"I love a good wager," Tristan said, sitting up, finally interested.

"If I miss, you get a chance to hit the target. And if you strike true…" Lucy looked around, trying to think of an acceptable bargain.

"You'll give me your bow," Wes said with a triumphant grin.

"Absolutely not!" Lucy retorted, gripping her custom weapon close to her body.

"Oh no, Luce," Tristan replied with a laugh. "Are you scared of losing?"

"No," she replied firmly. "Fine. The farthest target I miss but you hit, you get my bow."

Wes's smile spread wide as he moved into position, his swagger implying he would have an easy win.

"However, if you miss, and I can hit farther than you, then you have to tell Father that I outshot you." Lucy's smugness was palpable.

Wes narrowed his eyes in thought, and then gave a sharp nod. Tristan's bellowing laugh filled the open air.

This should be interesting.

Lucy resumed her shooting position as her brothers did the same.

Tristan remained on the grassy knoll, but this time, he sat up to watch.

"Go ahead," Lucy said, and Wes's Fae hearing picked it up even from his distance away.

Lucy readied her arrow, sought out the plate in the sky, released, and hit her target with a resounding crack.

Without hesitation, she prepared her next arrow from her quiver, excited to take on her brother in this challenge. The following target was even farther out, but still easy for Lucy to take down.

Then the next.

And the next.

And the next.

Her brothers looked at each other in confusion. Tristan stood, having to keep an eye on the far target.

"Lucy, you aren't charming your arrows, are you?" Wes asked steadily.

"No," she said breathlessly, invigorated by the thrill of pushing herself to her limits. "Prepare the next."

Lucy's focus was absolute, and her body hummed with energy. She had never hit a target at such a distance before. Her blood thrummed within her veins, and her eyes were wide with delight. Lucy clenched her hands around the fiery details on her bow; it was the epitome of force and eloquence.

Wes gave a contemplative look to Tristan as he took another step back, nodded, and magicked the disc so far into the air it could hardly be seen.

Lucy's release was so quick, the arrow whistled in the air, hitting the target and turning it into dust.

Tristan's hand lifted, attempting to bring the pieces back to the rubble pile, but nothing came. He pushed his right hand out farther, spreading his fingers wide to call back the shattered clay—again, nothing returned.

"Maybe it was too far away?" Wes asked. Lucy smiled from ear to ear. The idea that her ability outshined her brothers' magic made the power within her body rattle with excitement.

"Throw another," he told Wes. "Lucy, don't hit this

one." Wes careened the next plate even further, and Tristan held his hand out to retrieve the plate whole before it crashed into the ground. The disc came speeding back to Tristan intact.

"It wasn't too far." He looked at Lucy in question. "The disc you hit... there was nothing left of it," Tristan said, dumbstruck. "Luce—I'm not sure I understand."

Lucy's smile faltered.

How did I do that?

"I've always told you my bows outperformed yours," she said on a shaky breath.

"Let's call it a day, I think," Wes announced. "We will need more clay if you keep obliterating the plates." He shared a look with Tristan that Lucy did not miss.

They cleaned up and began the walk back to the estate. Lucy was unsure of what was happening and why.

My magic from The Elderwood must have something to do with this, she thought as she clenched her right fist. *I could really do with fewer surprises right now.*

Unfortunately for Lucy, more surprises were on the horizon.

Returning to the estate, Lucy hoped to find her father alone in his study so they could talk in private. Each time she had seen him since she left Joterra, he was flocked by her brothers or his staff. All she needed was one moment of her father's time without Jasper breathing down their necks.

She was convinced that showing Corvus her bow would be the turning point she was looking for. He would see this immaculate contraption and know that it was the best he had ever seen. No other Fae, female nor male, could construct such a refined bow.

This is it, she told herself confidently. *This is what it will take to get him to see my worth. This will get me back to Micah.*

Nervous excitement filled her heart, and she tiptoed quietly down the corridor to his office door. Her plan was to peek inside and ensure that he was alone—if Jasper or another staff member was inside, she would return later.

I only get one chance. I can't let anyone ruin it.

For once, the door was open wide, signaling that Corvus must be somewhere nearby. He would never leave his study unlocked and unattended. She walked in, planning to sit and wait for his arrival, when a barrage of voices threw her off course. Corvus boomed down the hall, arguing with a more faint voice that she almost recognized...

Tristan? Why is he here? Is he going to tell father we were practicing?

She quickly ducked behind a large cabinet, and immediately the memory of stealing the amulet came rushing back to her.

I am so tired of sneaking around.

She closed her eyes with a frown and dropped her head against the cabinet frame.

"Why won't you let her try?" Tristan said as they walked into the study and closed the door behind them.

"Tristan, why are you bringing this up now? After

everything we are trying to accomplish here, she does not need to hear that you agree with her. You need to stop giving her that hope."

"Unfortunately, Father, you're right about hope. I haven't expressed my opinions to Lucy about this, because I was fearful that you would do exactly what you are now."

"And what is that?" Corvus asked his son angrily.

"You're pushing any prospect of Lucy joining the business completely off the table. She is good, Father. She's better than all of us. Why won't you accept that this is right for her?"

Lucy's heart soared as she kept herself hidden in the corner of the room.

"You say this simply because you don't want to conform, either. You would rather join the Denoran army than involve yourself with the Baum Bowyer business."

"You're right. I would," Tristan argued.

Lucy held in a shocked gasp. She always knew that he wanted to become a soldier, but she never, in her wildest dreams, ever expected him to speak out against their father.

"That is the funny thing about this situation, Father. I am allowed to join the legion. I may leave and do whatever my heart tells me is right. You may not like it, but you cannot stop me. Lucy does not have that privilege."

The tension laid thick in the air. She had never heard her brothers speaking out against her father. She had never heard them actually admit that the Denoran policies regarding females were unfair. It was a much needed conversation at an inopportune time.

She panicked, looking around for an escape. Even if Tristan were to leave, she couldn't possibly speak to her father now; not after he was so riled.

How am I going to get out of here unseen?

"You do not know what you are speaking of," Corvus argued.

Tristan cut him off once again. "No, Father. I understand completely. It is you who chooses not to understand. Since it does not fit into your plans, you deem the entire concept unacceptable. You choose to not listen to Lucy, which means you choose to push her away."

"I am not pushing her away," her father boomed in response.

Lucy's heart stilled as the room went silent.

"When she is gone, she will not return. And it will be your fault." Tristan's scathing reply left Lucy breathless.

The door slammed shut and Lucy jolted in surprise. She calmed her breathing and focused her Fae hearing out as far she could. Realizing her father could hear her as well, she wordlessly pushed her concealment charm from the palm of her hand out to the rest of her body.

Sitting alone, she heard her father flipping through papers on his desk. He seemed agitated, but otherwise quiet. His movements stopped and he let out a deep sigh of defeat.

"I know you're there," he called into the room.

Lucy froze.

How did he figure it out?

"You may as well show yourself."

She hesitated, trying to determine what to say to her

father but coming up short. How could he take her seriously when he knew she was eavesdropping?

Just then, the outer door to the study opened. "My apologies, sir," Jasper replied.

Jasper? Lucy could have died from relief. *Thank the stars.*

She furrowed her brow as she focused on their conversation.

"You know I dislike it when you hover at the door," Corvus reprimanded.

"I understand. I simply did not want to intrude." The outer door clicked shut and Jasper walked to her father's desk. "This is all for the best, Master Baum. You will see in good time."

"You better be right about this, Jasper," Corvus ground out. He released a sigh again.

"I believe it is the most suitable course of action. Our Bowyer industry will spread throughout all of Denora with this pairing and the business will grow to reach all the realms. You will be the most powerful Fae of all."

An involuntary shiver raced down Lucy's back at Jasper's repulsive obsession with power.

"I'm not sure it will be worth it. Lucella does not want this arrangement. If she declines..." His voice trailed off. "I will have to reconsider."

"Sir, without the North, your business is at a standstill," Jasper interjected. "Beyond that, if Lord Sloan uses his ore in weapons from another industry, the Baum Bowyers will one day fade to irrelevancy."

"And what of Lucy?" Corvus's tone weakened, as if in surrender.

"She will come around," Jasper replied. "I will make sure of it."

Lucy's magic fluttered within her and her thoughts slowed as she put the pieces together.

Jasper.

FOURTEEN

MICAH

"What else does it say?" Micah asked as he leaned over Brax's shoulder in the study. They had been poring over the book all morning, but the majority of their time was spent with Brax ignoring Micah or telling him to be quiet.

"I will tell you when I find something worthy," she said in a bored tone.

"You've been reading this thing for hours and all you've said so far is that without the portal being guarded, things can come through."

"Correct."

"But we figured that out days ago."

"Correct."

"So you're telling me there's nothing new in there?" Micah asked incredulously.

"Wrong. There are many new things, just none regarding our current predicament."

Micah slumped into the chair across from Brax, staring at the blank shelves in the study. Only one thing sat upon the middle shelf: the picture of his mom, grandad and him. The only picture had left.

He sat there solemnly, thinking back to how things used to be—before he became the guardian.

"You know, before Wes and Jasper remade this room, it used to be filled with books." Micah's lips quirked into a sad smile. "At first I didn't mind starting fresh, all the old dusty stuff gone, room for whatever I wanted to fill the space... I honestly thought that having my grandad's things gone from here would make it easier for me, but I think it's actually harder."

"What is harder?" Brax asked, finally looking up from the book for the first time in hours.

"Being here without them. At least before, when all of Grandad's junk was scattered throughout the house, I didn't feel so alone. It felt like part of him was still here with me." He dragged his hand down his face. "I'm sorry. I'm sure this is not important to you."

"I am listening." Her voice was quiet.

"The books... they reminded me of my mom. The old furniture reminded me of Grandad. He was always patching something up." He gave a soft chuckle. "I thought moving my stuff in here would take away the hurt I felt when I was here alone, but now all I see are my things. There's no trace of him or my mom. There's nothing here to connect me to them. It all feels... empty."

Brax listened carefully, then sat back in her chair. Looking up to the ceiling, she closed her eyes and smiled. "I will tell you a story, Lumen."

Micah looked at her inquisitively.

"When I first became a Vytyrian warrior, the pride

inside of me swelled beyond belief. I had followed my dreams and made my family proud. However, after long years of traveling throughout the realms, I felt as though part of me was missing. I was not complete."

Micah's heart echoed with understanding, feeling like a shell of the person he once was.

"I came home for a visit and spent time with my family. I helped my mother cook our traditional foods. I assisted my sisters in their training. I felt happier, but I still could not fill that hole inside of me. My youngest sister, Noelia, has always been interested in art. Do you remember me telling you that?"

Micah nodded as he watched Brax's eyes brighten.

"I never fully understood it. She kept to herself and created her art, and I thought she was being foolish for chasing after such a silly hobby."

"I thought you said you loved her art?"

"Listen, you soggy cabbage."

Micah rolled his eyes and closed his mouth dramatically.

"I thought her art was foolish at first. Flowers and skyscapes? Waterfronts and plates of food? What was the purpose of such nonsense?" Brax looked at her hands, clearly wrapped up in a memory. "Then, Noelia brought me to the great willow tree, where she spent her days with her drawings."

Micah leaned in, giving Brax his rapt attention. It was rare for Brax to open up, and this conversation felt different from the others. It wasn't about business. It wasn't about The Elderwood or of any other Fae. It was about her.

"I didn't realize she quietly followed me around during my visit. I was always so busy, I didn't even notice… On a large sheet of white paper, my beautiful sister had replicated mine and my mother's hands, kneading bread, side by side. Each wrinkle of our knuckles, the shape of my mother's crooked pinky finger, my small beauty mark, right here." She showed him the small dark brown dot at the base of her thumb. Smiling, she rubbed it tenderly.

"That was only one of the many drawings she created for me. Another had my strong arms with my sisters, training in our Vytyrian uniforms. One with my feet kicking in the creek on a hot day. Each picture, one small body part, one small memory. Hands. Arms. Feet. The parts I love about me, like my strength, and the parts that betray me, like my eyes." She looked at Micah, with glossy eyes that refused to cry. "And it reminded me; I am not one thing. I am not just a warrior. I am not just a daughter or a sister. I am the sum of all of my parts, each one more intricate than the next."

"This is a beautiful story," Micah told her faintly. "But I am not sure why you're telling me this."

"Because, Lumen. You are not just the guardian. You are the sum of all your parts. A son. A grandson. A lover. A fierce protector, in this realm and all others." She leaned forward in her chair to look Micah in the eye. "You are Micah Lumen, and you cannot forget the parts of you that hurt. Take it all and let it shape you, let it fill you. Allow yourself to be both imperfect and whole."

Micah looked at her, speechless. An empty space inside of him swelled with gratitude for the Fae who sat before him and saw him for his imperfections and didn't judge. His smile warmed to the thought of their blooming friendship.

He was not alone.

She returned her gaze to the desk and flipped another page of the book. Her body went rigid.

"I—"

"Be quiet, Lumen," Brax interrupted in a demand.

"What?" Micah said in frustration.

Is she kidding me right now?

Micah tried again. "I wanted to say—"

"Whole."

"Yes, I heard you. I—"

"Lumen. Not whole; hole. The hole." Her eyes sprang to his. "I found it."

"You found what?" Micah asked, confused once more.

I cannot keep up with this chick.

"The hole, Lumen. Pay attention. Look." She pointed to the page. The words were in a language he could not comprehend, but the illustration was clear as day: a large shadow covering the base of a tree with sparking light, breaking away.

"What does it say?"

"Once the portal is broken, you must keep the realm contained. An open door that cannot be closed only leads to disorder. Find the basalt, smooth as glass, and build a wall. Combine purgheny, tormald, and golden crocidolite in a wooden bowl. Add water from a local source and leaves from the tree which holds the portal. Recite the incantation and protect the realm."

"An open door?" Micah asked.

"It says the portal is broken. How could your absence have broken an ancient door?" Brax stood and paced the room anxiously. "Something does not add up."

"What are all of those ingredients? I don't think I've ever heard of them before." He peeked at the book, trying to decipher the illustrations.

"Purgheny is a mineral used long ago for cleansing purposes. Tormald is a powder, inducing courage? Or strength? Then golden crocidolite is a gemstone of sorts —used to ward off evil. But I'm not sure why they are included."

"Why? Will we have trouble finding them? Are they odd Fae ingredients?"

"No. I have seen each of these ingredients all over your property. They aren't Fae at all. They are mortal."

"Why would a Denoran spell include those things if they couldn't be found in Denora?" Micah eyed Brax with doubt.

"It wouldn't." Brax's dark eyes met Micah's. "This is not a Denoran spell."

LARGE, smooth river rocks surrounded the base of The Elderwood tree and formed a large circle. Micah continued to find more and carry them over to the tree, creating a barrier three stones high. It wasn't much, but it rose to almost the middle of Micah's leg, and he hoped it was enough.

What else does this book say?

He flipped through the pages describing the protection spell written in a language he couldn't understand. It felt pointless.

Brax had read it for him and translated how Micah was to set up the stones. When she returned from securing the perimeter, they were to finish the spell and speak the words to keep the shadow creatures within the portal. He figured if he could get the rocks in place and the ingredients spread, then there would be only the one step left.

The sun was high in the sky and sweat poured down Micah's back. The rocks weren't overly large, but he needed two hands to lift each one. He spent the previous day finding the large, smooth rocks deep in the beds of the streams that ran through the property. Searching for them and bringing them to the tree took longer than he planned.

Brax left immediately after she gathered the ingredients and gave the instructions to Micah.

This better work.

Micah was hesitant to talk to Wes or Jasper. He knew calling for help in the mirror would bring someone, but he didn't have answers to any of the questions they would ask. He had no idea how any of this happened, and it was his duty to figure it out. The only person he would have been comfortable contacting was Lucy, and he sure as hell couldn't get a hold of her since their fight.

He kept trying to remind himself that even though it had been days for him; it was only one day for her. She was probably still stewing over their argument and sitting down to dinner; not even thinking about him because it hadn't been that long since they last spoke.

Not long for her.

His mind felt like it was being cleaved in two. On one hand, he understood Lucy had important things she needed to deal with at home. She left Denora and traveled to a different realm in order to get their attention, and now she had it—this was part of her plan.

Her plan never meant to include me.

Though, now that it did involve Micah, he struggled with the other side of it all—Laurent Sloan. How could she be spending so much of her time with him?

Was it that easy to forget me?

Micah heaved the rock into place and stepped back from the tree, watching the swirling black smoke as it writhed in the split in the ground.

This black, menacing fog seemed nothing like the green, swirling magic that came out of The Elderwood to help Lucy when the forest was under attack. He couldn't understand why The Elderwood's magic seemed so different this time.

It had been days since the crack in the ground appeared. When Brax examined it she couldn't identify the type of magic that caused it. All they were able to uncover about it from the book was that it was likely due to him leaving the property, allowing the creatures of The Elderwood to find their way out.

The only problem with that theory was that Lucy said that there were never any creatures in The Elderwood—so where did they come from?

A strange humming noise bubbled up from the

smokey, black pit. Micah leaned in closer, trying to figure out where the sound came from. The humming cleared, sounding more like clicking fingernails on a tabletop. The noise grew until Micah recognized it as the same chittering from when the base of the tree split open just days before.

He knelt on the ground in front of the rocks, and bent his head toward the dark, swirling mist, trying to see what was happening.

Out burst hundreds of black, shiny insects. Crawling with their many legs and arms, their sharp fangs dripped a dark red ooze.

Micah threw himself away from the rock wall. He crawled backwards on his hands and pushed the sight away as he scrambled to put distance between him and the barrage of shadow-like bugs. As he shoved himself from the wall, a rock shifted and nearly fell. He watched as the terrifying insects climbed up the tree trunk.

No, no, this can't be happening! Where is Brax?! We need this spell— now!

Micah's panicked breaths were barely heard over the calamitous noise of the disgusting creatures covering the tree with their dark shelled bodies. His eyes stayed glued to the chaos before him.

All at once, the rocks around the tree began to glow, first a deep emerald green, and then it radiated a bright violet. A high-pitched humming reverberated through the forest as the rock wall began to vibrate ever so slightly.

The bugs crawled from the tree toward the rocks and —*zap!* The purple glow became a hard barrier that the insects could not pass. They tried to climb over the rocks, but instead climbed straight up. An invisible wall kept the strange small, dark creatures contained, as they slowly spread out and covered the trunk of the tree—the sigil hidden under the many legs.

How did that even work?

The spell was not finished and the ingredients still sat in a bowl next to the tree.

A low rumble gently ruffled the leaves around him.

Not again, Micah thought as he looked at the ground in fear, worried that the earth would split further. Would the shaking cause the rocks to fall? Could it split the wall apart?

But it wasn't a rumble similar to what he had heard before. No. It was more of a purring growl. Deep in his bones, Micah realized exactly what it was.

The shadow beast.

Micah took another step back, but then stopped.

My purpose is to protect, he reminded himself. *It's the same as protecting and serving those in need in my precinct. This should be no different. I can defend The Elderwood.*

He looked at the forest around him and the cabin nearby, a surge of deference flowing through him.

"I can defend my home."

He picked up a thick piece of wood from near the fire pit. He prepared to use it as a weapon, but hoped and prayed that the creature wouldn't breach the rock barrier he had created.

An enormous black paw made of smoke emerged from the black haze and slammed itself down on the ground with a distinct thump. Micah stilled, looking at the sharp claws shining menacingly.

It was only made of mist and fog. How could the creature's paw have made that much noise?

The crack in the ground was only a few feet wide, and as the creature emerged, its body took shape. Another paw, then its muzzle and head—all hidden by the dense haze filling the circle around the tree. Once the entire body broke through the crack, it started to solidify.

The paws and legs were first, the swirling mist receding and revealing the dark fur of a large feline creature. Then the body, muscular and strong, sleek fur shining in the light of day, its tail swinging ominously. Last, its face came into view—dark, swirling misty eyes, shadowed with black and swirls of yellow. Its teeth, dark and rotten, dripped a foul ooze, just as the bugs had.

The shadow beast focused on Micah and crouched down low before leaping at the barrier.

BOOM! It struck the wall and Micah's body shuddered in fear. He searched frantically for a break in the barrier. His lungs squeezed with dread, knowing that once the beast was out, he would have more trouble than he could handle.

I don't even know what I'm looking for. Where the hell is Brax?

The enclosure strained, but the shadow beast stayed contained.

This only made the feline more angry, snarling so loudly it shook the leaves on the trees. The bugs chittered away, nervously crawling over one another, trying to run from the sinister beast, dripping in shadow and rage.

Micah stood his ground, staring at the creature, swinging his make-shift bat in his hand, prepared to defend his new life.

The shadow creature took a leap at the barrier again, and still, it held.

Damn, this thing is big.

It lurked down low, hiding itself in the smoke that had seeped from the crack since its arrival. The beast pushed its muzzle at the rocks, pawing some of them with quick, purposeful strikes.

It's testing the rocks, looking for a weak spot.

Micah scanned the rocks quickly, praying that there was no point of weakness to be found. Then, he remembered the rock that moved when the bugs arrived.

No.

He sprinted toward the wall, hoping to push the rock back into position, but the shadow cat got there first. With all of its strength, the beast swatted the stones. The barrier held for a moment, but the force of the hit was enough to cause the rocks to shift. The cat's eyes met Micah's in a terrifyingly intelligent gaze as he reached out to stabilize the rocks. Micah froze, and his heart shuddered in fear.

It's going to get through.

The beast slammed its paws once more, and the barrier quaked, the glow of the rocks blinking in and out. Micah held his breath. It slammed again. The barrier sputtered, the light dissipating before illuminating once more.

No, no, no.

His wide eyes watched as the yellow-eyed beast reared up once more. *SLAM*. With one final hit, and the rock tumbled away and the purple glow of the light died completely.

Micah's heart threatened to give out on him. He stood rooted to the spot as the dark mist spread further from the tree. He tried to listen for the sound of the prowling beast over his erratic breathing, but it was no use.

One of the chittering bugs crawled on top of the rock wall. Micah watched it closely, his eyes darting between the bug on the stone and the shadow cat crouching in the smoke.

The insect slowly crawled from the side of the rock to the top, and then flew away. Out of the barrier.

Fuck.

The cat pounced out of the boundary in Micah's direction as he took three large steps back. The beast seemed to grow with each second; its colossal head coming up to the middle of Micah's torso.

Glancing at the branch in his hands, Micah prayed it was thick enough to do some damage to this beast without breaking and leaving him weaponless.

The cat prowled around him, like a lion playing with its food. With each step the beast took, the muscles in its body seemed to shift underneath.

The creature was pure force, but Micah wouldn't back down. He had too much to do here. He was the guardian. Besides, he still needed to work things out with Lucy—for her, he would move mountains.

Man, I could really use some of that Elderwood magic now.

The beast leapt toward him with a snarl, its teeth dripping a foul slime, prepared to tear the flesh from his bones. Micah swung the wood with all of his might, steering the creature off course, but not leaving much of an injury.

"Come on!" Micah yelled, adrenaline surging through his body, prepared to end this.

Again, the shadow beast crouched down low, staring directly at Micah, and jumped with claws unsheathed, ready to slash into him.

Micah whirled the branch again, just hitting the muzzle of the beast. The oozing liquid coming from its mouth covered the edge of the piece of wood, making it fizzle and disintegrate before him. The wood splintered and popped as it shriveled into nothing, and Micah had to throw what remained at the beast, hoping to push it astray as sharp talons swiped at him once more.

Micah, weaponless, sprinted in the opposite direction. His heart pounded in his chest, threatening to burst. His wide eyes scanned his surroundings, desperately searching for a weapon he could use against the monstrous creature—anything to hurtle at the beast trying to flay him alive.

A small pile of wood was stacked on the border of the forest—remnants and small sticks from The Elderwood that did not make their way back with Lucy. Micah shot a look behind him as he continued to run and saw the insects crawling through the forest. Their clicking legs brought them through the swirling mist as they abandoned their sanctuary of The Elderwood tree, becoming a scourge on the forest. The leaves in the trees shook violently under the tremendous weight of hundreds of insects as they aggressively claimed their fresh territory.

The shadow beast slunk back and forth, weaving its way closer to Micah; a slinking prowl, making the hair on Micah's arms stand on end. He put his back to the trees and found the sharp edge of a branch. Micah held out the short, thick stick as if he were brandishing a pocket knife. His hands trembled as panic washed over him.

"So, you're not afraid of me, huh?" Micah taunted the beast. "Well, I'm not afraid of you, either."

It was a lie, of course, but Micah wouldn't run from this. His chances of getting into the cabin were slim to none, and the beast would not leave him alive. There was only one option left—he would not let the creature devour him without a fight.

The shadow creature paused and crouched to the ground. Micah barely spotted it as it jetted out of the grass, darting toward him with full force. Micah held his ground and then ducked and rolled out of the way, making the creature miss him and clamber into the trees.

"Here kitty, kitty, kitty," Micah jeered.

He stood firm, his knees and elbows bent, ready to change course on a dime. He clutched the scrap of wood tightly, desperate to come out of this alive.

The feline gripped its claws into the ground to steady itself, keeping its swirling gold and black eyes on Micah, refusing to move quickly, eyeing its prey in a slow stalk.

When it reached a close enough distance, the beast stopped, crouched, and pounced on him. Micah went down in a heap, the massive form of the beast crushing him beneath its weight. The snarl that escaped the creature made a trail of ooze slide from its teeth, falling to the grass just next to Micah's head, making the grass sizzle and burn.

The creature's head lifted with another deep growl. *THUMP*. Something shook the beast as it howled in pain. It took a step back, one paw moving from Micah's shoulder down to the ground.

With a freed arm, he sliced the face of the shadow creature with the stick he had grabbed, cutting across the beast's eye and causing it to shriek in agony.

It retreated from Micah quickly, getting away from the sharp piece of wood in Micah's hands.

"Lumen!" Brax called, running over with a spear in hand, her Fae speed astounding.

A silver spear stuck out from the back of the shadow beast, making it limp in pain.

"What the hell is happening?" Micah shouted as he and Brax kept their eyes on the creature. "Where the fuck have you been?"

The beast thrashed violently, shaking the spear loose. They stood, watching in utter shock, as the beast healed itself in an instant. The spear didn't affect it at all. There was no mark, no blood—nothing. However, the slice Micah left across the beast's face continued to gush a dark red blood, coating its black fur.

Micah backed up farther, thankful for Brax's timely entrance. There was no way he could have survived without her intervening.

The shadow beast looked at them with furious,

yellow eyes. Brax stood at the ready, prepared to engage the creature, and Micah gripped the piece of wood as if his life depended on it—because it very much did.

The creature backed away slowly, slinking into the shadows surrounding The Elderwood tree, and Micah raced over to the rocks to rebuild the barrier, checking each stone carefully.

Brax followed him, checking his body insistently.

"Lumen," she called as he kept checking the barrier. "Lumen, are you hurt?" She continued to scan him for injuries, but could not get a good look at him as he hurriedly moved from rock to rock.

"Micah, stop!" she yelled, causing him to finally halt.

He took a deep breath, sat down on the ground a few feet away from the rock circle, and sighed in defeat.

Brax knelt in front of him to get his full attention. "Are you hurt?" Her eyes were wide with concern.

"No," he said simply.

She placed her hands on his shoulders and closed her eyes. He waited as her silvery magic spread from her fingers, magically checking him for bodily harm. She nodded, opened her eyes, and released a brief sigh of relief. Finally appeased, she sat next to him, watching their surroundings: the tree, Micah, and whatever might creep up behind him.

"What happened?"

Micah chewed on the inside of his lip, looked to the sky, and ran his hands through his hair and down his neck. "I was nearly done with the rock circle, and some scary ass bugs came out of the crack. The barrier, though... it worked. It was glowing purple, keeping all the creatures in. Then that big ass cat appeared and tried to eat me."

"It worked?" Brax said in astonishment.

"Yeah, you told me to move all the stones and get the stuff where it needed to be, so I did." He pointed at the rock wall he created and the wooden bowl of ingredients needed for the spell off to the side of the tree. "No help from you, I might add," he murmured.

"But it shouldn't have worked." She stood in a rush, checking the barrier and spinning back to look at Micah, her hair flipping with her quick movements.

He stood angrily. "Why would you tell me to do something knowing it wasn't going to work? What the hell, Brax? I thought you were on my side here?"

"Lumen, enough with the misaligned anger. It shouldn't have worked because you are not Fae." She stepped up to him, meeting his gaze. "I assumed you would prepare it and we would call in a Baum or Lord Sloan to finish the spell... Even I cannot create Fae magic the way the ancients have."

"What?" Micah's head pulled back, trying to comprehend what she had just said.

"Micah. You did magic."

FIFTEEN

LUCY

Her exchange with Micah had upset her more than she cared to admit, but there was nothing to be done about it now. She understood he was far away, dealing with his own issues, but Lucy wished she could be there to help him. She couldn't believe another female was alone with him.

How improper.

She clicked her tongue as she shifted in her seat in the garden. Though really, hadn't she just done the same with Micah? And hadn't she spent alone time with Laurent, as well?

Laurent. She groaned.

Everything was becoming more complicated. She looked out at the many flowers in the garden, appreciating their beauty in this quiet space. It was so rare for her to have a moment of peace. Her mother's bright red roses made her stomach coil with unease... She still had not forgiven her mother since their conversation, but she knew she'd have to speak with her soon enough.

The jangle of chains announced Jasper's arrival before she laid eyes on him. "Your father wants to speak with you," his oily tone declared as soon as he walked onto the garden terrace.

Lucy had barely sat down to warm herself in the sun before she was ushered off yet again. She wasn't sure when she would get her much needed time to think.

Nodding begrudgingly, she walked to her father's office, Jasper tight on her tail. After overhearing their conversation the day before, Lucy was careful with her words around him.

She knew this conversation with her father was imminent since her evening with Lord Sloan—but what Jasper had to do with it; she had little idea. His presence steadily increased since she had returned from Joterra, and any time she saw him was always too soon.

"What did you do this time?" Jasper whispered to her in the hall as they walked.

"Excuse me?" Lucy whirled to look at him, the image of the burned corpse at the front of her mind.

What does he know?

"What happened with Lord Sloan at dinner that has your father so determined to see you?" He took a brisk step toward her. "What did you tell him? What did you see?"

Lucy took a compulsive step back, creating a distance between herself and this odious male who kept provoking her.

"I don't know what you're talking about," Lucy lied.

Don't worry, I won't tell my father about your secret discussion with Laurent. Yet.

Rolling her eyes, she spun away from him. "Get out of my way so I can speak with my father." And with that, she upped her speed, and made it to her father's office without another comment from Jasper, much to his dismay.

"Hello, Father," Lucy said politely, entering the room.

"My little flower," Corvus boomed with a smile on his face. "Sit, darling."

Lucy's heart ached. It had been so long since she had talked to her father with such ease. He was happy and light, and seeing him this way almost made Lucy feel the same.

"Lord Sloan called in and said he had a wonderful evening with you." His full cheeks rose on either side of his face. "He was insistent on seeing you again today and asked if you would be interested in a carriage ride around the countryside. He is very keen to get to know you."

A flutter of anxiousness filled Lucy and her heart sank. This was not what she had in mind when she had planned to sway him away from her. Now he wanted more of her company? A sudden and unexpected thrill ran through her.

When he could have his pick of any female in all of Denora, why me?

Lucy bowed her head to hide her sudden unwelcome blush. "When will he arrive?"

"Soon," Corvus said, looking fondly on his daughter. "Lucella, I know that you have had a hard time accepting the roles of life here in Denora after I have spoiled you for so many years, but I appreciate you being more open to spend time with Lord Sloan."

"Father—" Lucy began, trying to explain.

"No. There's no need." He held a hand up to stop her. "I know this was not what you wanted, but I hope that you are also finding joy in Lord Sloan's company. I want you to be happy, darling. I want you taken care of." The softness in his eyes was new to Lucy and made her heart hurt. "I only want what is best."

There was not a word she could say to combat that. Of course, a father would only want what's best for his daughter. However, now that she knew her father could be compelled to listen to her, perhaps the only person she had left to convince was Laurent himself. She was certain she could dissuade him of this agreement.

Then, I'll be free...

Her heart wouldn't allow her to think on the topic any longer as her father stood to give orders to Jasper. "Prepare the carriages, and put Thomas on escort duty."

"Sir," Jasper's smarmy voice creaked out. "I would prefer to go with Miss Lucella, if you would accept. I do not want Lord Sloan and his guards having to deal with numerous Fae while here, sire." He gave a deep, ass-kissing bow, making Lucy roll her eyes.

Please, not another moment with him.

Corvus barely gave him a second look as Jasper's head was so close to the floor he could have licked it. "No business; just keep my daughter safe," he said in a quiet, threatening voice.

Jasper rose from the ground and the two men's eyes met; there was no mistaking the threat that loomed in the air. Jasper quickly dropped his gaze, bowing once again as Lucy left to prepare, wondering what the day's events held in store for her.

Laurent's carriage was subtly beautiful. It did not have the bright red velvet of the Baum's carriage, nor did it have the exquisite brass adornments. The metal rails of the carriage were an understated matte black and the material of the cushion was a soft leather, lined with fur on the edges for comfort.

"I don't think I've ever seen a carriage like this," Lucy said as she fluffed the soft fur in her hands.

"The Northern Territory gets quite frigid," Laurent explained from his seat across from Lucy. "Here in the Central Territory, the weather changes over time, but in the north, it is always cold."

"Don't you miss the warmth?" Lucy asked, genuinely curious.

"There are ways to find warmth in the dead of winter," Laurent suggested with a glint in his eye.

Lucy blushed under her pale yellow gown. She opted for something simple with soft gold leaves embroidered in the hemline. She was still so far from Micah, but she was doing everything within her power to find ways to feel close to him. She even wore her hair down, the way he liked.

"But yes," Laurent changed the topic, looking out the open window into the grassy plains before them. "I do miss the warmth of the sun on a beautiful spring day.

Speaking of which, I hope you don't mind that today I have planned an outdoor adventure for us."

"Outdoor? Adventure?" she asked with sparked interest. His eyes met hers with intrigue.

"Yes," he laughed. "It seems to me you are not the typical female from Denora, and rumor has it you are involved in your father's business?"

Lucy looked away from Laurent and back to the landscape. They were approaching a tree line that reminded her even more of The Elderwood. She clenched her right fist.

"Unfortunately, my father does not believe females should be in the workforce and does not allow me to grow any further in the business." She looked at him, square in the eye, her face devoid of emotion. "He would rather I marry you."

Laurent's face dropped, but for a fraction of a second, his eyes flashed an emotion she could not read. It wasn't surprise, nor was it humor... was it... agitation?

"I'm sorry that you are put in this awkward situation, Miss Lucella."

"If you call me Lucella one more time, I am going to jump from the carriage and walk home."

Shock and surprise filled Laurent's face, causing Lucy to laugh.

"I'm sorry, it is habit." Laurent looked at her as if for the first time, smiling in astonishment at what sat before him. "You are remarkable. I really do mean what I said. I'm sorry that this is not what you want. If—"

"I would prefer not to talk about this topic at this moment, if you don't mind. It is a beautiful day and you've promised me an outdoor adventure and I'd much rather do that." Lucy couldn't believe she interrupted him, but she couldn't bear the topic a second longer. She was with Micah just the day before and now she was courting Laurent yet again?

Maybe Micah was right.

Laurent nodded and stopped talking. His lips still turned in amusement.

"However," Lucy stated as she looked around at the horses carrying Laurent's guards and the lone carriage ferrying Jasper. "I'm not sure my escort will be impressed with an outdoor adventure." She would do just about anything to remove herself from Jasper's presence.

"Ah, yes, about that." Laurent slipped from his seat and moved across to where Lucy sat alone. Lucy's breath hitched at the nearness. Laurent moved close enough to whisper in her ear. "What would you think about it just being me and you?"

She turned to look at him and he was mere inches away. When she went to speak, he delicately placed one warm finger over her lips to remind her to talk as quietly as possible—Fae hearing carried.

He removed his finger, and Lucy delicately bit her lip. The warmth of his finger lingered and her insides flipped with surprise.

Leaning in, she whispered in his ear in a challenge. "What did you have in mind?"

Without moving, she waited for his response as his mouth angled up her neck and toward her ear. His featherlight breath sent a chill down her spine, pebbling her skin and stirring an emotion she was not expecting.

"Stay close to me, and pardon my hands. I have to hold you close for this to work."

Her head jerked back in surprise as she met his ice-blue eyes. With her mouth slightly open, she nodded subtly.

Laurent looked from her open, pouty lips, back to her wide, eager eyes. He put an arm behind her, placing his hand on her hip, and with one quick swoop, lifted her onto his lap, keeping a firm grasp on her back. He put his other hand across her lap and clasped his hands together to hold her against him.

She wrapped an arm around his shoulders and allowed her hand to lie on his chest. He gave a mischievous wink and a second later, he was standing, holding her in his arms in the middle of a small clearing deep in the woods.

Lucy gasped, tightening her grip on his shoulders as he held her with his strong hands.

He gently placed her on the ground as she turned and looked at the scene around her. Off to one side, a blanket with a full spread of food was placed on the soft grassy earth, supplied with wine and simple goblets. A large swing hung from a nearby tree, large enough to fit four people, piled with blankets and pillows for added comfort. Beautiful red flowers decorated their space. They twined in the swing ropes and lay scattered around the forest floor.

Lucy looked on, astonished. The amount of magic and time it would have taken to create such a beautiful atmosphere was jarring. Each rose brought stunning allure to the space. No one had ever made such a play for her heart this way.

Is all of this for me?

Then, in the center of the clearing, rested an archery target with a bow and arrows.

"How?" was the only word she could get out.

"It seemed from our recent night, fine dining is not quite your area of comfort, nor mine." Laurent smiled and held her hand as she took a deep breath in, the perfume of the flowers filling her with so much joy. "I much prefer to get to know someone for who they truly are, and you are just captivating."

She looked at the bow, spinning around to face him, her face bright and youthful. "How did you bring us here?"

"I am a very powerful Fae, *Lucy*," he said, emphasizing her name without any titles. "I am able to use magic similar to a conjuring spell if I work the incantation just right. It is far enough from the carriages that they won't hear us, but close enough so that I can return us when they have made their turn to complete the trip back to your estate."

"We get to shoot out here?" Her smile lit up her entire face.

He nodded, and she involuntarily used her Fae speed to swiftly reach the bow and hold it in her hands.

Lucy's blood hummed when her skin came into contact with the delicate wood from The Elderwood—it was one of her father's bows. The rush she felt was immense. She twirled the bow in her hands once before lifting an arrow. Her eyes were wild as she took aim. The speeding arrow pierced the center of the target, exiting the other side of the hay bale holding it in place.

"Excellent!" Laurent cheered from where he stood by the food, his attention solely on her. "Where did you learn to shoot like this?"

"It's in my blood," she said, hinting at her family's history within the bowyer business, but also offering a subtle nod to the ancient magic bestowed upon her from The Elderwood. Her hand tingled with the memory, not so much a pulsing, throbbing pain like it usually was. It was as if the magic was giving a faint approval.

She placed the bow down and sat on the blanket, her knees curled in front of her as she carefully smoothed out her gown. The small clearing in the forest was set up entirely for them. He supplied the picnic with savory snacks and delicious sweets, and the pillows and blankets were soft and luxurious.

Laurent did all of this for me.

She toyed with a soft flower petal between her fingers. *Me.*

"Do you like it?" he asked her as she looked around, a smile softening her face.

"It's unbelievable," she shared in a daze. "This is..." She couldn't find the words. Never in all of her years had someone gone out of their way to make Lucy feel so treasured.

"I want you to know that I want you to be yourself around me. I don't want to change you. You are headstrong, but polite. Beautiful, but without vanity. I appreciate you allowing me your company, even when you do not wish to move forward with this arrangement your father has created for you."

Lucy looked away. He knew she didn't want to marry him, and yet he did all of this. Was he the one now trying to win over Lucy? His hand touched her knee delicately, making Lucy look up at Laurent.

"I do not fault you for these feelings," he said gently. "I merely want us to get to know one another."

"I would like that," she admitted. And it was true. Spending time with Laurent was a welcome surprise. Lucy reveled in the attention he gave her; his eyes that saw only her.

"As would I." His light blue tunic seemed to make his eyes brighten even more. "Please, tell me everything. I'd love to know more about you."

"Oh, there isn't much to tell," Lucy shared shyly, popping a cube of cheese into her mouth to avoid talking.

What is happening here? Wasn't I supposed to be dissuading him of our potential arrangement?

"I doubt that," he said as he helped himself to a piece of bread, removing his hand from her leg. "What I know of you so far is that you are the breath-taking daughter of Corvus Baum. You are an expert marksman, and you don't seem to be affected by wealth, status, or material things. Did I miss anything?"

"If you think a sentence could sum up my life, then carry on believing that," Lucy said with a devilish grin.

"I would never stoop so far as to assume you are anything less than enchanting," he said, looking into her eyes, trying to find an answer to a question he had not asked.

"I'm not sure why you keep saying I am this intriguing, enchanting Fae. I am not one to play humble, but let us please speak in realities. I offer no wealth, no great beauty, and no abundant knowledge. I am not sure what you gain from my presence."

The constant compliments were starting to overwhelm Lucy. He barely knew her and seemed completely taken with her—why?

He needs to see that we are not the match he believes us to be.

"I feel as though you are always truthful with me, and that is very odd for a male in my position," Laurent admitted. His arm hung over his bent knee as he spoke, his hair blowing freely in the breeze. "I have a knack for knowing when I am being lied to, though it doesn't seem to me that you have told me a single false statement since I've met you."

"Well, I did say it was a pleasure to meet you, didn't I?"

Laurent barked a laugh. "Well, my heart has been cleaved." He put two hands over his chest in mock heartbreak. "I guess that is true, though hopefully you feel differently now."

"I do," she said quietly.

"That was true?" he asked, full of surprise.

"I thought you said you had a knack for this?" Lucy teased.

"With you, there is just something I can't seem to put my finger on. I'm not sure I can tell with you," he said as he looked at her intently, trying to read her very mind. "I don't know why."

Lucy began to feel unnerved, being watched so intently. She hugged her knees close to her body and tried not to make eye contact, instead looking around at the beautiful afternoon before them.

Surely, he means no harm if he did all of this for me, could he?

"What do you want to know?" Lucy asked finally.

Perhaps I can twist my answers to get him to stand down. Maybe if he truly respects me, he will also respect my choice to say no.

He looked at her seriously, eyeing her attentively. "What's your favorite color?"

"What?" Lucy laughed. Her cheeks hurt from the smiles he uncovered.

"It is a very important question," Laurent said in false sincerity, a quirk in his lips admitting his humor.

"Well, then in that case I must answer honestly, now shouldn't I? Hmm. Some days I prefer yellow, because it reminds me of the sun. Others I prefer green, because it reminds me of the calmness of the forest. Red because it reminds me of the roses in my mother's gardens. Even brown," she said, immediately seeing Micah's deep brown eyes searing into her with intensity. She looked at the trees, trying to find the words she needed, but her heart was stuck on Micah.

She stood quickly, blood rushing through her body, making her lightheaded.

Micah. What am I doing here?

She walked over to the swing and sat, trying to create

some distance. Her fingers ran over the soft fabric, taking deep breaths to calm herself. Sitting back, she closed her eyes. With Fae finesse, not a sound was heard as Laurent came and sat beside her.

"Did I upset you?" he asked her quietly.

"It's just complicated." Lucy opened her eyes and looked at her company—a male of status and prestige, whose focus was entirely on her.

They sat in silence for a long while, appreciating the world around them. Even with the awkward moment they had experienced, the quiet solitude of the forest gave Lucy the confidence that she needed to say the words she had feared.

"I enjoy my company with you, Lord Sloan. I never believed that it would happen, but you are not the Fae I thought you to be, and I am sorry for assuming otherwise. However, I am not sure I am ready to wed." She looked at Laurent with honesty and fear in her eyes.

"I meant it when I said I just wanted you to be yourself. I would never try to change you. Life can be like this —easy and full of wonder. I want a wife who will never lie to me and a partner who shares the same ideals as I do."

He took her chin in his hand, lightly directing her eyes to his. Lucy held her breath, wondering how a male could have such an affect on her. It was as though his eyes looked through her, directly into her soul.

"I see so much life and adventure in you, and I feel you mirror so much of what I stand for. You are exquisite and truly one of a kind. Any would be a fool to ever pass up a chance at a lifetime with you."

"That is what you ask of me? A lifetime?" Lucy's heart fell as another male tried to dictate the landscape of her future.

"Perhaps a chance?"

"A chance seems reasonable." A small smile grew upon her face, as she looked into the eyes of this potential friend.

Laurent didn't want her to change, he wanted her as she was. Maybe her feelings for Micah weren't enough for things to work between them... Laurent wanted to make the realm a better place... Maybe this was a better path for her.

A chance.

"I'm glad you agree."

Lucy peered up into the sky—the sun had moved across the horizon, signaling the passing time. "We should probably be getting on our way, should we not? The last thing we need is my father's assistant realizing we are gone."

At the change of subject, Laurent's demeanor shifted. "Ah, yes. Jasper," he said with an annoyed sigh. "I find it interesting that your father had picked him as partner."

"Why do you say that?"

"He is not as he seems. It is as though he can't decide his true desire in life." His face twisted into a grimace.

"How would you know so much about Jasper?"

Why does it feel like there is something important I'm missing here... His true desires? Does this have to do with their argument at dinner?

"As I said, I can read people quite well, and that male is an open book. Be careful around him, Lucy."

His ominous suggestion made Lucy's stomach tie in knots. Hadn't she always suspected something was amiss with Jasper? He was the one pushing for this arranged marriage. Didn't she see Jasper and Laurent discussing something that clearly upset Laurent?

What could it have been?

"You know, others have warned me about you as well," Lucy said carefully. She wasn't sure if Lord Sloan would take this poorly, but she needed to know. "Why do others fear you? There has been talk of attacks on the Northerners."

"Ah," Laurent sat back and nodded, pursing his lips in a concealed smirk. "Let me ask you this, Lucy," he said as he looked deeply into her eyes. "If I were to tell you that there was a safe place in Denora, where females could make their own decisions in their life, where less fortunate Fae were not ignored, where wealth and status did not equate to importance, and where all Fae could pave whatever path they wanted for their future—not just follow in their family's footsteps—what would you say?"

"I would say that it sounds like a dream," Lucy said honestly.

"Yes," Laurent replied, nodding seriously. "Many would feel the same. But the other territories of Denora would then lose much of their population to the north, would they not?"

Lucy nodded.

"It is much easier for the majority of Denora to spread lies and create fear than deal with the reality that maybe something is wrong with how things are traditionally done here; maybe Denora has work to do."

Whatever Lucy had expected him to say—it was surely not that. She stared at him in awe, hesitant to believe such a male existed in Denora. And here, with her, no less.

"Let's get one more round of target practice in, shall we?" He cheerily changed the subject. "We can't let all the trouble of me getting this bow for you go to waste. I need to see the Queen of the Archers in her element."

"Queen of Archers is a bit extravagant," Lucy laughed. "Though I will never turn down practice."

She took his hand and followed him to the target. Lifting the bow and arrow, she looked at Laurent, who again watched her closely.

"Would you like a lesson?" she asked with a teasing lilt to her voice.

Laurent's smile spread across his face, lighting him up like a young boy. "From you? I would be honored."

He used his Fae speed to advance directly behind Lucy, his presence sending flutters down her center. He put his face close to hers, whispering, "I'm ready when you are, my queen."

Lucy's breathing came in uneven breaths now.

My queen.

It sent shivers down her spine and an ache of wanting need. She pursed her lips, taking a slow breath and lifted her arms into position.

Laurent slid his hands down her arms. "Hold the bow like this?"

Lucy met his gaze and nodded, biting her lower lip. She looked to her target and pulled her arrow back.

His hands slid on top of hers, heat seeping from his body, making her legs quiver. She feared her heart would combust; the intimate touches sending her body reeling.

Laurent slid his hand along her arm, then down her side, just missing the curve of her breast as it stopped gently on her hip.

"Show me your magic, my queen."

IF HE CALLS *me his queen one more time, I believe I'm going to combust.*

Lucy's head spun with the thrill of showing off her archery ability to Laurent in their secret cove in the forest. Arrow after arrow, she hit her target, and with each hit, Laurent cheered her on. He wasn't afraid to get close to her, and each word felt as though he placed her above him.

My queen.

Two simple words had never affected her this way before.

Her right hand throbbed, the magic begging to come out to play.

"We should probably take a break," Lucy said, beaming.

"Unfortunately, it is nearly time for us to return." Laurent tucked a stray hair behind her ear, the action reminiscent of Micah.

It sobered her thoughts quickly.

"What about all of this?" She looked around at the beautiful setting he created for them.

"I will have it taken care of."

"This truly was an amazing day for me," Lucy said gratefully. It was so easy to be around Laurent and she could see herself forming a friendship with him. "I'm sorry we did not get to talk more and that the majority of our time was spent with me shooting."

"You are a force to behold," he said with an earnest smile. "I could probably watch you do that all day long." He walked with her to the picnic set up and grabbed a small bundle of flowers, tucking them behind her ear. He paused and stared at her with wonderment. "You are breathtaking."

Lucy felt the blush come to her cheeks. As she tried to hide it, he delicately took her chin and pulled her face back to his.

"Don't hide your beauty from me," he caressed her cheek with his thumb. His eyes were hungry and his lips were parted. "I will be thinking about this day for a very long time. And the pink of your lips and cheeks is something that is sure to keep me up at night."

Lucy's core melted in his gaze. She straightened her posture to counter his unyielding stare with a show of confidence. Their smiles mirrored one another.

He took her hand and walked her over to the swing, sitting. "If you don't mind, you can take your place back upon my lap and I will transport us to the carriage."

Normally, Lucy would feel out of place and uncomfortable with such a proposition—but there was nothing uncomfortable about Laurent any longer. She blushed as she sat on his lap; not from embarrassment, but because her thoughts had strayed to an unladylike topic.

Lucy scooted her body so that her legs were high on his thighs. She wrapped an arm around his neck and didn't think twice about their intimate closeness. He put a hand around her back, his fingers gripping the top of her round bottom. His other hand slid up her thigh, keeping her in place.

He leaned in and whispered in her ear. "Don't make a noise." Then he inched closer to her until their lips were nearly touching. "Close your eyes," he whispered to her seductively.

She obeyed, a forbidden thrill of desire running through her.

His lips touched hers, lightly, and the surprise made her gasp. Laurent covered her mouth with his own, and he kissed her more deeply, firmly pressing his lips on hers.

To her utter astonishment, she kissed him back.

It was rushed, yet slow—their lips kissing and tasting each other. Lucy slid her tongue across his, and he gripped her hips more firmly as she remained in his lap. She let out a breathy sigh, and he captured her lower lip, silencing her again as he gently sucked on it, making Lucy's insides blaze with need.

His hands slid over her thighs, up the back of her yellow dress, until he held her face delicately in his firm embrace. Their passionate kiss grew as Laurent pulled her closer and closer. The movement caused Lucy to clench her thighs together, yearning for more friction between her and Micah.

No.

Laurent.

Oh my stars!

Lucy opened her eyes and pulled away from the kiss in horror. "I'm sorry, I can't," Lucy told Laurent, putting her hands on his chest to stop his advances, looking down in shame.

"I'm sorry, Lucy." Laurent's cheeks had a hint of red in them, more color than she had ever seen on him. "I guess we got a little carried away." He gave her a half smile with an apologetic look on his face. "That was much too forward of me," he shook his head. "It will not happen again."

She nodded as she slid from his lap into the cushioned seat next to her. She looked around in shock. "We are back in the carriage?"

"Yes," he smiled again, looking at her intently. "Are you... alright?" Concern laced his tone.

Lucy took a deep breath, straightened the bodice of her dress, and sighed. She looked at Laurent. He sat next to her with his hair tousled, his clothing slightly askew, and the most vulnerable look on his face. His eyes searched hers as he sat completely still, waiting with bated breath to hear her response.

"Yes, Lord Sloan —"

"Laurent."

Lucy looked at him in bafflement.

He is the Lord of the Northern Territory. Surely, he cannot expect me to call him by his first name.

"Sir, it would not be proper."

"Lucy, you just sucked on my tongue. I think we can drop the formalities when it is just you and I."

Lucy let out a huff of laughter, shaking her head. She hid her blushing face in her hands. "I did that, didn't I?"

He reached over and took her hands away from her face, holding one to his cheek. "You don't see me complaining, do you?" He smiled again. "Please, Lucy. Are you okay?"

"I am." She smiled at him. Though that was a lie, and not her first. She was not alright. She practically mauled Laurent right after she berated Micah for even assuming she would ever do that.

"Please. You can be truthful with me. You do not look fine." He kept her hand in his, bringing it down to her lap.

"I think I am just overwhelmed by our connection." *Truth.*

"That's all?"

"I want to get to know you more before things move in that direction." *Truth.*

"And you wish to move forward with the arrangement?" His fingers gave a small squeeze to hers as he held her hand.

"Perhaps. I have not decided." *Truth?*

How in all the realms is that possible?

"I'm sorry to keep interrogating you. I just want to understand. Is... is there someone else?"

"No." *Lie.*

"I appreciate your honesty with me, Lucy," he said with a sigh, leaning back into his seat with relief.

"Then maybe you can unleash one of your truths on

me, to even the score." Lucy said, scooting back, creating more space between her and the beautiful Fae male who made her insides curl with desire. She grinned to alleviate the tension she felt inside, but she wasn't sure if it was working in her favor.

Her cheeks flushed, and she fanned at her face, trying to rid herself of the redness she was certain covered her.

Laurent slid closer to her, returning her grin. "I have a secret, but I think I can trust you with it. If I share this with you, Lucy, do you promise not to share it with anyone else?"

"Yes, of course." *Lie.*

He smiled from ear to ear, then glanced out the window to see their location. "We are almost back, but I do not want others to overhear." He did a quick privacy charm, much smaller than his extravagant show in the restaurant. This bubble barely contained the two Fae, making it unknown to anyone outside of the carriage.

"I told you I have a knack for knowing when others are honest with me?"

Lucy nodded, remembering the conversation. Her heart raced with the urgency exuding from Laurent.

"Well, it is not just a knack. It is a magical ability."

Lucy stilled.

I've been lying to him.

"It is?"

"Yes. And you, my queen," he looked at her with adoration. "You are an open book. You are honest and kind and completely breathtaking. I trust you implicitly with this secret, as you are to be my wife." The color brightened in his cheeks once more.

Lucy stared at him in stunned silence, eyes wide. Her mouth popped open in surprise, unsure of what to say next.

No.

He spoke with a fervor she had not seen. "You are remarkable, and I cannot wait to marry you, Lucy. I've never met someone who didn't lie in my presence—even the smallest amount. You care for the poor the way I do. You do not think about wealth and status the way the other female Denorans do. You. My queen. My future wife. You are my equal."

He held her hands in his and kissed them tenderly.

Lucy had no words. She had failed miserably at getting Laurent to see her as unworthy. Why did she not try harder? How did she fall to his whims so easily?

The horses came to an abrupt stop and Laurent removed his privacy charm and slid to the other side of the carriage, creating the proper space.

Thank the stars, Lucy thought, relieved to not have to respond to that very surprising declaration. Her mind was racing. *How could he not tell when I lied?*

A sharp rap on the door made Lucy jump, but the interruption was greatly appreciated.

"Miss Lucella," Jasper's shrewd voice came from the other side of the carriage. He opened the door and stuck out his thick, sweaty palm for her to hold as she exited.

Lucy gave a quick apologetic glance to Laurent, opened the door to leave the carriage, then grabbed Jasper's hand for him to escort her out. As soon as her right hand touched his, her palm began to sting and burn.

"Ouch!" she gasped as she pulled away, taking a step away from him on the uneven path. She held her fist tight against her chest and peeked down, opening her hand so only she could see. The lines of her scar were bright red, the magic within her writhing in pain.

"Miss Lucy! Are you hurt?" Laurent sped out of the carriage to assist, but Lucy closed her hand tightly once more, hiding it under her other arm.

"I'm fine," she lied again. "It must just be sore from recent target practice."

Jasper's accusing glare landed on Lucy with disgust. "Your father has told you that you are done with the archery business." A wry smile came over his face. "Just wait until he hears about this."

Laurent forced Jasper out of the way as he grabbed Lucy's left hand and escorted her out of the carriage. Then he turned to Jasper with a look of utter rage.

Laurent's eyes were wide, his pale skin now devoid of any color—even his hair seemed more stark white than it had been. He quickly flicked his hand in the air, creating a privacy bubble around himself and Jasper, leaving Lucy and the guards to only guess what was being said.

Jasper seemed to crumble under Laurent's words, sinking low into a bow of apology and obedience. Laurent's shoulders shook with each word he spoke, and Jasper stayed glued to the ground.

A moment later, Laurent relaxed and straightened his shoulders, returning to full height. He removed the privacy barrier and turned to Lucy, leaving Jasper groveling in the dirt.

"I apologize for his rudeness to you, Miss Lucy. He will not speak to you in that manner again."

Jasper rose from the ground, giving a panicked look to Lucy and Laurent, unsure of what to say. He gave a slight nod to acknowledge Laurent and his eyes darted around nervously as he thumbed his oversized rings.

"Jasper. If you do not keep your word, I will find out." Laurent faced away from Jasper, but tilted his head to the side to ensure the sound carried to his weak Fae ears.

Jasper nodded again, looking at the ground.

I guess it pays to have the Lord of the Northern Territories as your betrothed.

SIXTEEN

MICAH

"This isn't working," Micah groaned. He lifted his hands again to The Elderwood portal, pushing as much energy as he could into his mind, but all it did was give him a headache. "We've been out here for days, Brax. Nothing works."

The chittering of the beetles in the forest put Micah's nerves on edge. They hadn't moved since they swarmed into the trees, but they hadn't quieted down either. It was as though they were watching; waiting for something.

"There is a reason you were able to channel that magic, Lumen. Now stop being a dried up mushroom and keep trying."

"Why are you always insulting me with names of food?" Micah stared at her, perplexed.

"Try. Again." Brax glared at him intently. She held the book in her hands, flipping through the pages, looking for an answer about his magic.

They were able to identify that his aches and pains were caused by leaving the property, but nothing about the shadow cat or the red magic could be found.

Seeing Brax sitting on the tree stump by the fire pit put an ache in his heart. He remembered his long nights with Lucy, sitting in the same place.

Damn, I miss her.

He paced back and forth, trying to find whatever strength he had inside of him that allowed the magic to come to the surface in the first place. It had happened more than once, he could make it happen again.

This is where I learned it all. This is where I will figure it out.

"Let's go through it again, Lumen. Think back to the first time you used your magic. What were you doing? Do not leave out any details."

"I was in the woods when the rumble started. The tree branch was falling down and somehow I was able to stop it before it crushed me."

Brax continued to flip through the leather tome, slowing as she reached pages with large pictures of glass vials and jars. "And the other day with the spell? What did you do?"

"I told you this a thousand times. I just did what you told me to do! I put the materials needed for the spell by the tree."

"But you didn't say the words."

"That's because I don't *know* the words," Micah ground out. They had gone over this so many times and always ended with the same result: they didn't understand how Micah was capable of the magic.

"Wait." Brax gasped as she read a page in the book.

"What is it?" Micah asked, coming near.

"Silence, you featherless chicken," Brax said.

Micah rolled his eyes, but kept walking closer. He tried to get a good look at the page she was reading, but he couldn't understand it.

"What language is that?"

"Ancient Fae…" Her voice was airy, as though she was afraid to speak the words aloud. "It has not been written for thousands of years."

"Well, what does it say?" Micah asked, exasperated.

She snapped her head up at him. Her gaze was wild, curiosity burning behind those dark-rimmed eyes. "Lumen. Did you ever go into The Elderwood?"

All at once, the entire forest went quiet. Micah looked up, the beetles in the trees still weighing down the boughs, but now eerily silent.

"Just once. Why?"

"What happened while you were there?"

Micah flushed, knowing well what he did there, but he wasn't ready to share that with Brax. "Uh, does it matter what I did?"

"Use your ears, Lumen. I asked what happened while you were there. I did not ask you what you did."

"I'm not sure if I understand the difference," he admitted with confusion.

She released an annoyed grunt and narrowed her eyes. "You got there. Did your body feel different? Did you see anything unusual while you were in the portal before you appeared in The Elderwood? Did you hear anything?"

Slowly, the insects began to chitter again. The rumble grew through the trees, passing through like a wave as though they were speaking to one another.

Micah replayed it all in his mind. Lucy held his hand as they walked into the portal, squeezing the amulet tight and preparing to be transported to another realm—as much as someone can prepare for that. He closed his eyes as he tried to remember.

"I remember seeing a bright swirling light—all different colors. My body felt weightless at first, but then it kind of felt like…"

"Like what?" Brax said, standing. She clutched the book to her chest. "Lumen. Tell me."

Micah looked at her, perplexed. "I was just going to say that at first it felt like I was weightless. Floating in a quiet void of nothing, then out of nowhere, my body felt suddenly heavy. Like the blood in my veins turned to lead. It was kind of awful." He looked at Brax as her smile grew. "It was just because I traveled through a portal into a new realm. It's normal, right?"

"No, Lumen. It's not." She opened her mouth and her eyes widened as a sigh escaped her. "I don't know where to begin."

"What was it supposed to feel like?"

She looked up to the sky, searching for the words. "Water flowing over you. Energy rushing through you. Air wrapping around you. Each portal is a bit different, but you… what you experienced was something else, Lumen. Something created specially for you."

"I don't know what that is supposed to mean," he said, a bit alarmed.

"Micah, what do you know about Alderic Lumen?"

"Other than he's my Fae ancestor who found The Elderwood? Nothing."

"Then I guess it is time for another lesson."

"Alchemy?" Micah said in confusion. "I don't even understand what that is."

"It's a source of magic that has been attempted by mortals for thousands of years," Brax explained.

She took a seat on the desk with her feet in one of the two chairs, Micah sat in the other, leaning over the book on the desktop, looking at the incredible pictures illustrated within it. Drawings of glass bottles and liquids, swirls and bubbles filled the page.

"You say *attempted,* so does that mean it didn't work?"

"Not for the mortals," Brax said, a smile slowly lifting on her face.

"You're losing me again," Micah said in annoyance. He pulled the beer he was drinking to his lips and took a long swig. It had been one hell of a week, and he really wasn't sure if he could take one more thing. The comfort of an ordinary beer helped stabilize him as he teetered toward the edge of insanity.

"The mortals tried using alchemy to create their own magic. They had heard of the gifts bestowed upon the Fae by the gods and wanted to even out the playing field. However, their focus was on transformation."

Brax pointed to the pictures in the book. "Minerals turning into gold. Metals into elixirs."

"Elixirs for what?"

"They wanted to create everlasting life." Brax said solemnly. "They wanted to live forever."

"Like the Fae?"

"We do not live forever, you absolute walnut." She let out an exasperated huff as Micah just rolled his eyes. "We live for a long time, yes, but not forever. Even Fae have an end, though expectancies differ."

"So what does Alderic Lumen have to do with this? And what does this have to do with whatever magic I have?" He chewed on his lip as he said it.

I have magic, he thought to himself, finally admitting it.

"You have to understand the alchemy first," Brax reiterated. "It will tie it all together."

"Then get on with it, you chicken nugget. We don't have all day."

Brax stared at him with confusion and disgust. "What did you just call me? What is a nugget of chicken? How can that even be an insult?"

Micah's face flopped with indifference. "You know what? It doesn't matter. Can you please explain this alchemy now?"

"Mortals," she sighed under her breath, shaking her head. "The alchemists of their time were able to create things akin to magic. Bright bursts of light that exploded in the sky in beautiful colors and pictures. Tonics to help heal life-taking wounds and illnesses. Some even believed in their potion making; creating love potions for those who they longed for. Do you follow?"

Micah nodded, following along, but still not understanding the connection.

"Alderic was always a very skilled Fae. His magic was strong and his natural passion for exploration is what guided him to The Elderwood. When I knew him, in our younger days, he had just found the portal to The Elderwood and used the wood to create the most amazing bow. He shot down more enemies than any other Fae to have ever crossed the battlefield. That is, until the wood from The Elderwood was shared with the rest of Denora, creating the strongest army in existence. Well—not stronger than the Vytyr. Soon after that, the amulet was passed down to the Baums, with the intention of allowing the Lumen line to fade from existence."

"In Alderic's letter, he said that he got married and settled on the land to protect the portal from the mortals who were moving in. What happened to him after that?"

"Now you are asking the right questions, Lumen." Brax had a twinkle in her eye, and Micah hoped it meant that they were finally getting to the point. "However, it is more than he just married. He married a mortal woman."

Micah's eyebrows furrowed in confusion. "Mortal?"

"Yes. That is why he became so interested in alchemy. His wife was the most breathtaking alchemist in all of Joterra. Her name was Sanni. She was incredibly gifted in alchemy, and together, Alderic and Sanni worked hard to find a way for their family to always be safe."

"Safe how?"

Brax ignored him and continued her explanation. "Alderic knew his Fae magic would stay within his bloodline, but not forever. Eventually, away from Fae lands, his ancestral line would have less and less of his Denoran heritage, until it was washed away completely. And, being that they were both incredibly intelligent, they created a fail-safe. And you, dear Micah, seemed to have found it."

Micah could have said that he was confused, but it wouldn't have made a difference. Everything about this made zero sense to him.

Brax showed Micah the entry on the page, pointing to the long paragraphs written by Alderic Lumen in a language he did not recognize, but Brax read it for him.

"In the book it reads:

The Lumen bloodline carries a strength in character that will last for generations. As Sanni and I live out our lives in Joterra, our lineage will be bound by the laws of mortality. The long-lasting love and devotion to knowledge and justice will strengthen our family as time passes.

While Fae magic brought me to the mortal realm, alchemy will bring us home.

With Sanni's knowledge, we will extract what remains of my magic and transform it. Together with alchemy and Fae magic, we will change the form of my magic, preserving it as it waits to be called on. We shall create a power so strong and unique that only the gifted shall be granted its magnitude.

As a worthy Lumen passes through The Elderwood, the magic will awaken. It will be restored in the Lumen blood-

line and reside there for generations to come, as long as their legacy shares Fae blood once again."

"I have his magic?" Micah asked breathlessly.

"Part of it." Brax nodded. "The other part is unique to any other Fae magic: alchemy. They found a way to allow their magic to live forever."

CHAPTER
SEVENTEEN

LUCY

"That's an interesting smile you have on your face, Lucella," Wes teased from across the dining table.

"Your face is quite interesting, too. You might want to see if you can have something done about that. May scare off the ladies," Lucy stage whispered.

Lucy couldn't hide her expression solely for the fact that she had no idea how she was feeling. Was it surprised? Worried? Quietly enthused?

The entire situation with Laurent had thrown her for a loop. This whole time she was so concerned with marrying someone without getting to know them. However, Lucy never considered that in getting to know Lord Sloan, she would find that he was a perfectly capable partner.

What am I doing? What about Micah?

She didn't have time to think about these intense feelings with her brothers there in front of her. Instead, she chose to ignore them until later, when she would be alone. While it had only been two days since she had her argument with Micah, she realized much more time had passed for him. It had probably been a week since their argument in Joterra.

She shook her head and refocused on her brothers.

Tristan laughed as he threw an apple into the air and made it hover with his magic. He juggled a few pieces of fruit as he made the apples twirl around Lucy's head in jest.

She swatted them away in annoyance. Tristan was never one to take things seriously. He enjoyed making his family laugh—even at others' expense.

Tristan pulled the fruit away from her head, back toward him. Lucy took the paring knife she was using to cut her apple and threw it at one of Tristan's. It hit dead center and lodged into the wall across the room, nearly six feet away.

The kitchen went silent.

Wes nearly choked. He walked over and stared at the apple wedged into the wall with the knife. The handle of the knife was halfway through the apple, pulp and juice dripping down the sides.

"What kind of strength training have you been taking part in?" Tristan asked in awe.

The pierced apple slid over the blade and dropped to the ground with a thud, making Lucy wince. The knife remained lodged in the wall.

"Luce—you sliced it in half from all the way across the room!" Tristan's eyebrows were halfway up his forehead.

"Lucky throw?" she suggested sheepishly.

"Nuh-uh, enough of this bullshit, Luce," argued Tristan. "Tell me what's going on. First, you demolish every clay plate Wes threw, and now you get a lucky throw with this apple? You hit it dead center, and this knife is so stuck in the wall it will take magic to force it out." He pulled and tugged at the knife without it so much as budging.

"Nothing is going on."

They can't find out.

"You forget I train with the best soldiers in all of Denora. Not a single male would have been able to nail that hit with a common kitchen knife, and definitely not in jest." He pulled over a chair, swung it around backward, and sat down next to her, pushing up the sleeves of his white shirt. His eyes narrowed and glued on Lucy. "Spill it. What happened in Joterra?"

Lucy got up to try to avoid the conversation when she met Wes's gaze. His brow furrowed, but he wasn't mad.

He's worried about me?

"Brothers... a lot happened in Joterra." She walked around the kitchen table away from them, desperate to find a way out of the situation. "I can't seem to find the words for most of it. Everything is changing now that I'm home. Especially with the impending betrothal to the Lord of the North." Her eyes darted around the room, never truly landing on her brothers. She couldn't lie to their face. She wouldn't. "Can't we just carry on?"

Wes picked up a plate and projected it at Lucy's head. Without thinking, Lucy threw her right hand up to block it, and a green force field radiated from her palm, protecting her entire body.

Wes stumbled backward and Tristan stood up in alarm.

Lucy gasped and closed her hand, holding it close to her body. She took a step back as the force field disappeared and the plate shattered on the ground. It was too late. Her brothers had seen everything.

"I knew something was different about you," Wes said quietly, taking careful steps toward her.

Lucy refused to hide from her magic, but also had no idea what to say. Their eyes met and Lucy could see the resolution in Wes's gaze. He was prepared to find out what exactly had happened.

"The orchards." He pointed to the back exit. "Out."

Lucy hesitated.

What did I do?

"Now," he barked. "No one says a word." He grabbed Tristan by the arm and led them both out of the kitchen, a backward glance ensuring that Lucy followed. He marched them past the gardens, past the grassy knoll where they had practiced, and straight into the apple orchards.

She realized why Wes picked this place—it would be empty and far away from prying ears at the estate.

Every few paces, one of her brothers would turn to look at her, their expressions filled with questions.

Fidgeting with her hand, she panicked, considering her options.

Do I tell them everything that happened? Do I pretend

that what they saw is something one of my teachers taught me? No, they would see right through that.

Over and over, on the walk through the estate grounds, Lucy debated what she would share. By the time they arrived in the orchard, she still had no answer.

Wes and Tristan stopped ahead in the clearing and turned to stare at Lucy, waiting for an explanation. Tristan and Wes stood across from her as she prepared for an interrogation she didn't know how to navigate.

"You aren't being truthful. What happened?" Wes demanded patiently.

Tristan, however, was much less patient. "What in the realms was that?!" he yelped. "I've never seen anyone do that before."

Lucy paced back and forth quickly, looking from her brothers to the sky, praying for a magical portal to open up from the skies and take her away from this incredibly strange conversation she was about to have.

Here it goes.

"Wes. I told you The Elderwood was under attack, did I not?"

"Yes, you did, sister," he replied with waning patience. "And what does that have to do with glowing green magic that emanates from your hand?"

"You see," she began, twisting her hands and looking from brother to brother. "When the land was on fire, The Elderwood called out to me... It bestowed upon me a kind of *borrowed* magic. At least, I think it was borrowed?"

"What is borrowed magic? That doesn't exist."

"Well, it did for me. The Elderwood sent magic into

my body so that I could control the flames of the fire and defend the land."

"You controlled fire?"

"I did. And…"

"There's more?!" Tristan's voice cracked.

"Yes, now shush," Lucy took a deep breath, trying to find the words to possibly tell her brothers that she levitated with all-powerful magic flowing through her veins. "When I was leaving, I placed my hand upon the tree that held the portal to The Elderwood, and it did this." She lifted her right hand, releasing the concealment charm to show them.

Square in the palm of her hand, red lines formed the Baum Bowyer sigil; the same symbol engraved on the amulet. The same symbol on the portals themselves.

Wes took her hand carefully to inspect it, turning it lightly, afraid to touch her. "What do you mean a tree did this to you?"

"Does it hurt?" Tristan asked, concern filling his voice.

"I'm okay, Tristan," she said with a weak smile, touching his cheek with her other hand. "It hurt when I received the mark. Since then, there are odd times when it may sting, but I don't know what it means. Sometimes it hurts for no reason at all. Sometimes I can feel the magic in my veins, writhing under the surface when I get angry, especially with Father… Then today it hurt when Jasper took my hand. But I don't know what that means."

"Did you say you *feel* the magic within you?" Tristan said, aghast.

"Truthfully, yes. I feel it all the time. It's... old magic. Ancient. It requires no spell work, no words. It responds to me, just knows what I need and when I need it. I feel it humming in my veins."

"Jasper?" Wes said with confusion. "He set it off?"

"I'm not sure. Sometimes it feels as though my body cannot control the magic when I experience heightened emotions," she said, remembering the anger she felt toward her father. It happened again when she experienced the thrill of using her bow. Her breath hitched as she remembered when she felt the magic begging to come out when she was propped upon Laurent's lap returning from their grove in the forest.

"Heightened emotions?" Wes said curiously.

"What else can you do?" Tristan asked. He grabbed her left hand and pulled her further into the orchard where there was a small clearing from a few chopped down trees. He brought Lucy to the center, then moved off to the side and stood by a tree stump—an expectant brightness in his eyes.

"Go ahead," he said with a flourish of his hands. "Show us what you've got."

"Tristan, this is absurd." Lucy crossed her arms in annoyance. "I'm not sure how this works! It just sort of happens."

He looked over at Wes. "See, Wes? This is all some big scheme. I'm sure she has no magic at all."

"Wha—" Wes began, but Tristan cut him off with a wave of his hand.

"No, no. It's fine. Luce here just clearly wants some attention from her big brothers since Father is so angry at her. And it makes sense! I'd probably do the same thing." He put his hands in his pockets and shrugged his shoulders. "I guess I just expected more from you, Luce."

"I am NOT making this up, Tristan. I—"

"Luce, Luce—it's okay! Really. We can pretend that you have some magic in you if it makes you feel better."

"Tristan, I don't want you—"

"Really, it's fine!" He sat on the stump and put his hands together in front of him on his lap. "You always were the least powerful of us all. It makes sense that you'd want that now." He gave her a sympathetic smile, as if he felt sorry for her.

"Tristan, stop interrupting me!" Lucy yelled, squeezing her eyes shut.

"I'm not, I'm just—" and suddenly he stopped.

Lucy looked up to find Tristan entirely wound in vines that sprang from the ground. His feet were tethered to the tree trunk, his hands bound at the wrist. The vines were swirling up higher and higher, encompassing his face so that he could not speak.

"Oh!" Lucy yelped. She lifted her hand and the vines fell away, allowing Tristan to breathe freely. "I am so sorry!"

He took in heaving breaths as he looked at the lifeless vines at his feet. "That. Was. Amazing!" Tristan shouted. He ran to Lucy and picked her up, swinging her around in a circle. "Luce! You beast! I knew you'd be able to do it!"

"You knew?" The spinning made her queasy and confused. She hit his shoulders, forcing him to put her down. "Did you just provoke me so that I would lose my temper?" Lucy asked in shock.

"Of course," he winked at her. "You're too easy. You do recognize that your most revealing trait is your constant yearning for others to regard you on equal footing, don't you? I just had to pretend that you weren't."

Wes walked up quietly. "Well, now we won't have to pretend any longer. You aren't our equal, Lucella."

Lucy took a step back, hurt by his words.

Wes took a step forward. "You are much more powerful, little sister." His half smile gave him away.

Lucy's heart soared, feeling the loving words leave a mark on her forever. Her father would have to listen to Wes; he would have to agree to let her follow her own path knowing how strong she was.

"Though, I do worry where this power originated and what it means for you... What does the magic feel like?"

Tristan huddled closer, wanting to hear it all, a keen interest twinkling in his eyes.

Lucy stood and stretched her fingers, closing her eyes to channel the magic within her. "It feels like the forest. Like The Elderwood. It's enormous, and airy—it feels cavernous inside of me, like there is no bottom to this power. But then, the feeling changes." She wiggled her toes in her shoes, connecting to the earth. "It grounds me, roots me in place as something thrills through me. Like my body is humming. Like something is alive within me, with its own mind. It wants to be released. It wants to be seen."

"Open your eyes, Luce," Tristan whispered.

When she did, she saw him staring with wide, awestruck eyes.

A green halo of light encompassed her body, emerging from her hands. Light poured from them, a string of brilliance darting around her body, as if a playful sprite. She looked around, then at her brothers joyfully. They seemed so far from her. She suddenly realized she was in the air.

"Oh, my!" Lucy exclaimed. She flailed her arms, worried that she would lose her focus and plummet to the ground, but the magic held her. She looked at her arms, the emerald light bouncing around like a rubber ball. Lucy giggled with delight, and the magic slowly lowered her to solid ground.

"What else can you do?" Tristan asked excitedly. "Can you call for things to be brought to you? Try summoning one of those apples from that far off tree."

She lifted her hand and thought of the apple from the tree. Immediately, the apple came to her and landed softly in her palm.

"Now send it careening as far as you can!"

Lucy lifted her hand, and with a sharp push, the apple flew so far it left their line of sight.

"Woo!" Tristan gave an exhilarated shout.

"Lucy," Wes said seriously, bringing a hand up to his chin in thought. "You mentioned that you were able to control the fire? Were you able to create it?"

"No. The fire was already there, and I couldn't extinguish it. All I could do was redirect it... that's how the house was destroyed. The fire wouldn't stop, so we sacrificed the cabin to save the forest."

"Maybe. But maybe you just thought you couldn't control it, since you never tried?"

"How would that change my ability now?" Lucy asked, confusion coloring her face.

"Luce, people don't just randomly get powers that make them exceedingly strong and precise. Nothing about this magic seems typical. Maybe you just need to train, learn how to hone it properly?" Tristan offered.

"I'm not sure I would know how," Lucy confessed, her heart beating erratically. This all seemed so impossible.

"Try this," Wes began. He pulled her away from Tristan and from the nearest tree. "Close your eyes," he whispered, calming Lucy. "Think about the spell we need to create a light orb. Don't speak it, just think about the effects of it."

Lucy held out the palm of her hand and did as he said, hoping something would work.

"Now, imagine that orb becoming a small flame. Small enough to control."

"What if it burns me?" Lucy worried.

"Don't let it," Wes ordered. "Control it. You tell it what to do."

Lucy focused her mind on a tiny orb of light, thinking about using that light to see her way in the dark. She remembered all the times she would sneak the light to read in her room when her mother told her to sleep. She thought of the nights in her father's office, working far into the evening, wanting to get her bow just right, needing an orb of light to see in the dark. She thought of Micah—when she created tiny glimmering lights that danced around the room like fireflies.

Then she thought of the small candles Micah used to

illuminate the study while they waited for the full moon to charge the amulet. The way the small flame flickered back and forth, giving a dim light to the room.

"Lucy," Wes whispered.

She opened her eyes, and in her hand, was a small flame. She looked on in awe at the fire, wondering how this magic could allow her such wondrous powers.

"Now try to douse the flame," he said quietly, eyes still on the fire.

She hesitated for a moment.

I can't do this. What if it grows and I can't control it?

The fear crept over Lucy, invading every thought.

The fire grew, changing from the size of an acorn to a maple leaf, slowly spreading to the width of her hand.

"Lucy, you have to douse the flame!" Wes commanded.

"I can't! I don't know what I'm doing!" Lucy panicked and tears stung the backs of her eyes. The flame grew higher in her hands. "You need to run! I don't want to hurt you!" She couldn't see her brothers through the tears.

"We aren't going anywhere, Luce," Tristan said calmly next to her. "You can do this. Close your eyes."

"No! What if it spreads? You need to go!" Her eyes darted around wildly, looking at the trees that were sure to be consumed by the flames in her palm that she could not control.

"Lucy!" Wes yelled again.

Tristan stood directly in front of Lucy, blocking her view of Wes and all the trees behind him.

"Look at me, Luce." His voice was calm and his body

was open to hers. "You won't hurt me. I know you won't. Close your eyes and get control."

"What if it spreads?" Her voice was breathless as fear threatened to take over.

"I will tell you. Right now I need you to talk to that magic inside of you—because I think it's trying to get your attention."

"What? What does that even mean?" The fire in her hand grew taller, blocking out Tristan's face from view.

"You said this magic is alive, and I know it doesn't want to hurt you, Luce," he said loudly through her panic. "And since you don't want to hurt me, I'm pretty sure it won't. You said it responds to you, right? You can feel this magic is different, but I think you're missing something. So close your star-damned eyes and figure out what's going on. Now."

Lucy felt the desperation in his voice, and her gasping breaths left her no other choice. She looked at her hand, the fire blazing out of control—but beneath that was something even more terrifying.

The lines on her hand were no longer red, nor did they glow green. The lines were now black, as if the magic within her had changed. Her fire changed from red to green, and the swirling black and green magic crawled up her arms. Her stomach began to churn, making her nauseous and dizzy.

This feels wrong. Something is not right.

"You can do this, Lucy," she heard Wes from far away.

Tristan gave her a stern nod of support through the growing flames, yet he never backed away.

She closed her eyes. The sound of her breathing made it difficult to focus, her panicked thoughts drowning her.

Stop it, she told herself. *You are Lucy Baum. Figure this out.*

She took three deep breaths, searching for the magic inside of her. Then everything went silent.

Lucy opened her eyes to an unusual dark mist. She was no longer in the orchard and no longer in the company of her brothers—all she could see was darkness and a soft green haze coming from somewhere far off.

She tried to follow the haze, since it was the only source of light for what seemed like endless darkness. Every time she took a step closer, it seemed to get further and further away. Her feet carried her farther, faster, desperately searching for the source.

"Where are you going?" she yelled into the abyss. "What are you?!"

She came to a halt, bending over to catch her breath. She looked around in dismay, each direction she turned was filled with shadows.

Am I even moving? she questioned.

She tried to take a step, watching her feet move, but knowing the misty green radiance was immobile in the distance.

I can't get to it.

Defeated, she put her arms on her head and screamed in frustration. "Why did you bring me here? What do you want?!"

The green glimmer bounced in response.

Her mouth popped open in surprise. The light

bounced the same way it did when she first returned to Denora, when her magic played as she explored. She took another step, and again the emerald light stayed far off in the distance.

Maybe I can't chase the magic... I have to invite it to come to me.

She stood still and closed her eyes slowly. Lifting her hands into the air, she opened herself to the magic.

"Come," she whispered into nothingness.

The green mist soared to her and hit her like a wave crashing into a rocky shore. A tingling sensation rocked her from head to toe and just like that, she saw what the green haze was hiding.

A gasp left her lips, and her eyes popped open. She was back with Tristan and Wes, the orchard was safe from her fire, and she was no longer afraid.

The magic entered her and felt like something completely new. It zoomed through her bloodstream, joined with her nerves, and trilled through her mind. Then, her magic showed her something that had been hidden from view. It showed her an image that she did not quite understand.

A ring?

EIGHTEEN

"Let's try it again," Brax called from the tree stump in the yard. "When the magic actually worked. What were you thinking?"

"Thinking?" Micah huffed out, clenching his fists at his side. "I was thinking I was going to fuck this all up. I was thinking that it was my fault that things were going wrong with portal and it was my job to fix it. That if I couldn't do this right, then people would get hurt. That Lucy would be hurt."

He looked back at the trees and let out a frustrated grunt, causing the insects closest to him to shift their weight on the branches. They still hadn't left. He kicked at the ground, looking at the barrier he constructed around the tree.

No one is going to get hurt on my watch. I won't let it happen.

"Now." Brax said suddenly. "Do it now."

Micah lifted his hands and tried again to summon the magic. He put all his effort into the task, focusing solely on the small stick from The Elderwood that was left in a discarded pile of wood.

Immediately, the branch radiated a red glow, then flew from the ground and bolted into his hands, causing him to stumble backward.

"That's it!" Brax announced with a wide smile, clapping as she walked toward him.

Micah stood speechless, an overwhelming relief washing through him nearly bringing him to his knees. He did magic.

It was real. All of it. There was something inside of him he could use to defend The Elderwood. There was something within him that connected him to all of this —he was no longer an outsider to it all.

Finally, a way I can help.

"Let's go again." Micah smiled with a fierce determination.

AFTER HOURS OF PRACTICE, Micah and Brax were at odds with his ability. Micah rested in the grass, exhausted from the endless attempts.

He did not have super strength at all times, he did not have the accuracy and precision of a skilled marksman, and he did not have the capability to do any special spells.

He had attempted to call a cup to him, but it stayed firmly on the ground.

He tried to create light, but all he did was stare at his sweaty hands.

Micah could not manage any spells that were common for Denorans, even with the correct spell work.

It was a fluke, he thought miserably.

"This is very interesting," Brax said at last, leaning against a tree stump in defeat. "You are as useful as a broom without bristles."

"What the hell is that supposed to mean?" Micah asked, disgruntled.

"It means you can't do anything worthwhile with it except use it to whack someone."

Micah's eyebrow raised in question, but then it came to him.

"You're right."

"I know I'm right," Brax said casually, swatting a fly away from her.

"No, listen," Micah interrupted as he sat up on the uneven ground. "I can't call the cup, because what would I do with it? Drink from it?"

"Are you new to cups?"

Micah gave her a look and ignored the jibe. "But I can call the stick. I can summon something I can use to defend myself and The Elderwood."

Brax paused, looking at Micah, considering his idea.

"I can't do spell work with Denoran magic because I am not Denoran. But I can ensure the magic of the barrier is firm, because I am working to contain the magic of The Elderwood."

Brax pivoted from her place on the ground next to him, put both hands on his shoulders, and looked him square in the eye with all the pride in the world.

"You are a guardian, Lumen. A protector. When you

channel that part of you, the magic comes naturally. It isn't about making the magic work for *you*, it's about making the magic work for *them*. For those who you desire to protect."

"This is about protecting?"

Brax's eyes lit up, finally putting the puzzle pieces together. "And you can channel your power to save yourself when it is in direct relation to The Elderwood; when it needs you to help." She smiled widely as Micah nodded.

She kneeled on the ground next to him, giving him a friendly punch in the arm that felt more forceful than he was used to, and stood up.

"Lumen. You are a force to behold." She reached down and offered her hand, pulling him up to stand.

"I am the Guardian." Micah said proudly. His heart ached with remembrance. "I wonder if Grandad had the same abilities?"

"I would not know," she admitted. "I presume Corvus would have the answers to your questions." She looked around the property, dusting off her pants. "Where is your grandfather buried? I did not see his grave."

"Oh, I didn't have him buried here. He's with my grandma, in the city. It was just easier to transport him from the hospital there, and I figured he'd want to be with her again."

Brax's face twisted in confusion. "That doesn't make sense, Lumen."

"It does." Micah took a step away to put distance between him and the kohl-lined, sympathetic eyes bearing down on him. He didn't want her pity, and he wasn't about to discuss his feelings. "It wasn't a far drive from the hospital where he died. They called me when he was sick, but he went very suddenly. I didn't get there in time—it was a matter of an hour. I lived right down the block. I basically just had to deal with the funeral and cemetery arrangements." He tried to shrug off her look, shaking his head like it hadn't been a problem.

She walked up to him again, calmly. Slowly. "Micah."

He was caught off guard by her words. She rarely called him by his name.

"Why was your grandfather in the city?"

"I- I don't know." He took a step back, his mind rapidly going through each reason he could be there.

Was he already sick? Did he have an appointment and things got worse? Was he in the city for business?

"Why does it matter?"

She took his hand and walked him over to the stumps of trees, and sat him down. It was unlike Brax to be so quiet, so solemn—Micah didn't say a word. She placed the leather-bound book in his hands and opened to the page where his grandad had inscribed his note. The letter about the curse.

Micah looked it over once.

Twice.

Then, realization hit.

He looked up at Brax in panic, and then back down at the page.

"No." It was all he could choke out. "Why would he leave here if he knew he wouldn't have survived it?

Maybe he got sick here and he called for an ambulance. Maybe someone brought him there?"

"I don't think any guardian would leave on their own, knowing the risk they would take. I'm not sure what happened, Micah. But it may be in your best interest to find out why he was so close to your home when he died."

His heart sank. His head swam with images of his grandad all alone, dying—desperately trying to get to Micah.

What did you do, Grandad?

But he had no time for his thoughts to spiral, because a second later, a low rumble began.

Both Brax and Micah swung their heads to the portal —they had been so busy talking and practicing these new powers, they didn't notice what had been building behind the barrier.

The sharp clawed bugs covered every inch of The Elderwood tree, but it was almost impossible to see because the entire wall of the magical barrier was covered with bugs and a thick, black mist. Its branches sagged down low with the weight of the insects—there had to be thousands.

Within the tunnel of mist, red sparks began to course through like lightning. Each strike set off a rumble within the ground. Every flash deeper and more powerful.

The bright sparks hit again, and behind the mist, Micah could make out illuminated yellow eyes staring at him through the deep cloud of smoke.

The shadow beast.

Its roar filled the forest, rattling the windows of the cabin.

Brax reached high into the air with two hands and called out in Vytyrian. From the palms of her hand, a silvery-gray mist formed, and within it, a spear appeared. It was as tall as she was, with a sharp metal point at the end. She gripped the spear in her hands and crouched into a ready stance.

Micah dug deep into the well of his powers, pushing his mind to focus on protecting The Elderwood, and called on two pieces of jagged wood.

Please work.

He stretched his hands out as a red rope sprung out to latch on to his weapons: one long branch, about as thick as a tennis racket handle, and the same small piece he used to stab the beast in the eye. He brandished his weapons with a fierce determination as confidence in his untapped magic rocketed through him.

Another roar and the insects vibrated so violently they fell off the tree branches. Micah's feet shook. The windows rattled again. The stones of the barrier quaked.

No.

Panic seized him as he stared wildly at the impending threat of the rocks falling and releasing the creature.

The shadow beast's dripping muzzle opened into a wide snarl that Micah could have sworn was a knowing smile. The beast roared again and Micah took off running toward the rocks, praying he would get there in time to keep them in place despite the shaking roar that threatened to topple the entire structure.

One last thunderous boom—a combination of beastly bellow and lightning—and two stones tumbled down and away from the structure.

The purple halo of light dropped from the boundary, and ever so slowly, the dark mist spread throughout the forest.

The shadow beast prowled out, with one resounding step after the other—its scarred eye searched for only Micah.

However, this time, it wasn't alone.

Behind it, three more monstrous beasts padded their way through the tumbling rocks no longer keeping them at bay.

"Well, now we know why it was such a loud growl," Brax began, but the scarred beast roared once again, making Micah's bones shake. "Or not."

"No, I think he's a bit upset with me for blemishing his perfectly black fur," Micah said quietly. "Don't worry, kitty. After I'm through with you, there will be nothing left for you to look at."

Brax stepped to Micah's right as she spoke under her breath. "You take Scar. I'll get the others."

Micah nodded, keeping his eyes on the beast.

As the leader snarled, the three fierce felines behind it came raging at Brax. She nimbly dodged the first, swinging her spear into the one in front of her, jumping over the creature as she tore the metallic point through its body. Its furious howl echoed through the trees as Brax made her way into a larger clearing, giving herself the space she needed to take on the three menacing brutes.

The wounded creature shook its body with a violent shudder, and in that moment, the gash was gone. Brax continued sparring with the beasts as they made their way closer and closer to her. Her Fae warrior speed kept her out of harm's way from their sharp claws, but it was anyone's guess as to who would tire out first.

"Lumen!" Brax cried. "My spear is doing nothing to keep them away!" She battled the felines as they snapped their oozing jaws at her.

Micah kept his eyes trained on the predator before him as they stood in a silent standoff.

Great, they fucking heal. How am I going to keep this beast away from me?

He looked down at the makeshift weapons in his hands.

I'm not sure how these sticks will help, but better than nothing.

He gripped the wood tighter, begging his magic to provide him with increased strength to have the slightest chance at besting the creature before him.

The leader of the shadow beasts crept toward him, his sharp, stained teeth more pronounced than before. The raging creature's eyes swirled with bloodthirsty violence.

It took a running leap toward Micah, and he stood with his feet firmly planted to the ground, refusing to leave the portal unguarded.

I am needed here. I'm not going anywhere.

He swung the larger branch toward the creature, cracking it on its side with all of his might.

The oversized cat went soaring away from him, a

loud whimper proving his injury. Micah felt the magic coursing through his veins—the power of the guardians was there with him. He bobbed on his feet; the adrenaline mixing with his newfound strength.

"Here we go," Micah said to himself, a warning of brutality in his sneer.

The creature let out a fierce bellow, letting its venomous ooze drip out of its mouth onto the earth below. Another leaping pounce and Micah quickly ducked under it as it flew through the air, stabbing upward with his smaller branch. Micah slashed into the underside of the beast, creating a long gash that spilled blood everywhere.

The shadow cat fell to its side on landing, and scurried back to its feet, slinking away from Micah on a limp. Micah braced himself and held his breath as he waited for the beast to heal and attack once more.

"Come on!" he shouted, but as more seconds passed, he realized it wasn't coming after him.

I hurt him.

Micah looked down at the weapons in his hands, then back to Brax. She was absolutely remarkable—screaming at the top of her lungs as she jabbed and stabbed each of the creatures as they got closer to her, fending them off with expert skill and finesse. Yet, every time she injured them, their wounds would heal and she would be back to the same battle.

"Brax!" Micah yelled, and when he knew he got her attention, he threw the longer of the two sticks he had to her. He watched as the crimson rope of magic carried the stick directly to Brax without effort.

Damn. Magic.

Micah wondered if he'd ever get used to it.

She grabbed the wooden branch, using it to pelt the beasts in front of her. Their advances slowed. Brax's eyes alighted. She abandoned her spear and broke the stick in half over her knee. She used the sharp points of the broken ends to stab and prod them as they attacked her. The creatures whimpered in pain as they continued to fight.

But they didn't heal.

"It's working!" she called out to him.

The trio of felines looked for their leader, finding it huddled in the distance, rallying its strength. Brax pushed forward in her attack, no longer having to take the defensive route. She swung, stabbed, lashed, and jabbed as the shadow creatures tried to fight back. They were finally showing signs of weakness.

Micah's insides leapt with a fierce hope. His gaze connected with the leader of the beasts. "Come on, Scar. Let's end this."

The beast began a canter and then a sprint as it raced toward Micah. To his surprise, it stayed low, not taking another running leap. The creature's snarling mouth opened wide and kept laser focus on Micah's legs.

Shit.

Micah bent low, bracing himself for the onslaught, and stretched his arm out as far as he could without losing hold of the dagger-like piece of wood. The beast butted Micah's hand out of the way and knocked him down to the ground.

The shadow creature crouched low and slunk closer

and closer to Micah. It snapped at his feet as Micah crawled backward, trying to regain his footing and give himself leverage—but the beast was too fast.

It bit into the side of his leg, grabbing his pant leg and large combat boot. It swung his head viciously, shaking Micah as it dragged him toward the misty void in the ground.

With as much strength as he could manage, Micah lurched up and stabbed the creature in its shoulder, forcing it to let go. The piece of wood got lodged in the beast's muscular body and Micah scrambled away, weaponless.

The creature's guttural growl was all it took for Micah to realize that this was the end. He held his hands out in front of him, hoping some magic would do something to save him. Anything.

The shadow cat's limping gallop did not slow it down, and it leapt high into the air—aiming straight at Micah.

His magic wasn't coming to him. Nothing was working. He was drained.

This is it.

A thunderous howl reverberated through the trees and Micah squeezed his eyes shut in defeat.

A high-pitched whistling raced past his ear just as he heard a yelp of agony.

Micah's eyes popped open just as the beast crumpled to the ground—an arrow straight through its scarred eye.

An arrow.

Micah's heart stopped as he looked back to where it came from.

Lucy.

She reached into her quiver and released another shot at one of the beasts coming close to Brax, successfully lodging the shaft into its back. Her eyes swirled with the same green magic from The Elderwood, with hints of darkness that weren't there before.

Wes ran out from behind Lucy, his hands swirling above his head, calling on his Denoran magic. He spoke loudly in a Fae language as he pushed the beasts away from Brax, grabbing them with some invisible force.

"Back to the crack in the ground!" Brax screamed over the chaos.

Lucy trained her eyes on the beast that nearly killed Micah. Her face was a picture of pure focus and intensity. Her hand glowed bright emerald as her fingers reached out to the beast and she lifted the massive creature with little effort.

Micah watched as the creature dripped oozing black blood from its injuries. It writhed in the air as Lucy flicked her wrist and sent it lurching toward The Elderwood, smacking its body on the enormous trunk of the tree.

Micah got to his feet and embraced the pandemonium around him. Lucy's swirling green magic kept the shadow cat behind the rock barrier as Wes and Brax worked together to force the last three beasts back into the void in the ground near the portal.

Micah staggered over and stacked the rocks to prepare the wall for the magic needed to reinstate the protection spell. The beetles scurried about in a panic, some of them following the shadow beast, and others making their way to trees farther away.

As the last beast's tail cleared the rocks, Micah pushed the remnants of his magic into the barrier— urging it to work and hold. A bright purple glowing wall signaled his success, and he fell to the ground in exhaustion.

Brax ran over to him, grabbing his shoulder. "Lumen!"

Lucy's green haze in her eyes cleared as she saw Brax embracing Micah.

She rushed over and pushed Brax off of him in fury. "What did you do to him!?"

CHAPTER

NINETEEN

LUCY

"Excuse me?" Brax grit out between clenched teeth. Her body hovered over Micah defensively, refusing to leave his side, even with Lucy's accusing remarks.

"What's wrong with him? What did you do to him?" Lucy shouted as Brax searched his body, her hands hovering above him with a silvery light.

Micah groaned in pain as Lucy neared his bloodied pant leg. His leg was pouring blood from the bite of the shadow beast.

Brax extended her arms toward his wound and Lucy's rage grew at the sight. The magic in her body vibrated menacingly, still heightened from its use against the creatures. Instantly, vines sprung from the ground and pulled Brax's hands away from Micah's body. This time, sharp thorns covered the vines, curling and tightening around Brax's arms.

"What the fuck, Baum!" Brax screamed.

Lucy's hazel eyes met her lethal gaze and the vines tightened again.

"Lu?" Micah's weak voice croaked as he opened his eyes, wincing in pain.

Lucy dropped her glower from Brax and searched Micah's face for a sign that he was okay. "I'm here, Micah. I'm here." Her hands landed on his chest, her fingertips pressing into his flesh, trying to convince herself that he was alright. She shook subtly with the terror of what a bite from that beast could mean.

"Lu, let her go." Micah held her hand weakly, looking over at Brax and then back to Lucy. "Let her go. She's my friend." He caressed her fingers, barely able to keep his eyes open.

If Brax's eyes could shoot daggers, Lucy would have been shredded. Lucy let the vines fall, but Brax's predatory gaze did not falter.

"Baum, I will allow you this one oversight, but make no mistake—the next time you attempt to harm me, you better succeed, or it will be the last thing you do."

"Is that a threat?" Lucy asked in a harsh whisper, her magic shooting through her like lightning, begging for permission to attack.

Instead, Micah interrupted. "Lucy, Brax is my friend. It's okay. She wouldn't hurt me, and I'd prefer if you didn't hurt her, either."

"Yes," Wes added, looking around nervously. "I think enough damage has been done today. Dare I say we work on fixing up Lumen here so we can talk about what in all the realms we just walked into?"

Micah groaned in agreement.

Brax went to put her hands on his leg again and Lucy eyes shimmered with green again, ready to stop her. Micah squeezed her hand tighter to get her attention. "She won't hurt me, Lu."

"If you don't mind, I'm trying to heal your lover. Now, if you would kindly leave me the fuck alone with your primitive magic, I can finish."

"Lover?" Wes asked.

"Primitive magic?" Lucy said in tandem.

Brax ignored them both as she placed two hands on Micah's leg and whispered a language Lucy had never heard before. It sounded like music and mystery—the magic inside of her hummed with recognition.

A soft, silvery glow emanated from Brax's hands as she passed back and forth, hovering over his wound. The silver light got brighter and brighter until Micah heaved a sigh of relief. Lucy had never seen healing magic like this.

Brax smiled at him and pulled him to stand. She nodded at Micah, the pair sharing in an unspoken conversation which made Lucy green with envy.

"How did you know the branches would work?" Brax asked Micah, shaking her head in disbelief.

"They were remnants from The Elderwood," he said to Brax and then looked at Lucy. "When you brought back a pile of wood from The Elderwood, you dropped the stack when we had to stop the fire. There were a few broken pieces that remained."

"So when you left that scar, it was from a piece from that pile?" Brax said as she nodded. "Of course."

"The Elderwood wanted to protect itself."

"No," Brax disagreed. "The Elderwood knew *you* would protect it. That's why it opened its magic to you."

"Can someone explain what those things were?" Wes asked, pointing toward the rock barrier Micah made. "And why there is a rock wall that glows?"

Lucy stood speechless, listening as the Micah and Brax spoke, sharing what had happened in her absence. She had been literally frolicking in the woods with another male and Micah had been here fighting for his life.

Her heart sank with every mention of the shadow beast and how it almost killed him.

What would I have done if he died and I wasn't here? She thought of Laurent. *Was I really ready to not come back to Micah?*

With the realization that she almost lost Micah, things seemed to click into place for Lucy. She didn't want Laurent and his pretty words and grandiose promises. If he were to die tomorrow, it would be unfortunate, but it wouldn't change Lucy's world. In fact, Lucy would daresay her life would be improved. But a reality in which Micah didn't exist was not a life she wanted to experience.

She couldn't.

With that sobering and distressing thought, the magic in her veins began to thrum, the dark lines along the sigil twisted beneath her skin. She held up her hand to look at the new black lines more closely, and the ongoing conversation abruptly stopped.

"What happened to your hand, Lu?" Micah said with concern, rushing to take her hand in his. He wasn't scared to touch her the way Wes had been. He held her palm in one hand and brushed her cheek with his other. It was his first time seeing the brand in her skin. "What is this? And how did you know to come here?"

At long last, she decided it was time to finally tell him about the connection she had to the tree when she left Joterra. Brax listened intently, not taking her eyes off the swirling black and green colors trailing Lucy's arm. Lucy did her best to explain, leaving nothing out even when Brax's unrelenting stare became too much.

"When the magic turned from emerald to black, it started acting differently—erratically. It made me queasy and everything felt off. I just knew I had to get to you," Lucy explained. "I knew something was wrong."

She kept her knowledge of the ring to herself. Lucy didn't know what it meant, but she was unwilling to trust Brax.

"Who did this to The Elderwood?" Wes asked, trying to regain control of the situation.

"That's the problem," Micah said at last. "I think it was me."

"What? No, Micah. It couldn't have been you." Lucy grabbed both of his hands with her own. "Besides, you have no magic. You couldn't have changed the portal."

"Last time you said that to me, I agreed with you. This time," he trailed off, running a hand through his dirtied hair. "Things have changed since you've been gone, Lu. I don't know how to explain it."

Wes pinched the bridge of his nose. "If you tell me you have some peculiar magic bestowed to you by some gnarled tree, I think I am going to need a drink." He kept his eyes closed as his face tilted toward the sky, shaking his head in dismay.

"No, I don't think that's what this is," Micah said. Wes let out a sigh of relief until Micah spoke again. "This is different magic—but I do think The Elderwood played a part."

"You have magic, Micah?" Lucy looked at him in disbelief.

"Yes, Baum. He does. Though it is very different from yours." Brax nodded toward her, surveying her with interest. "You have been gifted something very, very old —and powerful."

"You know what her magic is?" Wes asked urgently.

"Yes." Something shifted in Brax's demeanor and she stood before Lucy and extended one hand out in front of her. "May I?"

Confused, Lucy took her hands from Micah and cautiously placed one in Brax's.

Brax closed her eyes as the green magic rushed through her. She smiled and kneeled, putting one ear to Lucy's hand as if she was listening. A soft chuckle left her lips as she bowed deeper.

"What are you doing?" Micah asked her, looking between the females anxiously.

"You can communicate with it," Lucy realized in surprise.

"Yes. I can." She stood, still holding Lucy's hand. Her face was lighter, softer somehow. "I have not spoken to the primitive gods in many years. They have endowed you with something very special. Something I can't particularly understand."

"GODS?" Wes sputtered.

Lucy's face paled and her jaw went slack.

Gods?

"You speak to gods?" Micah asked her. His question seemed so run-of-the-mill. It was as if he were asking her if she knew how to fry an egg.

"The gods still exist?" Lucy in amazement. "No, surely this is something else."

"Do not underestimate me, Baum," Brax said sternly. "Yes. They exist. They are very wise and have been asleep for many years." She looked over at the tree. "I find it very odd that they had a connection within The Elderwood." She looked at Micah and poked him in his chest. "Why didn't you tell me?"

"Hey, I didn't know!" Micah said, rubbing his chest from her prodding. "So, are gods like, not around often or something?"

Lucy turned to Micah in surprise, and a nervous laugh passed between her lips. She forgot how little he knew about her realm. "Correct, Micah. In fact, they have been out of the public eye for centuries. I have never seen one, and neither have my parents. They left long ago. I've never met a Fae still alive who's seen them. Only our long forgotten ancestors would have been able to tell the tale."

"Then how could *you* speak with them?" Wes asked Brax, looking at her curiously. "You couldn't be much older than I am." He looked her up and down, a quirk of his eyebrow showing his interest.

"I am older than I look, Wesley Baum," she said with a tease. "Though, if you keep it up, I may invite you to do more than just look." She gave him a wink and Wes's cheek lifted into a half smile.

Lucy looked at her viciously. "I don't believe we have time for that rendezvous right now. What was your name again? Brax?"

"Let's not pretend that you don't know who I am. How infantile." She brushed her clothes off and looked over at Wes, speaking to him instead. "We have to figure out how to secure The Elderwood. We cannot figure out why it cracked open this way, though Micah's tome may have more answers."

"Each time we open it, we learn something new," Micah grunted in agreement.

As the three discussed The Elderwood, Lucy was distracted by a fluttering feeling that washed through her. She felt a pulling sensation deep in her chest, guiding her attention to the trees.

I need to see it.

"What?" Wes asked.

She didn't realize she had said it out loud.

"Can I see it?" Lucy asked at last. Her voice was small —completely at odds with how she arrived. They looked at her in silence.

She cleared her throat. "The Elderwood. May I see the split in the ground? My magic feels... connected to it somehow. It is as if I am being pulled toward it as we speak. Maybe it will know how to fix it?"

"I'm not sure, Lucy," Wes began, but Brax cut him off.

"She's right. The magic inside of her is more powerful than my Vytyrian and Micah's guardian magic." She looked over to Wes. "Even your Denoran spells are nothing compared to hers."

"I know they aren't," Wes agreed. "But we don't know what any of this means. We can't just have her go near the gaping hole filled with shadow beasts and expect for her to not get hurt."

"She can handle herself," Micah stated. He took a step forward and put his hand on Lucy's shoulders, standing behind her. He looked down at her and kissed her on the top of her head. "She can do this."

The words of affirmation swam in her heart, and Micah's proximity woke up parts of her soul that she didn't even realize were dormant. Her heart fluttered with joy. It wasn't simply attraction or lust; it was true acknowledgement. He saw her and believed in her, something that so many others struggled to do for so many years.

"So this is what you meant when you said he was important to you," Wes said to Lucy, still staring at Micah.

Micah held his ground and stared back, keeping his hands on Lucy's shoulders, refusing to back down from his place with her.

"Please," Lucy said to Wes. "Trust me this once?"

Wes broke his stare and nodded at his sister. Brax led the way to the portal.

Micah held Lucy's hand as he walked with her to the tree. Her heart beat a mile a minute, eager to see what caused these ebony and jade ribbons to flow over her skin in anguish. Something was wrong with both her magic and the portal. She hoped she could connect with The Elderwood to understand what was happening.

When she approached the glowing violet barricade, her magic flipped within her. A shimmering emerald stream of light leapt from her body, causing Lucy to gasp in alarm. It didn't hurt, but it felt like a part of her had detached from the rest of her body. Her magic crashed into Micah's barrier and melted into the other side, the violet force field doing nothing to stop it.

"What's happening? How did that get through?" Micah asked in worry.

"Like calls to like, Lumen," Brax said to him with calm reassurance. "The magic in Miss Baum knows it is coming home. Your magic did not feel the threat from hers, and it allowed entry. I would go so far as to assume they are old friends."

Lucy stood as still as she could as her magic wound through the tree branches, covering every surface. Though it was no longer part of her body, she still felt a vague connection to it. Recognition sparked through her as the magic swooped through the leaves, reuniting with The Elderwood's power again.

The deep black mist that swirled from the crack in the ground fled as the bright green magic invaded. She could feel her magic slithering through the leaves, searching... searching... but for what, Lucy wasn't sure.

The dark mist felt wrong to Lucy, as if something despicable hid deep within it. Her magic tried pushing it away, but it was unyielding. The darkness would run from the small specks of light, but there was so much of it compared to the minuscule amount of Lucy's light.

There just wasn't enough magic within her to penetrate whatever darkness overwhelmed this barrier.

She remembered connecting with the magic in the orchard. All she had to do was allow the magic to enter her, and she was able to see things more clearly. She tried opening herself up the magic once more to see if there was something she had missed.

Suddenly, a flash of bright white light filled Lucy's mind, causing her to gasp and shut her eyes tight. When she opened them again, a white mist seemed to float in front of her. Just as the black smoke she saw in the orchard called her to The Elderwood, this light mist was showing her something else.

In the misty air, a vision came to her. It was Micah, walking around the newly updated cabin, his eyes wide; shocked to see the magic that created such a masterpiece. Wes was there, installing the mirror for communication. It must have been the day Wes and Jasper returned to help him. But Jasper... where was Jasper?

As if the mist heard her question, the world around her seemed to zoom away from the cabin and into the woods. After focusing again, she saw him: Jasper, standing next to the portal to The Elderwood, placing something inside the base of the tree. His magic glowed orange and then turned black as the tree shuddered. He was hurting the tree with whatever magic he placed inside of it.

Jasper turned and looked around, making sure he was unseen. With a last look at the tree, he returned to the cabin sporting a depraved grin.

It was Jasper.

Lucy took a step back, pulling her magic back to her. She blinked her eyes again with a gasp, returning to the world around her.

The black and emerald magic that wound over her arms began to fade. Then suddenly, the black receded completely, the green light ebbing, leaving only her original mark from the tree. Her fingers traced the lines.

This will never feel normal.

"It was Jasper," she said breathlessly. "It was him. He did something to The Elderwood."

"What happened to the black marks on your arm? Why have they disappeared" Brax asked her curiously.

"I'm not sure," Lucy admitted.

"What do you mean *Jasper*?" Wes asked.

"The Elderwood—it showed me. He was here with you, Wes, when you created the cabin for Micah. And he left you alone, did he not?"

"He did," Wes murmured. "He did something while I was here?"

"I don't know what it is, but he hurt the portal. He added magic; dark, wrong, magic."

"I wonder how he could get the magic to hurt the portal," Brax thought out loud.

"You speak of magic as though it has its own thoughts," Wes said incredulously.

"Are you suggesting that it does not?" Brax challenged.

"How could it? I conjure it, I bring it into creation, and I douse it when I am through. I control it, it does not control itself."

"You're wrong, Baum. It does control itself, it just has

allowed you to learn the ways to use it. You speak its language, so it can agree to your terms."

Wes and Micah looked at her in confusion. Lucy remained shocked in place. It seemed impossible, but it was also only one of several impossible things to have happened to her that day.

Brax sighed and looked at Wes in question. "Have you ever attempted to use your magic, but the spell doesn't turn out right? Or perhaps you have to try two or three times in order for it to work correctly?"

"Yes, it happens to everyone," Wes said defensively.

"You're right. It does. But that is not because you are a weak male or unable to speak the correct Denoran words. It is because your magic and you are not on the same wavelength. You were not preparing your body to use it correctly, and therefore the magic decided to not come to you when called."

"That's impossible."

"It is not. You have worked your entire life to create beautiful magic; both strong and resilient. Where does the magic come from, Baum?"

"Well, every Fae has it," he said, scrambling for his words.

"Every Fae in Denora has your similar magic. Yes. And the Fae in Vytyr have Vytyrian magic. They are all unique, all separate. They all respond to different calls."

"That explains nothing," Wes retorted.

"The magic within us is gifted to us by the gods themselves. Do you not remember the creation story?"

"What story? I have never heard of such a thing."

"Come," Brax demanded, pulling Wes down to sit by the tree stumps.

Micah and Lucy walked after them to hear the story as well. Lucy's memory of this story had faded.

Could there be something to this?

"Before the realms became as we know them now, it was once one large territory. Creatures of all kinds roamed together, under the rule of the gods of lore. The gods had the power of unlimited magic. Some were skilled warriors. Some had healing powers. All magic was present in these gods—elemental, practical, some for beauty and good, others for evil."

Micah shifted nervously, pulling Lucy closer to him. His arm wound around her waist as she remained tucked under his shoulder. Lucy melted just a little in his presence, staying focused on the words Brax shared.

"When the gods tired of their day-to-day lives, they created life. They bestowed their magic on some of their creations—each group having unique abilities. The elementals could summon the four elements in order to bend air, fire, water, and earth to their will. Those with more practical magic conjured things from afar, created beauty and prestige, and brought light when there was none. A group was gifted the magic of healing others, and another group was blessed with warrior-like abilities."

"How does this explain my magic?" Micah asked.

Holding up a finger to silence him, Brax continued talking, ignoring his question.

"The gods did this expecting loyalty and adoration from their creations, and once they got bored, they sat by and watched them turn on one another. Those with elemental powers felt more important than those with more functional powers, like summoning. Those with powers that created beauty feared those who would destroy."

Brax paced, looking down at her feet as she walked. It seemed strange to see this powerful Fae so lost in thought.

"Each unit of Fae felt threatened by the others," Brax continued. "The warriors came together and left first, not wanting to be forced into battle with any of the other Fae whom they so loved and cared for. Many of the healers went with them, fearing others would take advantage of them. So became the Vytyrians."

Brax flourished her hands as she spoke of the Vytyr.

Lucy rolled her eyes.

"The elemental magic stayed fused with the realm. Those Fae who could wield water, fire, air, and earth felt that they were most strong when united. However, the functional Fae were terrified about what that meant. They bonded together and created what is now known as Denora."

Lucy and Wes shared a tense look as Brax's eyes darted to theirs.

"Your functional magic allows you to bring light in dark places, move objects of your desire, and protect you with spells and charms. The elemental magic is different. No one knows what happened to it, because we have not seen it in centuries. Though it seems Miss Baum has found it. We can't be sure, of course, but there are ways to test the theory."

"I have never heard that story," Lucy said breathlessly.

"Then what's the deal with Jasper's magic?" Micah asked.

"I assume Jasper has magic that has been tarnished with time," Brax lamented.

"He has very weak magic," Wes interjected. "In my presence, he has not been able to do so much as a summoning charm. We performed the magic on the cabin together, but his help was minimal."

"Then why did he have that reaction when I said Lucy's magic was stronger than his?" Micah asked Wes.

Lucy beamed at Micah.

He said that?

"Because he is a self-serving male," Brax said. "Anyone can see that. Besides, it fits right in with the majority of Denoran men." She scoffed at the thought. "He'd never admit to having weak magic. Especially compared to a female."

"What about my magic?" Micah asked again.

"Your alchemy is different, Lumen," Brax said quietly. "I have never met your magic before. I daresay it is unique to you, and you alone. The original archer's alchemy."

TWENTY

MICAH

"I think this calls for a beer," Micah said at last. Each time he thought he had heard the craziest thing, something new popped up. It was impossible to keep up with, and harder and harder to pretend that he was fine. He was so fucking far from the concept of fine that he wasn't sure if he'd ever be fine again.

"That's the first intelligent thing I think I've heard you say," Wes announced cheerily. Lucy glared at her brother, but Micah just rolled his eyes.

It wasn't worth the comment. For all he knew, Wes would call him a soup sandwich like Brax's ridiculous insults, and he didn't feel like going down that rabbit hole.

While Micah got the beers, Lucy started a fire. As all four magical beings sat around the campfire, it didn't take long for Micah to compare himself. Each person around the fire knew where they came from. Even Lucy understand her unique magic. But what about him? He knew he had magic, but he wasn't Fae—not really.

What am I?

The thought unnerved him. He was lost and confused and just a bit worried, which he didn't like at all.

"Brax is an interesting name," Wes said over the crackling embers. It wasn't quite dark out, but the night was not far off. Wes sat across from Micah, settling himself on the tree stump.

"I take it you haven't met many Vytyrian warriors?" Brax replied with a lift of her eyebrow.

"No, I have not," Wes admitted. "It is so odd for you to be here. In Joterra, of all places."

"I go where I am commanded," Brax replied casually, taking a swig from her bottle and placing it on the ground between her and Micah.

"That sounds awfully familiar," Lucy murmured.

"Please do not categorize me along with you and your plight, Baum." Brax's incensed tone drew an uncomfortable silence among the group.

Micah shifted uneasily. He knew the magnitude of power and viciousness that lay within Brax. Obviously, Lucy was a warrior in her own right, but there was no need for an all-out brawl right now.

Lucy's hazel eyes tinged with green as her expression hardened. "I would never want to side myself with a helpless soldier."

Brax's eyes darted to Lucy. "Say that again and see how helpless I really am," she challenged.

Micah grabbed Lucy's hand before she attempted to stand up and create a real fight. "We don't have time to bicker," he said softly.

Lucy looked at him in betrayal. "So you side with her?"

"I don't have to side with anyone. Neither of you are helpless—I think we can all agree on that. But both of your situations are very different. We don't need to jump to conclusions here."

"Why were you sent to Joterra?" Wes asked, trying to break the tension that filled the air, shifting uncomfortably on the tree stump.

"My employer entered a new business arrangement and had stakes on this property. I came to ensure nothing happened to it as he finalized the deal."

"Here?" Wes looked baffled. As if a lightbulb had turned on, his eyes alighted. "Your employer is Lord Sloan?"

"Lumen, why can't you be as intelligent as this male?" Brax replied in her deadpan way.

Micah laughed for the first time that day. It had taken a while, but he finally understood Brax enough to get her jokes. They were usually at his expense, but they didn't feel so bothersome anymore. Brax didn't have an affinity for compliments.

"Why are you so rude?" Lucy interrupted. "He is very intelligent. You know nothing about him."

"I know plenty," Brax said as she leaned forward, placing her elbows on her knees. "It is you who needs to learn, Baum."

"What do you mean you know plenty?" She looked between Brax and Micah accusingly. "How well do you really know one another?"

"Lu-" Micah began, but was cut off.

"Lucella Baum, age 122. Lives in Central Denora with her father, Corvus, mother, Anita, and four brothers, Wes, Tristan, Simon, and Henry." Brax spouted off facts about Lucy as if she were reading a report. "Brothers Gregory and Hugh live in the Southern Territory, directing the southern branch of the Baum Bowyers. You are betrothed to my employer, Lord Laurent Sloan, and apparently things have been going swimmingly, according to him. You spent a Joterran week here, with Micah, falling in love and bringing a mortal to The Elder-wood, unescorted by your family."

Swimmingly, Micah repeated in his mind.

Piece by piece, his heart shattered, discovering more had been occurring than Lucy cared to let on. He wanted to be mad but he had no claim to her. Nothing had been discussed about where they stood—he couldn't even call it a relationship.

Of course, *he* had no interest in anyone else, but he would never expect to control Lucy's thoughts or feelings about it.

Lucy stood up in a rage, the bright green light dancing along her hand and curling up her arm.

"You are a female in Denora which means you have no say in the matter," Brax rattled on. "You are destined for a life of idiotic males telling you what to do and, from the looks of it, you are more powerful than all of them combined."

At that, Micah and Wes looked to Brax in confusion. Lucy stilled as she stood above her.

"So tell me, Baum." Brax stood up. "Are you going to

let those males control your life?" She took a step closer to Lucy.

"Never," Lucy said adamantly.

Brax's eyes lit up wickedly, a small smile forming on her lips.

"Good. Maybe you are closer to learning than I thought."

"And what is it exactly that you feel I must learn?" Lucy demanded.

"That you are the only one in charge of your life. That you must never let a male determine your fate nor your future."

"Didn't you just say you were commanded here? How is that being in charge of your life?" Lucy spat.

Brax sat, unaffected by her anger. "Because I chose to come here. I chose the contract from Lord Sloan knowing that I could complete my job and be paid handsomely."

"You chose? What do you mean?" Lucy looked dumb-founded.

"Ah, yes. I know. It is such a foreign concept for a Denoran female," Brax continued. To others, it seemed as though Brax was being crass, but Micah knew she meant the words with sincerity. "Lord Sloan is an honorable Fae. He creates the contracts and sends them to Vytyr. Any of the warriors can apply for the position. I've had a longstanding partnership with him, and he agreed to my request for payment. I signed the contract and arrived here soon after."

"Your request?" Wes asked curiously.

"Yes," Brax murmured.

"What did you request?" Micah asked, equally curious.

Brax looked at Micah as though he was the only one there. "I requested a payment big enough so that I can go home." Her words were simple, but Micah heard the words she didn't say. Just like she mentioned before—her eyes betrayed her.

They softened as a barely noticeable shimmer foretold withheld tears. It wasn't for her to go home for a visit. It was for her to finish her days of being a warrior and be able to live out the rest of her time with her family.

"And Laurent agreed?" Lucy asked. Each time she spoke of him so casually, Micah felt as though he took an arrow through the chest.

"Yes," Brax said simply. "He differs from the Denoran males. Though I expect you've already figured that out." Brax's usual mocking tone was gone. She shifted her eyes to Micah, seeing his hurt. Brax looked down to the ground, grabbed her beer and took another drink.

Lucy was quiet. "Yes," she replied. "I suppose I have."

Micah refused to look up from his gaze on the fire.

Swallow me whole, he asked the flames.

"What makes this male so different?" Wes asked, oblivious to the fact that Lucy just admitted something life-changing for her and Micah.

Lucy looked at Micah in question, but when he didn't meet her eye, she turned to Wes instead. "He supports the poor in his territory. He is of high status, but does not flaunt it or abuse his power. He doesn't believe that females should have no voice in their life."

"As long as they aren't his future wife, right?" Micah spat.

"Micah," Lucy began, but Micah threw his hands in the air and stood.

"It's fine. I'm glad he's a good person. I wish you all the happiness in the world."

Then he grabbed another beer and stalked off into the trees, putting as much distance between him and Lucy as he could.

"Micah!" Lucy stood up and tried to follow him, but Brax took her arm.

"Give him a minute," Brax told her calmly.

"I need to talk to him," Micah heard Lucy say as he got further from the fire pit.

"Well, I need to talk to you," Wes said to Lucy in annoyance. "Someone needs to explain more of this to me, because I clearly am missing some major details."

The voices carried through the trees as they argued, until they all faded away. The last thing he heard was Brax stopping Lucy.

"You can talk to Micah soon, but he needs a minute to calm down. After everything that has happened, it's the least you owe him."

IF MICAH WASN'T SO angry, the forest would have looked much more imposing. However, his mind was not on the broken portal, the shadow cat, or his alchemy. None of that mattered to him right now. All he could think about was Lucy in the arms of that asshole, and how he was stuck here pining after her while she went to Sloan.

She actually likes him. She defended him!

The wind in the trees was subtle, and the lightning bugs made their appearance alongside the stars. Night had fallen quickly, but this one felt different. For so long, Micah looked at every night as one step closer to Lucy, but it didn't seem as though Lucy had the same plans in mind.

His feet led him to the old tree house. He regularly found himself there when in need of refuge—half of the time he didn't even realize where he was going until he arrived. It was as if his mind knew it was the one place he could find solace. The one spot that remained that would connect him to Abe.

What I wouldn't give for a sliver of advice right now, old man.

He climbed up the weathered rungs of the tree house, skipping the third one that had rotted away to nothing. Balancing carefully, he shuffled over to the far corner that was most supported by the massive tree trunk. He slunk down and sat, staring up at the sky through the broken rooftop, watching as the clouds covered the moon and stars.

"Typical," he said to himself.

More things being hidden from view... Is that all my life is now? A series of events that are hidden from me until they come crashing down?

He closed his eyes and let the crickets lull him into calm. Micah wasn't happy with how things were going, but he also knew when there was nothing he could do.

He couldn't force Lucy to feel a certain way about him, and he'd never pressure her into something she didn't want. He couldn't master his magic without practice. He couldn't change his path in life; he was the guardian, and he accepted that for himself. He'd be lying to say he accepted without the thought of Lucy—he had hoped she'd be there with him every step of the way. He thought this visit to Denora would have been a hiccup in their future, not change its course completely.

Lucy is fierce and adventurous. She has big plans for her own realm, it's selfish to consider that she'd leave her old life behind and be forced to stay here with me.

"I am such a fool," he murmured into the dark.

"No, you aren't."

Lucy.

Micah sat up straighter and looked away from her as she climbed the ladder with ease. His body tensed as she sat down next to him. His emotions were in an uproar—he couldn't figure out if he was mad at Lucy or himself.

"Micah, please talk to me," she whispered.

He looked at her with despondence. "What is it you'd like me to say, Lu? That I'm fucking broken knowing that you want this other guy? That I can just accept that you're going to run off into the sunset with him? You know I can't do that."

"That isn't what this is," Lucy said. "I'm not running away from anyone."

"But you want him."

Lucy bit her lip as tears came to her eyes. "It's not like that."

"Then what's going on with you and him? You seem pretty fucking interested in all of his good deeds."

"I don't know how to explain." Her voice faltered.

Micah remained quiet. With his arms propped up on his knees, he held his beer bottle with both hands. Each thing he considered saying wouldn't change reality.

He wouldn't ask for specifics, because he didn't think he'd be able to handle it. He didn't want to know what her plan was, because if it didn't include him, he might scream. All he needed to know was how she felt about him. He needed to know it wasn't all just a ploy to get what she needed from The Elderwood—but he couldn't ask that. If the answer was what he feared, there would be no mending his heart.

Not now.

Not after everything.

"This place has so many good memories," Lucy eventually said, breaking the silence. "Abe and I were in this tree house all the time... I miss him."

"Me too," Micah replied. "I've been so busy I haven't even been able to read all of the letters he left me... He mentioned you in a few of them."

"You remind me of him sometimes, you know," Lucy said as she took his hand and held it in her lap.

Their touch ignited a fire in his heart, but he couldn't act on it.

"You have his eyes," she said quietly.

He finally looked up, meeting her hazel eyes, rimmed with red, tears shimmering.

"Please, don't cry," Micah whispered, touching her face.

Lucy leaned into his hand, crying more. "I'm sorry," she sobbed. "I wasn't sure what to do and I really thought I could help make a better Denora with Laurent. But when I got here and saw that shadow beast hurting you, it was as if my world was falling apart. I don't know what I would have done if anything happened to you. I'm so sorry."

Fuck it.

He pulled her into his lap and cradled her there as she cried. He stroked her hair, caressed her arms, and held her as if she was the only thing in this universe that could save him. And maybe she was.

TWENTY-ONE

LUCY

Micah held Lucy's left hand firmly as they walked through the cabin upstairs to his bedroom; his broad hands fit in hers like a perfect puzzle piece. She felt the gritty mud and dirt that covered him from his encounter with the shadow beast. His steps were sure, no trace of the injury, but something lay heavy on his heart.

Releasing her hand, Micah walked further through the bedroom and pulled his shirt from his back. As he reached the bathroom, he turned the water on to the shower. He didn't look at Lucy, but she couldn't keep her eyes off of him. She followed him in and stood near the sinks, taking in the view. His tall frame slumped. His hair was a tangled mess as he peered through the room with vacant eyes.

I can't believe I hurt him like this. I don't deserve him.

His broad shoulders rippled as he made his way to her. His face was stoic and untelling—something that Lucy was surely not used to. She remembered his anger, his flirtation, and his adoration; but not this. Not an empty vessel.

Her brows furrowed, leaving a line of worry in the middle of her forehead. Sadness filled her, unsure what this all meant.

They didn't speak a word as they found each other in the dark room.

He reached for her and brushed her hair back from her face and off her shoulders.

"Micah," she began, but he silenced her with a kiss. Soft, immediate, and filled with all the words they could not say.

She melted into him, and he put his hands on her face, his thumb caressing her cheek. Lucy would do anything to hold on to this moment of contentment— they never seemed to last with him. Wrapping her arms around his shoulders, she pulled him toward her, needing him closer.

Micah slid his hands down her back and to the hem of her shirt, pulling it over her head. He threw it to the floor next to them, then he picked her up by her waist and abruptly sat her on the edge of the sink. The forceful movement caught her off guard, their gaze snapping together.

They stared into each other's eyes for a moment and thoughts of everything that had happened since she had left filled her mind.

Her time spent with Laurent, kissing him in the carriage.

Her dreams of both of them seemed at war in her heart.

Her constant state of indecision when it came to the marriage arrangement.

She thought of Brax and anything that could have happened with Micah.

It doesn't matter.

None of it mattered now that she was in his arms once again. Her fingers traced the tired look in his eyes that had appeared since her absence.

"Micah?" Lucy whispered to him in the solace of the dark bathroom.

Micah pulled back and kneeled in front of her. Each time he put more distance between them, her heart ached.

He untied her shoes, taking them off one by one and placing them on the tile floor with the other clothes. Lucy stared at him from her seated position, afraid to speak. He peeled off each of her socks, then stood in front of Lucy again, looking at her body, at her hands, every-where but her eyes.

Micah moved in closer to her and her heart raced as he reached around to pick up one of her legs. He cradled one leg at a time, pulling her leggings off slowly, as though he was peeling each layer of distance away between them, leaving only them.

When she was left in only her undergarments, he grabbed two towels, put them near the shower door, and returned to her.

His eyes trailed her neck to her lips, and stopped on her eyes.

The hurt that lived there was like an arrow to her heart.

If Lucy didn't know any better, she'd think there was nothing there behind that darkened gaze. But Lucy did know Micah, and she knew this was about more than the shadow beast. It was about more than their time away from each other and the devastatingly confusing information he was gaining each day.

No. This was not Micah feeling nothing at all. He was feeling too much.

He was doing his best to keep it all in without breaking, but he was cracking. And Lucy wanted to put him back together.

Lucy stepped down from the edge of the sink and padded over to him, her bare feet cold on the white tile. She dragged her hands down the sides of his arms and stopped at his waistband, pulling his pants off. She stood and removed the rest of her undergarments, wordlessly telling him she needed him, too.

Her skin pebbled even as she opened the door to the shower and the warm steam filled the small space.

Lucy tugged on Micah's hand, and pulled him into the shower with her, the hot water spilling over their naked bodies, cleansing them from the filth of battle. His eyes remained unfocused as their bodies pressed together. He looked down, behind her, at his hands; but never at her.

The reality of the situation hurt, but the fault was hers. He waited here for her, while she allowed herself to be distracted by the possibility of a new Denora in the arms of another male. Of course he was hurting.

How could I have been so selfish?

Lucy grabbed the soap and lathered a sponge, then

turned Micah so she could clean his back and his arms where he was covered in dirt and blood. With each movement, Micah relaxed a little more. She turned him to face her, so she could get his chest and shoulders, her breathing hitching at the proximity of him.

She scrubbed away the dirt. The quiet unnerved her. Feeling his eyes on her, she held her breath as she finally looked up, making eye contact with him. He stared at her, unblinking.

All she had to do was say it.

Tell him you love him, she swore at herself.

She felt it in every bone in her body, every ounce of her being yearned for him and him alone, but telling him now would be unfair. She couldn't manipulate him like that. Not after he had been through so much.

Micah took the sponge from her and turned Lucy. Slowly, he smoothed her hair over to one side and washed her back, then her arms, mirroring the movements from Lucy. Ever so slowly, he washed her as Lucy took shallow breaths, afraid to speak.

Look at me, she begged, terrified to say another word.

His eyes trailed to her lips. "Did you pick him?" he finally asked her.

Her heart sank like a falling stone in a bottomless sea.

"No," she whispered.

It's you, the words silent on her lips.

Micah squeezed the sponge on her chest, watching the bubbles cascade down her breasts to her navel. "Do you still want me?" Micah's eyes burned with hurt as they trailed her neck, her lips, and finally her tear filled gaze.

Lucy nodded, tears falling and blending with the stream of water from above.

Micah crashed into Lucy, pulling her into a deep kiss and grabbing her body with his large, firm hands.

Lucy gasped as she opened her mouth to his, tasting sweat, and soap, and Micah. He gripped her thighs and picked her up, pushing her up against the wall of the shower to keep her in place. Their soapy, wet bodies slid over one another as the cold tile warmed with the steaming water and their heated skin. With each possessive stroke of his tongue, Micah claimed Lucy as his own and with each moan, Lucy accepted.

She was his, and he was hers.

They didn't speak after that, the only sounds coming from the room being breathless cries, full of lust and love lost. Their joining bodies gave them the comfort they both needed as each processed what had happened.

They needed to know they were still rooting for one another. They needed to know the other was still there, still present—even if they were realms apart.

The water turned cold by the time they were done.

As Micah slept soundlessly next to Lucy, she stared at him and took in all of his features. His face seemed so relaxed as he slept, the stress and tension not present in his dreams.

Lucy realized in the dark of the night the importance

of Micah... He would never be a great Lord of Denora, making the realm a better place for all those who needed a champion—but he was *her* champion. Micah was the one who would always be there for Lucy's battles, supporting her and giving her whatever she needed. And more than that, Lucy would give Micah the same love and affection in return. She didn't need lavish outings and fine dining. She needed a partner. Someone who would sit with her and stare up at the stars, discussing the beauty of the world around them.

Lucy looked through the window to the night sky just outside, and from the comfort of Micah's warm embrace, it was so very beautiful.

"We need to test the magic to see what it can do," Brax announced as Micah and Lucy walked outside the next morning.

Lucy wore one of Micah's t-shirts with her leggings, and she hugged it tightly to her chest, taking in the smells of Micah.

Micah was still quiet, but there wasn't so much distance between the two of them now. His hands kept finding Lucy, touching her arm, her back, her hair. Lucy's body leaned into every touch, yearning for more of his attention.

"How do we test it?" Wes asked through a mouthful of eggs.

"We push it to its limits and see when it breaks," Brax replied.

"Can it hurt him?" Lucy asked, watching Wes move his plate to the side. She didn't have an appetite—her mind kept reeling with the same thought over and over.

I hurt Micah.

She barely slept, worrying over what would happen next; knowing she'd do whatever it took to regain his trust.

"No. We won't let him get hurt, I promise," Brax said, no jeering in her tone. "If anything happens to him, I can heal him."

Since their argument over the fire the previous night, they had seemed to come to a truce. Both females wanted to protect Micah and The Elderwood. They were both on the same team—for now.

Lucy nodded in assent.

"Glad to see you two have finally joined us," Wes said with a raised eyebrow in irritation.

Lucy's eyes widened at her brother's tone. What was she supposed to say to that? Obviously she and Micah needed time away to talk things over. Could he really be so unhappy with her over this relationship?

"Don't worry. I've already talked to Brax and she's explained everything, with no help from you." Wes took a dramatic bite of his breakfast and put his plate on the ground next to his place on the stump.

"I'm sorry." Lucy took a step toward her brother. "I didn't mean to disappear on you like that, I just had things I needed to take care of..."

"Yes, it seems as though there was much more going on here than I had realized." Wes gave Micah a cursory glance and refocused on his sister. "I don't think I'll ever approve of anyone you wish to be with, but what matters is that *you* want it. Right?"

Lucy's heart soared. She nodded.

"So, testing this magic," he said in a change of topic. "Can I start?" He wiped his hands clean and walked over to Micah.

"You seem a little too excited for that," Micah replied with a laugh. Lucy heard the sadness in his tone. It wasn't a genuine laugh, just another show.

I hurt him.

"It's good to release some magic when you're stressed. You'll see, it'll be fine."

Lucy stood off to the side as Micah and Wes faced one another in the yard. The Elderwood barricade glowed a faint purple in the background, reminding Lucy of the importance of Micah learning.

He needs to know how to protect himself when he is alone. He needs to learn as much as he can.

That reality struck Lucy with a heavy dose of fear.

If he doesn't learn, there may not be someone around if he... she couldn't even finish the thought. How could she leave him again?

Wes started by using his magic to lift a large branch from the forest floor, then hurled it at Micah. Lucy's breath got caught in her throat as she watched Micah's magic respond without delay.

Before Micah's arms flew out in front of him, an enormous red shimmer created a wall before him. The tree branch smacked against it and was projected back toward Wes. With exceptional Fae speed, Wes jumped out of the way to dodge the hit.

"Interesting," Wes mused, his hair windblown from his sprint. He walked back to his starting position with a smile on his face, nostrils flared and breathing hard. "Drop your shield and let's see if you can get past this next one."

"I don't always know what the magic is going to do," Micah replied. "I didn't mean to call on the shield... it just kind of happened."

"What were you thinking of, Lumen?" Brax asked from the sidelines.

"I thought the branch was massive and I wasn't sure if I could stop it," he admitted.

"You didn't trust your magic, so your magic did it for you. This time, *know* you can do it. Even if you miss, your magic will stop it on its own. Understood?"

Micah nodded and scrunched his face in concentration, forcing the shield to drop. He stood at the ready, his arms outstretched and prepared.

Lucy watched with bated breath as her brother lifted a variety of rocks into the air. Some were as small as an acorn, and others as big as Lucy's head.

Micah gestured to Wes with fierce determination in his eyes. Wes pushed his two hands toward Micah, and the wave of rocks came careening at him all at once. Micah's crimson magic latched onto each stone, stopping them midair. The rocks wavered as Micah stumbled over what to do next.

"Focus, Lumen!" Brax shouted in support.

"Find the thread that connects you to your magic," Lucy called to him, taking a few steps closer. "It will be deep inside of you and feel different from the rest. Your alchemy will be connected with the earth—find the connection and pull."

Micah's face contorted as he put all of his effort into the task. He squeezed his eyes shut tight. Lucy watched as the stones began splitting—one by one, each rock dividing into smaller and smaller pieces. Suddenly, the rocks disintegrated entirely; the dust suspended in the air. Micah opened his eyes, his eyebrows furrowed in concentration.

"Good, Micah!" Lucy cheered him on. "Now, what does your magic want to do?"

Micah's eyebrow rose in surprise, then he closed his eyes once more and his mouth set in a grim line. The speckles of rock remnants moved toward each other, creating one large sphere of dust.

With his hands stretched out and knees bent, Micah was clearly exhausted from using so much force at once. These were not minor spells and charms to move a chair or create an orb of light—this was critical life-or-death magic.

Micah set his sights on the sphere. He pulled his arms toward his chest, then together with a large step forward, he pushed out with vehemence, grunting through the exertion.

The cloud of dust was no longer a cloud, but instead an enormous boulder that cannoned toward Wes. Lucy knew he wouldn't get out of the way in time, and she pushed her magic in front of Wes, creating a green field that protected him and demolished the rock with a resounding crash.

Wes stared at the force field before him in shock. He looked between Lucy and Micah, panting heavily.

"You almost crushed me," Wes barely got out.

"Just returning the favor," Micah replied, equally breathless.

"Perfect. Now we know if you need to use your magic, you can," Brax said. "Interesting addition to the alchemy though," she looked at Lucy. "I'm very curious about what this all means."

"You and me both." Micah groaned and sat on the ground.

"No, no. Get up, Lumen. We saw how you responded to Denoran magic. Now, it's my turn." Brax gave him a crude smile and cracked her knuckles. "Let's play." She rolled her neck in a stretch.

"This is sure to be interesting," Wes whispered to Lucy as he stood next to her, still panting.

Brax gave Micah no time to rest, pouncing at him with a warrior's call. Micah rolled onto his side to avoid her knee as it came thundering down into the ground, cracking the earth beneath her.

"What the hell?" Micah shouted as he leapt to his feet.

"No time to go easy on you, Lumen." Brax said as she stood. "Give me everything you've got."

Micah stood tall, curled his hands into fists, and rolled his shoulders back. "I'll do my best."

Brax came speeding after him. Lucy held her breath as she watched. Brax's fist flew out in front of her, but Micah dodged it in a flash.

He can move like the Fae?

He sped behind Brax and pushed her, causing her to turn. With a swoop of her leg, Brax kicked out and knocked him to the ground.

"Not bad, Lumen," Brax spat. "The Vytyrians can move quickly, with speed, finesse, and accuracy. See if you can hit me."

"But I don't want to hit you," Micah argued.

"Oh, but you wanted to pulverize me?" Wes called from the sidelines.

"If you don't hit me, I'm going to break apart your rock wall and let the shadow beasts take you down."

"You wouldn't," Micah said, standing up straight to speak with her.

She sped forward with a punch to his gut as she whispered, "yes, I would. We will do whatever it takes to pull the magic from you."

Micah spun and took the legs out from under her, causing her to crash to the ground. With Brax on her back, Micah brought his fist down to punch her. Just as his fist was inches from her face, she rolled away, causing Micah to put a divot in the dirt.

Lucy felt the ground rumble under his strength.

Brax did a flip, skirting away from him, a look of surprise and pride on her face. She zoomed to his left, ducked and popped up on his right, prepared to hit him.

Micah caught her fist midair with his hand. Brax pushed more of her force into her arm, trying to hit Micah. Instead, Micah held his ground, sweat pouring down his face as he kept her away from him.

She tried to punch with her other fist, but Micah caught that one, too.

It was an even stand off, neither stronger than the other.

"That's enough," Lucy shouted. "Let go of each other —there will be no winner."

Micah nodded and released Brax hesitantly. As he relaxed, Brax followed up with a quick head-butt. Micah fell to the ground in pain, and Brax acted as though nothing had happened.

"What was that for?" Micah groaned.

"We both know I couldn't let you win," she winked. She placed her hands on his head and healed him, giving him a firm clap on the back when she was through. "You were a worthy opponent."

"That was exhausting. Is this always what magic feels like?"

"Sometimes," Lucy said, bringing him a bottle of water. "Over time, you can build stamina so it doesn't feel so exhaustive. But all Fae need time to recharge. I'm curious what your magic will need to replenish."

"That is a good question," Brax said thoughtfully. "Denorans need to be in a Fae realm and limit time between usage to restore their magic. Vytyrians need to strengthen their body, keep themselves moving. We recharge during battle, which makes us hard to take down."

"You recharge during battle? Man, your adversaries are out of luck." Micah took a big drink of water. "Wait. You checked the perimeter like three times a day. Were you recharging then?" Micah asked.

"Sometimes, yes. Other times I was just bored." Brax

waved off his comment. "Lucy, what about you? How do you replenish this magic?"

Lucy had never thought about it before. This particular magic that flowed inside of her felt different than her Denoran magic. It felt like it was always alive and ready to be used. She felt tired after the initial battle at The Elderwood when the land developers were trying to burn down the land, but that could have also been shock.

"I don't think I have to recharge it," she said, surprising even herself.

"That is impossible," Wes said, walking over to his sister. "All magic needs to recharge."

"Truly, I don't think I need to? Though, I haven't had to use much of my magic since I've received it."

"Show us," Brax said as she stepped back and leaned against a tree.

"You want me to go against Micah?"

"No, I think Lumen needs a break," Brax shared. "But your elemental magic would be a splendor to behold."

Lucy nodded solemnly. She kept forgetting that this magic wasn't just from The Elderwood, but it was likely the long lost elemental magic. Something completely different from anything she had ever known before.

"Remind me, elemental... that means I can control all four elements?"

"Yes, Baum. Fire, air, water and earth."

"I have an idea," Lucy said with a smile. "But Micah, I need your assistance."

"I'll try, but I'm not sure how much help I'll be."

"Sit here," she directed him to a place in the dirt. "And put your hands on the ground."

Micah looked at her inquisitively, but obeyed. Lucy's insides jumped with excitement. She could feel her magic moving inside of her, knowing it was going to come out to play. Her eyes glimmered with hints of green.

"I'm going to try something, and if you can feel it, I want you to pull it toward you. Alright?"

Micah nodded, and Lucy knelt in front of him. She called on her magic, and the green swirls of light bound from her hand and encircled her entire body. Lucy closed her eyes and placed her hands on the ground next to Micah's.

That was when she felt it. The ground trembled beneath her; the earth shifted subtly far below.

"Is that you?" Micah whispered to Lucy.

"You feel it, don't you?" Lucy asked, pleased with herself.

I knew this would work.

"I do, but I don't know what it is."

"Pull," she reminded him with a smile.

Then, with all of her might, she pressed down hard into the ground, her fingers clenching the dirt as her magic obeyed her thoughts.

Brax's gasp cut through the rumbling.

Wes swore.

Lucy opened her eyes and saw the emerald green magic swirling around Micah's ruby red, and under his hands, exactly what she had hoped for: liquid metal.

Micah opened his eyes and looked at ground in shock. Beneath his hands were small metallic pools of gold, settled among the dirt.

"What is this?" Micah asked in disbelief.

"I loosened the ground so you could find the precious metals."

"There was gold under Grandad's property?" He looked around in shock.

"Not exactly," Lucy said with a smile.

Brax came over and bent down to see the liquid hardening now that Micah lifted his hands. "You used your alchemy, Micah," she said in amazement. "How did you know how to do it?"

"I didn't," he told her. Then he looked at Lucy. "Did you plan for that?"

"Partially." Her smile grew as she looked at the astonishment on Micah's face. "I asked the ground to separate from the minerals and metals so that you could find them."

Brax turned to Lucy suddenly. "Did you just say you asked the ground? Or you asked your magic?"

"The ground, I guess." Lucy saw the concerned look on Brax's face. "Why?"

Brax stood up in a rush, still staring at Lucy. She walked away from Lucy, then turned back—words lost on her lips, her eyes wide. She paced back and forth, a panicked look across her face.

"What is it?" Micah asked her.

She ignored him until Micah walked over and held her arm gently. "Brax. What's wrong?"

"What's going on?" Wes asked in worry.

"Lucy, if you didn't tell your magic to do that, then..." Brax couldn't seem to say the words.

"Just say it," Lucy pleaded. Brax's reaction was

scaring her. Lucy's heart thudded loudly in her chest as everyone waited silently for Brax to share why she was so thrown.

"Your magic has actualized."

"What does that mean?" Micah asked.

"It means Lucy's magic has joined with her body. They no longer need to communicate because they are joined as one," Brax explained.

"But that hasn't happened since the Originals," Wes argued.

"You're right." Brax bent respectfully into a low bow. "She is an Original."

TWENTY-TWO

MICAH

"Y**ou're wrong,"** Wes said furiously, pointing his finger at Brax. "Take it back."

Micah watched as the three Fae in front of him panicked as they spoke.

What does any of this mean? Why is Wes so mad? Why is Lucy so scared?

Brax stood up from her position in front of Lucy, looking at her with adoration. She turned to look at Wes with sympathy. "I'm sorry, I cannot. What I said is true."

"How can you be sure?" Lucy asked, a tremble in her voice.

"You can see for yourself," Brax said, nodding her head encouragingly. "Tell the rain to fall," she whispered joyously.

"What?" Lucy took a step back. "I can't do that. No one can do that."

Brax remained silent, staring at Lucy expectantly, a smile playing on her lips.

The only time Brax is quiet is when she knows she doesn't have to argue.

Micah's heart raced with anticipation. "Try it and see what happens?"

He wanted to encourage Lucy, but their reactions were concerning. He needed Lucy to be safe, but wouldn't this protect her? To have powers beyond all other Fae?

He placed his hands on her waist, offering support and reminding her he was there.

Lucy looked up to the sky and closed her eyes. Seconds later, small droplets of rain fell from the blue, cloudless sky. She gasped and opened her eyes when she felt them on her face.

Micah stood in awe of the woman in front of him. She was perfect in every way, and now her magic was otherworldly. Her once hazel eyes swam with emerald.

Wes stared into the sky with wide eyes, his mouth hanging open in surprise. "This can't be," he murmured.

Brax gently touched Lucy's arm to get her attention. A soft smile reserved for very few appeared on her face as she spoke again. "Now, tell it to stop."

Her eyes were frozen on Brax. "Stop," Lucy whispered.

The rain ceased and Lucy fell to her knees. Micah caught her and held her in his arms.

"Lucy?" he asked in concern, but she covered her face, a gentle sob muffled from behind her hands.

He had never seen Lucy this weak before. Even in their time together, she was nothing but strength. If she was supposed to be all powerful now, why had she collapsed?

"Is she okay?" Micah asked Brax, fear coursing through him.

Brax bent down low, putting a hand on Micah. "She will be." He looked at Brax, seeking answers from her solemn look.

"But you aren't doing your magical thing," Micah argued. "Heal her." His voice was demanding. "Does she need to recharge her magic? Did she do too much?"

"She's not in need of healing, Micah. She is in shock."

"She's okay?" Micah asked breathlessly.

Brax nodded, then her eyes found Wes. He was still staring with unblinking eyes. Brax walked over to him and punched him in the stomach. He keeled over in two.

"What in the realms was that for?" Wes wheezed.

Brax put a hand on his shoulder and healed him from the pain. "Needed to help you take your mind off of it for a moment," she said with a wink.

Lucy shivered in Micah's arms, her panicked breaths increasing with each second. Micah had not seen her look this pale before. She uncovered her face and looked to Brax.

"How did this happen? Wouldn't I have realized?" Lucy asked her. "Why me?" Lucy's hands trembled with fear as she rattled off her questions, one by one, without pause.

Micah held her close and kissed her forehead gently. "We will figure this out," he reassured her. "Come on, let's go inside."

Lucy could barely move. Tremors racked her entire

body. He lifted her into his arms and led the way back into the cabin as Brax pulled Wes inside after them.

Placing Lucy down in a chair at the table, Micah went to the sink to get a glass of water. "It's not uncommon to have a physical reaction to shocking information," Micah said calmly as he filled the glass. "When I had civilians who had experienced extreme trauma, this was a typical reaction. You need to drink some water, and I'll get some sugar in you." He looked through the cabinets for some candy as Lucy sat shivering, staring out the window past Wes, who sat across from her.

Micah's calm demeanor on the outside was just a show of strength for Lucy. Inside, his mind was reeling.

What does it mean that her magic has unified with her? Why is she having this reaction? Does the magic hurt her? Why is Brax so damn quiet now?

He shot her an annoyed glance as Brax stood near the kitchen island, watching the two men dote on Lucy.

"Luce," Wes said quietly. He took her hand in his and rubbed his thumb across her fingers.

"You haven't called me that since before you joined Father's business." Lucy's eyes were on Wes as Micah placed the glass of water down in front of her and sat to her left.

Wes gave a weak, tight-lipped smile. "Sometimes I try to be the Fae Father wants me to be, and sometimes I forget where my heart truly lies."

"And where is that?"

"With those that I love," Wes replied. "Tristan was right about you. You're more worthy than all of us combined."

Lucy looked away from Wes and continued to stare out the window.

"What does it mean, Brax?" Micah whispered, afraid to speak the words if the answer was not something he was prepared to hear. He looked at her, searching for answers; for hope.

Brax sat down next to him and took his hand. Micah couldn't recall a time that Brax touched him as a show of sentimentality. Her hands were softer than he expected. "Micah Lumen, you are a defender, so I know this is hard to accept—but Lucy doesn't need your protection."

"What happens when magic actualizes like this?"

"I have never seen it firsthand," she admitted. She looked down at her lap, deep in thought. "I have read little about it, and heard rumors for the rest. The Originals were the Fae who were given magic by the gods. They were more than Fae, because their power was absolute. You see, as years pass, the magic within us dilutes as it transfers from generation to generation. But Miss Lucy was gifted with magic that was looking for a home, straight from the gods of lore."

She withdrew her hand and moved her chair to face him. Wes leaned in further to listen.

"Once the gods ascended, some of their magic remained on the living planes of existence. Lucy's magic was living in The Elderwood for a very long time."

"So she isn't an elemental?"

Brax shook her head no in response. "No. This magic from the gods... It found its home with Lucy and has decided to form a symbiotic relationship with her."

"What does that mean?" Micah asked, confused and

frustrated at never understanding any of these Fae terms.

"It means," Wes said slowly. "Lucy has changed."

The words should have rocked Micah right out of his seat, but in the same second, Lucy stood up quickly, scraping her chair across the tiled floor.

"Someone's here," she said as her magic crept out from her hand and twined around her arms and torso.

Brax stood as well, looking out the window. "Who is it? I see no one."

"The Elderwood is showing me," she said in a whisper. Her eyes were a bright emerald. "It's Jasper."

"What does he want?" Micah asked. One by one, each person stood up, looking through the glass, searching for Jasper's arrival.

"I'm not sure, but we need to call my father," Lucy directed. She seemed more confident than just seconds before, her eyes clear and her hands no longer shaking. "Wes, Brax, and I will go out to speak with him. Micah, you use the mirror and tell my father that his arrival is urgently needed. He will be able to stop this charade—we will take Jasper's power out from under him."

"What are you going to say to Jasper?" Micah asked.

"We are going to tell him The Elderwood is not his to take," Lucy said, taking a deep breath.

"We are going to tell him we will go down fighting," Brax said.

"We are going to tell him to fuck off," Wes added angrily.

Micah looked back to Lucy, his eyebrows furrowing in worry. "Are you sure you'll be okay?"

Lucy looked at Micah and gave him a soft smile. She leaned in, kissed him gently and whispered to him. "I am alright. I promise." Her voice was strong.

Micah nodded.

"Let's go take Jasper down," she added.

Micah couldn't help but smile as Lucy, Brax, and Wes left the kitchen to meet Jasper on the property. He watched as Lucy walked over with a determination that could not be destroyed.

There goes my badass warrior.

His heart thudded with pride.

He swiftly turned and reached the mirror, threw the calling sand and called out to the empty room. "Corvus Baum! The Elderwood is in danger!"

Only a second passed before the face of Lucy's father was clear in the mirror.

"What is the meaning of this?" Corvus asked, his wide body taking up the majority of the looking glass. He was regal in a deep navy suit jacket that only made his reddening cheeks look brighter.

"Hello sir, my name is Micah Lumen, I'm the new guardian of The Elderwood?" Micah was doing his best not to stutter, but he was not prepared for Lucy's father to be such an intimidating man.

"I know who you are." He eyed him judgingly. "What is the problem? Why are you saying The Elderwood is in danger?" The stern look on his face prompted Micah to jump right in.

"Mr. Baum," Micah spoke clearly. "There will be time to explain it all later, but The Elderwood is in trouble. We need you now."

"We?"

"Wes and Lucy are here, sir," Micah said, gulping.

"They are there? I told-"

"Please, sir," Micah interrupted. "I don't know how much time we have."

Tight-lipped, Corvus nodded. "I'll come at once." Corvus's face changed from anger to worry. "I need to find Jasper."

"He's here, sir."

"Why is he there? Did you call him first?"

A loud crash thundered. Micah ran to the window to see what had happened. Outside, Jasper stood alone in front of Brax, Wes, and Lucy. Wes was on the ground and Brax was helping him up. Lucy's green magic swirled, and from all the way where he was, he could sense the rage growing from Jasper.

"No, Mr. Baum," Micah said, racing back to the mirror. "He's the one threatening the portal. Lucy and Wes are out there right now trying to defend it from him. You need to hurry."

Corvus's face paled with fear.

"Do not underestimate him. There has been a change in him lately. We are on our way. Keep my children safe," he said solemnly. Then, just as quickly as he appeared, he vanished.

TWENTY-THREE

LUCY

Lucy's magic curled around her body in anticipation. Her heart thumped steadily in her chest as she stepped across the flattened grass to meet Jasper. They agreed to bring the fight to him in fear of Jasper getting too close to the portal. Ever since The Elderwood showed her Jasper's involvement, she knew there would be an uncomfortable accusation, but she did not expect it to be so soon.

"Are you sure he's out here, Baum?" Brax asked quietly from behind her.

Lucy had placed a privacy charm to ensure Jasper wouldn't hear them approach, but she wasn't sure what good it would do. He was still here, and there was still a serious problem they needed to rectify.

They needed Jasper gone.

She closed her eyes and asked The Elderwood to show her where he was, and clear in her mind, the vision came to her. Just like in the kitchen, her magic filled her mind with trees and leaves until suddenly, Jasper's face came into view. His menacing sneer made her stomach coil. He was just behind the line of trees.

"He's here." Lucy dismantled the privacy ward and watched as Jasper came around the bend—the house in the distance behind them.

"To what do we owe the pleasure?" Wes asked as Jasper arrived.

Lucy expected to meet Jasper with his eyes bulging at the surprise of them halting his progress toward The Elderwood, but instead, Jasper smiled. Not his usual devious look, but happiness—elation, even.

"Oh, this is wonderful," Jasper called as he walked up to them. "All of you in one spot. This will allow things to move much more smoothly." He looked at Lucy. "It's such a joy to rely on you to never do as you're told."

"Nothing will go smoothly for you, Jasper," Lucy bit back. "You aren't getting anywhere near The Elderwood."

Jasper howled with laughter, bending over at the waist. His laughter unnerved Lucy—she had never so much as seen him smile before, and this overt display made a chill run down her spine.

"I don't care about The Elderwood, you naive female."

"What are you doing here, Jasper?" Wes demanded, taking a step closer.

"Just coming to get what I am owed." Jasper's eyes looked full of rage as they bulged from their sockets. He turned the rings on his fingers, his hands moving greedily.

"And what is it you think you are owed?" Lucy asked.

"Oh, there is no doubt. The magic here is mine, and I will not be leaving without it."

"You aren't coming anywhere near that portal," Wes ground out.

Jasper thrust his hands toward Wes, knocking him down in a crash, the ground rumbling from the force.

I thought Wes said he was weak?

"Are you not listening? I don't want the damn portal." Jasper snapped, his neck flushing red in anger. His view looked beyond Wes and Lucy, back toward the house. His eyes narrowed and he curled his lip in a depraved smile.

"You," Jasper's voice shook with rage.

Lucy turned to see Micah rushing toward them, using his newfound Fae speed to meet them. He gave a swift nod to Wes, letting them know he reached Corvus. An ounce of relief filled Lucy, but she worried it wouldn't be enough.

"I should have taken you out when I had the chance," Jasper snarled.

Brax stood defensively in front of Micah, as Lucy took a step toward Jasper. Rage bubbled in Lucy, sending her green magic writhing like hungry snakes around her torso.

"You will not touch him." Lucy's voice carried on the wind.

"There is only enough room for one Lumen," Jasper's oily voice replied.

What?

"You just had to make everything more difficult, didn't you?" Jasper took a ring from his finger and squeezed it in the palm of his hand. Immediately, bright orange sparks flared from his hold.

Lucy took a step away from Jasper, slowly getting closer to Wes, Brax, and Micah.

One Lumen?

"Don't worry—I can rectify that." Jasper pushed his hand out in front of him, and a orange orb of magic trapped all four of them. Immobile, their arms were down at their sides as if they were bound. Their mouths were closed and their faces' expressionless.

Jasper chuckled with delight as he neared the orb, pushing his hands up higher into the air, lifting them so that they hovered above the ground.

Lucy tried to speak, but she couldn't move her mouth. She couldn't move anything at all—she was frozen stiff in this orb of light.

"Yes, I imagine you're wondering how poor little Jasper, with his mediocre magic, could pull this off." He walked slowly, circling around the orb as he guided them through the trees to the house. "You see, my magic has been trapped, no thanks to the false Lumen ancestor."

False Lumen?

Lucy tried to scream, but nothing worked.

The only thing she could do was move her eyes to see that the others were captured just the same. Micah's eyes were wide with fear. Brax perfected her murderous gaze. If looks could kill, she would have taken out Jasper by now. Wes though, he looked as though he was trying to tell Lucy something, his eyes darting back and forth. But what?

"As soon as Alderic pulled his magic from his body,

he took it from the entire Lumen line—hundreds of Fae lost their immense power because Alderic thought some fucking trees were more important than his family!" The words thundered among the forest. "My mother told me the stories for years—about how her horrible uncle ruined our lives. Stole our magic and stole our status among the Fae."

Uncle? Who is he talking about?

"This worthless mortal is not the last of the Lumen line," Jasper spat. "You see, I took my father's name—even after he abandoned my mother and her child. The Lumen name was tarnished by that point anyway; a legacy of weak Fae, our magic trapped."

Lucy's heart raced as Jasper spoke. Her eyes searched the trees for a sign of her father, but he was nowhere to be seen. She struggled, trying to move beneath the powerful spell. Nothing seemed to work.

"I've spent my entire life trying to find a way to unleash the magic. I think good ol' Abe was onto me after some time. Thank you for that, by the way," Jasper continued, looking at Micah. "If he ever successfully got to talk to you to tell you the truth, you might have been able to stop me. He knew once you refused the phone calls and letters for so long there was only one way to get to you—in person."

Micah's eyes opened wide in horror.

Lucy's heart shattered.

No, no, no. Please, do not let this be true.

"He got so far as a block away from you before his heart stopped completely." He paused to admire the jewels adorned on his hands. "Some mortals found him on the sidewalk and sent him to your healers, but they couldn't save him. The only thing that could have saved him was returning here." Jasper's eyes were on the house as they walked, not even looking them in the eye as he told them this devastating news.

He was the one at fault for Abe's death. Lucy's mind raced.

Micah's eyes overflowed with tears that ran down his face, frozen by Jasper's magic.

"I tried to come to The Elderwood after that to figure out how to release the magic, but it wouldn't let me in." Jasper shouted as he lost his temper. He stopped to regain his composure as they got closer to the cabin.

Go ahead, Jasper. Show us the real you.

Lucy always knew there was something off with him, and now he was ready to show them all. She silently prayed for Corvus to hurry.

"Luckily for me, mortals are fools who are motivated by riches. The J. Pearson Land Developers tried to push the false Lumen into making the decision to sell. I needed him to quickly finish going through Abe's hoard of garbage to find the book." His eyes flared with wicked desire. "And like a bee to honey, you found it."

Jasper took a deep breath and stretched his neck, regaining his composure once more.

"I told those foolish mortals to keep a close eye on you, and they waited too long to return. I was notified after you had already entered The Elderwood, so I directed them to burn the property to the ground." Jasper's evil eyes looked back at Lucy. "Thank you for killing one for me. It made it much easier to dispose of the others."

He killed them all!

Lucy's heart shuddered. But then, a fiery rage grew.

He is going to pay for this.

"I should have killed you when we found you huddled in the rubble," Jasper sneered at Micah. "But you seemed so powerless at that point. It would have been easy enough to get the book from you when you didn't expect it, but then the portal betrayed me again."

Lucy's mind flashed to what The Elderwood showed her, when Jasper did something to it—ultimately opening the portal. She wanted to scream. Not being able to talk was pushing her to her limits.

Wait. Didn't Brax say if I wanted something, I just had to ask for it?

She focused her mind on the world all around her.

Let me speak.

Her mouth popped open as she took a deep breath in. "What do you want from Micah?"

Jasper stilled, his body going rigid. "I sensed there was something different about you when you returned… something wrong." He walked nearer to her, looking her up and down, trying to figure her out. "No matter now, you won't be around for long…"

"Tell me!" Lucy screamed.

"What do I want from him? I want what I am owed!" Jasper screamed back. "What is rightfully mine!" The veins on his forehead pulsed with rage.

"And what is that?" she asked.

"The magic!" he screeched. "Once I kill him, the magic will go to the only other Lumen. Me."

Lucy glared at him in disgust.

He will not touch Micah.

"Why would you admit your entire plan to us? You just love to hear yourself talk?"

"It doesn't matter anyway—you won't be around to do anything about it. Say goodbye now," Jasper taunted.

No, this isn't the end.

Lucy's panicked breaths came quicker. There was nothing anyone could do while they were confined.

There must be a better way.

That's when it hit her.

She closed her eyes.

Release me.

Suddenly, she was dropping like a rock in the sea, escaping Jasper's orb. Lucy thrust her hands out, her magic coming to her aid immediately.

An enormous gust of wind caught Jasper off guard and pushed him through the air, his necklace flying from his hands as he was tossed like a rag doll across the forest.

Lucy threw her hands to the orb, driving a blast of magic into it, releasing her friends from the spell. They dropped to the ground in a frenzy, Wes landing on his back, Micah and Brax landing on their feet, their magic preparing them for battle. Micah's hands misted with scarlet.

Brax sprinted toward Jasper, Micah tight on her heels. Lucy hesitated for just a moment to ensure Wes was fine.

"His rings," Wes gasped. "Stop him."

"His rings?"

"Go!"

Lucy took off running, catching up with Brax and Micah. What was she to do with Jasper's rings?

She realized Micah must be battling difficult emotions, but all he shared with the world was a mask of rage. His face was drawn and his eyes dead set on Jasper.

Jasper will pay for all of this.

Brax got to him first. With a tightly clenched fist, she thrust her arm at him to land a devastating blow, but she was thrown back with a bright orange gleam. Brax screamed as she flew through the air, unsure of when or where she would land.

"Save her!" Lucy called out in a screech. The green magic that twined itself around her shot through the air like a shooting star, catching Brax just before she collided with a tree trunk.

Micah lunged at Jasper, pushing him back down to the ground. Jasper's rings started to glow, then the swirling amber mist grew around them, creating a force field that shoved Micah away.

How is Jasper capable of this?

Lucy stared at the odd magic, trying to understand where he got it. She had never seen his rings glow before, and she definitely had never seen Jasper's magic this strong. He himself said that he was a weak Fae because Alderic locked up the Lumen magic.

So if it was true that he was a Lumen, why does he suddenly have more powerful magic?

Micah's red magic began swirling around his hands,

preparing to attack Jasper. It was the strongest she had ever seen Micah. She took a step back as she watched the confrontation. Then, a small voice tugged in her mind. She couldn't place it, but she knew she heard it once before—when she had left Joterra for Denora.

Immediately, another vision came rushing to her. A group of Fae males dressed in dark clothes were making their way across the forest, leading straight to them.

"Tell me what you did to my grandfather," Micah roared. His crimson magic grew again, swirling around his entire torso. Lucy watched as Jasper snarled with contempt.

"I did nothing to him," Jasper spat. "His death was your fault, not mine. All you had to do was talk to him. You and that Baum bitch are a perfect match—so hard-headed that you don't care at all about the people around you."

Micah drew his hands in a circle and pushed his power out with all of his might, pushing Jasper to the ground again, making it impossible for him to get up.

"Don't you dare talk about her," Micah growled. "This is about me and you, you weak piece of shit."

"Oh, maybe you missed that last part," Jasper sneered. "Since you woke up the Lumen magic, I'm not so weak anymore." His hands thrust toward Micah, making his footing stumble just enough that his magic pulled back.

Jasper got to his feet, twirling the rings in his hands. "Yes, my Lumen magic has awoken, and I've been dabbling in something a bit different. Though you may be familiar."

His rings began to glow a bright orange.

"What is that?" Lucy asked.

A tidal wave of light grew from Jasper's hands, the orange magic from Jasper mixing with the red of Micah, creating a collision of magic that rung through the forest.

They stood in a raging battle, each trying to over-power the other—the magic seconds away from obliter-ating everything that came in its path.

Lucy's rage could no longer be tampered down. The anger within her grew, spreading throughout her body, reminding her of every single thing that Jasper was responsible for.

He was the one who forced this arranged marriage.

He was the one who scared off Abe, causing him to die.

He was the one at fault for burning down Abe's prop-erty and putting Micah's life at risk.

He was the one who damaged the portal, causing the shadow beasts to escape.

And now, he was the one who was trying to hurt Micah. And she would not have that.

The wind kicked up around her, and the emerald light danced along her limbs. Slowly, she was lifted into the sky, her hair blowing around her wildly.

She continued to rise into the air, searching for the intruders.

Jasper will not come out of this unscathed.

TWENTY-FOUR

MICAH

The look on Jasper's face was pure hatred—it was so clear now that he was the one who was behind all of this. Micah should have seen it from the beginning when Jasper snooped around the property talking about the J. Pearson Land Developers.

Micah's power surged through him more than ever before. He wasn't sure if it was from his absolute rage at what Jasper admitted or something else, but his magic felt strong and ready to be used. Feeling powerful, he pushed more of his magic toward Jasper, throwing him to the ground.

Wes and Brax moved closer to join the fight just as a bright gust of power spread from Jasper's hands. Another tidal wave of orange magic forced the pair onto their knees.

Micah tried to push more of his power into Jasper, but he just wasn't sure how. He stood above Jasper, sweat pouring down his face, screaming at him to stop.

Jasper remained sprawled on the forest floor,

pushing magic out to Micah with one hand and to Wes and Brax with another.

Straining to stand, Brax crawled behind Wes, stood and used his crouched body to project herself into the air, escaping the blast of magic. As she flipped, she called on two short swords, swinging them toward Jasper's outstretched arms.

The movement caught Jasper off guard as he was torn between who to fight off first: Micah or Brax. Jasper's magic faltered as the Vytyrian warrior came swooping down on top of him.

Wes stood, no longer being weighed down by Jasper's oppressive force. He looked into the air at his sister, seeing her levitating by the godly magic that flowed through her body. Meeting Micah's eye, he gave a quick nod that he was okay.

Brax's silvery magic was breathtaking—fluid like a dance. She swung the swords in front of her as they moved gracefully in her hands. Jasper sent small branches from the ground toward her like bullets as she closed the distance between them. Brax blocked each dart that came her way.

Even with his immense effort, Micah's magic was not enough to stop Jasper from his onslaught of attack.

"Enough of this, DeValey!" Brax shouted as she came close to Jasper and brought her boot down onto his face, forcing Jasper's concentration to end and his power to stop.

Thankful for the short reprieve, Micah quickly shook his hands out and rolled his shoulders back, returning to fighting stance when he saw Wes sprint away from the corner of his eye.

With his Fae speed, Wes ran to the vines that Lucy had previously used to hold Brax, his hair whipping behind him in the wind that Lucy created. Using a manipulation charm, he lifted them and hurried them over to Jasper, who was subdued by Brax.

"Lucy!" Wes yelled, trying to get her attention, but Lucy's eyes were on the distance beyond.

"More are coming," her calm voice boomed through the forest at a volume Micah couldn't comprehend. "Protect the portal."

Micah scanned the woods, looking for the incoming intruders, but saw none. However, when his eyes landed on the portal, he knew he would have his hands busy with his own problems.

The battling magic made the ground quake, and the swirling black mist grew restless, twisting and twirling and growing with each passing moment. The beetles that never seemed to have left the tree branches were flying around nervously, refusing to land—the mass of them casting a shadow over the property.

Micah rushed over to the tree that held the portal, eyeing it carefully, trying to determine what needed to be done to properly protect it.

A low growl traveled through the smoke. The shadow beasts were prowling just on the other side—he could hear them, but could not see them. For now, they were not a problem. Though it would only be a matter of time until they returned to break through the barrier once again.

The rocks had shifted ever so slightly with the battling magic. Micah got down on his hands and knees to stabilize the wall.

There's got to be a better way than this, he thought to himself.

He continued to twist and turn the rocks, hoping this new formation would hold under pressure.

How many times have I fixed these rocks for them to topple over and let these beasts out? There's got to be a better way to close them in.

From his place on the ground, he could see past the rock wall to the base of the tree. There was a gold ring with a black opal in the center shoved between the tree roots, almost lost in the swirling black mist.

Where did this come from?

He reached in quickly, picked it up, and turned it in his fingers as he inspected it. It was definitely not his grandad's.

From behind him, a branch snapped. He spun around, seeing two large men in black tunics.

Before Micah even said a word, the taller of the two shot out his hand and a blast of energy came careening toward Micah. He didn't have time to jump out of the way, and shouted in fear as the magic neared him.

A ruby force field spread around Micah with a flash, protecting him from the Fae magic. The energy seemed to ricochet away from Micah and back to the caster, shoving the stranger deeper into the woods. The ring fell to the forest floor, away from the portal.

Micah kept his back to the tree as he watched the

other Fae slowly stalking around him, looking for a weakness.

"That's an interesting trick you have there, Lumen," the Fae man said, eyeing the force field.

"How do you know who I am?"

"All of Jasper's recruits know you and the Baum female. We had to get to know our adversaries in order to break them down from the inside."

"What does that even mean?" Micah asked, confused. He kept his eyes on the Fae, worried to lose his focus. Using magic was new to Micah, and he didn't need it wearing thin.

"It means that everything you know will change," the Fae replied with a smile.

"If you think you are stepping one foot closer to this portal, then you're wrong. I'm here to protect it, and I will," Micah growled with fierce determination.

"Don't worry. Soon you will find yourself without a tree to protect and without a meddlesome bitch to get in our way." His sneer grew as he crouched, prepared to attack Micah.

Micah stood tall, looking at the piece-of-shit Fae in front of him. "What did you call her?" He felt the energy inside of him shift, preparing for the complete destruction of the man in front of him. His eyes narrowed as he pushed his shoulders back, ready to unleash the magic building within him.

The Fae's mouth popped open, his face contorting in fear. His eyes were wide with horror.

Micah lifted his arms, just as an enormous beast leapt over him and mauled the stranger right before his eyes. The Fae screamed in terror as the shadow beast ripped him limb from limb. Aghast, Micah looked on.

Taking several steps back, Micah walked directly into the rock barrier as it tumbled to the ground. The shadowy mist seeped further out into the forest, making it hard for him to see anything at all.

Shit!

He continued to crawl backwards until he pushed his back all the way against the tree trunk, watching the shadow beast tear the Fae apart. Directly next to him was the enormous crack in the ground.

His panting breaths were sure to give him away if he didn't calm down soon.

Why didn't it come after me?

He looked around, terrified, expecting to see more of the beasts. Everything around him was impossible to decipher with any clarity—the shadows spread too quickly and the rest of the battle was too far from where he hid.

The visceral snarl of the shadow beast echoed throughout the property, sending a shiver down Micah's back.

How am I supposed to use this alchemy when I don't understand any of it? Think, Micah, think, he told himself angrily.

He went back in his mind through everything he learned about the unique magic his ancestors bestowed upon him.

He thought back to the pages he read about the combination of power that was able to preserve Alderic's magic and send it into Micah. The magic had been altered through alchemy, granting him more abilities than the average Denoran. The force field he created seemed different from Denorans, but there must be more to it.

What were the abilities?

His mind ran through anything he could remember.

Alchemy. Metals into gold. Transformation. Curing diseases. Long life.

He thought of his mom and grandad. His entire life would have been different if only someone else was granted this magic... His grandad or his mom would have been better suited for this. His mom would have been cured from her cancer. His grandad wouldn't have died.

I wouldn't be here alone messing things up.

A scream got his attention. He searched through the dark mist, but could not see his friends. Wes and Brax were fighting together as a team, taking on a horde of thugs from the sound of it.

Where was Lucy?

He searched further, seeing only the flashes of bright orange and green light: Lucy and Jasper in a vicious fight for power. Lucy's magic was devastating, but Jasper had years on her. Could she best him?

He squinted through the dark shadows, searching for the ferocious animal that tore apart the Fae. He listened as Lucy and Brax took on attack after attack, refusing to back down and give up. His mom was like that, always refusing to back down from a fight.

And that's when it hit him.

Micah wasn't alone. Not really. Brax was his friend, and Lucy loved him. He knew she loved him just as much as he loved her. They would help him. They wouldn't let him down, and he couldn't let them down either.

He tried to calm his breathing, hoping to clear his mind and find a resolution to his problem. The rocks continued to shake slightly under the chaos of the forest, and the snarling beasts in the smoky shadows that surrounded him did not seem to be improving his situation.

I can do this. My magic is different. Alchemy.

He repeated the word in his mind, over and over.

What is Alchemy? Changing? Creation.

He looked at the rocks again.

Transformation.

Micah took a deep breath, climbed to the outside of the rock wall, and put his hands on the vibrating rocks, hoping that his idea would work. He pushed all of his focus into his hands, imagining the rocks changing— transforming into something more sturdy. His heart pounded, the repetitive *thump, thump, thump* slowed his breathing more.

"Protect," he mumbled.

Thump, thump, thump.

"Defend," he said louder.

Thump, thump, thump.

"I am the guardian!" Micah screamed.

Blazing hot energy surged through his hands, and a blinding purple light blasted through the trees. The force threw Micah away, knocking him down onto the ground in a daze.

He looked up to see the barrier, and he gasped for breath. There in front of him, where there used to be a falling rock tower sat a solid metal wall, half the height of Micah, completely encircling the tree. It glimmered and shined in the dark mist, the silver and purple-tinged metal dutifully encapsulating any of the beasts who tried to break through.

All except one.

The dark mist that surrounded him faded, giving Micah the ability to clearly see the forest around him.

Micah stood tall, searching for the shadow creature with the terrifying putrid yellow and black eyes. Though, it didn't take long to find it, because it was searching for Micah, too.

"Come on, Scar. Let's get this over with." Micah crouched down, panting. The amount of magic that he was using was wearing him down. He wasn't sure how much more he would be able to take, but he had to keep trying. There was no giving up.

The shadow beast looked at him for a long while, pitching its head with a curious tilt, and gave a slow blink.

Micah dug his feet into the ground, preparing for the onslaught.

The shadow beast stretched back from its front paws, then sat in the dirt.

What?

It looked at Micah lazily, as if waiting for something.

Micah took a step forward, ready to fight, but the creature just sat there, watching him.

What the fuck is happening? Is this the same creature?

He took a few steps closer to look at the beast more clearly. It blinked again as Micah came near, seemingly unfazed. Micah saw the scar left on the beast's eye, looking at him intently.

It must be the same... but why is it acting so differently?

Something was off about the beast... its eyes. They were more gold than black, as though the shadows had been lifted.

The beast stood again, and Micah quickly got into a defensive position. It took a few slow strides toward Micah, and then stopped. The gold swirling magic in the beast's eyes faded. The shadow cat leaned forward, grazing its jaw against Micah's head. Then, just as suddenly, the entire beast turned into a misty shadow.

Micah jumped back in surprise, watching as the mist returned to the void in the ground at the base of the tree.

Why did it leave?

He was breathing heavily, watching the black mist fade behind his new metallic barrier. Looking up into the trees, he watched as hundreds of black bugs flew around chaotically. They were nearly crashing into one another until they all flew at The Elderwood at once.

Micah ducked, throwing his hands over his head and... silence. Nothing happened as each bug returned to the portal, becoming dark mist once more. As the last beetle passed the barrier, the black mist dissipated completely. The forest looked normal once again—except for the giant metal wall, that is.

He crept closer, one step at a time, prepared for any other creatures to escape from the large crack in the ground.

Gently placing his hands on the metallic wall, he felt

for the rumble of the creatures. He focused intently, but there was no sound.

Tilting his head up, he could see the sigil on the tree trunk. It no longer had the blackened outline—it looked back to normal.

At last.

A few feet from the barrier, a glint of gold flashed in the light. Looking at the ring more closely, realization hit. Only one person would wear these gaudy rings.

Jasper.

Micah's rage bubbled up again, taking the ring he squeezed it in his fist. Without warning, his red magic burst out from the palm of his hand, more recharged than ever. He looked down at the ring that had been reduced to ash.

That's how Jasper's magic grew, he realized. *Alchemy.*

CHAPTER

TWENTY-FIVE

LUCY

Lucy threw her magic into Jasper again, pushing him farther and farther away from the cabin; and away from Micah. Jasper would never use magic on him again.

Jasper crashed into the ground, each time taking longer and longer to recover. Lucy was granted a moment to scan the property for her friends, The Elder-wood's magic gifting her sight.

Wes and Brax were taking on a much smaller group of Fae now. The scattered bodies of the dead sprawled out among them.

Good, she thought bitterly. *The realms are full of enough evil already.*

She could see Micah in the distance near the portal, but shadows disturbed her view. Seeing him moving was enough for her to know he was okay. Enough to allow her to focus her thoughts back on the weak excuse for a Fae in front of her.

Pushing more magic into Jasper, Lucy kept him

firmly planted to the ground, unable to move. From her place high in the air, she descended, keeping her eyes locked on the one who threatened to end the man she loved.

"You will never lay a finger on him," Lucy said to Jasper, using her magic to send her thoughts into his mind. She glided closer, preparing to end his existence. A shadow of a smile appeared on her lips as she stepped back onto the ground.

With widened eyes, Jasper looked at her, terrified. "What magic is this?" He stumbled over his words, watching her as she approached. "What are you?"

"I am your worst fucking nightmare," she spoke into his mind. Her eyes shone green with magic and her hair began to stand on end, as if a field of electricity buzzed through the air. She rose her hands in front of her as emerald darts of light hovered all around her.

Jasper got to his feet and came stomping toward her, ready to fight back. He grabbed his rings, preparing to use his alchemy on her. Lucy knew better than to allow that. She lifted her hands higher into the air, garnering her power from within, ready to release it on Jasper to end him once and for all.

"Enough!" A booming voice carried through the trees, shaking the branches.

Jasper and Lucy both whipped their heads toward the sound.

Father.

Corvus Baum stood menacingly near a small clearing of trees. His purple shadowy aura exuded power and strength. With Fae speed, he stopped short in front of Jasper and Lucy. He snatched Jasper by the collar and lifted him from the ground, holding him by his scarf and chains around his neck. Lucy watched as Jasper's feet dangled in the air.

"How dare you attack my family," Corvus said in a lethal whisper. "It is the last thing you will ever do."

Lucy couldn't take her eyes off of her father as his enormous stature grew. He lifted his free hand, curling it into a fist as he drew upon his power, preparing for a fatal blow.

"Or not," Jasper whispered, his eyes glimmering with malicious intent.

Suddenly, Corvus shouted out in pain. His eyes squeezed tight as his magic wavered, dropping his fist and using two hands to try to detain the traitorous Fae. Corvus screamed once again as he dropped Jasper, cradling his hand to his chest.

Jasper fell to his knees with a strangled laugh, coughing as he tried to catch his breath.

"Father!" Lucy screamed, running to him. The hand he used to hold Jasper up by his neck was now covered in large, red welts—burn marks sizzling and melting his skin.

"Brax!" she yelled out. Lucy spun, anxiously searching for her and Wes.

She can heal him. Where is she?

"Brax!"

Corvus fell to his knees in pain, grunting in anguish. A sinister laugh echoed on the wind as Jasper clambered to his feet once again.

Corvus's glare, full of hatred and disdain, landed on Jasper.

"You traitor! After all I have done for you—you turn your back on me and do this?" He grimaced as he stood before his disloyal assistant.

Jasper met Corvus with a mirthless smile. "Turn my back on you? Me? No, Corvus. You have it all wrong." He inched closer, rage twisting his face. "You have turned your back on me so often that you have no idea what happens when you aren't looking."

Corvus glared at Jasper, squeezing his hand to his chest, using his free hand to try to pull Lucy behind him.

"There's nothing left to say, Corvus. I am no longer the weak Fae you can push about. I am stronger than you now." He took a step closer, a crazed smile breaking across his face. "I am more powerful." Another step.

Jasper's magic began to swirl in his hands.

No.

Summoning as much magic, power, and strength from around her, Lucy lifted her hands in the air.

I am more powerful than Jasper DeValey.

Lucy merely had to look at Jasper, and at once, he was trapped inside of a green orb of light.

Let's give him a taste of his own magic.

He was lifted off the ground, floating higher and higher. Lucy simply pushed off of the ground and levitated in the air before him.

As Jasper banged on the walls of the orb that confined him, Lucy tilted her head in amusement. The otherworldly magic seemed to take over her entire being, turning her into a feared predator on the hunt.

"Jasper," her primal magic spoke for her, taunting him. *"Your magic has no chance."*

She spread her arms wide once again, pulling more magic into her. The trees on the Lumen property rattled under the force of her power. The sky darkened and lightning streaked ominously through the horizon. Bolt after bolt of lightning crashed through the clouded airspace, terrifying Jasper.

"No!" Jasper shouted, falling to his knees.

Lucy nodded her head in reply. Turning her wrists ever so gently, she twirled her fingers through the air as little bursts of electricity jumped along her fingers. She focused her magic onto the green orb in front of her, and with a wicked gleam, she pushed all of the lightning into Jasper, striking him. With heaving breaths, she watched him writhe within the orb.

"You will never hurt anyone I love ever again," she screamed within Jasper's mind.

"This is bigger than you and me," Jasper tried to explain between bolts. He began to plead for his life. "Please! Please listen to me!"

"This is for Abe," Lucy finally spoke aloud, her voice hoarse as though she had been screaming for all to hear. Her heart ached, but this act would avenge the death of her best friend, and it would keep Micah safe forever. She raised a single finger, pointing it directly at Jasper's heart, the electricity surging down her arm.

"Lucy!" Corvus bellowed from the ground. Lucy's eyes darted to the sound as she watched as Brax and Wes rushed over to her father, healing him and pulling him to stand. From high above, she saw Micah run to the group, worry clouding his beautiful face.

They all turned, speaking to someone who had just arrived. Lucy tilted her head to look around Jasper's confining orb.

Laurent?

He and his most trusted guard, Roger, walked toward the group quickly, sending a burst of magic to take out a lone Fae straggler of Jasper's.

What is he doing here?

Laurent looked up and made eye contact with Lucy, a question in his eye, but amazement clear upon his face.

Beside him, Micah wore the same expression.

At the sight of them, something in her heart cracked in two, and her magic gave way. She felt the wind rush past her as she came plummeting to the ground.

"No!" Corvus shouted, his hand reaching out for Lucy.

"Jasper!" Brax warned them all.

Lucy turned her head just enough to see him falling along with her. The orb of light that had contained him failed when her magic sputtered, sending them both into a free fall.

Jasper's rings glowed bright orange as he sent a beam of magic directly at Lucy. She held her hands up before her in a panic, hoping her magic would come to her aid, but nothing happened. Her magic had gone dormant within her, she couldn't even feel it humming inside of her.

"No!" Micah screamed. His swirling red magic shot toward Jasper, grabbing at the rings on his hands. With an enormous tug of power, Jasper's rings came flying to Micah—taking Jasper's fingers along with them.

Jasper's piercing scream rang through the sky as he was left powerless, staring at his bloodied hand.

They did it. All that mattered was that they stopped Jasper.

Now that the threat of Jasper had passed, Lucy focused on the magic within her, but she couldn't seem to manage a single spell to slow her fall. Her mind raced as she thought of Micah and Laurent standing side by side, watching her magic with awe. But all that magic was gone now. There was nothing left to do; she was going to crash into the ground. Lucy squeezed her eyes tight, bracing herself.

Suddenly, a soft breeze ensnared Lucy. The magic curling around her felt warm and safe and vaguely familiar. Her falling slowed, and she knew she would make it to the ground in one piece.

She opened her eyes to find a shimmering ice-blue magic dancing around her. Her eyes found Laurent as he used his magic to bring her to safety.

Micah held the extracted rings in his hands; Jasper's amputated fingers scattered on the ground in front of them. His eyes were on her as well.

Brax detained Jasper in a magical lock with Wes, securing him and ensuring he wouldn't get away. Without his connection to his alchemy charged rings, he had lost his power. The vise on her heart seemed to lessen, knowing at least Jasper had been stopped.

Corvus ran to Lucy as she descended to the ground,

his face full of fear and worry. Lucy had never seen her father so pale.

"My flower," he gasped. "My sweet Lucy, are you alright?" He scooped her up into his arms and embraced her tightly, hugging her so close she could barely breathe.

"Father," she sobbed. "I'm okay. I'm alright." She hugged him with a fierceness she had never felt before. Jasper attacked them and they had almost been killed. They almost lost everything.

Relief washed through her as the reality of the situation struck her. This entire time Jasper was the one who had put a wedge into their family. Now with him finally gone, they could make amends. They could rebuild the relationships shattered by Jasper and his need for power and control.

"I don't know what I would have done if I had lost you, Lucy," her father said into her hair as he held her tight. "I am so sorry for everything. I'm sorry I didn't see it all sooner."

From over Corvus's shoulder, Lucy watched the scuffle unfold almost as if in slow motion. Jasper stood, gripping something tightly around his neck, causing an explosion from the space between Wes and Brax. They both flew backward, releasing Jasper from his magical hold.

Corvus turned around just as Jasper ripped the chain from his neck and blasted a bolt of amber-tinted magic straight toward Lucy.

But the magic didn't hit her.

Corvus, with outstretched arms, stepped in the line

of fire just in time, sending the magic directly into his chest.

He fell back with a thud.

Lucy moved to catch him and was assisted as Laurent sped to her aid, gently lowering him to the ground. Wes, Micah, and Brax sprang into action, trying to fight off Jasper in vain.

Lucy couldn't breathe.

Corvus lay in her lap on the ground—unmoving. Unblinking.

Jasper created a tidal wave of magic to push the Fae away, allowing him time to run.

Laurent squeezed her shoulder and tried speaking to her over and over.

But this was it.

Jasper killed Abe.

Jasper killed my father.

She gasped for air, searching for answers. Each glance around her felt as though the world was spinning. Then, all was dark.

TWENTY-SIX

LUCY

The bright light from the fire was too much for her eyes to endure as she came to. Lucy had no idea where she was or how long she had been asleep.

She propped herself up on one arm, her head swimming in pain. Glancing around, Lucy saw the familiar furniture of her father's study. The enormous fireplace roared from her place on his settee.

"Father," she croaked. It must have all been a bad dream. She shot up from her place on the couch, looking around the dark room.

Tell me it was all a bad dream.

Wes jolted awake at the sound of his sister's voice. "Lucy?" his groggy voice choked out, leaning toward her from his position on a nearby chair.

"Wes, where is everyone? Why are we home?" She searched the room for answers to the one question she couldn't bear to voice.

Where is my father?

Her heart broke at the reality. She knew the answer—but it couldn't be.

She stood, looking around.

"I'm sorry, Lucy," Wes's voice broke off in a sob.

"No," she begged. She crashed to the ground, grief weighing her heart down, shattering it to nothing. "No!" Her soul could not take another moment of pain—of hurt. She pulled her knees to her chest as she sobbed for the reality of this enormous loss.

Wes sat on the ground next to her and pulled his sister in close, holding her until there were no more tears left for her to spill.

Lucy stared at the fire, her existence feeling as though it was in flames itself, the only feeling left from the hollowness within her.

Long after her tears ceased, Wes spoke to her. "Brax and Micah are safe in Joterra," he cleared his throat. "I thought you'd want to know..."

Lucy nodded subtly.

"He wanted to come with you, but Brax was adamant that he stayed for his own safety."

Lucy tucked her chin closer to her body.

"Brax tried to heal you, but when you didn't wake up, we weren't sure what happened. We thought it'd be in your best interest to return to a Fae realm to recharge."

"How-" her voice croaked. She cleared her throat. "How long has it been?"

"You've been asleep for three days."

If she had any more tears left, she would have cried again. She had been away from Micah for almost two Joterran weeks.

Lucy sat up slowly, seeing her brother clearly for the first time since waking. He had bags under his eyes, and his hair was a mess. It looked as though he had not bathed since their return.

Lucy looked down at herself. She was in a clean gown—someone had been taking care of her while she was asleep.

"Mother came to care for you," Wes shared as he noticed her lightly touching the fine cloth.

"And Laurent?" Lucy asked in a whisper.

"He helped transport us home as quickly as possible. He has a magic unlike anything I've seen—he was able to travel through the realm with a blink of an eye. He took us from the Lumen property to the portal. Then from the other side of the portal right to our estate."

She knew of this power and was thankful for his presence, but why was he even there?

Her head spun with questions... but there was really only one that mattered.

"And Jasper?" she ground out at last.

"We..." He couldn't say the words. "We couldn't find him."

Taking his hand in hers, Lucy squeezed tight as she spoke to her brother. "We will get him. I promise you."

"You don't have to promise me that. It is a deal Jasper sealed in his own blood. This will go beyond vengeance—this will be a brutal punishment dealt straight from the Baums for every betrayal Jasper has ever committed."

Wes and Lucy sat in silence, holding each other's hands, staring at the flames that seemed to flicker and grow as they promised the death and destruction of their family's greatest enemy.

Knowing that Jasper was alive somewhere, Lucy could not sit still. It was not acceptable. He had to pay for his crimes.

The magic within Lucy that usually soared and surged with her emotions barely ebbed. Now that she was well rested, she could feel it deep within her, but it was dimmed somehow, like the rest of Lucy's life.

She had hardly left her father's study since her return. There was something about being close to his things that made her feel close to him. His massive wing-back chair that held his imposing stature, the large fire-place that warmed all on the coldest nights, the divot in the couch where he always sat... How could it be that this larger-than-life Fae just ceased to exist?

She would never hear his hearty laugh again, watching as the apples of his cheeks rose to crinkle the corners of his eyes.

She would never make another bow with him as he leaned over her shoulder to comment on ways to improve her technique.

She would never see the ire in his eyes when she upset him or the remorse they shared as they would make amends.

There would never be a new memory of the male who had shaped her into the steadfast, determined female she was today.

The pain seized her heart as she thought of him. She clung to the edge of the couch as the hurt became overwhelming.

How can this be real?

Moving from behind the couch to sit, she squeezed her eyes tight to rein in her tears. Taking deep calming breaths, she felt the weak flutter of her magic as it came to soothe her.

A gentle emerald mist presented her with a vision... Her father and mother, sitting on that same couch, cuddled next to one another, drinks in hand as they warmed their bodies from the heat of the fireplace. She couldn't hear a word they spoke, but their smiles were stretched across their bright faces, their cheeks red with laughter.

They were so happy.

She opened her eyes. Lucy wasn't sure why that vision surprised her—of course her parents loved one another, didn't they? They had been through so much together...

Lucy stood to go to her mother. Words couldn't describe what she must be feeling, to have lost a spouse... What could Lucy say to make anything better?

It is my fault that he died.

She dug her knuckles into her eyes to try to shake the thought. Deep down, she knew it was Jasper that had killed Corvus, but the same thought kept popping back up... If it wasn't for her, he would still be alive.

There was nothing else she could focus on. She needed to find Jasper and destroy him.

But how?

A knock on the door startled her from her spiraling thoughts.

She straightened and took a deep breath. "Come in," she called.

Lucy wasn't sure who she was expecting, but it certainly wasn't the Fae who walked through the door.

"Laurent?"

"Hello, Miss Lucella," he replied sheepishly, bowing his head and diverting his ice-blue eyes.

Lucy noted the formal greeting.

"I wanted to see how you were doing." He carried a bouquet of white roses, almost the same pale color as his flowing hair.

He looked completely put together and Lucy was sure she looked like she had been trampled by a stampede of horses, but she didn't care. She was no longer interested in concerning herself with love and the false lives she could picture for herself.

The only thing on her mind was vengeance, and she would have it.

Lucy crossed her arms over her waist, pondering her response. He knew she was not fine, she knew she was not fine, and he held the ability of knowing when someone lied to him.

She looked everywhere but at him. There was nothing to say, and she didn't care to play games anymore.

At her silence, he nodded in understanding.

"I've also come to offer my services," he said seriously.

That got her attention. Their eyes snapped together

as her interest grew. He was a few steps closer to her now, his height looming over her frame.

"Services?" She asked. "How can you help me?"

"Miss Lucella," he said softly as he neared her. "I am in control of the entire Northern Territory as well as a vast army. Any battalion will walk out to battle at my very command."

Lucy still looked at him in confusion. Why would a group of soldiers put her at ease?

"Miss-"

"Enough with the *Miss Lucella* if you want to finish your next sentence," Lucy snapped, her patience thoroughly diminished.

A smile broke through Laurent's serious exterior. "Lucy. I wish to put my best Fae soldiers on the task of finding Jasper DeValey and bringing him to justice."

Lucy's eyes popped open in shock. A Denoran battalion exclusively formed to capture Jasper?

Of all the things that Lucy considered, there was only one word she could form.

"Why?"

It didn't make sense for the Lord of the Northern Territory to utilize his resources for something so trivial to the masses of Denora.

He got down on one knee and spoke to her in a near whisper. "If there is anything I can do to comfort my betrothed, I will move the moon and the stars themselves." He took her hand in his, smoothing his thumb over her fingers. "Come with me, my queen, and help me lead the soldiers in finding this cretin. Together, we can accomplish anything."

Her heart stilled.

Laurent did not realize what he offered her. It was not only vengeance on the table, but real partnership. Equality in the face of Denoran custom. Would he dare push back centuries of tradition?

"It is not the Denoran way," Lucy replied, carefully choosing her words.

"For you, I will take down every Fae who stands in our way and says it cannot be so." His words were a promise.

Her heart thought of Micah. She pictured his brown eyes that melted into her soul. There was no way that she could ever be with Micah unless Jasper was gone. She would do anything to keep him safe and keep The Elder-wood out of the hands of those who wished to do evil.

The best way to keep Micah safe... was to say yes to Laurent.

And so she did.

CHAPTER

TWENTY-SEVEN

LUCY

The carriage clattered over the uneven terrain as the Leithe Mountains appeared in the distance. Laurent sat in the seat next to her, which gave her the freedom to look out her small carriage window. Facing away from him, she managed to poorly mask the devastation upon her face.

Leaving her home was harder than she ever could have imagined. Her mother cried, but that was not a change from her waking moments mourning her husband in deep wailing weeps that penetrated her privacy charms when her magic failed from exhaustion.

"I'm sorry to be leaving so soon, Mother," Lucy had said to her in a near whisper. "I promise I will return for Father's funeral." Lucy's words shook as she held in her tears. Her mother had been through so much, Lucy needed to be strong for her.

"Sweetheart," her mother had replied with tear stained cheeks. "It is alright. Take care of yourself. Lord Sloan will keep you safe and return you to me soon."

The news slightly lifted her mother's spirits. All Anita wanted for her daughter was love and support and a future.

Saying goodbye to Wes went nothing like she imagined. Instead of sending her off with well wishes, he had tried to change her mind. The conversation replayed constantly in her head.

"Don't do this, Lucy," he had told her. "This isn't what you want."

The desperation in his voice rang in her ears even now. She knew he was right to some extent. She didn't want Laurent. However, she needed Jasper found and brought to justice—and for that, she would do whatever it took.

She told him to take care of Micah—to apologize for her. Lucy was too ashamed to go herself. There was nothing she could say to make this right. Nothing anyone could do. This was the only way.

Hugging her younger brothers goodbye was a challenge all on its own. Henry and Simon tried not to cry, telling Lucy they were mature now, and had to step up and serve the family business. Wes had swatted them over the head and sent them out to play. He would not steal their childhood from them in the face of such tragedy.

Oddly enough, Tristan was the only one who understood her position. As she said her goodbyes to him, he slipped her a silver dagger with a striking amethyst set into the pommel. The purple was nearly the same hue as their father's magical aura.

He ran his hand through his shaggy hair, still

refusing to cry after all the time had passed. "Do whatever it is you need to do, and find a way home."

She wanted to tell him that there would be no reason to come home, but she had no more energy for words that would go unheard. Instead, she held her brother in a tight hug, slid the dagger into her boot, and left the Baum Estate to leave for the Northern Territory with her intended.

Laurent shifted in his seat next to her in the carriage, sliding his hand over to where hers sat on the leather cushion. The heat of his skin met her frigid fingers with a shock.

"My queen," he said in concern, sliding over to her. "Why didn't you tell me you were so cold?" He wrapped his hands around hers, offering her warmth.

Lucy offered a small smile in reply. "It's fine. I'm sure I will get used to the cold." Truth be told, she didn't even realize she was as cold as she was. She paid little attention to herself these days. Everything about her was numb.

"Once we get past the mountains you will see the castle," he told her, holding her close to warm her in the face of the brisk snowy mountains just outside of their carriage. He carefully pulled the curtain back a bit more to allow her to see.

The Leithe Mountains were monstrous, looming over them with malevolent prestige. The mountainscape went on as far as Lucy's eyes could see, crevices and plunging valleys hiding the boreal beasts that inhabited the land. The calynx prints in the snow were nearly as big as the carriage, and Lucy was grateful that they were largely nocturnal.

"How much longer?" Lucy asked. It had been almost an entire day of journeying. They left before sunrise, and the deepening shadows of the mountainside hinted at the night that swiftly approached.

"Just on the other side of this peak we will see the castle, and then enter the underground tunnels leading us to the carriage bay. I can bring us to the eastern wing once we are within the property lines."

"Why not do it from here?" Lucy didn't understand why they were taking this long journey when she knew Laurent had the capability to transport himself far distances with his magic.

"We have wards within the Northern Territory that prohibit magic. Even I cannot wield magic within the boundary lines. It helps us to fortify our borders and keep the people safe."

"You really would do anything for your people, wouldn't you?" Lucy asked, true understanding dawning on her for the first time.

It wasn't just that Laurent wanted his people to be protected, but he did everything he could just to make it happen; even if it meant making life more difficult for himself.

"I would," he said seriously, turning to look Lucy in the eye. "And you will, too. These will be your people as much as they are mine. Together we can create a realm where all are cared for—it's all that matters."

He turned away from Lucy at that last sentiment, staring into the distance, clearly deep in thought.

Lucy took the moment to study him. Strong angles lined his face, a seriousness that Lucy was sure came with a difficult life of safeguarding an entire nation. His posture was so at odds with how he was with her in the grove on their intimate date alone.

So much rests upon his shoulders, yet he finds time for the little things that make life meaningful.

His eyes lit, life coming back into them. "There," he said with barely hidden relief. Lucy followed his gaze.

Nestled high into the rugged, snow-covered mountains, the Fae castle sat as a testament to both nature's beauty and the elegance of Fae magic. The sight was breathtaking, with glistening ice crystals hanging from the windows like precious stones. The pale turrets nearly blended into the mountainside if it were not for the ice which sparkled like frosted glass.

An enormous bridge covered in ice suspended over a chasm, connecting the castle and grounds to the rest of the Northern Territory. Lucy watched as snowflakes flitted down slowly from the gray clouds blanketed above them.

If The Elderwood was the embodiment of springtime, this was winter incarnate.

"It's beautiful," Lucy said in awe. "Does it always look like this?"

"Yes," Laurent replied, suddenly looking concerned. "Is that acceptable? I know you are fond of your forests and warmth... I promise I will do what I can to ensure your comfort while you are here."

"It's wonderful," Lucy replied with a reassuring

smile. "Thank you for bringing me here to see its magnificence."

"Of course I would bring you here, my queen. It is your home now."

Lucy didn't reply, but her frozen heart cracked at the reminder. She refused to think about it for long, but Laurent was right. Lucy had agreed to this; to a lifetime. And if it meant it would keep Micah safe, then so be it.

With each passing moment, the carriage moved closer and closer to the castle, and Lucy knew there was no turning back. Her tensed muscles were the only outward sign of her panic, but she knew she could blame it on the cold. The air was biting, and she wasn't sure how anyone could get used to the frigid temperatures.

A sentinel guard stood at an outpost, bundled up with furs and leathers to fight off the cold. He stood tall, taller than any other Fae Lucy had ever come across. As they passed him, she stared into his deep blue eyes and was shocked to see tusks coming from his mouth.

"Your guards are not Fae?" Lucy asked in surprise.

"They are. I employ the Fae from a variety of realms, not all of them look the same as Denorans. My exterior guards are from Karroz. They can handle the extreme temperatures better than most other Fae."

Lucy just nodded. That seemed to make sense, especially since he employed Brax from Vytyr.

Brax.

Micah.

Her frozen heart ached. There was no time to think of them now, but she hoped Wes took good care of them as promised.

"The guard's outpost is the boundary line. We are free to enter the castle now. The carriage will next go to the underground tunnels, but there is not much to see for the remainder of the journey," Laurent told her. "Are you ready to relocate to the east wing?"

"Yes," Lucy said with a weak smile. She played the role of future-wife, hoping that Laurent would keep his promise to find Jasper. Every second of her time in the North should be focused on finding Jasper and getting back to her old life... or what was left of it.

Laurent slid one hand around the back of Lucy's neck and the other held her arm. In a blink, Lucy found herself standing in the foyer of an extravagant room decorated for royalty.

"Do you like it?" Laurent whispered to her, standing close over her shoulder. She felt his warm body press ever so gently to her back, reminding her of his comforting presence.

If I have to leave everything I know to be with a male I may never love, at least it is in a beautiful place with a partner who will care for me. At least I won't be alone, she tried to convince herself.

She smiled up at him, the closest thing to a real smile than she had had in days.

"It's wonderful."

Laurent beamed, his bright blue eyes bringing more warmth to Lucy than she had felt all day.

"Welcome home."

~

FINALLY GETTING AWAY from Laurent was a breath of fresh air. From the moment she agreed to go with him, from packing and through the carriage ride, he had seemed to always be nearby, waiting to dote on Lucy as though she were a breakable, fragile thing.

I've slayed men who have tried to hurt me, wielded other worldly magic, and have made the rain fall from the sky. I am not fragile.

She looked into the mirror with a huff and took a surprised step back at the image. Her hair was flat and dull, her skin pale and lifeless, and dark circles rimmed her eyes from lack of sleep. There was a heaviness about her that she had never seen before.

This is why those around me are walking around on eggshells, worried to upset me.

Her empty eyes devoid of emotion trailed her reflection.

I look breakable.

The admission, even if only to herself in the privacy of her quarters, hurt. She had been trying so hard to just keep moving. Trying to convince herself and others that she was perfectly fine. It was clear now that everyone could see right through it. And everyone had... everyone but her.

Her room was as extravagant as the rest of the castle. An enormous four-poster bed sat in the middle, delicate designs of flowers and leaves carved into the posts. The bedding was a soft silver, shimmering in the candlelight of the sconces. A wardrobe, bureau, and floor-length mirror were placed strategically around the room, and across from the door was a wall of velvet curtains.

Curious, Lucy walked over to pull back the velvet to see what was behind. A panorama of northern life was displayed in the wide windows. Far below lay a small city with a bustling town square, Fae walking to and fro, buying things at shops or walking with their families. It seemed almost too serene to be real; everyone calm and joyful. The only thing out of place were the sentinel guards roaming amid the citizens.

She watched those happy Fae as she sat alone in a castle room, trying to gain the courage to be the Fae she needed to pretend to be.

A KNOCK on the door startled Lucy, who sat in a silent panic. Her heart beat irregularly, but she did not know what else to do. She was dressed in a fresh gown and had cleaned up as best as she could, adding a little make-up to make her drawn face seem less sallow.

"Miss Lucella," Roger's voice sounded through the great wooden door. "I am here to escort you to dinner."

Of course, she realized.

Quickly, she walked to the door and opened it, greeting Roger and another servant.

Lucy smiled and nodded, following the pair of Fae through the castle as they navigated her through the corridors. She did not feel much like talking, but Roger was always overly friendly and did the talking for her this time.

"The castle is separated into three wings, Miss Lucella," Roger explained. "We are currently in the east wing, which holds the private living quarters of our more permanent residents."

"Who else lives here?" Lucy asked, genuinely curious.

"Lord Sloan, a troop of his most trusted guards, the lead housekeepers, and now you." He explained in a gentle voice, almost as though he was cautious of scaring her off.

They continued walking to the foyer where the corridor divided into three.

"That direction will take you to the center of the castle," he said, pointing to the middle passageway. "That is mostly for visitors and where the majority of the wait-staff live. There are small historical areas, a library for all who live within the castle, and a few other common areas. You must pass through the center to get to the west wing. This is the passage to the dining room and kitchens," he continued, pointing to the right. "It's toward the back of the wing."

"What's down the other corridor?" Lucy asked, curious why that was left out.

"That section is off limits, I'm afraid."

"What does it hold?" Lucy glanced to the hall on the left.

"Oh, nothing of concern. It's mostly old construction. Nothing particularly of consequence."

Lucy nodded in reply, seeing the tension in his stance.

"The west wing is where most of Northern Territory business takes place," he continued. "There are offices, conference rooms, battle rooms, a ballroom; pretty much anything you can imagine."

"Battle rooms and ballrooms, huh?" Lucy replied dryly. "Quite the juxtaposition."

"Lord Sloan must be prepared on all fronts—the politics of Denora are... precarious."

Lucy did not speak again as they approached a wide archway with oversized wooden doors with cast iron handles. Roger opened the door for Lucy, and she entered a room with an overly large dining table.

At the far end, Laurent sat with papers and scrolls surrounding him—his advisors whispering in hushed tones. Upon seeing Lucy, he excused the advisors, stood, and smiled.

"Lucy, you look splendid," he politely greeted her. "Please, sit. Dinner is just about to be served. I hope it isn't too late."

"No, no, it's fine," she reassured him. The day's journey was long, but she was ravenous after not eating much. It was, indeed, late, but she couldn't sleep now even if she wanted to. She was happy to have something to do.

However, once she looked at the table setting, her happiness faded quickly. Laurent sat at the head of the table, and eight chairs down, Roger seated her at the complete opposite end.

This was nothing like the dinner where he refused to sit far from her. This was nothing like the moment where he gifted her the head of the table as his honored guest. Similarly, this was nothing like the intimate lunch they had in the grove of trees, surrounded by flowers and sunshine.

No. This was typical Denoran business.

Lucy took a deep breath, holding back the disappointment, and sat with a fake smile pressed upon her lips.

"I'm sorry I wasn't able to help you settle into your new quarters. Are they acceptable?" Laurent asked her in between bites of dinner.

"Yes, thank you. Your castle is lovely." Lucy's insides churned at the fake niceties she was using.

Why am I acting this way?

She couldn't figure out why she went from being unabashedly herself to now hiding behind a simpering smile—something she would have refused to do before.

"I have been catching up on some business that has been on hold since I was gone," Laurent continued, not noticing that Lucy was behaving differently. "I anticipate that it will be like this for some time, but Roger, here, will help you get a lay of the land when I am unavailable to assist."

Another one of Laurent's advisors came into the room and began whispering in Laurent's ear, interrupting their conversation. Ordinarily, this would not have bothered Lucy, but she did not understand why his staff felt the need to barge in on their dinner and act as though she wasn't even in the room.

Once Laurent nodded and the male left their presence, Lucy asked the one question that had been consuming her every waking moment.

"How is the search for Jasper going?"

"Nothing so far, I'm afraid. But you need not worry. I have my very best troop on the frontlines, looking for any indicator of his whereabouts."

Lucy nodded and smiled, but inside her heart was breaking.

TWENTY-EIGHT

MICAH

"What do you mean she's gone?" Micah shouted at Wes. It had been weeks since Micah had heard from Lucy and there was no way that she had just disappeared.

"I'm trying to explain," Wes said, desperately. His hair was a mess and his face looked as though he had added years to his life in just a few short Denoran days. He dragged his hands down his face.

"Try harder," Micah said angrily, his body tense with barely subdued ferocity.

"She wanted to do the right thing... She wanted to keep you safe from him. Lucy hadn't slept a wink from the moment she woke up to the moment that she agreed to Lord Sloan's offer."

"What did he even offer her that I couldn't give her?" Micah roared in reply.

"Hey, slow down, Lumen," Brax said, pulling him back from Wes.

They were on the front lawn of the cabin—that's as

far as Wes got before Micah saw him and charged outside, looking for answers.

"No! I won't slow down. This is bullshit!" Micah pulled away from Brax, shoving her hand off of his arm. "This isn't what she would have wanted. What is it? Huh? What did he offer?"

"He offered your safety, for fuck's sake," Wes said curtly. "Jasper is out on the run and he wants you dead, Micah. Do you understand that?"

"Yes, but we could work together to take him down!"

"Micah, he killed the strongest Fae Lucy and I have ever known!" Wes shouted back, his voice cracking. "Lucy did what she thought would keep you safe."

"She wouldn't pick him, she wouldn't!"

"Well, she did!" Wes screamed, stunning them all into silence as his exterior crumbled. "She's gone, trying to fix what Jasper ruined! And my mother is in fucking agony over losing her husband. And now I am the one who has to try to fix all of this mess, and I don't even know how! Is that what you want to hear? That we are all doing things we fucking hate trying to make things better?"

Micah's heart pounded in rage, but it couldn't have touched the agony Wes was going through. Micah remembered that pain... losing his mother. Then, hoping beyond hope that his grandfather could have been there for him to help make the grief bearable, but then he left Micah, too. That's exactly what was happening to Wes.

The realization subdued Micah's thoughts, draining his anger and replacing it with a sullen understanding.

Wes stood panting, trying to calm himself, looking down at the ground with clenched fists.

Micah took a slow step forward, and then another, until he was only a step away from Wes. He extended his arms and pulled Wes in for an embrace, wrapping his arm around Wes's shoulders.

At first, Wes stood as tense as a rooted tree, refusing to accept the offer of camaraderie.

"Death is confusing," Micah said gruffly. "You don't have to hold it all, man. That's what friends are for."

Friends.

The word felt foreign to Micah, but right nonetheless.

"Yes, Baum," Brax said gently, placing her hand on Wes's shoulder. "We're here for you."

Wes dropped his head on Micah's shoulder and finally let it all go. His silent sobs wracked his body as he released the pressures of leading his family business without a mentor, the sadness he felt for his mother and siblings, his sister's sudden exit from his life, and his devastating grief of losing the most influential male in his entire existence.

"You don't have to hold it all."

TWENTY-NINE

LUCY

Walking the halls of the castle was turning into Lucy's only pastime. It had been nearly a week of life in the Northern Territory, and each day was more depressing than the last. There was never any news about Jasper's plans. No one knew where he was, and each time she asked, Laurent changed the topic—and that was when Laurent was around.

Every day she saw less and less of him. At first, it was him being present for all three meals, then moved to just dinner and tea. Now it was a toss-up if she would see him at all.

Part of Lucy wanted to be offended by his lack of attention to her, but quite honestly, she was happy to not have to pretend in front of anyone anymore. The only constant in her life had been Roger these past few days, and she didn't care what he thought about her. He didn't force conversation and was happy to speak without her responses. He was easy to be around, because he needed nothing from her.

Each morning she planned her route at breakfast, ate alone for lunch, and then wandered the more interesting places she found before she broke away for dinner. Roger didn't seem to mind and narrated all the interesting, and more often than not the uninteresting, things about the castle. It gave her something to do, kept her body moving, and her mind off of her reality.

She had never been in a position where she felt there was no way to solve a problem. Even when she felt that her back was against a wall, she fled to another realm just to prove herself. When faced with violence, she exerted her power and strength and came out on top. When she missed her mortal lover, she snuck away and found the time to be with him.

Yet now, holding all the magic of the gods inside of her, she sits as a simpering female betrothed to a powerful Fae and therefore has no opinions? It didn't add up, and she couldn't figure out what in all the realms was wrong with her.

Today, she was pleased to be truly alone. Laurent needed Roger's presence and, surely, Roger was happy to no longer play the role of tour guide. Lucy promised to not wander off too far and mentioned perusing the library. However, what she didn't mention was that she was far more interested in the one area she was told not to explore. It was the only place in the entire castle that made her take pause, and each time she did, she felt the gentle tug of her dulled magic trying to breach the surface... She didn't know what it meant or why it happened, but she looked forward to finding out.

Taking the route to the center of the castle was easy

enough, and when she came to the fork in the corridor that led to the portion of the castle that was off limits, she hurried down as quickly as she could.

If anyone asks, I got lost, she told herself.

The adrenaline rush from running in the hall was enough to almost make her smile. It was by far the most exercise her body had gotten since before her father died… At the realization, the smile that nearly made its appearance swiftly left.

The hallway changed from soft carpeting to bare wood and the walls became more barren as she progressed through. Roger had mentioned this area was under construction, but it seemed as if it had been forgotten all together.

What was wrong with this area of the castle? Surely, there must be a reason it looked abandoned.

Her footsteps echoed in the bare hallway, shadows shrouding her sight. A flutter of curiosity swam within her veins, her magic slowly waking for the first time since her arrival. The relief she felt was all-encompassing, feeling herself come back to life.

She brought her hands to her lips and whispered the Fae spell for light, and a small orb lit in her hands. Since the incident on Micah's property, she could not get her magic to work how it once did. Just weeks prior, the gesture was not needed any longer since she had actualized, but now she could not wield magic without the words. Lucy could not understand why, but she took comfort in the magic all the same.

The small light cast a dim glow all around her, but it was not enough to see in the dark space.

I should have listened more to my mother, she thought.

She froze in the middle of the corridor. She had been working so hard not to think about her family, pushing away the feelings of grief and depression that weighed heavily on her heart. But now, with that one little thought, emotion flooded her, making it hard to breathe.

My family.

She put both hands to her chest and closed her eyes, thinking of her family and what they must be going through as they plan out her Father's funeral without her.

I should be home with them.

Laurent's words from the day she arrived echoed in her mind, *"welcome home"*.

This was not her home. Her home was with her family. Love sprouted from her heart at the thought of her six brothers and how fulfilling it would be to finally see them again.

All at once, her emerald magic came to her, caressing her arms in a gentle greeting. The sentiment rattled her insides, tearing her presentable facade apart at the sight of her magic returning to her.

Tears fell down her cheeks as she choked out a small laugh, smiling at the comforting presence she had missed so very much.

It glided over her face in a warm nuzzle, then darted down the hall, guiding her way.

"Wait!" She called in a whisper, hoping it would slow so she could follow at an easier pace, but the green light did not slow. She had to run to keep up, wondering where it took her.

Soon, Lucy found herself at another forked path, with a corridor going to the right, or stairs leading down. She peered in each direction, wondering which way her magic fled. Instinctively, she closed her eyes and asked within her mind, *where did you go?*

She opened her eyes and the stairwell down glowed an ominous green. Lucy used quiet footsteps as she descended, unsure of what she would find at the end.

She could have listed a thousand things in her mind, and not one of them would have led her to what she found in the middle of the long passageway at the bottom of that stairwell.

As her magic tenderly receded back into her, Lucy took one step closer to the scene in front of her. Huddled in the back of a cell, a male Fae with disheveled clothing and dried blood covering his body, shook and whimpered in fright.

"Please, please no more," he cried. "I have nothing else to say, and no more alchemy to give. Please, Sloan, you will drain me to my death."

Lucy gasped, and at the sound, the Fae male sat up attentively at the sight of his visitor. His eyes bulged in recognition and relief.

"Lucy! Please, Lucy! You need to get me out of here!"

Loud footsteps from the other end of the corridor made their way toward them, and Lucy looked up in terror.

Backing up a step at a time, Lucy nearly fell over as she ran from that basement cellar. Up the stairs, back down the dilapidated passageway, through to the forked hall and back to her bedroom quarters, where she threw the door closed behind her and tried to catch her breath. Disappointment threatened to drown her.

"Jasper has been here all along?"

HER MIND HAD BEEN RACING with disbelief and distress, not quite understanding how that pile of ragged bone and muck was really Jasper. It couldn't be... just that morning she asked how the hunt for Jasper was going and Laurent had told her that they were still on the search with no updates.

Her magic raced through her veins restlessly, causing discomfort and unease in her soul. Lucy didn't know how to slow any of this down—her thoughts, her emotions, or her magic. She was rapidly veering toward a mental breakdown if something didn't calm her soon.

She washed her face and fixed her hair once, twice, three times before a soft knock on her door made her nearly jump out of her gown.

"Yes?" She called with a shaky breath.

"Miss Lucy, Lord Sloan is requesting your presence for tea," Roger's voice sounded from the other side of the door.

Perhaps he is prepared to tell me of Jasper's arrival?

Lucy's heart soared with hope. She opened the door and offered a sheepish smile and nod in reply. She couldn't risk speaking when she was so wound up inside.

Her magic beneath her skin would not quiet, and it took all the concentration she had to keep it within her body. Lucy was not prepared for it to make an appearance in front of Laurent and have to explain any of it.

Following Roger down the hall, her eyes darted to the off-limits passageway, remembering the battered Fae found in the depths of what must have been their dungeon.

A fucking dungeon.

Her stomach threatened to bring up her earlier meal. Dungeons were not unheard of, but they were only found in the homes of the most ruthless Fae.

Once near the dining room, Lucy's heart felt as though it might explode at the impending conversation she would have with Laurent. Would this be the end of her fears? Now that he was captured, could she go home? The idea grew like a warm flame melting her frozen heart.

Seeing Laurent sitting so calmly piqued Lucy's curiosity and caused her to still.

He does not seem as though he has anything positive to tell me.

"Ah, my love, please come sit," he said cheerfully. "I am so sorry to have been neglecting you so much these past few days. I am happy to see you."

"Thank you, my lord," she said in a curtsey. "I'm happy to see you, as well. It is good to see you in such a jovial mood. Do you have good news to share?"

"Good news?" Laurent asked, bewildered. "Not particularly, I do not think."

"Any update on Jasper DeValey?"

Lucy's heart stopped, waiting to hear him say the

words; that Jasper was captured and he would take care of the rest. That she no longer had to fear.

But that relief never came, for instead he replied with sadness.

"No, Lucy. I am so sorry. We think we have a lead in the Southern Territory," he said, taking another sip of tea, a new gold ring on his finger. "Don't worry. We will find him and have him pay. I will tell you as soon as I hear anything, I promise."

Lucy's magic flared in her body at the deliberate lie. She felt the heat of it flash in her eyes for only a moment, and Laurent looked at her with interest.

"Are you feeling alright, my queen?" Laurent asked her in concern.

The words made her stomach roil.

She would never be his queen.

"Yes, my lord," she said, her mask of meekness covering her contempt. While he could tell when others lied to him, he was never able to detect Lucy's deceit.

As for Lucy, she didn't need a magical skill to tell her that the Lord of the Northern Territories was lying to her face.

"Don't worry, Jasper may be a strong Fae, but I am stronger by far. You are safe here with me."

Lucy continued tea with Laurent as he filled the room with unimportant chatter, but all the while, she dove deep into her thoughts, her magic coursing through her, alive and ready to pounce.

I may have been so foolish to believe him once, but I will not be taken as a fool again and I will not be used as a pawn. Lord Laurent Sloan may be one of the most powerful Fae to have ever walked the realm, but I know something he does not.

Lucy smiled at the Lord of the North as he sat across from her, a green shimmer in her eyes.

I am no longer Fae.

Acknowledgments

Writing this book was a crazy journey that profoundly altered my identity as an author. Primarily, it was my first full length novel, which held a steep learning curve. However, writing a sequel brought me so much joy and a wealth of valuable lessons. The landscapes of Joterra and Denora are so real to me, and it is because of readers like you who have breathed life into these stories that I get to do this. My heartfelt gratitude flows to each of you.

I must offer a huge thank you to my personal assistant, affectionately known as my mom, who has provided unwavering love and support throughout my author journey. She has been not only my rock, but also the best friend a girl could ask for–I appreciate you more than you'll ever know. Thanks for doing the hard things for me so that I could do the fun ones.

Throughout this process, my author colleagues and friends have been instrumental. My friends within the FaRo world, Mom's Who Write, and our Fantasy Author Collective – thank you for your wisdom and your advice.

Elayna, your unwavering support has been a beacon of light amid the chaos. The friendship you offer is invaluable. Please never stop writing amazing stories!

My beta readers who stuck by my side will always have a special place in my life. Kate, Clara, Sarah F,

Stephanie, Natalie, Sarah D, Veronica, Emily, Janet, Drew, and Anna–thank you for believing in me and giving me the time and feedback that helped me turn this story into something truly special. You are wonderful–no wet noodles in this bunch.

Thank you to my beautiful children, who graciously encouraged me through book one and saw the hardships of a parent with two jobs during book two.

Even my loyal pup deserves recognition for this novel. She faithfully kept my feet warm during many writing sessions, offering silent encouragement amidst the solitude of the writer's world (also, happily hiding from the loud noise makers. See paragraph above.)

Lastly, my husband. Without you, I am not me. You helped me to find who I truly am in this world, and each year you help me unlock more and more. Everyone who knows you, loves you–and I'm the luckiest, because you love me back. Thank you for this life.

About the Author

S.A. Heiden has always lived in her own fictitious world with her nose in a book. She thrives off of coffee, fantasy, and wine and indulged in all three as she wrote her first of many books for you!

When she isn't writing, she's hanging with her family and her dog, Penny.

Keep an eye out for more books to come! Make sure to stay in touch on her website www.saheiden.com, join her newsletter, and follow her on Facebook, Instagram, and Goodreads!

www.ingramcontent.com/pod-product-compliance
Lightning Source LLC
Chambersburg PA
CBHW032113310726

48972CB00001B/210